Them That

A no

R. Allen Jervis

My wife told
me to write this,

Them that Live Below.

This is a work of complete and utter fiction.
The places and names aren't there anymore so don't bother looking.
Though once when I was a kid…

To Juliet:
Thanks for signing me up for that Creative Writing course.

Printed in the United States of America

First Printing, 2012

ISBN 978-1478128748

Cover Art ©2012
Linda McLachlan

SECTION ONE:

The Past.

Chapter One: Dick Wellman's Writing Assignment. No.1

Stuff my dad says that makes no sense:

My dad has very little to say to me and even less of a profound nature. Still over the years he's come to repeat several aphorisms or "Ol' Sayin's" to me that he hopes will someday sink in.

Here's three off the top of my head that he uses a lot. I can't say I understand any of them but as you know Old Sayin's are always true else how would they get to be old? I should note that I've cleaned these up for general viewing. I don't see the need to be foul mouthed about something when it's uncalled for.

Old Sayin' number One: "If a man doesn't use his brain he might as well have two arses."
I get the impression he brought this one home from the Service with him. Perhaps some high-ranking naval officer berated him with it as much as he uses it on me. I remember hearing it from a very early age and while the meaning is clear I just can't seem apply it to his satisfaction. I honestly do try to think things thru but the man has a terrible habit of assuming that everyone around him has the same basic knowledge of the world that he has and that goes double for his son of few years and fewer experiences.

Tie this to his impatience with questions and delays and it is more luck than anything that helps me successfully do his bidding. Yet it seemed I've heard this one often enough that its ceased to carry any import. I've don't dare ask him where it came from. He would assume I am being 'smart' with him and that would have started me down the Path of Pain. He would say "Boy, I'm gonna get with you like Karo got with syrup: We're gonna mix!"

Second Old Sayin': "Never sleep with someone crazier than you are."
I think he started telling me this when I was barely eleven or twelve years old and at a time when he himself was between wives. There's a rumor that he has a whole nuther family some place and at least one girlfriend so its very likely this little tidbit (or is this a bromide?) came to him honestly. Still it strikes me as the sorta thing you'd read on

the wall at a bar someplace which is just as likely a place as any for him to discover it.

Third Old Sayin': "Don't coon dog what's already been tree'd." Nobody I know has ever heard this one before so I believe its an original. I have a story where this one came in handy and I'll tell you about it next time. But it turns out that by the time I knew what this meant I had already made the moral decision not to "coon dog what's already been tree'd" and moved thru that little adventure unscathed. When my dad gets old and I'm sure I can outrun him I'll let him know that at least one tidbit of his wisdom made an impression on me. For those who can't wait to read on "Don't coon dog what's already been tree'd" simply means, "Don't chase after married women."

I know very little about my dad's personal life either before or after I came along so I'm kinda hard put to say whether he has followed any of these aphorisms himself. My father, Ray Isaac Wellman, ran away to the Navy at the age of 14 by lying about it to the draft board. He left school with an Eighth grade education. Everything he learned after that he was taught in the Navy. I can't help but wonder if that qualifies him to wax philosophical or not.

I came up with an "Old Sayin'" of my own that I will share with my children someday. But I will leave it to them to decide if it qualifies as an "Old Sayin'" because it just isn't that old yet. It goes like this: "There are always more fries at the bottom of the bag, you just have to dig for 'em."

Hey I just remembered he has another one he likes to repeat: "If you don't get a good education you'll die digging a ditch." I am not sure if that counts as an aphorism but I think about it every time he puts me to work draining water off our flooded property by--yes--digging a ditch. Being at least part superstitious hillbilly at heart I studiously avoid any other offers to take up a shovel.

Chapter Two: Dick Wellman's Writing Assignment No. 2, Pt 1.

I hadn't intended to get into this stuff, but it feels like the floodgates are open so I'm writing it all down and waiting for it to make sense later.

My brother KellyRay stabbed me once and I never quite got over the shock. But this isn't the story about how my brother stabbed me its about the fallout afterwards. It involves a swing. A rope swing with a tire on it which hung in a park next to the elementary school where we both played. The swing went out over a hillside and it was our habit to grab it or dive into it, swing in a wide arc twenty or thirty feet in the air and then at the last moment twist around to plant our feet on the hillside where we had started. You couldn't go completely around the tree but you could come close.

Sometimes older boys would come around and chase us off the hillside and stand around smoking and talking about girls, cars, or drink. Sometimes they would talk one of us (usually my brother Kelly) into getting into the tire while they spun it around or pushed it too hard to stop. The tire was a bit like a shock absorber but he would always come away dizzy, sick to his stomach and bruised from rolling down the hill. This didn't stop him from coming back for more, he was always so desperate to join in with the older boys.

Later that summer someone cut the tire off the swing and left us with just a big knot in the end of the rope. We still managed to find some fun in it, by running off the hillside while holding above the knot then swinging out wide and letting go. We would land in leaves we'd piled up or on big sheets of discarded rubber we'd found by the nearby American National Rubber plant.

I was never the first to do these things but I was keen to be seen to be just as brave as the boys I hung out with. But not even a tiny bit more. Being third or forth in line was about the norm for me. I think if we'd been moon explorers I wouldn't have even made the first journey. But I would have definitely been there somewhere around Apollo 14.

The first boy to do things in our group, the one who always thought of stuff for us to do was named Smith. It was our habit to call each other by our last names: Smith, Hatfield, Kretzer, Neace, Tripplett. At least when we weren't calling each other Git, Bernie, or ErnBob. Smith produced a kitchen towel from somewhere and tucked it into his gym shorts so it would look like he was wearing a loincloth. He gave a mighty Tarzan yell and swung outwards, let go and solidly landed on the rubber mats and just rolled off the other side.

Hatfield was always contending with Smith as to who was leading our jolly little band and so had to go one better. He not only jumped and yelled, he tucked a long stick in his belt and swung out yelling "For Helium!" and landed on the rubber mats, bounced once like John Carter of Mars, then drew his makeshift sword as he landed just shy of putting Smith's eye out.

Then it came my turn and I howled my best jungle howl, swung out and immediately realized that I didn't have a very good grip. It would have really helped if I'd had anything resembling upper body strength and I think I would have made it if I'd gotten both hands on the rope above the knot. But instead I swung off center in a wobbly orbit and it was clear that I was going to land much more horizontal to the ground than the other two jumpers and I wasn't going to hit the mats square on if at all. I did manage to hit them but then I bounced off to the side and landed hard on my arm.

There was a crack like the sound of a tree with too much ice on it and I yelped much louder than before. Even before I stood up I knew I had broken my left arm. It was odd cause it didn't really hurt much at first but there was a definite bulge where the bone was splintered, almost poking thru the skin. I remember thinking "This should hurt." and then suddenly it did.

I told everyone around me it wasn't hurt that bad, it was just a sprain. Smith and Hatfield almost chimed together "Yep, its broke, don't it look broke?" They didn't seem to know what to do and frankly neither did I. Everyone seemed to be afraid to get closer as if it was contagious. My brother KellyRay was no where to be seen. Suppressing the desire to break out crying right then and there I took off my sweat socks and wrapped them around my arm where the bulge was. I walked away saying I had to go home all the while worrying how my dad was going to react, that I'd probably get beat for it, and that it would hurt especially bad with a broken arm. All the denial in the world wasn't going to save me from a confrontation and I broke into a sweat either from fear, shock, or both.

When I got home I sat at the kitchen table for a long time cause it helped the pain to hold it perfectly still. My mind was full of angst and apprehension; imagining all the myriad ways Dad might react. My brother KellyRay came in and laughed at my pain, even trying to poke the bump on my arm just to see if I was faking. Jerking my arm away from his fingers made it hurt even more. I really hated him at that moment. The incident with the knife was still fresh in my mind; heck the cut hadn't even healed properly yet. And even though he had been there when I broke my arm he hadn't even bothered to see if I got home OK he just played in the park like he always did waiting till the last minute before Dad got home.

So when Dad came in a few minutes later and he asked where we'd been, who we talked to, and what had we done that day to disobey him. ("What did you F-- up this time?" It was a kind of litany.) I turned to show him my arm and said the first thing that came into my mind. "KellyRay pushed me out the door and I fell on the concrete steps!"

"What?" He snapped, shooting a look at KellyRay who's grin rapidly slid off his face as he paled. This wasn't going to be the entertaining show of force he expected and before he recovered enough to deny it, Dad told him to Shut UP. Using a tone of voice I would later associate with the Bene Gesserit in Dune or perhaps just Darth Vader. He turned back to me and demanded I repeat myself. "What did you say boy?"

"I was trying to keep KellyRay home like you told me to but he wouldn't stay so I stood in the door to stop him and he pushed me out. I landed on those steps there and broke my arm!" That scene had actually happened up if you replace the break my arm part with 'stabbed me with a knife.' I still had scratches on my knuckles and shoulder where I'd fallen on the concrete steps which gave me some convincing evidence to back my story up. I hadn't told my dad that KellyRay had stabbed me cause I figured dad would out and out kill him and get arrested and then where would we be? I told myself this was payback for the torment, the stolen money, and the chores I had to do while he ran around with older kids and especially for stabbing me with a pocketknife. You just don't do that. You can shout and you can argue or curse and even fight with a brother but you don't pull a knife on them and you don't ever ever draw blood. Not in anger and not in jest.

I had never before been successful at diverting the Discipline Juggernaut once it locked onto a target, mainly because I had never dared to lie about it before. And usually punishment at my house was more like a grenade going off than a missile where there was some hope of guidance or accuracy. I didn't know what to do except step back and try not to be in the way while Anger ran its course.

Things were kind of a blur after that. KellyRay was running around the living room in tight circles, my dad holding him by one arm and beating him with a belt in the other. It didn't go on very long though because I started crying which drew Dad's attention back to me. "What are you bawlin' about?" He asked, still holding onto KellyRay who was still vainly struggling to get away. "He's the one getting his ass whipped!"

I held my arm up with the other hand, half hiding behind it. "Swelling up... hurts..." is all I managed to get out. He pushed my brother toward the back of the trailer "Get to your room and stay there till I get back." KellyRay went, a look of hatred on his face for both of us, and Dad turned to me. He didn't offer to examine my arm just quickly looked it up and down then told me to get rid of the dirty socks and wash my arm off. While I was doing that he got into his car and left.

KellyRay came out of the bedroom as soon as Dad left and tried to punch me in my bad arm. "I'm going to get some big kids to come over here and beat you up! Break your other arm!"

"Well you shouldn't have stabbed me last week!"

"You were in my way."

"That's it? That's why you stabbed your brother in the stomach with a rusty-assed pocket knife?"

"Yeah...well...its your pocket knife anyway and besides you're so fat I wasn't going to hit anything vital and *laugh* it got the job done didn't it?"

"Job? What job?"

"You got out of my way..." And with that he went out the door. I shouted after him "What about when you stole my bike and sold it? What about when you hit me in the kneecap with a Coke bottle and I couldn't walk for a week? What about when I helped you sneak past dad thru the back window?" How is any of that fair?"

Chapter Three: Dick Wellman's Writing Assignment No. 2, Pt 2

My Dad returned a couple hours later with my stepmother Jean, who had moved out some months before and was now training to be a nurse. She didn't hesitate in her diagnosis: "That's a broken arm alright. Look at the bump sticking out. His arm isn't even straight anymore." Dad did not look happy but he was trying to get back together with Jean and this was a way to get her back to the house. I was a pretext I realized, but maybe she actually could do something.

We did not have insurance that I know about or at most the minimal coverage given veterans and their families. Dad told me to get in the car and I sat in the back gingerly balancing my arm on my lap and trying not to make any noise when we crossed railroad tracks or hit bumps. Jean suggested we go to the veteran's hospital but my dad just grunted and drove on. We went to the far north side of town where there was a small 3-storied building with only one light on above a sign marking a driveway down into the ground. The sign read "Emergency vehicles only."

We went down that and drove up to the door. Jean wasn't happy about being there and sat turned away from my dad agitatedly blowing smoke out the window. He told me to get out and we walked up to the back door of the building. He rang a buzzer and we had a long uncomfortable moment to look around before an elderly nurse came to the door. I was looking at the parking spaces reserved for hearses and wondering just what sort of hospital my dad had taken me to?

He quickly explained our situation and the nurse told him this was a private hospital and asked if we were one of Dr. SoAndSo's patients? Dad said something rude and pulled me forward into the light. "The boy's arm is broke. You could fix it if you gave a damn."

The nurse's look softened a bit when she saw me but she quickly recovered: "I'm sorry, he should go to a real hospital." Then she closed the door on us. My brief hope that the pain would soon go away faded as I followed him back to the car. Jean called something to him and he gave her a stony look. I don't think he yet knew how to play this situation to his advantage. I got in the back seat again and gasped from the jolting as we shot back up the ramp and back onto the main street. It was dark by now and I found myself trying to get some distance from the pain by focusing on the pool of light under each streetlight as they went by. There were several blocks with no lights on at all and it made me curious but not curious enough to ask about it. Instead I wondered how things like this were handled in other families and thought that if this was TV there would be a commercial or two about tooth whiteners and then the next scene would be of me on the steps of the schoolhouse getting my cast signed by all the cool kids.

At the next stop I didn't even get out of the car. My dad went up to another hospital door and talked to someone there. My stepmom said something she thought was re-assuring and reached back without looking to pat me on the head or shoulder. It was her left hand and all I could see was the red ember of her Virginia Slim arcing toward my face. I leaned back and dodged it. She looked back when she realized she'd missed me entirely and saw my look of fear. She gave me a half smile and said "Hang in there, your dad just has to go thru a thing."

Dad eventually gave up on hospital number two and we went to Collis P. Huntingon General; the main hospital in the area. I was lead to a seat in a crowded waiting room and Jean sat down next to me and tried to fill out some forms. My dad left, calling over his shoulder that he needed to get back to finish a paint job at the shop before morning. Jean complained loudly to everyone around us about the wait and went up several times to try and befriend the staffers since she was a nurse trainee and she supposed there was some sense of sorority about the whole thing.

After more than two hours they either had pity on us or they got tired of her going back up to the desk to ask about the wait. They put us in an examination room and told us to wait for x-rays. Jean thanked them but also observed that she didn't need any X-rays to tell my arm was broke but do what you have to do.

Two hours became three, became five. Jean went out frequently to talk to grownups and borrow cigarettes since she'd run out some time ago. Each time she was gone longer and longer and I finally said something like "Thanks for waiting with me...but umm...is it usual to wait this long?" She looked at me and thought about what she was going to say for a long moment. Finally she stubbed out her cigarette and exhaled the final puff from the side of her mouth. "Honey you're not a priority. There are other people here who were in worse accidents and they get to go first. Plus the main power was cut off in this part of town so they're running the whole hospital on a generator. That's why a kid with a broken arm has to wait."

I said something about understanding that but if they added in the hours since my accident it would surely put me ahead of someone. Jean asked me when I last ate and I said before lunch, meaning breakfast but not wanting to be exact since it was one of the 'issues' between her and Dad.

She hmmmned and looked in her purse. "Well I'm going to call your dad and let him know we're STILL HERE and get some smokes. If you'll promise to be good I'll go get you something to eat." She left with a wave and closed the door quietly. I looked around the exam room for the 100th time wondering if I really did prefer having her wait with me instead of my dad. Yes I decided, thinking of the food about to come, yes I did.

I was standing on a short stool testing my eyesight with a chart on the back of the door when it opened and a young intern in a lab coat stuck his head in. He looked around the room and at me for a second then closed the door again. A few minutes later he came back asking, "Who's supposed to be with you?"
"My stepmom is here, she's looking for a cigarette machine or something."

He closed the door again and came right back with a chart. I got the impression it was hanging on a hook outside the door. "When did you get here?" he asked looking at the top sheet and frowning as he leafed thru the others.

"I don't know. It seems like hours." He shook his head still not looking at me "It doesn't say here."
"It was just after dark when we came here." I offered, "Is it still dark out now? There's no windows in this room."

He looked at me still frowning and seemed to come to some decision. "Alright." He said, holding the door open. "We can get you x-rayed while we wait for your mom."
I followed him out, swallowing my reply of "Step-mom." cause Jean had told while she was filling out the forms "If anyone asks you're my son, not Ray's."

He took me to a room with a big table in the middle, larger than the one in the exam room and I wondered if someone in here was finally going to look at my arm? That hadn't actually happened yet. The intern spoke to someone else, a tech I guess and then left. The tech told me to sit in the chair next to the table. He went into an alcove where a female tech was waiting and he chatted to her while he adjusted the x-ray machine. He moved it up and down some and called out "Lie your arm flat on the table!" I tried to do as he asked though it was very difficult to position my arm flat and in the center of the table. He said something to the girl tech and they both laughed. I didn't know what about but it bugged me. I alternated between watching the x-ray machine move over me and watching the two techs in the control room talking to each other.

He looked towards me and frowned. Medical professionals seemed to do that a lot and I made a mental note not to seem happy around them lest it break their professionalism. "Try again your arm isn't flat yet!" I tried again, now kneeling in the chair and bent over the side of the table from the waist up. "Should I get on the table?" I asked trying to be helpful but didn't get a response. The girl was showing the tech something in a manual or maybe it was her purse but either way they weren't looking in my direction anymore. The lens of the camera came down closer and closer and I thought I could see crosshairs projected onto my arm by the lights around it.

The square of light got smaller and more intense as it got closer and I wondered if this was the X-ray beam itself? On TV they said X-rays were invisible so I called out "I can see it?" a bit nervously and tried not to move my arm as the lens dropped within inches. Maybe they needed really strong X-rays for bone. "Are you supposed to be able to see it, the X-rays I mean?"

I lost my nerve when the lens touched the hairs of my arm and I jerked it back out of the way. That made me cry out and the tech finally looked over and tried to figure out what was going on. The camera started making a whining noise as the motor pushed it into the table's surface. He jumped forward, hitting a switch to reverse it and yelled, "What did you do?" I looked between the table and my arm unclear what he meant. Maybe he was talking to the other tech but he was looking at me. "I moved my arm cause it got really close and looked like it was going to hurt." The female tech said something and they argued for a while and then left. The X-ray machine went back up and the lights on it went out. I didn't know what to do so I put my head down on the end of the table almost accustomed to the throbbing of my arm by now. I fell asleep telling myself it wasn't that bad, that maybe we could just go home and it would heal OK. The kids at school might even think its cool to know someone who could reach around corners and stuff.

The intern who took me from the exam room came in and woke me. He spoke to me much nicer this time and took his time x-raying my arm. I didn't have to sit bent over the table either, I got to lie down on it, which seemed the proper way to do it all along. I wondered if the trio of them had gotten into trouble for not paying attention. I don't think I'd been in a hospital emergency room before but I had a good idea from TV that they were usually run better than this, power outage or not.

When I got back to the hallway where my exam room was my stepmother was asking people passing by if anyone had seen a fat kid leave in the last hour? I mentally tallied the hours up and decided it must be after midnight by now. The intern spoke to her and sent us back into the exam room to wait. I immediately smelled the wondrous odor of Burger King in the room and fell on the food she'd brought me, eating it one handed and needing help sticking the straw into the cup of soda. It tasted so good after all that time with only swallows of water from the hallway fountain between now and breakfast.

An older man I assumed was the doctor on duty came in with my chart in his hand and some x-rays in the other. He stuck them up on a light board and spoke to my stepmother without actually looking at my arm. I really felt someone should have by now as there was bruising and swelling all the way up to my shoulder. They started arguing and I got the impression I had done something wrong when he turned and asked me "When's the last time you ate son?"

I pointed at the crumpled bag in the trash and said, "Just now, my mom brought me Burger King!" I smiled brightly at her to let her know I was thankful and remembering to pretend to be her son but she wasn't smiling back. The doc turned to her abruptly and said "That was...unfortunate." He explained to her and her 'training" that because the break was so severe they'd have to put me asleep to set my arm. "It will hurt a lot so we put them under. Now though...and he looked at me for a long moment as if he could will the food out of me. "I'll have to admit him. He can't be put under with food in his stomach. He might choke on it. That's why he was put in here for 8 hours, ma'am."

Jean and the doc talked more even as he was writing things on my chart and walking out. I looked out the door more worried than before. I had no clue as to what was about to happen to me. Whatever it was though the only thing I was glad for was that I didn't have to be the one to tell my dad.

Chapter Four: Dick Wellman's Writing Assignment No. 2, Pt 3.

I was taken upstairs alone, weighed, and made to change into a hospital gown. I was on the children's ward but put in a section meant for kids who had to stay a while for one reason or another. There was a big age gap between the really young kids at one end who were barely out of the crib and the other end that held me, the guy I was gonna share a room with, and a girl about our age across the hall.

My roommate was a boy a year or two older than me named Roger. He had been badly burned somehow and the doctors had just grafted skin onto his neck and chin. He watched while the nurse got me settled in the bed leaving me a big plastic tumbler with shaved ice in it. He said "Hey...my name's Roger, what's yours?" I told him RJ. (I didn't know how far to carry the ruse of being Jean's son, so I didn't answer with his name.) I waved from my bed and asked what happened, gesturing to the gauze bandages around his neck. He seemed to be in a good mood and wasn't in any pain that I could tell. "Let just say that if you're ever tempted to light a cigarette from a gas stove don't do it. They'll graft skin from your ass onto your neck!"

That was an impressive summation of his problem and not to be outdone I replied back: "And if you're ever told that monkeys have the strength of 10 men believe it or you'll end up like me!" I gestured to the arm now supported by a gauze sling and shrugged. I could tell he half believed me or at least wasn't going to question what I said in front of the grown ups. I immediately took a liking to him.

Roger had been there a week or two already and he let me know what was what. He knew about the power outage, he knew which nurses to ask for treats or 'cigs' and especially knew when his favorite volunteers came on. He had a likin' for a buxom candy striper named Helen. He told me if I was in long enough I could ask for a sponge bath on Thursdays and she'd be the one that would have to give it. I remembered he fell back on the bed sighing and squirming a bit "I'm pitching a tent just thinking about it!"

Well I had no idea what a sponge bath was, why I'd want a mere volunteer to do it, or what it had to do with camping at all. But I wasn't going to let on like I wasn't just as clued in as he was. I said "Yeah? That good is it?" which was about all I could safely contribute to the conversation. Fortunately that didn't slow Roger down at all. He was full of advice and tidbits of trivia. Mostly about girls and sexual positions neither of us had actually tried. Apparently he had access to the dark materials that I had only heard rumor of. He described his accident in great detail and how he couldn't wait to get back to his girlfriend in Kentucky cause he was shore itching to give it to her doggy style. I was just nodding and saying "Hell yeah" at what I thought were the appropriate pauses in his speech but apparently at some point I admitted to being a big fan of doggie style too. He got all-serious for a second and said "That's not why you're in here is it? How you really hurt your arm? Oh man I'm sorry!" He paused for half a second to let me to tell my story but I never even got close to the whole swing and concrete stair thing before he was off again. He talked nonstop till the nurses came around and made us go to sleep, admonishing us that it was 3:00 am and other patients needed to sleep.

I realized I was very tired soon as it got quiet but startled awake every time the nurses came in to check on us. I don't know why I had to be awakened every 2 hours and asked about my pain. I'd had enough adventure for one day and just wanted to sleep. Come 7:00 am or so a huge black lady pushing a cart full of food came in. She gave Roger a tray with a metal lid on it. She was surprised to see me and said "I don't have an order or nuthin' for you honey but I'll go check at the desk." Roger started eating right away and when he noticed me watching he offered me his dessert. It was yellow Jello and had a small dollop of whipped cream on top. "It's supposed to be diet so you can have it." he said, leaning over in bed to reach my table. He slid it across to me and it stopped against my beaker of ice shavings, now mostly lukewarm water.

Thanks I said and had it half way to my mouth before I remembered what the doc had said the night before. I didn't want to be here another 8 hours, even in good company and I certainly didn't want to face my dad when he found out I had screwed up again and cost him another day's stay in the hospital.

So I sat it on the windowsill where it would stay cool though I was very reluctant to give it up. "I'll wait till the food lady comes back and when they tell me I can eat I'll have it then. If she brings me a different kind you can pick which flavor you want." Roger said I was all right between mouthfuls and I looked around for something to read or look at for a while.

I didn't have much luck finding reading material and the food lady didn't come back. About 10:00 am another doctor came by to talk to Roger. I sat up on the bed waiting expectantly for him to come over and ask how I was and to tell me I could eat something. That Burger King meal was a long gone memory and I hardly regretted it at all by now.

The Doc looked at me and checked his watch. "Someone from the nurse's station should come by and check on you." He said then left. Right behind him two members of Roger's family burst in: His mom who was a big roly-poly woman barely my height and his younger brother John who immediately reminded me of my brother KellyRay but perhaps not quite so evil. His dad was down the hallway with his sister cause she was too young to be allowed on the wing where sick people were. I was told that's cause children carry more diseases. It didn't seem logical to me that more germs would stick to a child than a grownup with a larger body but I filed this info away for later consideration.

Roger's mom had brought him some home cooking. A big pot of slow cooked cube steak simmering in gravy with onions and potatoes all around it. It smelled wonderful. His mom introduced herself to me, told Roger to share the food with me, and slapped John's hands as he tried to dip into the pot and take a lick. This was easily the closest, messiest, loudest, friendliest bunch of people I'd ever met. I think to this day I have a soft spot for Kentuckians as a result.

Roger's dad came in to see him once his mom was done visiting. He was a tall thin man with round thick glasses that gave him an owlish demeanor. He offered to shake my hand and I shook it back weakly in surprise. Grownups didn't shake hands with kids in my neck of the woods. This seemed to disappoint him on some level and he asked what trouble I'd been into to break my arm? I told him I fell out of a swing, for some reason unwilling to lie to him. Roger looked at me over his shoulder and I could tell from the look on his face that the news that I hadn't actually been arm wrestling with a gorilla was a complete and total surprise to him.

After his family left I could still hear them down the hall chatting with the nurses and even other patients. His mom had a loud easy laugh that I found both surprising and comforting. She sent John back around to our room and he stuck just his head in: "Mom says the girl across the hall is her first cousin's daughter so you'd better go over and say hello." Then he grinned and said "Bring a pillow case with you, you'll want to cover her face before you jump her bones. She's as ugly as four miles of bad road!"

Roger told his brother to get the hell out and apologized for his coarseness. Still, I got the impression this was important news to him. His younger brother John was even more girl obsessed than he was or maybe Roger just hid it better thinking that a touch of suave might improve his chances. I could see the door across the hall from my bed but both doors were never open at the same time. Roger asked me to keep a look out just the same and gave out a mock sigh "Its a shame you can't eat, my dad fixes the best cube steak you ever had..." Then he proceeded to tuck in and had everything eaten and cleaned up before the noontime meal came around.

A candy striper came by and filled our water jugs with shaved ice. Roger chatted her up though she was clearly several years older than he was and he had little to no chance of getting anywhere. My odds were less than zero. He used my plight to prolong her visit, leaning over close to her and trying to sound all confidential like. "Rich over there hasn't eaten in days, someone out there should sign a form. I understand he's taken to hoarding Jello against the forced dieting policy they have here..."

My ears reddened and her eyes got big and she asked if that was right? I said in all honestly I hadn't eaten yet that day and could not tell her the exact hour of my last meal. Roger nodded encouragingly behind her but I didn't have anything else to say. She promised to ask the head nurse what was going on and left. Roger said "Man you should have said something, anything! Tell her what your favorite position is, girls love doin' it on all fours." I looked at him crooked and pointed out he hadn't mentioned anything about sex either. He assured me that was only because she would probably know Helen and he was saving himself for her and her sponge.

Just then the food lady pushed open the door and I sat bolt upright in the bed. "Finally!" I cried out. "Uh Oh!" cried out the food lady and she backed out again taking the cart with her. Even Roger was surprised. She held the door open and shouted down the hall "Does 13-B get food?" "He doesn't?" "Sure smells like food in there, you sure?" She looked back in at us and Roger was pretending to read a newspaper his dad had left and I was leaning forward like a hound waiting for his master to throw him a bone. My ears were pricked up and I had the scent, just let me at it!

Food lady came back in carrying only one tray, which she put on Roger's table. "I'm sorry honey, they have an order from the doctor not to give you any food but the nurse is going to call down and see if you can have an IV."

I said "OK...thank you." though it was done half heartily. I had already watched Roger eat two meals that day and I wasn't looking forward to round three. I looked out the window at the parking lot wondering which direction the Burger King was from there? I was formulating a plan to get my clothes and escape that I'd put into action if this Ivy thing wasn't tasty and filling. I turned the dish with the Jello in it and licked my finger. It was lemon and artificial but it tasted great. I had to get up and stand looking out the door of the room to avoid eating it and to diminish the sounds of Roger devouring whatever passed for hospital food.

The door to the room across the hall was open and I saw a young man about 20 or so holding the hand of someone in the bed. He was talking quietly to her and all I could make out was a spill of long blonde hair. He looked up at me, reached over and pulled the privacy curtain across and sat back down. I could see his arm moving in the shadows on the curtain. He was stroking her hair slowly, over and over as he talked.

I looked down the hall at the nurse's station. It was circular and looked like it could have been a library reference desk if it weren't for all the women in uniform standing around it. Our school librarian Mrs. Justice didn't have a uniform but she did wear the same green sweater every day, hot or cold.

I went down there keeping my backside tight against the hallway wall to avoid breezing my gown open and said very softly "Excuse me, I think I'm supposed to get an IV? I haven't eaten since yesterday and I'm very hungry." The nurse I spoke to asked another nurse and she looked up and asked my name? "Wellman." I said and pivoted as a group of visitors walked by. I would have liked to sit down so my butt wasn't in danger of sticking out but there wasn't anything on this side of the desk for people to sit on.

"You mean Burns?" she asked, looking at me over her glasses.

"Oh, Yes I think so."

"You can't have anything to eat because we don't know when the power will come back on. They'll want to take you into surgery right away." She paused as if she had more to say but could tell the talk of surgery had upset me. Then she said "Did your parents visit today?" I couldn't answer right away. I wondered if anyone at home had noticed I was gone, if someone at school might miss me, or even that one of my friends would have thought to ask my brother why I wasn't on the bus? Wasn't it normal to be visited in a hospital? Wasn't it normal to eat? "No." I said trying to hide my confusion and sadness. "That was someone else's family."

She waved me back to my room with a metal clipboard. "Well I'll try to find out who your family doctor is and see if he can authorize an IV. You go back to your room and wait now, hear?" I went back down the hall muttering under my breath. "Family doctor?" I haven't seen a doctor in 5 years. My family doctor's back in Virginia."

I almost walked past Roger's bed before I noticed it was empty. I looked up and down the hall and couldn't see him. I didn't think he'd gotten past me while I was at the nurse's station but maybe he had. I inspected his tray and found there wasn't so much as a crumb left over. That didn't help my mood, not that I would have eaten it anyway. I turned to go back out and heard laughter from across the hall. I stood outside the door for a while until I heard Roger's voice clearly over the other. I opened the door and he was leaning over the bed, showing the girl laying there the newly grafted skin around his neck. It was bright pink and looked tighter than the rest of his neck. He looked up at me, winked and looked back down. I followed his gaze and could see he had a great vantage point for staring down the girl's gown from where he was. I blushed and walked over noisily bemoaning the fact that I still hadn't eaten.

"This here's Rich. Rich say hello to Sherri!" Sherri was frail and easily the palest person I'd ever seen at that point in my life, but she wasn't ugly. She had wide blue eyes and a firm, prominent chin. And there was a calmness about her I wasn't old enough to fathom. I smiled and made a mental note to never listen to John's opinion on what a girl looked like ever again. I said hello and she asked what was wrong with me? I said I had a broke arm and she waved a hand weakly in my direction "Oh, they don't admit people to the hospital for a broken arm they just put a cast on it and send them home."

This was the same thing I'd heard Roger's mother say and it embarrassed me not to have something more exciting wrong with me. Before I could return the question in a kindly manner Roger piped in "She's got blood poisoning Rich, real dire stuff." Then he looked back down at her with a solemn look on his face but unable to keep her gaze his eyes rolled down to her chest. She caught on this time and tutt-tutted at him, tugging the woolen blanket up around her neck. "And Roger was showing me how he has ass skin on his neck!" She laughed at his distress at being made fun of in front of me and I laughed too, served him right I thought.

"Is she your...cousin?" I asked, not sure what relation she was to Roger, if any. He said "Shoot no, I could kiss her or anything." He grinned at her shocked look and said in way of explanation "We don't really kiss on our cousins back in Kentucky despite what the rest of the world thinks."

Sherri tried to sit up in bed, gave an exhausted sigh and pushed the buttons to raise her bed up instead. I was surprised by this and stepped closer. "Your bed folds up?"

"Yours does too silly, they all do in hospitals!"

"Mine doesn't have a thing with buttons like that on it. I don't think it moves."

"Well...." Roger started, trying his luck on the other side of the bed. "That's partly my fault. When they put me in that room I played with the controls so much it quit working. So I moved to the other bed and some guys took the broken bits away with them. Sorry."

I gave him a look that said "Well that's just great! Not only do I have a broken arm and I'm admitted into a hospital instead of getting a cast and being sent home which apparently never happens and all the while I'm not allowed to eat and to top it off now I have a broken bed." I turned to go back to my room and sulk when Sherri said "Don't go yet, I think y'all are funny." then she paused and said softly "They're gonna come get me for some more tests in a bit. Please stay till they do my husband had to go back to work after his lunch hour."

Needless to say my eyes got as big as saucers when I heard that and I looked down and noticed a small thin ring on the correct finger. That guy I saw holding her hand must have been her husband. I looked over at Roger who seemed unfazed by the revelation. He'd probably noticed the ring right away and maybe he'd come over there before Sherri's husband had left. I pictured him bumming a cig and trading knives right there in the hospital all while ogling another man's wife. I was so out of my depth I didn't know what to do. I was pretty sure Roger was 110% BS but he was fearless and entertaining. I sat down across the room and listened to Roger re-tell his story of using an old mobile home as a hangout and lighting up stolen cigarettes from the propane stove only to have it blow up in his face. Sherri laughed softly at all the right places and I did too, despite having seen his 'eyebrows blown off' look six or seven times by then.

I got my first IV later that day and I couldn't possibly communicate to you the disappointment. I had envisioned some sort of space age diet, something akin to astronaut food or maybe even whole meals in a pill or from a blender like on the Jetsons. What I got was a stab in my good arm and a drip of saline water. I pointed out to the nurse hooking it up that if all I was getting was water I could drink it faster from the jug they've gave me, especially if I still had use of my good right hand. This had as much impact as you'd imagine it would and she told me it was Doctor's Orders. I hadn't even seen a doctor yet but I was pretty sure I wasn't going to like him when I did.

Chapter Five: Dick Wellman's Writing Assignment No. 2, Pt 4.

I spent another night without food in that place. Roger and I tried to play cards after the nurses chased him out of Sherri's room. This didn't last long cause he got tired of flipping the cards over for me since I was real slow doing it myself. Late at night I woke to find my stomach was chewing on my liver. It was that or it was a nurse coming around to see if we were asleep. I still hadn't worked out how that was supposed to help since opening the door to see if we were asleep always woke me. I got up quietly and looked out the window again. There were very few cars out there and no sign of anyone bringing food up to my floor. I remembered the Jello dish on the shelf and determined to eat it. I was at the end of my endurance and 8 more hours from now wouldn't make that much difference. I slid back the curtain to get the dish and pulled it out triumphantly only to find it was empty. It had been licked clean; there wasn't even any dried cool whip on the dish. I glared at Roger in the dark and went back to bed, if he hadn't eaten it his brother had. I began to think all this bad luck was because I'd lied about KellyRay pushing me down the stairs and determined to come clean once my arm had healed even if it meant getting it broke again when my Dad found out. No amount of deal making or promissory oaths to the higher powers made food magically appear before me so I fell back to sleep wondering if you could eat your shoes like I'd read about and if they actually had to be made from leather?

A doctor did see me the next day and said the backlog from the power outage should be caught up by 3pm and I could eat anything I wanted to then, after the operation. Roger's family didn't visit him that day, which was all well and good cause they would have found him across the hall in Sherri's room. I admit I was in there too, though I felt a bit predatory about it. Roger however, was in his element.

A man came in to take a blood sample from Sherri and she turned to Roger and said "Y'all distract me from the pain please." He leaned in like he was gonna kiss her and just hovered above her face whispering, "Should I do it? Should I not? Do you want me to kiss you?" Damn that boy was smooth beyond his age and it did have the desired effect of distracting her. It was distracting me too. Part of me wished I'd thought of that but the best I could come up with was to keep watch at the door in case her husband came back.

I cannot tell you whether Roger kissed his so-called cousin or not though he would want me to say he did. The intern finished taking his sample and looked at us both a bit sternly, "You boys should behave yourselves." Then he left. I heard the food lady coming down the hall and decided I'd go stand at the opposite end of the hall till she left. I couldn't even look at food at that point cause it hurt too much to know I couldn't have it. When she got to the end of the hall she told me she'd sneaked an extra tray out of the kitchen just for me. I told her I knew for sure I was due in surgery in a few hours and dared not eat it. I asked her to leave it by my bed and told Roger to leave it the hell alone. He knew what I was on about cause he said "Hell son it was just Jello." I started to say, "It wasn't just the Jello..." when we were both distracted by loud voices and something being thrown in Sherri's room. We stuck our heads out and nurses were dashing in to see what had happened. The head nurse pushed us back into our room and closed our door. "Stay in there till we see what's what."

I thought gossip about Roger's escapades across the hall had gotten back to her husband and I said so to Roger. He looked scared and uncertain for the first time since I'd met him and he slipped his jeans and shoes on under his gown and got ready to make a run for it. I couldn't think of anything to say that would be helpful so I shared one of my dad's ol' say-ins: "Don't coon-dog what's already been tree'd Roger, don't coon-dog what's already been tree'd."

I never did hear what was going on because I was prepped for surgery shortly after that and wheeled down to a part of the hospital I hadn't seen before. I was moved from a wheel chair to a bed on wheels. A nurse injected something into my IV and someone else coached me to count backwards when the mask was put on my face. I was worried that there would be another power outage and said so. The doc said, "Don't worry about that the surgery and the gallery above are on separate power." I was still trying to sort out how this jived with my earlier info and my three day stay at the hospital when they came over with the mask.

I remember my friend Hatfield telling me once about being put under and how he'd seen a white rotating light passing before his eyes. He said that before it made three revolutions it was suddenly hours later and he was in Recovery. I started counting backwards, closed my eyes and waited for the white lights to come. I counted back to the lower 90's and I still had no light. I gave up on that and thought it might be a good time to test Astral Projection. I determined to try and contact my friend Tripplett using just the power of my mind. Of all my friends he was the one most into such things and would be the most likely to receive a visit from my astral form without too much shock. And I could count on him to swear it had happened. Once it actually had that is. I pictured his house across the river from mine and tried to will myself free of my earthly bonds. Someone out there asked, "Are you still counting?" and I said "Yes, 89...80...." and then I was out.

I woke with no white lights, no successful separation of body and soul, and no clear idea where I was. Someone was calling my name and rubbing my good arm. I tried to focus and found a beautiful blonde candy striper leaning over me and smiling a big smile with her perfect white teeth. I was half convinced she was an angel come to take me away but it was Roger's favorite volunteer, Helen. I grinned like a fool and said "It must be Thursday, can I have a sponge bath before I die?"

Unfortunately I never got the sponge bath or the chance to lord it over Roger that I had spent quality time with his dream girl while he was hiding from an angry husband. As soon as I recovered they put me in a room identical to the first exam room I'd been in days before and my stepmother was already in there. She told me to get dressed soon as I could and stepped outside to grab a smoke. She added thru the door: "Ray is outside waiting in the car."

I managed to get dressed quickly despite a fresh cast on my left arm and Jean finished her cigarette and led me out of the hospital and into the car. I got into the back seat and my Dad immediately drove off in his usual breakneck fashion. He didn't say a word and I couldn't tell right away if he was mad with me or not. Jean turned around and asked how was it? I said everything was fine except for the fact that I hadn't eaten anything since I was sent upstairs. My dad thought I was trying to get more Burger King from my Stepmother so I just shut up. The comment about Burger King started up another argument so I sat back and leaned to the side so I couldn't be seen in the rear view mirror. My dad's steel blue eyes were just as hard to meet in a reflection as they were straight on. Eventually I was asked for details and why exactly it took 3 days? I worked in the bit about not getting to eat with the fact that I was low priority due to the power outage. My stepmother said, "Well I won't be bringing anyone Burger King anyway soon that's for damned sure!" My dad just said it looked like it hadn't hurt me none, I was still fat enough as it was. I was starting to have a real dislike for those TV endings as they were so far from any reality I knew. My reality was waiting for me back on Airport road and I hoped someone had remembered to get in some groceries.

Chapter Six: Dick Wellman's Writing Assignment No. 3, My Dream House.

I don't recall many reoccurring dreams over the years but there is one that sorta keeps coming back to me. The thing is, it isn't really the same dream, but the same house. I can recall first having it when I was 9 or 10 at the time and I've had a dream involving the same house just a few weeks ago.

The house is a two-story Virginian farmhouse with a large living room divided into sections by French doors. There was a bay window on one side that I recall let in a lot of light. Beyond the living room was a bathroom and master bedroom on one side and a dining room on the other. Behind this was a kitchen and pantry where the back door was. Upstairs there was another bathroom and a large bedroom that took up most of the second floor. There was a smaller bedroom and bath where the stairs started, and the rest of the second floor was unfinished attic. There was no basement under the house, but it did set up on blocks several feet off the ground. It had a deep front porch made of wood and supported by columns. There were also several buildings and a barn nearby. The property it sat on must have been several acres' worth.

In my mind, thinking about the house in the waking world I realize that it is a mix of the house where we lived before my brother Randy died and the house we moved to a few years later. Both are in the same area of the country (or was.) I can't tell them apart after so many years. The point being that it is this house or this style of house that keeps showing up in my dreams.

I remember the first dream very clearly. Probably because I had it several times:

It was a very warm and windy day. I was playing with our dog Sparky at the side of the house while my mother hung washing up to dry on the clothesline out back. I was trying to coax him out of the shade to play in the sun with me when I noticed a flying saucer go over the house. I was just like the ones in the movies; pie-pan shaped and all shiny with no windows or lights. I watched it frightened into silence and not able to move or even breathe. I just stood there staring after it as it disappeared out of sight behind my house.

I ran to the backyard to warn my Mom but she wouldn't even stop what she was doing to look at it. I was very excited, jumping around and pointing behind her "Look! Look! There's another one!" But she just smiled and kept doing the laundry. "There are flyin' saucers all the time RJ. They land at the air force base back there." I looked again and now there were dozens of flying ships of all designs in the air. I remember thinking that the warm air on my face might have been the exhaust from so many aircraft. I turned to ask her why everyone had let me think flying saucers weren't real before but she was gone. I wanted to go see where they landed but the land between our house and the air base was swampy and I needed someone to take me. When I awoke I was still watching the skies for more flying saucers to go over.

There was another dream set in the same house where I kept finding doors I hadn't noticed before. Not the standard dream imagery of the endless hallways with doors repeated ad infinitum off into the distance but more like there was a door to the pantry off the kitchen in the real world but in my dream there was a further door that led to another unused pantry or closet beyond that. They were always darker, unkempt rooms, as if no one else in the house knew about them. Clearly my mother hadn't noticed that they were there or she would have cleaned and brightened them immediately. Let in some natural light, as she would say. I remember finding an extra attic door, an extra bedroom, and even a basement that the real house didn't even have. It was the same house though from the look of the exterior and mainly the Feel. I just sorta knew it was the same house as before.

The world seemed a bit clearer in these dreams compared to normal dreams; everything was sharply defined like it had been colorized after the fact. And I seem to be more lucid in them than I am in most of my dreams. I don't mean lucid as in sanity, but lucid as in aware that I am dreaming, actually participating instead of observing. With other dreams I wake up right after I realize I'm dreaming but in this series of dreams I have free will. What usually wakes me up from them is thinking too hard about not wanting to wake up. Then I would drift into consciousness wondering why the dreams are so mundane -- except for the flying saucer bit-- when there could be so much more interesting things to dream about or why I never got to see the space ships up close.

In other dreams the house had been split into two apartments but I still had free access to all the former rooms. I remember being offered a chance to sleep in my old bedroom in one dream even though some cousins of mine were sleeping there at the time. Many of the dreams during this period picked up within moments of where the last one left off despite occurring months apart in the real world.

For example in one dream there was now a radio station's studio where the big living room had been and I was sent to the basement to get some old vinyl records. I remember going downstairs and being surprised to find another family living in the basement. It was a full apartment down there now and this new feature woke me.

Some time later; months or possibly even years later, I picked up the dream at the bottom of the stair, asking someone there where the records were kept and being directed to a room lined with wooden shelves full of music. There was a Hispanic woman showing me around in this series of dreams though I was unsure how she was related to me or to my cousins still living there.

In one dream I found the basement had flooded several feet deep and we -- the cousins, their dad and their Hispanic mother-- walked on wide boards they had put across till the water went down. I should point out at this point that I'm using the term cousin very loosely. It was habit to refer to any adult friends of my parents as "Uncle Soandso," or Aunt 'Thisandthat.' So its very likely these other kids weren't related to me at all but were just part of the extended family around me.

Once in a related dream the house was attached to one of those grand old buildings like you see in movies featuring a private school of some sort. The type of building with a hundred rooms and huge grounds all about. A Stately Home I think they call it. At the start of the dream I was in a classroom or meeting room when the power went out. I was heading to my workshop to get a fuse and someone told me to take a shortcut thru the tunnels in the basement of the building. Apparently all the buildings connected together. I met several students along the way who all knew the way to the tunnels but I didn't so I must have been new at my job. The tunnels quickly led to some natural caves each larger and longer than the first. There was even a hot spring and some sort of animal playing in it but I recall being afraid and giving it a wide berth. In that dream I never made it to back to the House.

I can remember being lucid enough in a few of them to try and discover where I was. I would leave the house and try to walk to school or into town where I might see a sign with the town's name on it. I tried this several times but never got out of sight of the House. The road always seemed to become unpaved and overgrown and more than once dogs would jump out and bark viciously at me. Or they would force a standoff preventing me from going any further. Once I even asked someone in the dream if flying saucers were real and they said yes but everyone calls them UFOs now. That's pronounced "You-foes" by the way. It seemed like an important point of distinction to the person I was talking to. Equally strange was that flying saucers were everyday things but no one mentioned aliens. That seemed like a whole different subject.

There was even a dream in which I was driving on an elaborate cloverleaf highway that had been built in route to the House. Sometimes in the dream I was driving and sometimes I was just a passenger but we never found our way there. We could see where we wanted to go from the elevated highway but not how to get there. After trying several different exits I determined to try each one in order. Then I noticed the exits were no longer numbered so I couldn't tell them apart. I turned to the person in the passenger seat and said "Ok, This is just too ridiculous." and woke up.

This series of dreams spans several years and at one point I toyed with the idea that I was contacting an alternate universe where "Everything was exactly the same as here, except now there were UFOs." I tried to will myself to have these dreams but I don't recall it ever working that way. I found I had the dreams more often if I slept on my side with one arm under my head and my other hand touching the headboard or the wall beyond it. Maybe the constant firing of the nerves in that arm when it went numb under me was triggering this particular dream state. I don't know enough about dream research to do more than guess. I expect I'll have these dreams all my life and I don't mind really, except for the dogs.

SECTION TWO:

The Present.

Chapter Seven: Stop in, Get Gas.

RJ pulled his Honda Civic into the roadside Park and Shop. When he was last here this was a one-man repair shop run by some guy named Shorty who did all the car repair, drove the wrecker and snow plow, and sometimes even the school bus. RJ guessed you need similar skills for all three.

Getting out of the car, RJ paused with one foot on the ground and looked down. This was the first time he had 'set foot' in West Virginia in over ten years. Should it feel so strange? It wasn't really ground or soil he was touching just oil stained concrete but still? Shrugging he popped the gas tank open and turned to swipe his card thru the card reader but the pumps weren't new enough for that feature. They were dingy and rusted and you had to lift a lever on the side when you wanted to start pumping fuel. They were probably old when he left had left this town and it surprised him that they still worked.

He decided to take a chance on whether they would only accept cash inside and started the pump. The only money he'd spent on the drive down was for a quick toll road burger for lunch. As he filled the tank RJ noticed the cost per gallon was higher than in Indiana. Some things he guessed had kept up with modern times. He could have done with seeing some pre-1999 prices on a few other things he might pick up and take back to Indiana with him.

He went inside blinking in the sudden dark of the shop. The floor of the place still carried a hint of oil-soaked sawdust from its days as a garage. The floorboards were old and grey and they creaked as he walked down a few narrow aisles. He had a look at the meat counter; it bore a handwritten sign proudly proclaiming, "Get your deer butchered here!" The mental image made him a bit ill so he moved toward the register and picked up two small bags of peanuts and a Diet Coke. Apparently Diet Dr. Pepper was still a rumor in these parts.

The chunky lady at the register wore a stained butcher's apron over a voluminous t-shirt and blue slacks. Maybe she did double duty, there didn't seem to be anyone else in the shop. RJ tried to remember when deer season was and couldn't quite place it, sometime in the fall or winter he thought. Late October might still be too early. Didn't really matter, he was as likely to go hunting while he was here as he was to do car repair or coal mining for that matter.

The lady snapped him out of his reverie with a loud "Is this gonna be cash or charge honey?" RJ noticed he was being closely scrutinized but wasn't sure what the lady thought of his rumpled clothes and road weary face.

"Charge please and I topped off my tank out there too." The lady nodded, "Hee! "topped off!" That little car doesn't hold much Go juice does it? I saw ya out there trying to figure out the pump. Didn't know if you were thinkin' about driving off without paying since I didn't recognize you or the car."

Good Grief thought RJ; this town is so small they know people by their cars. Guess it makes a bit of sense; I'm probably the only one here with a Honda Civic and this is probably the only place to get gas without driving back into Huntington. He smiled back without comment as he handed her his credit card. She looked at it -- actually looked at it -- front and back, then looked back at RJ, one eye squinting and the other owlishly wide. "Just whose boy are you?" she asked critically, tilting her head to the side as if that helped her hear his response.

RJ was taken aback at the unexpected challenge and he blushed before answering. He wanted to say something flip like "I'm nobody's boy, Lincoln freed the slaves years ago." But he wasn't sure just how that would go over. No need to antagonize random people here he admonished himself, despite their nosiness.
"I'm a Wellman, I've come home for my mother's funeral."

The lady leaned across the check out lane and looked closer at RJ's face. He tried his best to return the gaze. "One of Gerri's boys? You're the one that's been living in Indiana all this time aren't you?"

Again it bothered RJ that this lady somehow knew about his family business without his knowledge. He reminded himself that she might have been a close friend of his mother's and would have heard all about her family. Mom had always been proud of her family no matter how fragmented it had become. He swallowed his outburst and said, "Yes. I'm from Indiana now."

The lady laughed harshly and shook her head. "No you're not, Once A Local, Always A Local. Can't run away that easy, especially you Wellmans. You have roots in the earth here, if you know what I mean." She paused as if waiting on some confirmation that RJ did indeed know what she meant but he was clueless how to respond. It was if he was being singled out in Sunday school and asked what some parable meant while the whole class watched. He picked up his things and signed -- signed -- the credit slip before heading back out the door. "Well...they don't know I'm here yet, so I better go. Nice to meet you...bye!"

He stepped back out into the sun noticing that she watched him from the store doorway as he walked around his car. Another pair of eyes belonging to an equally rotund mechanic sitting back in the shade was following his movements too. The man called out "How far did you drive from Indiana?" RJ wanted to confront him and ask how the man knew he was from Indiana then realized as he walked up to his car that the mechanic could see his Indiana license plate from where he sat.

"453 miles in nine hours." RJ answered, wondering why he bothered to be so accurate. Diving back into the car and latching the door he saw the man stand up and move toward the car. He quickly put his Honda in gear and called out "Say hello to Shorty!" as he drove off.

Chapter Eight: Over the Hill.

It was a short drive down the hill from the Park & Shop across the bridge and up the winding road that led to town center. The roads looked in a bit better shape than he remembered, the hills looked unchanged. They were mostly covered in maples, sycamores, and a few oak trees. But where a road cut thru the hills or construction took away the topsoil there were small rock slides exposing dull yellow clay and grey sandstone shot thru with thin black coal seams.

RJ didn't remember there being so many pick up trucks in town but then reminded himself that he wasn't even driving yet when he last visited Wayne West Virginia. Not being one of the cool kids with encyclopedic knowledge of car models he was unlikely to have noticed what sort of cars anyone was driving. Still it struck him as stereotypical of the region. There didn't seem to be many SUVs which was funny because as this was exactly the kind of "urban" landscape SUVs were meant for.

As he continued on into town the few things he recognized seemed to have either suffered drastically over the years or remained impervious to the wearing effects of time. There were a few more trailers in the trailer park though most looked exactly like the ones that were there 10 years ago. He remembered playing with the kids that lived there without ever knowing their names. They would just meet up at random times among the piles of gravel and sand the DRW kept at their site across the road. The road crews chased them off regularly but they always came back and played there. Once RJ had slipped on a small pile of road salt and scraped up his arm badly. The salt crystals added their burn to the sting of the injury, but even that wasn't enough to deter him from visiting there the very next day. For a brief moment he considered turning down that road to see if the gravel piles were still there but drove on past consoling himself with the thought that there would be time enough to visit around town after the funeral. Besides, there was a place just ahead he was going to stop regardless of the time spent.

RJ cursed under his breath as he passed a shiny new gas station complete with electronic signage and a well-lit interior. The price for unleaded gas was a few cents cheaper too. He hadn't needed to fill his tank at that strange little station after all. He shook his head and made a mental note to stop here on the way back out if need be. Growling to himself he sped up a bit anticipating the bridge ahead and near it the place where he spent most of his time while living in Wayne. It was a small house with two bedrooms situated on the hillside overlooking the "Brinkley Bridge." So-called because of the ticker-tape noise it made as cars traveled across its rickety frame. Some time later the bridge fell and was replaced with a concrete and steel structure but the memory and the sound was still fresh in RJ's mind. He crossed the bridge as slowly as traffic would let him, glancing down over the side to see if the floodwall was still there. Unable to resist the draw of his memories he pulled over next to the railroad tracks as soon as he crossed the bridge. He got out to look down at the bend of Twelve-pole Creek where it flowed under the bridge and back the way he came.

He half expected to see the iron framework of the old bridge still in the waters below the new one but there was no sign of it or the pylons it once stood on. He couldn't tell if there'd been any change to the 20-foot high floodwall holding back the waters from the lower course of Twelve-pole. Gone also were the large blocks of stone he had laboriously chiseled to free fossils for high school projects. There wasn't supposed to be any substantial fossil finds in the area but he had found six or seven bones in the rock that were the size of a man's hand. RJ made a face at the memory. He'd probably destroyed any value the fossils had by using ten-penny nails as chisels and clumsily hitting them with a common claw hammer. Still he wondered as he stood there what had become of those fossils and the really superb one of a dinosaur footprint he had found in nearby Dunlow and carried around for years?

RJ shrugged to himself and turned to get back in the car. He'd probably given those fossils away as he did so many things he once valued, in order to curry favor with some friend or group he wanted to hang out with. His eyes traveled up the hillside opposite looking for his childhood home but in its place was a billboard proclaiming "A ghost town is dead!" He stared at it for a while trying to work out what it was trying to sell and the nearest he could come up with was something about advertising on the billboard itself. The clock display on his dash caught his eye as he started the car. He would be late for the funeral home if he didn't get moving and he needed to find a place to stop for the night afterwards. He was still puzzling over the words on the sign as he gave his Honda some gas to climb up the last hill before Wayne's main street. "A ghost town is dead!" What the hell did that mean?

He felt a bit of confusion as he topped the hill not remembering which way around the courthouse he should take. The only landmark he recognized was a small pizza chain called Gino's and that seemed to have moved across the street from where he remembered it. He paused at the stop sign a bit longer than normal trying to get his bearings and it was the presence of an old battleship grey artillery cannon that cleared things up for him. He mock-saluted it and drove slowly downhill past the Methodist church and along the bus garage where the middle school now stood. It had been a "Junior" high school when he went there but now the parking lot was all that was left of the old building on the hill and its hundreds of steps. He spared it a lingering look suddenly remembering a near brush with kissing the Dalton twins on a dare…their dare, not his. Someone had built a nice multi-level home on the grounds and the sign above the bus garage proudly proclaimed "Wayne Community Center." RJ wondered when Wayne had developed a sense of community; he sure didn't remember one. There had been nothing more elaborate than "Hobby Days" at the one room public library to distract children from the dismally uninteresting landscape they found themselves in.

The town center was soon behind him and he turned at another new bridge on this end of town. Not as new as the Brinkley Bridge but still not resembling the one he thought he would find here. He remembered there was a second place near this bridge where his family had lived but couldn't spot it from the car. The coincidence had never before struck him that he had lived next to the bridge leading into town and then moved from there to a place next to the bridge leading out of town. It was too late to ask mom if there was any significance to the choice. Again he was jolted back to facing his task here and he started looking for the funeral home. He was pretty sure where it was since it was the same place that held his father's funeral and his brother's before that. Soon as he made a turn and saw the parking lot and the low, unassuming building marked Moore Funeral Home he knew he was in the right place.

Chapter Nine: Inside at last.

The foyer of Moore Funeral Home was slightly cooler and much darker than the afternoon warmth of October just outside it. RJ stood blinking for a moment and tried to read the announcements on the wall while his eyes swam. He could hear indistinct music coming from some other room, something vaguely spiritual but not immediately recognizable. He wondered as he walked forward if there was such a thing as "Ambient Gospel" just for funeral homes. Still half blind he moved near a couple of doors trying to determine where everyone was and spun in surprise when a soft voice behind him said "Mr. Wellman?" He blinked rapidly trying to focus on the small, smartly dressed woman before him who was holding a door open and giving him a slight smile.

"Yes, I'm Mr. Wellman, one of them anyway."

"Come this way, your family is downstairs." He followed her down a short flight of stairs into an open area that would not be out of place in anyone's basement. Comfy, overstuffed sofas sat in a circle around an oval coffee table. Along the walls were discrete speakers and religious symbols set back in shallow alcoves. Sitting at one end of the coffee tables were the owners; Mr. and Mrs. Moore, and at the other end his two brothers, Ronnie and Kelly-Ray.

Ron exclaimed a bit too cheerfully as he walked in. "There he is! Come have a seat son." And KellyRay chimed in "About time too. We can't get anything done here without you." Ron stood up and hugged him, following it with a slap on the back then looked around sheepishly, as if the extra noise and quick movements were discouraged in this place. KellyRay fished in the front pocket of his coveralls and stuck something in his cheek. "We can't get anything done cause none of us has any money. I hope you brought your check book cause its going to cause a helluva lot to bury mom."

Ron sat down and gestured to the seat next to him. RJ swallowed, surprised to be confronted with financial issues so soon after arriving. "Good to see you too." he replied gruffly while eying his middle brother. KellyRay looked back at him critically while shifting whatever it was in his mouth from one cheek to the next. RJ seriously thought he was going to spit on the carpet, or possibly on RJ.

"Well you're the Big City One, living in Indiana with your Hoosier wife and all, clearly doing better than either of us S.O.B.s."

RJ looked around the circle of people about him all expecting him to say something encouraging. "I wouldn't call New Carlisle a big city, there's barely 3000 people there and besides I have 2 kids and a wife in school, there's not much leftover...." The comment was answered with silence and uncomfortable shifting by everyone. RJ noticed Ron sat rigidly and he wondered if he'd hurt his back recently. He wasn't going to ask though he desperately wanted to change the subject. There was no real choice though; it was the Big Question of the night. He frowned at his brothers and the professionally passive faces of the Moores and said "So ummmm, how much money are we talking?"

Mr. Moore cleared his throat and said, "Usually the surviving family members of the deceased split the costs. I think we offer a very reasonable funeral for community members such as your mother starting at $20,000."

The silence got longer and the looks at RJ deeper. KellyRay sat forward and barked out "$20,000! Mom made less than that in a year and I don't make much more. Why's it cost so much to dig a hole and put someone in it anyway?" He leaned to the side to spit, looked at the horrified faces around him and thought better of it. "How much is that each anyway?"

"Call it $7000 from each of us." offered Ronnie who was trying to be helpful even though he had turned slightly green at the number. Mrs. Moore stood and excused herself, flipping thru papers on a clipboard as she left. KellyRay got up as well. "That's no damn good either." and walked back into the room where muted signs could be seen for the toilets. RJ watched him go and said "What else did I miss? Is her insurance handling any of this?"

Mr. Moore looked more uncomfortable and said "Mrs. Wellman didn't seem to have any...active coverage."

KellyRay walked back up and barked out "Stephens! She'd got remarried after Dad died. Where are any of them now? She'd given up being a Wellman when she did that. They should have to pay, not me."

Ron gave KellyRay a withering look and turned to RJ "I called our half-brother Glen and told him about mom. He hadn't heard from her directly since the adoption but I've stayed in touch. Even took him hunting with me last fall."

RJ tried to conjure up an image of his half brother while KellyRay proceeded to tell the story of their abortive hunting trip. "Boy has hay-fever or something...couldn't stop sneezing, had dirt and dried snot all down his face by the end of the day." Then he laughed harshly, "Sounded like a buck in rut!"

RJ couldn't picture what his half brother Glen might look like now, he was only 18 months old when he'd last seen him. Nor could he imagine what was going on inside Kelly's head. Clearly he was doing a poor job of dealing with the situation. Relations between RJ's middle brother and his mom had been strained since their father's death and KellyRay pretty much stayed on his side of Wilson's creek and Mom on the other. He didn't seem to care much for anyone or anything save his dogs, his pickup, and his son Justin. RJ wasn't even sure he had that order right.

RJ stood up and stretched still stiff from the long drive and too tired to think. He felt like he'd been here hours and since there were no windows to let in the light, he just might have been. It could be any time out there. He cursed the state things had fallen to here and wanted to confront his brothers about not taking care of their mom but he wouldn't do that in front of Mr. Moore. No airing family laundry here, though he was sure his brother KellyRay was itching to get into it. The last time RJ was here, KellyRay had decided to bring up some childhood slight 25 years after it happened. Never mind that his father was laying in front of him in a casket with all his relatives gathered round. Any time and any place was good enough for a scrap where KellyRay was concerned.

A delicate clearing of the throat announced Mrs. Moore's return. She said "Mr. Wellman...Richard, there's a phone call for you." RJ blinked at her not understanding for a moment. "Who knows I'm here?" He asked no one in particular as he walked toward the hallway door she was holding open. If he was feeling less fatigue he might have gently corrected her with a "Call me RJ, everyone else does." But instead he silently followed her thru the hallway and back upstairs to an office facing the entrance. She gestured to the phone lying off its cradle and stepped out of the room closing the door behind her. She apparently did a lot with doors in her job. RJ watched her go and then picked up the phone.

"Hello?"

"Mr. Wellman?"

"Yes."

"You're the eldest son of Geraldine Wellman-Stephens?"

"Yes, I believe I am."

"Wellsir, I have good news for you. I managed your mother's insurance policy and it appears that she was still covered at the time of her death after all. Not by much, but it should cover a SMALL funeral and her hospital bills."

"That is good news. I'm sorry...I didn't get your name sir?"

"Wilson, I represent Private and Casualty Insurance.

"And my mother had a policy with you?"

"She was a close and dear friend. I am so sorry for your loss Mr. Wellman."

RJ had never heard of the company but he could dimly remember a salesman coming by years ago when he was in college. He was certain the company name wasn't P&C Insurance though. He was about to ask about the actual amount when the silence was interrupted.

"I won't keep you long. If you could put Mrs. Moore back...put Mrs. Moore on the phone I will make all the arrangements with her."

RJ looked up from the phone to see Mrs. Moore standing silently in the door. She looked as if she expected RJ to be ecstatic about the insurance news. In fact, the slip-up Mr. Wilson just made led him to believe she had called him, not the other way around. He gestured her forward. "He wants to talk to you now."

"Good news, yes?" she said as she took the phone from him. RJ was determined not to be manipulated into gushing his relief so he nodded solemnly. "It appears so. Thank you for taking the time to talk to him."
She looked disappointed at RJ's reaction but then waved it off. "Its nothing, we talk to insurers all the time in this business."

RJ went back down the hall to the basement and Mr. Moore nodded at him and turned to his brothers. "I think your brother has something to say." Both brothers quit bickering where they stood and looked over. RJ had made up his mind not to say anything but it seemed he was being guided along a path whether he wanted it or not.

"That was an insurance company. He said mom had a SMALL policy that should help." Ron showed immediate relief and sat back down. KellyRay eyed RJ suspiciously. "How SMALL is SMALL Big Brother?" RJ shrugged "I didn't ask for an exact amount, he's talking to Mrs. Moore right now. RJ gestured to the door. "Go and ask if you like." He let the offer hang for a long moment but KellyRay made no effort to move towards the door.

Mr. Moore cleared his throat again and said, "The evening grows long. Let us proceed under the assumption that a...modest funeral can now be afforded. Please look at the brochures I have placed on the table for you..."

RJ's mind was trying to shut down on him. He didn't want to be here picking out a dress for his mother to be buried in, he didn't want to be awake at all at the moment but every question came around to him, what he wanted. His brothers were either being mute on the subjects of coffins and color schemes or turning the question around on him. He remembered the final amount barely fell short of the estimate Mr. Moore had originally put forth. He must have had years of guiding people thru difficult questions at a time when they were most in denial, the most emotional. KellyRay left during a discussion of makeup and skin tones saying he had to get back up Wilson's creek before it was too dark. Ron stayed thru the final decisions and they got everything covered but picking out a tombstone which had to wait till the next day anyway now that it was long after closing time. When the Moore's walked them to the door and said their goodnights Ron turned to RJ and said "Son you look like 45 miles of bad road."

"Isn't that just 4 miles of bad road?"

Ron grinned and thumped the top of his pickup. RJ noted he was walking stiffly and holding his back rigidly. "In this case Bro, I mean every mile of it! Follow me back to my place. You can crash on the sofa. Pay no mind to the sound of gunshot, just stay close."

RJ gave him a startled look and he laughed again. "You are so easy to rattle Big Bro, I'm just pulling your leg."

RJ turned his car around in the parking lot and pulled up behind his brother's pickup. Ron hit the gas and spun out in a cloud of dust and gravel as he got traction on the hard tarmac surface. RJ was hard pressed to stay close as his brother sped confidently thru town in the half-light of the evening. Someone waved to Ron from the drugstore doorway and he drove around the courthouse and back to talk to whoever it was. RJ pulled into the spot behind him and waited while his brother talked and joked loudly out his passenger window. He had time to read the bumper sticker on his brother's truck just before it pulled wildly away again. It read, "If God is your co-pilot you need to move over."

Chapter Ten: Overnight on the Hill.

It was full dark by the time RJ had followed Ron back thru town, down the other branch of Wilson's Creek and climbed up this side to just shy of the very top. RJ stayed close behind his brother's truck till he stopped which meant there wasn't much chance for a look around. Ron's house wasn't actually a house at all but a doublewide trailer he'd somehow perched on the top of Wilson's Creek hill. RJ knew that somewhere directly below his brother's house was his Uncle Bob's house. Both of dad's brothers had given Ron some much needed guidance after their father died. RJ hoped that Ron's trailer was further up the hill from his uncle's than it looked in the dark because the slope of the hillside made it look as if it might slide right down and settle on whatever was below it. There wasn't much choice in where he could to leave his car; the widest spot off the road was where Ron parked his truck. RJ stepped out in the dark and felt the ground give wetly. He squished and slid his way to the trunk, retrieved his suitcase and tried hard to keep it out of the mud all the way up to the door. His brother apparently had cleared several acres of land for his trailer but none of it was paved or even had flagstones to step on.

Ron was holding the door for him and saying something but he couldn't hear what it was over the sounds of gunfire coming from inside. RJ looked past Ron and saw that a wide-screen TV took up most of the living room area. A thin young man wearing a ball cap and balancing a tin of snuff on his knee was sitting on the couch and rewinding thru the movie "Terminator 2."

Ron grinned and made room for RJ and his suitcase. "Told ya there would be gunfire. This here's Albert, he's a Useless Fart that I can't seem to get rid of. Useless Fart, this is my Big Brother RJ." RJ nodded and leaned his suitcase against the side of the couch and took the proffered hand. RJ tried to hear the man's reply over the blaring TV but gave up and just said "Nice to meet ya." Albert went back to his movie and started running the movie backwards looking for where he left off. RJ could tell from the scenes going by that it was still early in the movie and realized there wasn't going to be a quiet evening for chat or an early bedtime.

Ron offered him a soda and some snacks and they sat down at either end of the couch to watch the rest of the movie. Albert was propped up in the middle with his feet on an ottoman and a can of beer cradled in his crotch. RJ sank back in the chair and tried to stay awake, answering questions as best he could but not hiding his yawns or pretending to be interested in the movie. He noticed that Albert and his brother spoke to each other in street lingo, and it amused RJ greatly to hear them try to sound 'ghetto' when they were 40 miles away from anything resembling a city, let alone a ghetto.

Somewhere near the last third of the movie Albert paused it and apologetically asked if RJ wanted him to run it back to the beginning since he came in late? RJ assured him he knew the movie well and it wasn't necessary to replay the first hour and a half. Albert started up the movie again and pushed the volume up another notch. RJ could count six speakers in just the space around the sofa. The vibrations along his back indicated there were more behind the sofa itself. Ron noticed RJ counting and bragged on his stereo system stating proudly that he had paid a lot to bring them back from Germany and counted being able to play the TV as loud as he wanted to one of the key benefits of country living. RJ had to agree with him on that point and wondered if Uncle Bob agreed too.

Finally the movie ended and Albert lingered just long enough to finish his third beer before heading off into the dark. RJ's head rang from a combination of the noise he'd just sat thru and his need for sleep. Earlier it had been the long drive that wore him out but now it really was past his bedtime and he felt every inch of those 45 miles of bad road.

Ron pointed out the bathroom and told him to sleep in as long as he liked since he was going to do the same. He apologized for the couch not folding out and then went back into his bedroom for a spare pillow. RJ hugged a cushion and shifted his feet up, stretching his legs for what felt like the first time in days. Ron launched the pillow at him and it slammed into the right side of his face causing a painful snap against the curved arm of the couch. He said, "Think fast!" about 5 seconds too late. RJ was too tired to even give him a dirty look. He waved surrender with a vague gesture of his hand calling out "I remember I remember!" He decided against showering before bed and gratefully closed his eyes. As his mom would say he was asleep before his head hit the pillow. He smiled in the dark briefly and then suddenly felt very sad and miserably alone. He wished he'd come home sooner, he wished he'd never left, but mostly he wished he'd never needed to come back.

Chapter Eleven: The Day Of.

Morning came earlier than either of them wanted it to. RJ did not feel the least bit rested. It was long after 1am before he fell asleep on the couch and a steady parade of noises woke him every hour or two after that. First a car drove up the hill just outside with a loud muffler or possibly no muffler at all then a truck loaded with people pulled up and shouted for his brother to come out and party with them. And finally it was his brother's snoring interspersed with shouts out the bedroom window to tell his dog to go to sleep. RJ hadn't even noticed a dog, let alone one making noises. He tried to go back to sleep one more time but that just earned him a stiff neck and a short dream about storm winds blowing thru some pine trees.

He gave up and straightened his clothes, pushed the couch cushions back to roughly where they were before and peeked around in the kitchen for coffee supplies. An old percolator sat on the countertop near the sink but there wasn't any sign of coffee or filters. RJ gave up and hefted his suitcase onto the ottoman. His back complained bitterly and he knew he'd pay for the exertions of this weekend long after his return to Indiana. He dug thru his bag for some painkillers and recalled Ron's rigid stance and his favoring of his left side. He wondered if back problems ran in his family. His brother KellyRay didn't seem afflicted by it though, he carried his weight well. RJ couldn't remember Ron ever complaining of any back problems before now so he decided to ask him if he'd injured it in the military.

RJ walked quietly down the hallway and opened the bathroom door, shaving kit balanced in one hand and clothes tucked under his arm. As soon as he opened the door a dog started barking loudly from somewhere nearby. RJ sat down in the small room listening and realized that the dog was underneath the house, somewhere right below him. He tried to will the dog to be quiet and not wake his brother but after a minute or two of constant barking his brother shouted from the bedroom next door "SHUT UP you USELESS bag of BONES!" There was no sound for a few minutes and then the dog began growling lowly just beneath RJ's feet. The sound was close enough for RJ to wonder if the dog could see thru the vents in the floor or something equally bizarre.

He sat his clothes and shaving kit on the toilet and stripped down to get into the shower. He turned the knob marked "H" and the plumbing creaked and a shudder ran up the handle and along RJ's arm. Eventually a thin stream of water came out of the spigot and puddled on the tub's bottom. It took its own meandering time to find the drain. He tried the other knob and all this did was slightly increase the flow of water. He pulled up on the lever that should send the water to the showerhead and nothing happened. When he let go of it the lever fell back down and water continued to flow leisurely into the tub, swirl a bit and then go down the drain. RJ looked for a stopper for the tub and there was nothing around the right size. He was clearly missing something here. He used a washcloth to plug the hole, sitting on the edge of the tub while he watched its progress. It didn't take him long to realize it would take hours to fill up at this rate. He debated waking his brother but decided to kneel across the tub and wet his hair with water by catching it in his cupped hands. This process took a long time and his ribcage hurt before he was able to wash and rinse his hair.

The rest of his ablutions were equally abbreviated and with a sense of defeat he packed everything up and went back to the living room. The clock on the wall above the stove read 9:37 am and Ron was still not out of bed. There was nothing to do for hours before the viewing started and RJ felt restless and hungry. He peeked into the fridge again and noted that it was well stocked but not much in the "eat quietly' category. He sat back down and looked out the bay window facing down the hill, settling for a few stale chips and a sip of lukewarm soda.

His brother's yard stretched down the hill several hundred feet all rough-cut trees and bare patches where the sandy yellow clay showed thru. RJ could just make out the backyard of a house at the bottom of the hill and several cars parked at odd angles around it. Occasionally a car or truck would chug its way up the hill but no one turned up the lane that led to Ron's house. RJ turned around and looked to either side thru the diamond-shaped window set in the front door but could not see if there were other houses further up the hill behind this one. He opened the door and started to step out when a brown and black hound pushed its way in between his legs and trotted down the hallway. RJ looked after it curiously and moments later there was a loud "Dammit dog, keep your cold-assed nose to yourself!" RJ suppressed a laugh picturing the scene down the hall and decided it would be a good idea to step out onto the decking.

The air was crisp and cool and the hill behind the trailer presented RJ with a steep slope leading to a gravel road that curved up and around the house and further on around the ridge. Deep ruts in the clay marked the road to his brother's trailer and he wondered how he had managed to drive up here without sliding into them in the dark. Most of them were deeper than his car tires and had standing water in them from somewhere. Wincing he remembered a few bad scraping sounds as he came up the hill and he resolved to have the undercarriage looked at when he was back in town. A town. Any town.

Ron came up behind him dressed only in a pair of gym shorts and booted the dog out the door. "Mornin' Bro. May I politely ask you what the HELL was the noise coming from the bathroom just now?"

"Ummmn, the dog growling?"

"No sir, it was not a dog. It sounded like you had a small aircraft engine in there with you."

"Oh, that was my blow dryer."

"BLOW-dryer!" Ron exclaimed looking skeptically at RJ's hair.

"Yes it was a blow dryer Mr. "Chainsaw.' You got a lot of nerve to complain about a blow dryer with all the noise going on around here last night."

Ron grinned at the use of his military nickname. The guys at the base gave him the nickname Chainsaw because of his loud snoring. He wouldn't be diverted though and asked incredulously: "You use a BLOW dryer?"

"Well normally, there wasn't much use in it today. I couldn't get enough water to fully wet my head let along take a shower."

Ron looked back down the hallway towards the bathroom. "You couldn't? Did you turn on the pump first?"

"What pump?"

"Son we're at the top of Wilson's Creek Hill where do you think the water comes from? It has to be pumped up out of a well 154 feet below this trailer."

"You didn't tell me about a pump. I didn't see anything in the bathroom to turn on a pump." Ron ran his fingers thru his short cut hair and stomped down to the bathroom. He looked around in there for a while then came back out and reached under the kitchen sink. There next to a box of cleaning pads and a bag of dog food was a switch hanging loose from the wall. Two heavy looking wires ran down from it thru the floor next to the drainpipe. Ron flipped the switch and listened to something far off chugging and whining before standing back up.

"It'll take a while to pump up enough water for a shower. You've used up most of what was in the pipe is my guess. Doesn't look like you hurt anything though..."

"Sorry, I didn't know."

"Well leave it for now. It'll take a while to fill up the pipe, but there ought to be enough for coffee."

"Yes! I couldn't find that either."

Ron shook his head sadly and opened a cabinet over the fridge and took out a small jar of instant coffee.

"IN-stant coffee!" RJ mimicked his brother's earlier shock perfectly. "YOU drink IN-stant coffee? Now I know I'm in the boondocks!"

Ron looked at the jar and then back at RJ. "Its mom's."

RJ stared at the jar as if some essence of his mother was still there deep in the brown crystals. He had often wondered why his mother drank this cheap store brand of instant instead of real ground coffee. Its harsh taste was the main reason he hadn't learned to like coffee before leaving home. He realized suddenly that she probably would have preferred a better brand but could not afford it. He looked across the jar at Ron and said softly "I'd be honored."

Chapter Twelve: Among the Living.

RJ recognized the room.

This was the same room where his father's funeral was held a decade before. Though this time there was no hiding in the back row with his school buddy Tripplett. In fact the seats were gone completely though a few folding chairs had been brought in for some of the elderly family members who couldn't stand long.

RJ immediately noticed that there was a sort of unspoken division going on in the room between families. It reminded him of the odd sort of layout you see at a wedding. The reasons and motivations aren't much different in either case. There was a knot of men to the right made up mostly of uncles from his father's side and a few first cousins. On the left were small groups of people from his mother's side of the family. They weren't as tightly knotted as the other group. RJ walked into the open gray area in between and noticed that there was no one from the Stephens family in either group. Maybe they felt like they wouldn't be welcome. RJ had no idea if his mom still had any contact with her second husband's family after he died. Out-lived them both, didn't ya mom? he thought to himself as he walked slowly toward the dais where his mother's casket was displayed. Her sister Mary was just walking away from it and there was a tall man of slim build bent over the edge of the casket crying into his handkerchief. RJ waited respectfully and got a few hugs from his Aunt Eleanor and her husband Bill. The man turned around and straightened himself. RJ noticed he easily topped seven feet tall. He looked over his handkerchief as he moved forward and extended his other hand to RJ.

"I'm deeply deeply sorrowful for your lost." RJ returned his handshake solemnly and tried to place the man. He wasn't a family member, at least not one RJ recognized and he was certain he hadn't met the man before. His accent was definitely southern but perhaps from deeper down South. Even so it sounded completely out of place here. RJ searched the man's tear-streaked face questioningly hoping an introduction was forthcoming. "Ah...thank you sir, that means a lot. " The man said nothing further and started past RJ then turned back, gripping RJ's shoulder. He said loudly "You may have lost a mother, but I have lost a dear dear companion, and I am bereft! Simply bereft!"

RJ blinked back at him, his questions silenced by the man's outburst. He watched the man's tall narrow back as he walked away into the crowd but before he could ask anyone who the man was his cousin LindaKay nudged him and nodded toward the line of people behind him. "Go on up RJ, say goodbye to your momma."

RJ took those last few steps as if the all the fatigue he'd felt in the past thirty-six hours were suddenly piled up on his back. He focused on the dark blue dress with roses printed on it and tried not to cry. It was no use. He stood there for what was probably only 10 minutes gazing at his mothers face, seeing that she was at peace at last. Inside it felt like an eternity before he could look away.

Suddenly he was shocked out of his mourning by the sound of his mother's voice coming from somewhere behind him. She was saying "Hello RJ it's been too long!" He wheeled around and saw his mother standing before him in a muted floral dress and a dark cabled sweater. His mouth dropped open but no sound came out. He took a step back to look at the body in the coffin and then over at his mother. She was still standing there, smiling and holding out her arms to him. With a strangled cry he rushed forward and hugged her tightly, crying even more tears. The woman hugging him patted his back and said, "I'm sorry I didn't let you know I was coming back, I just got here myself."

"Coming back? From...from?" RJ's mind started working again after several moments and he felt his brother's hand on his shoulder. "Bet you forgot mom had a twin sister didn't you? I know I did. There here's your Aunt Irene."

RJ looked at her face again. He could see she looked like a less travel weary version of his mother and he blushed deeply. He managed a soft "Of course." Aunt Irene was still a bit surprised at RJ's outburst and she patted him on the back as she untangled herself from his hug. "Now I know what people mean when they say someone looks like they've seen a ghost! But I'm here to tell you that the only shock bigger than that is looking over there and seeing myself lying in a coffin." Her voice trailed off and RJ followed her gaze over his shoulder and back to where several of his cousins were hugging each other and crying over the coffin. Irene walked over and spoke to them then they all hugged at the same time and a new bout of tears and sobs started up.

RJ felt he needed air or he was going to explode and he didn't dare look over at his uncles to see if they had witnessed his shock at seeing his mother standing before him only to find it was her twin sister from Ohio. He went quickly up the stairs and out into the too bright day. He walked over to his car and rummaged in the glove box for a tissue and wiped his face. He put a spare in the pocket of his suit and took several deep breaths.

"You're not leaving already are you?"

RJ looked around and saw his brother KellyRay leaning into the back of his pickup, an older and more beat up twin to Ronnie's. KellyRay spat tobacco juice on the dry ground and nodded to a young man standing on the other side. "Do you remember him? He's your half brother Glen. Hey Glen, remember RJ? He's the one too good to live in West Virginia anymore."

Glen walked around the back of the truck and offered his hand to RJ. RJ took it and pulled him into a hug. Glen had short dark hair, no beard, and wore crisp new jeans. He smelled of denim and Old Spice. KellyRay said "Remember changing his diaper when we were living on the Vaughn's farm back in Mentone?" RJ did remember but he didn't choose to mention it just now. RJ was really glad Glen had come and told him so. He saw none of his mother's face in Glen's but thinking back to his father Glen Sr. he could place the hair and the smile.

"Have you been in yet?" RJ asked nodding toward the open door of the funeral home, the darkness within masking anything beyond the shaft of sunlight in the hallway.

"No I haven't. I've been trying to convince KellyRay here he needs to go in." RJ turned to face his brother with a stern look. "Why haven't you gone in yet? Everyone's down there." KellyRay shifted his tobacco from one side of his mouth to the other and answered. "Two reasons, and that's reason number one. Reason number two is 'cause I don't want to come out looking as stupid as you do right now."

RJ realized his face must still be red and tear streaked and he was certain there were stains on his shirt as well. He glanced in the side view mirror of Kelly's truck and resisted the urge to try and pat his hair into place with his fingers. "There's nothing stupid about crying at your mother's funeral."

RJ could see KellyRay was working up something more to say but he wasn't going to debate it with him. He said, "Suit yourself!" and turned to Glen putting his arm around his shoulder. "C'mon Glen, I'll go in with you and nobody will say ANYTHING. Its the right thing to do." And with that he led his half brother down to see his mother one last time.

Chapter Thirteen: Hillside.

The line of cars creeping up the hill was short compared to how many were parked outside the funeral home. RJ was fourth in line and there was maybe another four behind him. Many of the people who came to the funeral would not make the climb up to Johnson's Cemetery and there were several more with cars that shouldn't try to navigate the unpaved road in any case. RJ's Honda complained and whined in several spots forcing him to downshift and fishtail on the unpaved road but he eventually made it to the top of the hill and parked in the grass along one side.

There were already people at graveside and a trio of singers from a nearby church was filling the air with hymns. He walked along the row of the graves finding the Wellmans interspersed among the Johnsons, Marcums, Robinsons and Stampers. His brother Randy's grave and his father's had a bit of unused space around them that had been recently cleaned. Whoever did the cleaning had even scraped a layer of moss and soil off the top making the two graves look sunk-in and fresh. They were not of course; his father had died ten years before and his older brother Randy had died as a child of 13. RJ had been seven at the time but he remembered standing in that very same spot all those many years ago.

The gravesite dug for his mother's casket was about twice as far from his father's grave than his brother's was on the other side giving the layout a definite sense of being off center. Possibly the caretaker was showing some deference to the Wellman family. How would you decide that RJ silently pondered; closer to her first husband or closer to her father? Or possibly back down the hill at the Damron cemetery where her second husband was buried? Clearly some negotiation had gone on without his input. RJ wondered if there might be the same seating strategy used in a cemetery as there was in funerals and weddings? It must make a weird kind of sense to someone.

After the preacher said his piece the choir started singing "Rock of Ages" and RJ broke down into tears again. The sound of his mother's favorite hymn brought back too many memories to hold in. He sat down on a hardwood bench and watched a few of the people who did not attend the memorial service setting up a tarp and pushing tables together for a meal. RJ had stopped trying to figure out who was who hours ago and he just thanked people for coming and accepted hugs and handshakes automatically. The emotion of the day had already left him feeling raw and ready to be alone.

Someone he thought was his Aunt Ruth had taken up a collection and she pressed a handful of bills and change into his hand, said everyone was so so sorry and turned quickly away. RJ didn't know what to do with it. He didn't remember any money changing hands when his father or brother died though if it had it probably went to his mother. He stood for several moments looking around for someone to ask, silencing the urge to call out to Aunt Ruth as she walked back down the hill. He was afraid he'd gotten the names wrong and the woman might be his Aunt "C" instead. Another branch of the family he remembered fondly but had no idea how or even if they were actually related to him. He glanced at the tangle of crumpled bills in his hand and remarked out loud to no one in particular: "What a strange ritual this is; part funeral, part church revival, and part family reunion!"

After the meal he gave the roughly sixty dollars and change to the preacher and asked him to share it with the choir. Brother Damron was just as surprised and embarrassed by the gesture as RJ had been. He asked if RJ was sure? RJ nodded and patted him on the shoulder and said, "She would have loved this!" and walked away. They both were left wondering why he'd said such a strange thing. His mother had mentioned death just once to RJ since Randy had died: "I'd rather you were dancing a jig on my grave than spend the whole blessed day crying and wailing. The time to feel sorrow for me will be long past." RJ wondered how that wish and her Irish roots had mutated into the event he was seeing around him today? RJ came to the conclusion that the death of Geraldine Wellman had made more of a stir in the small community of Wayne West Virginia than she'd ever done while alive.

He walked back towards his car and found his brother Ron at his truck getting out some tools to help clean up the cemetery. RJ wondered where the energy came from since he himself felt weak and didn't even want to stand let alone do yard work. It seemed everyone wanted to do something, wanted to help in some way. Quietly he helped Ron take down the "Funeral Today" banner that was hanging between two identical pine trees that had been planted for the purpose years ago.

The two brothers stood talking softly about nothing in particular for a long time as they looked down at the hillside and across the river. They could just make out Granmaw Wellman's house from the hilltop and the tiny speck of her dog Sparky running around in the yard. Ron reckoned she was feeling poorly and since she was blind and Aunt Chrissy didn't drive it was unlikely either of them would make it up to the cemetery anytime soon.

"She's become more reclusive since she had to auction a lot of her belongings to pay taxes on that tiny piece of land. Everything went up in value after the Military moved in and there's word they're thinking about flooding half of Wilson's creek to put in a reservoir. Anyway she'd probably think it a great pleasure to see you since you've come all the way down from Indiana and all."

RJ agreed and said he would stop in there before he left town. He said his goodbyes and promised to come by Ron's house again before leaving town. He was certain they both knew he was lying. He drove the car out of the cemetery and started to try and find his way back down the hill. He didn't really care where he finally came back to the main road, which was a good thing since he ended up going miles out of his way. He passed a sign for Dunlow and realized he was on the wrong side of Twelve-pole creek to be headed out of town. He decided to stop in at Granmaw Wellman's so that tomorrow he could go back into Huntington and stay a night in a hotel before driving back to Indiana. He deserved that much. With a possible stop in Kenova if any of his high school buddies were still around to chat with.

The road was in better shape than he remembered it but one whole section of highway 152 was closed now having become the entrance to a military base of some sort. RJ seemed to recall there was a microwave tower up on one of the highest ridges but wasn't certain if he was near that now or not. It wasn't as easy to find Granmaw Wellman's house as it had looked from up on the hill and he found himself slowing down in several spots trying to see familiar landmarks. Several times someone in a truck behind him beeped harshly to remind him that he was the only tourist around.

Eventually he pulled up to Granmaw Wellman's house and eyed it closely before he got out to be sure he had the right place. The yard looked a bit like he remembered though there were no crops planted in the small field next door. He got out of the car and looked the place over slowly. It was the right place, though the porch looked even more saggy and worn down than before. A new roof of tarpaper gleamed in the sun and there was a large patch of gravel where most of the grass had been before. It looked like some large trucks had parked in the yard and then back-filled the grooves with gravel. He expected to be jumped on by Granmaw Wellman's dog but Sparky was nowhere to be seen. Unless he missed his guess, Sparky was probably hiding under the porch amid a pile of stolen toys.

His Aunt Chrissy met him before he got to the top step of the porch, shouting back over her shoulder "Lord its Richard Allen, come to visit his Granmaw!" He hugged the rotund woman and was struck by how much shorter she seemed than he remembered. The smell of lilac water that went everywhere with her became more pervasive as she led him into the small living room where his grandmother sat in her rocker exactly where she had been decades before when RJ last saw her.

Chapter Fourteen: Seven Across.

Granmaw Wellman was blind. That in no way slowed her down but people visiting her had to be precise where they put things and mind whether their feet stuck out or not. She had a reserved space on the end of her sofa within hands reach of her rocker. That was the Visitor's seat.

People said that she went blind from doing the crossword puzzles in Grit magazine. People also said that she had killed a bear with a frying pan full of bacon one day. People had a lot of respect for Granmaw Wellman and nobody messed her around.

When he was a child RJ had been frightened to meet someone so old, but once he got over the shock he spent a lot of time in her Visitor's seat. He looked at her now and realized it would be hard to tell if she'd aged any at all since then. She still looked older than dust, regarding him with her hawk-like gaze. Back then she wore tri-focals -- that was before she lost her eyes--not her eyesight mind you, she claimed she still had that, she just didn't care see things that didn't matter. Granmaw Wellman looked for all the world like Granny Sweet in those old Sylvester and Tweety cartoons. And that was just fine with RJ.

RJ came forward and sat down in the Visitor's seat noting that his grandmother looked so thin and fragile he was worried he'd hurt her with a warm hug. He spoke a bit too loudly as he sat down. "How're you doing Granmaw?"

"Not so bad as to complain about it nor so well off that I'd go about bragging." She gave him a long look with her blind eyes. "Been a long time since you've been to visit your Granmaw, what do you have to say for yourself?"

"Oh well, you know..."

"No, I don't know or I wouldn't have asked." She looked over her left shoulder as if she had a secret audience or maybe a parrot on her shoulder and said "Tsskk! Kids!" Then she said "Where's that wife of yours, and your kids? Don't they go to funerals back in Indiana?"

"Well, actually they are at Disneyland."

"Disneyland? They can't interrupt their visit to see a cartoon mouse long enough to go to your poor momma's funeral?"

RJ looked down even though he knew she couldn't see it and said softly "That is...the gist of it. Her work is paying for the transportation and one of her co-workers has a house down there. She said it had been planned too long to change." He left it at that and looked closer at Granmaw Wellman's face. The way she focused on you it was like she really could still see. Maybe that was why she made everyone who came to visit sit in the same spot. She knew where that was in her head.

Granmaw Wellman huffed and folded her arms across her chest. She shifted forward in her seat and RJ saw a sign on the other side of her chair written in Aunt Chrissy's deliberate hand: "Do NOT tell my Mother Bad News." RJ sighed and wondered why that sign wasn't out on a table or tacked on the door as you come in? Maybe it had been and Granmaw moved it out of sight. He looked around to catch Aunt Chrissy's eye and let her know he'd seen it but she was nowhere in sight. That was unusual for her, she usually hovered right on the edge of your vision, ready to step in if there was any conflict or question that might upset her mother.

"I suppose the plan is for you to go join the merry-making after you leave here? Anxious to get some sun are you? You know you have relatives down there; your first cousin's husband Conrad drives a truck shipping oranges."

"Uh, No ma'am, I'm headed back home. Work gave me just the Monday off."

"Please Don't UH and pause like that. You have my permission to completely form an answer before starting to talk."

RJ grinned and felt like he was back in grade school. She really did sound like Granny Sweet at times. He felt himself sitting up straighter in his chair and leaned a bit forward, hands folded in his lap.

Granmaw Wellman reached over to a worn, yellowed newspaper folded up on her magazine stand. RJ could see it had a half-completed crossword puzzle on it. He was about to ask about it when she said "You still working nightshift at that Notre Dame place?"

"Yes Granmaw, in Computer Operations." She paused and run her thumb along the edge of the newspaper. RJ was struck how the gesture was exactly the same as if you had a knife in your hand instead of a rolled up newspaper. She unfolded the paper and spread it on her lap. "You ever see anything strange there son?"

"Strange Granmaw?"

"Like Shadows. Ghosts. Spirits and Principalities?"

RJ thought long and hard about the question. Sometimes on nightshift he felt like he was on the bridge of a spaceship, carrying future settlers to some habitable star. He wasn't sure he wanted to explain that concept to his grandmother so he tried a different approach. "The reflections on the glass sometimes make it look like people are outside the building when they're really not, is that what you mean?"

Granmaw scoffed at that and muttered over her shoulder again. "Reflections...that's the best he can do." She held out the newspaper. "Read me the clues, I'm workin' on Seven Across. Five letter word for "Ghost Dancers."

RJ looked at the paper, it looked like several different people had tried to help finish the puzzle. It had been written on and erased in several colors of ink, pencil, and even marker. He wondered just how old the paper was and started to unfold it to see the date on the top.

His grandmother touched his hand and said, "Stay focused! And I know what a cheater sounds like. A cheater flips thru that crossword dictionary over there and finds the answer without any effort, without thinking." RJ looked at the pale, almost translucent skin of her hand and felt a bit panicked. He tried to think about the answer and looked at the other bits of finished puzzle. "It has a U in the middle." he offered helpfully.

"Yes yes, I got that far with your Aunt Chrissy. Chrissy! Bring RJ a glass of milk with some cornbread tore up in it."

RJ blinked at the strange request and called into the kitchen "Just some water will be fine Aunt Chrissy." He wondered about that combination of food and before he could ask his grandmother said "You told me you liked milk and cornbread, don't you remember? I do. T'was on your 5th birthday. Gerry brought you over to see us for the first and last time before you all moved to Virginia to be near the naval base where that no good father of yours was stationed."

RJ spread his hands out in surrender almost knocking the glass out of Aunt Chrissy's hand. She had silently appeared beside him with a tumbler of water and ice. He nodded his thanks to her and took a sip. It was icy cold and tasted of minerals. It was strange but not unpleasant and the taste came back to him over the years. He remembered helping draw water from a deep well in the back yard. He took another drink, the ice making the only noise in the room. He sat it down on a doily and said, "You know, I don't recall that at all..."

"Hoo Hoo! I do! Sharp as a carpet tack your Granny is!" She slapped the arm of her rocking chair and smiled right at RJ. He was sure she was looking out at him thru her veiled broken eyes. Looking thru him maybe.

"Now, she said, tapping her fingers on the newspaper. "Seven Across. I'll give you a hint. It has to do with Indians." Then she got quieter and patted his hand "As do so many things around here if you go back far enough." RJ had the distinct impression she already knew the answer. He was back at school and this was some kind of oral test.

"If you guess it right, I'll tell you a story about Indians, but not this kind of indian, oh no."

RJ went on to other hints, working around the missing word with his grandmother who often paused to tell him local gossip and how things were done back in her day. But listen as close as he could RJ couldn't exactly place when her day was. Sometimes she would talk about being a young girl during the Depression and sometimes she'd talk about such and such president and the arrival of the railroad in this county and it would sound like she was much much older. He only knew she looked to be about a hundred when he'd first met her, and that was 38 years ago.

He focused again on what she was saying, half fascinated by her font of knowledge and half wishing he could think of a way to leave without hurting anyone's feelings. Of all the attempts to get him to linger in Wayne County he'd been thru so far, the dry almost weightless touch of his grandmother's hand on his had shackled him to the spot. Finally he got a word that intersected Seven across. The last letter of the missing word was an X. Granmaw Wellman looked at him expectantly "Can't be many words that begin with an S, end with an X, and has an U in the middle. RJ looked at what he had written down. S _ _UX. He thought to himself "Suuux!" and he said "Sorry Granmaw, that doesn't help me any."

"Well you'll just have to work on it tomorrow then, too late to start out for Indiana now anyway. "

RJ looked up with a start and saw that it was pitch black outside. He must have sat for hours in the Visitor's Seat trying to do a crossword puzzle with his grandmother when he should have been heading out of state. He picked up his untouched glass; it still had ice floating in it. He took a slow drink and tried to think of an ironclad excuse to head back to Huntington tonight. The mineral taste refreshed him and seemed to feed some unspoken hunger deep within him.

"Ice doesn't melt very fast here does it?"

"Its Deepice, takes longer 'cause of the minerals. Good for you. Helps you sleep."

Aunt Chrissy was suddenly there, taking the glass away from RJ. "Oh now Mother, Richard Allen doesn't want to hear your tall tales about ice."

Granmaw Wellman looked up and bit her lips; she had no teeth so it looked very severe on her face. RJ could tell she wanted to say something but present company made her think better of it. She stuck out her tongue to wet her thumb. The gesture was lost on RJ, but he could tell Aunt Chrissy knew what it meant.

"Go and get your bag young-un, Chrissy will turn down the spare bed for you."

"Already done Mother." Aunt Chrissy said as she stepped to a beaded curtain and held it aside for him, smiling at his confused look. "A foregone conclusion I'm afraid. I knew you wouldn't disappoint your Granmaw."

Granmaw Wellman slowly got up from her chair and stood by the screen door looking out at the dark or perhaps just listening while RJ went to his car. When he came back in he moved past her, freshly assaulted by the smell of lilac water and she said "I believe I will sit on the porch a while. It is cooler out there and we're likely to get more company if my bones have any say in the matter."

Chapter Fifteen: A little Night Visit.

The close, warm air of Granmaw Wellman's spare bedroom reminded RJ of having a fever. Of childhood diseases and the long dry years flowing back into the dark around him. He couldn't see a thing that had changed in this room since he'd spent a week in bed here sick with both the measles and the chicken pox. The walls held the same World War memorabilia, (WWI,WWII? He couldn't tell.) some faded fabric samples and a shelf of old dolls in crochet'd dresses with yellowed china doll complexions.

The railings on the bed were worn down to the brass and the bedding felt cool and possibly damp. RJ smiled wryly as he slid into bed, they always had felt like that, like camping in a cave. Aunt Chrissy had seen to it that the sheets were tucked in tightly on every corner, which was a real problem for RJ since he'd grown too tall for that bed years ago. He felt certain that the pillows and comforter in the 'wedding ring' quilt pattern were the same as the last time he slept here. The pillows smelled of musty feathers. RJ seemed to recall that his granmaw once kept chickens at her place, maybe this was what had happened to them?

Directly overhead were two low watt light bulbs mounted in between twin sets of deer antlers. He registered the skulls with a start remembering the fear those hollow sockets invoked in him as a child. In all the years since he'd never seen anyone keep that much of an animal's skull for decoration. Usually it was just the antlers by themselves or maybe the full head but this was the entire skull except the lower jaw. It looked as if the deer skull was biting thru the wooden plank they were mounted on. RJ began to doubt he could sleep at all with his mind running back and forth thru all the memories this house brought him.

He wondered if they were all bad memories and try as he might, he was hard pressed to remember any good ones. His mother only seemed to come here in hard times. When trouble was closing in she would head for the little house on the hill with the tarpaper walls and corrugated tin for a roof. It was her sanctuary. RJ guessed that if he'd lived in any one place as long as his mom had lived here he'd feel the same about it. He grimaced to himself with the realization that he had no such sanctuary, had never had. He pulled the chain dangling down past the deer's gaping eye sockets and the dark rushed in around him. As an adult he felt uncomfortable to be cared for by his elderly family but deep inside he knew this was as close as he would get to his mother from now on.

RJ wasn't sure when he fell asleep. He drifted off listening to the distant soft sound of Aunt Chrissy's old Philco bringing in some station that carried news of her "Sisters of the Eastern Star" and their projects with the poor children around the world. RJ was amazed to hear it still worked. Anything with a wooden case and tubes had no right to still function in 1999. Maybe this house preserved things as well as it had his grandmother? Its tinny voice faded in and out and at some point was replaced by the sound of his granmaw talking to someone outside. He lay still and listened, almost asleep but wondering who would have come by at that hour for surely it must be long past midnight by now?

"Well come on up if you're coming. " Granmaw Wellman was saying, "I don't think you mean any harm or you wouldn't stand there waiting to be invited."

Hello Granmaw...do you remember me?"

"I know you were laid to rest next to your daddy way too early son, is what."

The visitor walked up the porch steps, each one creaking and releasing slowly as if the stranger had problems moving without aid, without pausing to rest his full weight on each step as he went.

"Sparky remembers you, even though he's no longer a pup."

"None of us are...well...none of you all are..." RJ could hear the collie's tail thumping rapidly against the wooden floor of the porch. He was distracted by trying to remember when they'd given Granmaw that puppy...14...15 years ago? The stranger's dry breathing filled the pauses as he spoke and RJ wondered if this was an elderly friend of the family, ruined by black lung like his grandfather had been.

"Little brother is here...but he doesn't know why yet does he?"

"No young'un. I have been fixin' to tell him and we've all been wishing mightily we wouldn't have to, that you were still here to take up Gerry's work."

"I know Granmaw...that's why I came. Besides, its been so hot lately...the ground's all cracked up...a feller can't hardly get any rest. What with the funeral not a stone's throw away..."

"Did Gerry ask you to come see me young-un?"

"She sure wishes she could...come herself Granmaw...but you know there's a time of wandering...before you find your way... isn't there?"

"That's what the songs say boy. I reckon I'll find out for myself afore too long."

RJ dared not breathe; he listened intently, trying to picture the scene out on the porch. There was the creak of a chair taking weight. Then he heard Sparky whine and his nails clicked down the steps as he left for his place under the porch.

"Why you're soakin' wet and smell of the river! Were you in such a hurry to see your Granny that you couldn't cross Twelve-pole at the bridge?"

"I reckon I was Granmaw...and I have to get back right soon...I just wanted you to know...how sorry I am that I can't do this for you...for the family. Plus Gerry...mom… wanted me to tell you not to fret none...that she's in a well lit place now...among friends."

"Oh your Granmaw knows that Randall Lee, and she knows its not gonna be easy to find a replacement for her. You four boys were to sort it out between yourselves once you were old enough. Its such a pity you got bit by that tick and died..."

There was a long silence. RJ shivered despite the heavy comforter clutched to his chest. His mind rebelled with the thought of what was on his Granmaw's porch. But it couldn't be. Someone was playing a trick on her, a cruel vicious trick. Granmaw Wellman was blind he reminded himself, but sharp as she was, she would still have a soft spot for anyone pretending to have news of her recently departed daughter. RJ's heart ached as it dawned on him that Granmaw HAD lost a daughter, a loss just as intimate and painful as losing a mother. That thought pushed thru the dread he was feeling and clinched the deal in his head. He slid back the covers and turned slowly, trying not to let the bedsprings creak as he shifted one leg over the side.

"Ronnie'd be a good choice...KellyRay's strong enough...but too stubborn to listen...when he needs to...How are you going to convince RJ...to stay here and not go back...to Indiana?"

Granmaw hummed and chanted to herself for a bit "mmmn mmmn mmmn.... Quite a few people are studying on that very question." She sounded like she was drifting to sleep then said more clearly. "He can be loyal to a lost cause at all the wrong times and he takes so long to make up his mind on the little things, and not one to take chances. I'm am of two minds on whether Them that live Below would prefer him or not." Then she paused and hummed some more, the only other sound the creaking of two rocking chairs moving in tandem. "They are so anxious to have things sorted before Harvest time."

RJ had one foot on the floor, he braced on the bed knob to stand and it creaked loudly. He froze, listening to and not liking what was being said about him. The voices went on though he thought he heard the rocking chairs stop as someone stood up.

"Ronnie's got that bad back and there's a lot of hauling and crawling to do. Plus he's had military training and you know how that broke your father's mind."

RJ set his other foot on the floor and looked toward the beaded curtain. It would be impossible to sneak thru it without everyone in the house hearing it so he determined to push thru quickly. Half a dozen steps would take him to the screen door and then another two and he would be on the porch between the steps and whoever it was pretending to be his dead brother.

"It will be...the death of him."

Granmaw Wellman sucked in her breath. "Say what you mean clearly young'un; the training or his back?"

"I...."

RJ stepped to the beaded curtain and it opened before him as he reached out making him startle. His aunt Chrissy was standing there in her heavy cotton nightgown. She held her fingers up to his lips and whispered urgently "Not now RJ, please Jesus don't go out now!" RJ tried to look around her to the screen door. He could see the outline of someone standing there, looking back at him, but he could not make out who they were. The figure seemed to shrink a bit as he watched to barely the height of a child. A dry, dark hand touched the screen, and then another as they cupped a face pressed up against the wire, outlined but indistinct. "He's still fat as ever...fatter!"

"WHO are you?" RJ called over his aunt's shoulder. She was pressing hard against his chest and praying loudly trying to muffle the sound of everything else. RJ wanted to push her aside and confront the stranger on the porch but she cried and wailed against his chest, gripping his shirt so tightly that she pulled chest hairs in her distress. He looked down at her and pried her fingers from him, not able to get past her in the narrow doorway. The screen door creaked as it opened and then banged as it was let go.

"Too soon!" Aunt Chrissy was shouting between gospel lyrics "We will all meet up yonder over there! But its too Soon RJ, Lord Jesus please!"

The figure at the door walked down the steps into the yard and RJ forcibly sat his aunt down in the Visitor's seat. He burst out onto the porch and peered into the dark. His eyes wouldn't adjust fast enough and he stumbled down the steps, slipping and falling hard on the last one. He scrabbled at the railing and took a couple steps into the dark yard. He thought he heard rapid footsteps on the road just beyond and childish laughter.

"Never could catch me little brother!" Granmaw Wellman stood, felt her way to the door and hugged Aunt Chrissy to calm her.

"Its alright Chrissy, its alright. Those two said their goodbyes years ago. They aren't going to set things to happening by crossing paths now. No ill will come of this so just calm down." RJ stood in the dark wishing he had a flashlight to shine down the road, maybe catch a glimpse of who had just left. He thought that he knew who it was, really knew, and the thought chilled him to the bone. No way he thought to himself. NO F--ing Way. He went to his car and hit the headlights; they shined out across the sidewalk and over the tops of the plants in the un-tended garden. They weren't pointing in the right direction to help but he felt calmer by breaking darkness' grip around him. He noticed that even the insects were quiet now and no wind moved the leaves of the crab apple tree directly in front of the car.

He shivered and looked around, every dark corner of the yard suddenly suspect. He could see the hillside's black outline behind his Granmaw's house and the squares of light shining out from the kitchen and bedroom stood out like holes cut in the night, letting the light of the next day shine thru. RJ's fear was settling deep in his chest, in his stomach and he was wondering how to leave the lights of his car on so he could walk that path of light back to the house and then turn them off without ending up in the dark. Maybe he should sleep in the car for the rest of the night? Maybe he should drive away as fast as he could and not stop till dawn? No, driving would mean going down the road the same direction the visitor went and the thought of who might be walking along that road now, maybe putting out a thumb for a lift was the most frightening thing RJ had ever considered in his waking life.

His Granmaw's voice broke the freezing grip of his fear. "Come back inside RJ. Chrissy's put water on to boil for coffee. I see right now that no one's going to get any sleep till we have ourselves a little talk." RJ turned off his car and quickly walked up the sidewalk to the steps. He slipped in a puddle of water he hadn't seen on the way down and wiped his feet on the rug outside the screen door. It was wet too. Granmaw Wellman felt out for him and gave his hand a squeeze. The cold pit of fear inside him melting as he was led into the kitchen. Aunt Chrissy wouldn't catch his eye and busied herself with the coffee. Granmaw Wellman sat down in a precisely positioned chair and said "Looks to me like you're gonna get your story about Indians after all."

Chapter Sixteen: A mad Irish poet and some Indians.

"Long before your Granmaw or any of us came to these hills our ancestors were walked on Irish soil. There was this mad Irish poet who roamed all over this old world...Heaney, Sweeny, something like that. His story is still told today for those who know where to hear it but far as I know he didn't come to America. He inspired a lot of other people to take up the Lord's work, to go out and missionary to people all over. One of them was directly related to you, a lowly monk whose name was Brother Padraig Wellman.

"One thing I've always wondered since I was a child and my granddaddy told me this story was how that monk got washed up on the shores of Chesapeake Bay so many years before white folk were supposed to be here but he didn't rightly know. So, I can't tell you that either. He might have been going to Iceland or Greenland or headed to some monastery on a wild piece of rock those Irish abbots tried to set up. Mad every one of them! But they were mad with their convictions, their religion."

"You mean a place like Skellig Michel, Granmaw?"

"Eh? Yes yes, Skellig Michel. I told you about Skellig Michel when you were little didn't I? Well that's just the sort of place I'm talking about. Picture people trying to do that all over and each abbot trying to outdo the previous one. I believe there was some stiff competition for monastery space back then or maybe they were just trying to show how pious they could be. But I digress and I am sorry. It's just hard to think of where to begin this so that when it's done you'll understand it and not think your granmaw is any battier than she is. Do you know how far back I'm talking RJ? Before Columbus, hundreds of years before Columbus, and yet he gets all the credit."

RJs eyebrows went up over his cup of too sweet coffee and he smiled indulgently at his Granmaw. She looked back at him with her un-seeing eyes and said, "I'll be able to prove all this when I'm done, just hear me out."

"No, go ahead. I knew it would have to been a long time ago if it involved Indians."

"Yes, Indians. They hadn't ever seen a white man, specially one who took after that mad Irish poet, climbed trees, sang to the sun, prayed over odd things. They reckoned he might be good to keep around cause the spirits they believed in were either amused by such things or frequently sent mad people to vex the tribal leaders. Again I don't rightly know. Those Indians, the Algonquins...I think thats how its said 'AL Gone Quinns' yes, the Algonquins either took him or led him deep into Virginia away from the coast. Following first one river and then t'other till they came to where they had made a huge camp for the summer. It was deep in the woods near what we call Wyoming County nowadays." Granmaw Wellman paused and stirred her coffee not even tinkling her spoon against the sides of the cup. "Course there weren't no West Virginia back then you know...they did teach you that much didn't they?"

RJ nodded, looking at his aunt who was standing behind Granmaw Wellman slowly undoing the plaits in her mother's silvery grey hair and letting it fall about her shoulders. RJ had never seen his grandmother's hair down; it had always been in a tight grey bun at the back of her head, shot thru with dozens of hairpins. Now that it was down he could see it reached almost to her hips and rippled in waves of platinum under the weak light of the kitchen bulb. "Yes Granmaw, I took West Virginian history in the 9th grade."

Granmaw Wellman tut-tutted and rolled her neck sending ripples thru her hair. She turned her head over her shoulder toward Chrissy and said "Boy thinks he's already had an education. Wait till he hears all I have to say on the matter!" RJ refilled his cup and warmed up his grandmother's. Aunt Chrissy's hands had never stopped combing and stroking out her mother's hair. RJ realized this was a calming ritual for her and probably explained his grandmother's habit of commenting over her shoulder all the time.

"Where was I?"

"The Indians had captured the monk Granmaw."

"Yes. Well, nobody's sure how it happened but they had a falling out. This monk, probably meaning good musta tried to preach the Gospel to those Indians and it got him into some hot water so they chased him off. He didn't go far though; there was a cave near there that the Indians feared to go into. They called it Bear-skull Cave because something had killed a big bear at the entrance and the birds had left nothing but the skull and some bones lying about. The monk, Brother Wellman mind you, had the power of the Lord about him so he just went in and set up house. He made that cave into his church not being able to build anything out of wood or stone what with the hostiles just outside. But he kept it the Lord's house and said his prayers and sang his songs. The Indians came to listen and he preached to them in his tongue and they talked back to him in theirs. I imagine this went on for a long time each picking up a bit of the other's language." Granmaw Wellman felt out for her cup and paused, crinkling her brow and leaning toward RJ critically. "You're not asking a lot of questions RJ, does that mean you believe your Ol' Granny?"

"I learnt not to contradict you years ago Granmaw. I can still feel the sting of that wet wash rag you've got sitting right over there." RJ smiled and wondered where she was going with this story? An Irish monk in America before Columbus was a strange idea but it wasn't completely out of the realm of possibility.

"The carvings are still there on that cave in Wyoming county RJ."

RJ looked up at his aunt and said "What? You actually know where this happened? Its not...lost in the mists of time?"

"Oh no, we've been to see it, years ago. It's got carvings all along one wall that are prayers about the birth of Jesus written in an old Irish script."

RJ sat up and frowned, thinking hard at this news. "And no one thought to have a historian check it out, an archaeologist maybe? Confirm that it's from that time period and not..." He hesitated to call it a hoax since it was clear his family believed in it so strongly. "Not something written later, by someone else?"

Aunt Chrissy looked offended and stopped plaiting her mother's hair. Her fingers poked up thru the silver skein of hair like tiny pink islands on a gray sea of time. "We don't have to have it proven RJ, we Wellmans were there." Then she paused and said, "Besides your Uncle Jack at Marshall University had pictures took and sent them to people in Ireland for translation. They say its canon RJ and it dates from the year 960, not 1960, just plain as you please Nine-Six-Oh."

"Almost 700 years before Columbus? You're telling me a monk was trying to convert Indians here in Virginia 700 years before the first Europeans came to America?"

Granmaw Wellman shifted a bit in her chair and said "Hoo hoo! Maybe Columbus took the long way round! By all accounts he landed a considerable distance to the south of West b'gawd Virginia!" She took a tiny sip from her cup, looked up at her daughter and repeated "First Europeans" then looked back in RJ's direction. "If you're having trouble accepting that I'm not sure I should go along any further."

"No please do, I'm hooked now. What happened to Brother Wellman?"

Chapter Seventeen: Them that Live Below.

"Well somebody should tell people. They have these big murals at ND depicting Columbus discovering America and things that happened afterwards. Wouldn't it be a shocker for people to learn that a Wellman discovered America?"

Granmaw Wellman made a face "You sound like your brother KellyRay. And No, it wouldn't be great. We've gone to a lot of trouble to leave things as they are and you're about to find out why."

RJ sat back and placed his hands in his lap. He was feeling a bit amused by this whole thing but had to admit he was no longer frightened by the night's events and certainly not sleepy anymore. He took a long swallow of his coffee and sat it down a touch too loudly. "Sorry, go ahead, I'm all ears."

Granmaw Wellman put her hands flat on the table and took a deep breath. "After some time the monk stumbled onto a way to get the Indian children to sort of say their prayers, figuring to guide them into the faith as time went by. He would play a mimicking game with them. One where he would sing a few verses of a song and then have them mimic it back to him. Echo it back like prayers in a church are sometimes done. Say he'd sing 'Glory to God, creator of all things.' and the Indian children would sing 'Glory to God, creator of all things' back to him. He would do this with verse after verse till they had learnt all the sounds of praise even if they did not know the meanings behind them. Baby steps RJ, that's how you proceed in cross cultural things. You remember that, hear?"

RJ nodded and then blushed and said as seriously as he could. "Yes Ma'am."

"Good. Now we don't know how long this went on but he must have been there some time. He was there long enough to carve the story of the Nativity onto the rock face. Many many years if he found it necessary to mark Christmas coming around again and again. But those Indians let him live and the children continued to learn from him. Then one night he heard his song being sung not from outside the cave but inside, way down below. And it weren't no echo.

"He listened and listened then called out and the singing stopped. The next night it happened again and he tried to sing along, sing the reply back to whoever it was. I reckon he believed that some of the Indian children had snuck past him and into his cave while he was sleeping and they were trying to reverse the rules of the game on him, least-ways that's how it were told afterwards. So on the third night he walked deeper into the cave; singing his song, waiting for a reply, and advancing a bit further. He found it difficult to pinpoint where the sound came from but always it led him deeper and deeper into the earth. Soon he had lost his way and had no choice but to go on, imagining that there must be some other way into the cave and that the voices could lead him to it."

RJ's coffee grew cold, his face a picture of rapt attention. His grandmother's head was tilted back and to the side like she was trying reach the past, the place in her history where she had heard this story. He felt her dry feathery touch on his hands and he held her fingers firm in his. She seemed to draw strength from the contact. He wanted her to go on but feared speaking would break the storyteller's spell she had on him. Aunt Chrissy had disappeared without notice and RJ was taken by the grayish, almost silver halo caused by his grandmother's hair as it spread out over her shoulders and down the back of the chair. He had no idea how long the silence lasted before she spoke again.

"Before long his torch was spent and he made progress slowly, spiraling down, down past the Cold, down thru the Dark, and into the Warm. The singing was all around him now and it was only his faith in the Lord Jesus that kept him from despair in that dark place. Soon the song was done and voices spoke to him in words he did not know, words even the Indians have forgotten. They touched him, touched his clothes, his face, his cross. He was sore afraid but he kept up the singing. Sang every song he had been taught at the monastery and even those from childhood his mother sang to him. When he could not sing anymore he whistled and then hummed and then just clapped out the rhythm. He was filled with the Spirit and it calmed him in the dark though he might just as likely have been surrounded by demons as regular folk, but he soon found out they were not that much different than he was. A people of paler, cooler skin, and able to get about in the dark with a skill he never quite developed."

Granmaw Wellman let go of RJ's hands and tapped the spot between her eyebrows. "There's a spot where you can feel a tingle, just a tiny one but if you focus on it you can feel it spread out, change...takes a long time to make sense of it but it can help where your two eyes can't. And the deep ice helps too, there's minerals in it and of proper amounts...it all helps them get about. They never would tell me how out right but your granny had sight before she lost it and I still see plenty!" She paused closing her eyes and moving her finger in a slow circle just above her eyebrows, not quite touching.

"But I digress again and it's getting early. Ahem! They fed him, these people of the Dark, though he did not know what meat they had and they made him to lie on beds of moss and lichen. After a time a host of people had come to see him or just touch him I guess and he was made to sing till his voice failed him. Have you got a singing voice RJ?"

RJ blinked at the odd question then said "I freely admit I do not but that doesn't stop me from trying to sing when I feel like it."

"Good, good! So Brother Wellman, he made to leave many times and at least once he fell and broke his leg. That much is in the record, the story as it was told down the years, and for the rest of his days he walked with a crutch. Many days, months, even years passed and each time he tried to find his way out he was stopped by something. One way was blocked by an underground river, another an un-climbable rock face, the third was the Web and the Weave..."

Granmaw Wellman's voice took on a sing-song nature as if the story she was telling was some epic saga, some lay by a bard that RJ had never heard of. His questions quieted in him as the story went on and he no longer tried to rationalize everything though he made a mental note to ask what the Web and the Weave was referring to. He didn't like the idea of a spider being there in the dark with Brother Wellman. Not if this story was leading where he thought it was.

"It did not first occur to them--Them that Live Below--that he could not see as they could. But eventually they realized he was as lost in their world as a child born sightless is in ours. They took him on a long journey thru the dark and this is where we reckon he made his way from Wyoming County to these parts and there, wherever there really was, he met up with their priests of sorts. Now these priests, they did not worship the Lord Almighty as we do but they were priests all the same and they tried to give him sight in return for the songs he had given them. These priests had their own rituals, their own songs, and their own gods. They gave him draughts to drink, herbs to chew, and all sorts of remedies, which gave him a sort of sight in the Dark, or at least a Comfort. It's unclear if he gained sight as you have or if he just learnt his way around in his head like your granny does.

"He learned some of their language, and some of their intent. At first their priests were very concerned when they learned he wished to teach about his god to their people but he had learned from his mistakes with the Algonquin and so he remained silent as to the exact meanings of the songs he sung to them. But when he had learnt enough he proposed a sort of covenant, an agreement based mostly on trade and he was to become the conduit. If he would be allowed to preach the Gospel to their people he would bring them things from the surface they could not create for themselves. Somehow he convinced them he would not try to leave but would become a tie between our two peoples, between the people who have always dwelt in shadow and those that walk beneath the sun. The sun holds a powerful place in their religion RJ and they will not tolerate its gaze.

"They took him back to his cave with the bear skull and gave him some things to trade to the Indians. There was every sort of mushroom you can imagine and lichen lining moss covered capes to keep off the winter's chill; tiny stone pots of draughts and spirits such as he had been given, meal made from ground up albino frogs and blindfish. These he traded for blankets and feathers, hide and bone, and things to make torches with. A drum was given him as a gift. His own items were still in the cave untouched and after his visit to the surface he took those with him and went back to the People as promised."

RJ surprised himself by blurting out "And you say they didn't have fire Granmaw? These people live their whole lives in complete darkness? That doesn't make sense to me."

"Oh no son they know fire, and light, and some things that just naturally glow in the dark as you well know. But only their priests carry fire, and it is only the priests who have the secret of fire making. It's as essential to them as water is to us. And that's a very basic difference you'd do well to remember. And they believe an area of darkness protects them, a sacred area that no light can be carried thru. If Brother Wellman's torch had not gone out when it did he would have never made it to their land. Why they even paint themselves with oils and ground up cave crickets, which makes them shine and glow in the dark like heathen Halloween masks. I bet Brother Wellman thought he had gone mad to see it or that he truly was surrounded by demons!"

RJ noticed his grandmother had started talking in the present tense but chalked it up to everyone being tired. He was trying to think of a way to subtly correct her when Aunt Chrissy re-appeared dressed for the day. She took the bucket from the counter by the stove and started out the back door. She did not turn to look at RJ or her mother as she said "No point in trying to sleep now, dawn's here. I'll get some water in and see about breakfast shortly." Granmaw Wellman tutt-tutted. "I've taken too long to tell the tale but there's more you must hear. Then I think, some biscuits and gravy will cure what ails you."

Chapter Eighteen: Where there is coal, there is fire.

In short order bacon, biscuits, gravy, eggs over easy and homemade jelly in huge portions were placed before him. RJ was given a glass of milk and had to hide a smile at the thought of it. He honestly couldn't remember drinking a single of glass of milk in the past ten years. He also had a tall glass of well water but he drank sparingly from it now slightly suspicious of what it might contain.

Aunt Chrissy would not sit at the table with him but nibbled from the stove and tested the bacon to see if it was OK to serve. She even dipped a warm biscuit in the bacon fat, caught RJ looking and laughed as she turned away blushing. It was probably the first color he'd ever seen in her cheeks and he was struck by how pale she was compared to his other relatives. As a child he was confused by the things his relatives did and said in this house and it was hard to ask questions even now. Those quirky things that didn't make sense were just 'how things were' and left at that.

Granmaw Wellman remained at the table and made a big show of smelling each item of food as it arrived but she did not take anything for herself. Occasionally she would take a small sip from her coffee, wetting her lips but nothing more, just going thru the motions. RJ thought hard back thru his memories and couldn't recall a single time he'd seen his grandmother eat anything. The tradition in her house was to feed the men and the women folk at different times so it was not unusual for her to be absent when RJ sat down.

He cloed his eyes behind another cup of coffee and admonished himself for getting wrapped up in this bizarre story. When he thought about it, he realized he hadn't met a single relative on this trip who was completely normal. But maybe to themselves they were. Maybe this crazy X-File belief system they had going and all these superstitions *was* the norm for them and it was only because his perspective was from the outside that he found them so strange. Not for the first time since this visit started RJ found himself wondering what his life would have become if he hadn't been in such a hurry to leave West Virginia? He dabbed up some gravy with his last bite of biscuit and asked "How do you know of these things if they happened so long ago?"

Aunt Chrissy froze with a tin dipper of well water half way to her lips and looked at her mother. When Granmaw Wellman said nothing she sat it down slowly and said "We've been piecing it together for many a year. There's no written record, nothing that can be traced back that far but the story has been told unchanged from generation to generation...Orally." She paused as if the word caused her pain. "The Wellmans have worked these hills as far back as anyone can remember. But much was lost once coal was discovered here."

Granmaw Wellman sat quietly drawing circular shapes on the table with a bony finger. RJ watched her as the silence built up between them. Then she abruptly pointed at RJ and asked, "Do you know when coal was first discovered in West Virginia?"

"Not exactly, I have a feeling they found coal here sometime before the Civil War?"

"Close enough. There is a long break in our records like Chrissy said, during the dark times when the Covenant was not observed. Brother Wellman, he lived a long life and a pious one but eventually he had to die as we all do. Someone took over in his stead but it never really got back up to speed. The Indians were driven away and the story of Brother Wellman was lost for hundreds of years. The Europeans that came here didn't go very deep under the hills; they found what they wanted right near the surface. And that was coal. And they blew it up, dug it out, and carted it away with no thought that there would be anyone else about to lay claim to it. A steady stream of coal has been taken from West Virginian hills since the 1750's and it's been the death of many a good man like your grandfather George Wellman Jr.

"Oh RJ, it was not a good time for them or us. Whole families were lost here and many places in the Below were made unlivable or were completely collapsed and cut off by the taking of the coal. The Covenant was long broken and while I daren't call it a war, a lot of anger was taken out on the coal miners. For those Below saw the very layer of darkness that had protected them for centuries was being stolen away from them. All sorts of evil were worked to drive us away. And by us I mean all of us here above ground." Granmaw Wellman gestured her hands around as if patting the soil, the ground, and the land all about her. "Safe mines were made to collapse, clean air was poisoned and even rivers were re-routed to wash them...us away. But it did no good, we just brought more men, more dynamite, and machines big as a house to drag off every bit of coal we could lay our hands on. No one in the Above knew of Brother Wellman, or of the Covenant."

"So how did you come to know it or hear the story from someone else?"

Granmaw Wellman smiled a toothless smile and said "My grandfather's grandfather. Mason Stamper Wellman. He brought an end to the hostilities though it cost him his life."

RJ screwed up his face. "My...Great Great Great Grandfather...no wait, add another Great in there...he did what exactly?"

"He was a coal miner from right here in Dunlow but he moved out and worked the Boss Hosie mine in the southern part of the state where Wayne, Mingo, and Lincoln counties meet. The west fork of Twelvepole has its start right near there and they used a water wheel to pump out the lower levels. He married an Irish girl newly arrived and settled down. By all accounts he had a good life till the cave-in.

"He was trapped inside that mine with 15 other men and he was the onliest one to come out alive and that was by strange circumstance. See they were closing off a section of the mine--robbing it as they say--before abandoning it entirely and Mason was the last to leave that section. It was the furthest back of the whole mine, a mile from the entrance, which was about as far back into the mountain as they dared go in those days. He was looking for anything left behind when the roof began to working and there was a far off rumble followed by the worst sound a miner can imagine. Thunder underground! The last sound many a man ever hears down there.

"When he dug himself out and got his senses about him he found he was trapped behind three dozen feet of mother rock with a broken leg. He had no real hope from that exact moment but he kept his head and felt around to find his pick. Course there was nothing for it but to say a prayer and start digging. Some men might have lain down to die right then and there and some would have wept and pulled their hair. But Mason didn't, he started to dig and sing to keep his spirits up. He sang a merry tune or two and others that he remembered from church or from his mother's side. He dug in the dark, scooting along and singing loud and long maybe hoping he would be heard on the other side. And heard he was but not by the other miners, they were all dead RJ. He dug for hours or maybe days, how would he know? And at one point he uncovered a horse's body; one of several that was used in the mine and it saddened him to the point that he stopped digging his escape and spoke a little prayer over it, dragging it gently aside as best he could with a broken leg and removing the ruined harness. He sank down at the back of the little space he had, sang some nonsense childhood song about a reluctant pony and prepared to meet his own reward.

"Them that live Below, they were never far away. They could hear him singing prayers for a dead horse because it was them that had caused the whole mess in the first place you see? Now though they had themselves a problem. As you already know, these people put a lot of stock into song and there were those among them who had been taught the songs Brother Wellman had brought with him. Songs that they knew the sound of but not the meanings of the words like I said. They began to wonder among themselves if Mason might be a priest too? If this was at long last another Brother Wellman or a member of his order come back to honor the Covenant? This discussion went on a long time with some advising the side of caution and some wanting to kill him outright. And all the while what little air he had was being used up. Ah but then he did something that settled it for them. Can you guess what that was?"

RJ closed his eyes and tried to picture himself sitting alone in the dark with a dead horse, a broken leg, and a miner's pick. He sipped his coffee but found it cold and pushed it away. "Well if I was playing Dungeons and Dragons I'd probably decide to eat the horse!" He shrugged and smiled trying to lessen the mental image but Granmaw Wellman was not sidetracked.

"I see. Well now. Let me ask you this. What's the one thing that they say you should never ever do in a mine?" Before RJ could form an answer Aunt Chrissy leaned in to take away his cup and plates. She said, "Whistle! Its bad luck to whistle in mines RJ, always has been."

Granmaw Wellman thumped the table. "Chrissy! I wanted to hear what the boy would say to that! You already know this story so hush up and let RJ hear it thru, please!" RJ watched his rebuked aunt retreat into the sitting room and snatch up a bible as she headed for her room. He was suddenly very glad he didn't live with a retired schoolteacher. He leaned his head on his elbow and asked half jokingly, "What's wrong with whistling? The vibrations cause harmonics and crack the rock?"

"No RJ, nothing so dire. But remember our family and many many others who came here for work were born in Ireland or Scotland and even Wales, and they brought their beliefs with them. From the earliest times that men have worked the rock they were advised two things: One: not to bring women into a mine, and Two: not to whistle lest they drive away the Good Luck Spirit that lives in each mine…or everywhere underground to be more precise."

"Huh…and these people living in the mine, what did they do when they heard him--Mason--when they heard him whistle?"

"Say 'Them that live Below.' They wouldn't live in a mine RJ any more than you would live in a graveyard. Yet here's where luck was on his side. Those priests Brother Wellman met hundreds of years before, they whistled to each other. No one else among them is allowed to. I think that's why they took Brother Wellman to meet their priests in the first place. I don't know if this prohibition somehow got to the miner's back home or who thought of it first. In fact I asked that selfsame question when I first heard this tale and you know what they told me? They said 'That's neither here nor there.' The point is this lucky happenstance affected enough of them to decide the issue. They would spare his life but they would not make open contact. Memories run deep as underground rivers with Them that Live Below and time passes or not at all. I often smile thinking about my great Grandaddy Mason whistling some tune that was more likely 'Rigs o Barley' or 'Devil among the Tailors' than it was anything of a religious nature and it was that sort of song that got him spared.
"They were none too gentle about it though. They let him pass out from lack of air and then came into the mine and took him from near Warriormine, West Virginia where the entrance was…that's down on highway 16 near the state border…clear up here to Moses' Fork just a few miles shy of where he was born. And they came all that way underground. That's a drive that'll take you over 3 hours by car RJ so you can imagine how long it would have taken to walk.

"Mason woke to find himself in the crook of a holler, cold and wet and covered with clay and the cold breath of a cave breathing out over him. He was chilled to the bone but he was alive. And all he had with him was the clothes on his back and the broken harness from the horse. So he made a splint from a dogwood tree and worked his way back towards his momma's place. His father had long Passed Over from the black lung you know. His wife Louisa was there too and they were all mourning his loss and those other 15 fellas caught in the mine collapse. Oh you could have knocked them over with a feather when he limped in the door, every one of them!"

Granmaw Wellman chuckled to herself and began to sing some nameless tune under her breath. RJ thought maybe the story was over for now and quietly slipped away to the bathroom. He washed his hands in the cold-water basin staring at all the faded and curling photographs tucked into the edge of the mirror's frame. He had no idea how far back they went or even if the hilly country in the background of the photos--the mines they showed--were here or back in Ireland, Scotland maybe? He suddenly felt very tired and leaned his forehead against the cool glass. In the reflection he could see his grandmother sitting there with her hands folded in her lap. She turned her head toward him and reached out for him and gesturing to the seat next to her. The seat was a wooden hand carved bench of some old dark wood. RJ remembered when both he and his two brothers could fit on that bench. Soon as he was settled his Grandmother began again, her voice softer now, almost conspiratorial. Aunt Chrissy had not resurfaced.

"Mason had been missing for a week and soon as they got him all cleaned up and fed they had a revival right there. Even set up a prayer tent to celebrate his being spared. He got asked lots of questions about how he survived and some of the folk who lost men in the mine wanted him to lead them back the way he came but he kept the location to himself and told everyone God had led him out. It was the talk of the county and people said he had a blessed life from that day on. Once things had calmed down and he got his wife and mother alone he told them what he remembered about his escape, about voices and songs and him being carried thru the dark for days on end. He had a vivid memory or vision of someone whistling in his ear over and over as if calling him back from the edge of death.

"His wife and mother did not agree completely on what should be done as wives and mothers often find themselves disagreeing on the subject of the husband. His wife Louisa became convinced that he had been aided by the Fey, by the faerie folk that live under all mountains. She felt he should make some gift, an offering to them as thanks for saving his life. This Mason agreed to do though his mother was one of God's strong women and advised against it.

"They took his father's wagon and told his mother that he would do as God saw fit. But when they got close to the place where he woke up he stopped the wagon and made his way up the hillside to the cave entrance and sat down some goods. Just to be sure you see? He brought with him blankets and a miner's lamp, a toy horse and a wooden top and some good whisky. Remember his leg was broke and it agonized him sorely to manage these items up the hill. So much so that before he started back down he decided the faerie folk wouldn't miss a swallow or two of whisky. Ahem! He was a long time on the hillside and his wife who was left waiting with the wagon became very worried for him. For a while she could hear him singing somewhere up on the hill and then just the occasional whistle and then just silence. But she was a superstitious girl fresh from a small Irish village after all and she didn't have the courage to go looking for him till the next morning."

RJ smiled and said "I'm guessing he had more than just a swallow of whiskey just then, didn't he Granmaw?"

"A considerable amount RJ, by all accounts! In fact he passed out and woke the next morning with his wife glaring down at him, angry that he had kept her waiting all night while he put a drunk on. She felt he had made light of her beliefs and gave him a good piece of her mind I'm here to tell you!"

RJ chuckled at this and looked past his grandmother to see Chrissy was standing near the curtains of the spare bedroom listening silently. She made no sign that she noticed RJ looking in her direction. RJ thought she looked like an actress waiting for her cue to come on stage. The image of her standing there the night before came back to him and he frowned and looked away feeling just a tiny bit manipulated by this whole thing. His grandmother said nothing till he looked back as if sensing where his mind was wandering to and then she carried on, touching RJ's hand to keep his attention.

"But then they noticed the blankets and the lamp and the whiskey-- what was left of it--was gone! In its place there was a rolled up piece of flattened mushroom and a cane. The cane was intricately carved and made not of wood but of a single piece of Mother rock, trending up into a crystal or geode rubbed smooth enough to see into and there was a pocket of water trapped inside. No one has seen its like before or since."

RJ looked back at his grandmother and thought about this last piece of info. "The cane was made of rock and it had a crystal full of water on the top? That sounds...well unlikely."

Granmaw Wellman leaned across the table and tut tutted at RJ "Much of what you've heard this night sounds unlikely young man but this I can prove. That cane was precious to Mason Wellman and he carried it till the day he died. Then it passed to his son and so on down to my husband and it is still in our family...still in this very house!"

RJ stood up and tried to apologize quickly, not meaning to question his grandmother's story, not meaning to offend but Granmaw Wellman tossed her head over her shoulder and called out "Chrissy! Bring Mason's Crutch in here so RJ can see it."

Chapter Nineteen: Mason's Crutch.

Chrissy brought out a footstool and squeezed it between the sofa and the door to the bathroom. She sighed and puffed as she said, "I knew she would ask for that old relic but you will have to fetch it down. These legs aren't as steady as they once were."

RJ got up and fiddled with the stool trying to get it to sit steady across the doorframe. It was old and looked dry rotted to RJ but it held as he tested one foot on it so he braced his hands on the doorjamb and stepped up onto it. The floor between sitting room and the bathroom didn't match exactly. It must have been added on sometime later when they first got indoor plumbing. "Some settling may occur!" He grimly thought to himself and shifted his weight back onto his heels so the one short leg wouldn't tip the whole thing over. Aunt Chrissy took down the heavy curtain and rod that hung between the rooms and RJ could see there was a space in the ceiling that had been hidden by the frilly bunting of the curtain. Behind it was yellowed newspapers rolled into tightly bound sticks and each held with a piece of string or rubber band. RJ looked down at his aunt and said "Behind here?" Aunt Chrissy waved a handkerchief around her face to fan away the dust he had already dislodged and nodded. "Just dig that stuff out, it's what passes for insulation between these walls."

RJ handed them down to her, most of them flaking away at the edges as he did so. He tried to catch a date here and there but couldn't find one and even the font on the paper was odd, almost gothic in nature. He tried not to breathe in the cloud of dust around him and muttered under his breath "Now I know what you've done with your lifetime subscription to Grit magazine." There was no reply so he kept working one-handed, the other braced on the doorframe. It was several sweaty minutes before he came to what he thought was a bit of cardboard or plasterboard. "There's something here alright. I can make out some writing on it."

RJ pushed away some more paper shreds and a few ancient cobwebs to see the word "Flyer" on the side of the box. More digging revealed a picture of a low-slung sled with wintry winds blowing along the sides and a cherub-faced boy grinning back at him. His aunt stepped back to get a better view into the space and said "Don't try to get the whole box down, we'll never get it back in. Just flip that side up and reach in for something wrapped in a baby's blanket."

RJ's eyes got wide and he had to steady himself at this last comment. He exclaimed "Oh Lord"!" before opening the side panel and peering in. He had to take a deep breath and look away before sticking his arm into the dark space before him. He tried to look back at his Aunt and as he did so his fingers touched something hard cold and smooth. It felt like bone to RJ and he nearly fell off the stool jerking his hand back. His cry of surprise was cut off by his Aunt's frantic chanting of "Careful! Careful! Careful! Lord, don't let him drop it we would all have the Devil to pay! The very Devil himself!"

RJ put his hand back into the box and closed them around the blanket, pulled a bit toward him and then tried again getting a better grip on the object itself. He freed the cane from the blanket and slid it out a few inches. Then he stepped backwards and down off the stool dragging it un-ceremonially out into the light.

He held a grayish white cane just a bit over 3 feet tall. It was maybe two inches in diameter at the base and carved as if there were 4 vines or roots moving up the central post till they bulged out to make the pommel. Inside that was a crystal geode of some sort. It was white as salt at the bottom and translucent across the top where many hands had rubbed it smooth over time. Sunlight coming in from the kitchen window struck it and shards of color bounced up against the ceiling. As he shifted it, RJ could see there was indeed water or some liquid inside a small pocket within the crystal. He was dumbfounded and silent for minutes, just turning it in his hands and examining every inch. The lattice work made it amazingly light to lift considering it was carved of stone and it looked and felt like gypsum though that mineral would not have been strong enough for such a purpose. He looked up to see his aunt and grandmother standing nearby with hands folded against their chests as if praying expectantly for something to happen. RJ finally managed to whisper "I feel like I'm holding Gandalf's staff!"

Granmaw Wellman stepped forward and said "That is Mason's Crutch and you should count yourself among the lucky few to have seen it in the light of day. I was twice your age before I ever saw it and that was the day it passed to my father. Mason was the only one to have used it for its purpose and I pray that you never need its support."

RJ propped it against the floor like a walking stick, judging that it was just a bit short for him. Aunt Chrissy had not moved but she smiled at RJ and said "The men in this family stand a bit straighter now that they don't spend their whole lives in a coalmine."

"'How long it must have taken to make this! There's no tool marks anywhere on it, not even where the crystal is. It's a single fluid piece!" RJ held it out at arms length and turned it side to side to watch the liquid inside slosh around and cast shards of light about the room. "Granmaw, Aunt Chrissy this is...this is priceless! It should be in a museum or something, not shoved into your pantry wall."

Granmaw Wellman gave RJ's shoulder a hard firm grip as she moved past him to her rocking chair. "That which is of the Hills always comes back to the Hills." She settled herself and rocked loudly for a bit then reached over to her family bible and said, "You should put that away now. There's a bit more story then I think you need to go see your brothers."

Chapter Twenty: Not by his own hand.

RJ took another long look at the cane and even put his ear to the crystal and listened. How such a thing was made was beyond him and he wondered why his grandmother and aunt lived so poorly if they had access to items like this? He took much more care returning it to its resting place than he had taking it out, Aunt Chrissy silently handing him each bundled newspaper as if he were interring someone in a mausoleum. She set about clearing up the dust and putting the stool away immediately and before RJ could take his place in the Visitor's seat there was no sign anything had been disturbed at all.

"Where was I? Well-sir after that Mason returned on a regular basis. Bringing different things with him, drinking till he passed out and then taking away whatever was left him the next morning. When he wasn't in the cave he took work as shift foreman in a nearby mine. They caught him whistling in the back of the mine once and that started the rumor that it was his whistling what caused the Boss Hosie cave-in. After that they encouraged him to look for other work. So he bought the land all around the cave and fenced it in. Went about telling people he was going to try raising cows. Hoo hoo! It would have been hard times indeed if not for the "Indian relics" and the steady supply of rock salt he brought home from his secret cave up there on the hill.

"The relics.... some things he'd leave would be rejected and sometimes the trades were things that had been taken before. 'Returnables'...he had no real idea what they wanted and no idea why they wouldn't show themselves so it was all trial and error you see? The whisky and later the moonshine was always gone the next morning. I don't intend to make any excuses for his behavior but that's the only way he knew how to make 'Them' come. "

Granmaw Wellman paused and sniffed loudly. It was clear her opinion was that blessed little of the alcohol had ever made it Below. RJ's mind was spinning, trying to recall everything he had heard this night. He looked over his shoulder at the spot where Mason's Crutch was hidden and still couldn't comprehend what he had seen, what he had been told. He picked up an embroidered cushion from the other end of the sofa and hugged it to him, comforted by its familiarity.

Granmaw Wellman looked down her nose at RJ as if she could see him and said, "Then something happened that changed the relationship he had worked years to create. A bitter cold winter hit us the third or fourth year after the cave-in. One that hung on into late spring and a lot of people round these parts were suffering from consumption and the croup. There was no doctor in all of Wayne county back then and getting someone into Huntington usually meant they were so bad off that they weren't likely to come back. "Mason had two kids; Jason and Brittany, boy and girl both under two years of age. Jason caught the croup and it seemed he never would shake it. His daddy sat up with him night after night watching him get weaker and weaker. When weeks of croup turned to consumption he couldn't stand it no longer. He took the boy against his wife's wishes out into the wintry night and carried him up to the cave. He was ahead of his regular visit but he feared waiting any longer. He took the boy and all the things he'd traded for and all the alcohol he could lay his hands on and sat down in the mouth of the cave with that child hugged to his chest and sang as loud and long as he could. Them that live Below, they'd fixed his leg didn't they? It healed in a week's time well enough to walk on. So maybe they had a cure for consumption too. Some of the things they trade us RJ are meant to be remedies or poultices but we can't ever be sure what they're for. It's like eating mushrooms when you don't know which to pick and which is poison. Hold your nose and take your chances, that's all!"

Granmaw Wellman paused, eyes closed and letting the morning sun play on her face while she was lost in thought. The lacy curtains made a strange shadowy tattoo on her face, all spiral vines and leaves. She ceased to look like an old woman to RJ and became as timeless as a carved face on a mountain or perhaps just the pattern of lichen and moss growing on it.

RJ waited as long as he could stand it before softly asking "Then what?" His grandmother shivered and sat up again rocking energetically. "Eh? Then? Oh...sorry, I think... " She rubbed her nose hard enough to press it flat against her face and said, "I think my nose is itching and that always means we're going to have company. Yes, well Mason woke up and the whisky was gone. The knives--they always want knives of one sort or the other RJ-- were gone and everything else was gone too. And so was little Jason Wellman." His grandmother paused to let that sink in and RJ was afraid she was going to stop there. He felt a chill pass thru the house as Aunt Chrissy went out the back door towards the clothesline and he leaned forward anxiously.

"Well that was not the result he was after of course so he gets all fired up and starts yelling into the cave how he'd been robbed and about kidnapping and generally making a mess of things since he was still hung over and stumbling about. Oh but he was mad as an old wet hen! He calls out for them to show themselves, for them to bring back his son and basically curses them till a fly wouldn't lite on'm! "That gets him nowhere so he rushes in determined to find his boy. And of course his light has gone too and he gets lost soon as he's away from the cave mouth. When he doesn't come home at daylight his wife gets some neighbors to help look for him and she tells them she thinks he's gotten lost looking for more relics. Pretty much has to show them where the cave is but keeps mum about Them and the baby. His brother David and a neighbor man spent all their time looking thru the cave. They didn't find anything till nearly three days had passed when finally they hear a baby crying. They follow it to a deep dry shaft in the cave and there in the bottom they find Mason's body all twisted up and the child in the crook of his arm crying for its momma. Mason's neck was broken in the fall but the child was unharmed, cured of its consumption and wrapped in what Louisa said was "lace so fine it was like spider web." Which I wish I could show you some of but it yellows and gets brittle quickly once the sun gets at it."

"Louisa got the men folk to not talk about what happened in the cave putting it all down to the drink finally driving Mason over the edge. She was glad to get her baby back but she decided that was the end of that, Fey or no Fey. The cave wasn't visited again for some ten years or more but when it came time Jason took his father's staff into the cave and sang what songs he knew to Them and they accepted him into the Covenant. And so it passed down father to son more or less continuously until it came to my husband who had it but briefly before the Black Lung took him. "

Granmaw Wellman turned her head back towards the window and RJ saw her eyes flicking back and forth under her eyelids as if she was reading or perhaps dreaming. Somehow he felt it would be some time before she came back to the here and now. He shifted uncomfortably and looked about, reaching over slowly to where the crossword puzzle still lay from the night before and caught a moment in the corner of his eye. He looked out thru the half open front door and saw his Aunt Chrissy gesturing to him silently from out on the sidewalk.

RJ got up quietly and walked to the front door, opening it further and came face to face with the screen door for the first time since last night. Looking at the old stiff wire and the moiré patterns it made as he moved made him uncomfortable with sudden memories. With a frown of anxiety he pushed the door open causing the oval imprint in the wire to stretch taught and be erased. He did not like thinking about what made that mark, what he thought made that mark. And he didn't want to think about what accepting that fact would mean to him personally. He slowly descended down the old stone steps as if at any moment they might collapse under him. His aunt stood smiling tightly at him from the shadow of a dogwood tree near the mailbox. She looked as if she was losing patience with his cautious progress. She put one hand on her ample hip and said "You're not gonna fall RJ, your grandmother climbs those steps all the time!"

RJ shrugged sheepishly and joined his aunt on the sidewalk. She pinched some blossoms from the tree and said, "Can you believe how warm it is for October? This poor tree thinks its spring already. I hope it doesn't lose all its strength and die off when winter comes. And winter will come sure as I'm standing here."

RJ looked closely at the tree and squinted thru the sunlight at his aunt. "This tree's been here all my life. I don't think it'll die from Indian Summer. But it might not bloom again till next year." Aunt Chrissy looked at him thoughtfully for a long moment and said, "Not bloom again..." Then the memory of something came over her face and she started again. "RJ you're not exactly right. You and your momma brought this tree from your place in Virginia back in oh...'67 I think. That's when we got Sparky you know, one of the litter your brother's dog had before he...before you all brought him home to rest."

RJ looked around for Sparky and saw him lying just under the porch in a patch of shadow chewing an old red ball. The dog looked tired and long overdue for a haircut. RJ couldn't imagine that this was the same dog his family had brought here 30 years before. He turned to express his doubts to his aunt but she had moved along the edge of the garden patch to where an old tractor tire could just be seen lying among overgrown weeds. He walked over and had a pang of guilt wash over him, first wondering why none of his brothers had come to mow the yard and then wondering if his mother's house was in a similar state. Things needed doing here or it wouldn't be long before 'the old home place' wouldn't be fit to live in no matter what secrets it held hidden inside.

"RJ do you remember this? This here tire held a cactus my brother Forrest brought back from Arizona. You fell in it once when you were little and we had to pull the spines right outta your rump! I never heard such bawling! Your momma came running over the ridge from your place like she was on fire. Do you remember that?"

RJ looked down and saw Sparky had silently trotted up and dropped the drool-covered ball at his feet. He bent down and picked it up with two fingers and gingerly tossed it down the sidewalk. Sparky shot after it and disappeared into the higher grass. "Yes I DO remember that and curiously enough I've yet to see another cactus in real life. Outside of greenhouses that is."

"This one lived a long time till the winter cold got to it. We didn't get snow back then like we do now. I reckon everything changes a little from year to year. " Aunt Chrissy kept walking as she spoke, her voice carrying easily across the tiny yard. She walked around RJ's car and up the hillside a bit with RJ following quietly behind and Sparky bringing up the rear. He could see in the window where his grandmother sat, the sun still holding her immobile as a statue. His aunt paused by a bit of rock sticking out of the hill just to the side of the house, all pockmarked with lichen and looking like the bones of some huge animal washed up on the edge of the mountainside.

"RJ, do you remember that Easter when we had an egg hunt here and you found the prize egg in one of those holes? I thought I was being so clever hiding it in there but you found it in nothing flat! "

"You always hid the prize egg in one of those holes Aunt Chrissy! And I remember you always gave each of us a prize whether we were the one who found it or not. The one thing I was good at and you...neutralized the fun of winning because everyone got the same thing regardless of how hard they tried."

Aunt Chrissy nodded as if expecting that response. "Your mother said the same thing on this very spot but I make no apologies for it. My game my rules." Then she softened her face and said, "The point I'm trying to make RJ is that your momma made her mark, her history right here, and so have you. Even though you haven't been back in years and it wasn't your intent at the time you left part of yourself here and here it will be till this land of ours rolls back under the sea..."

RJ stood looking down at the rock and all its little pockets like rooms in a museum or a time capsule. He wondered if his aunt knew something about archaeology and fossils or if she meant what she said in biblical terms? Sparky was back with his slobber covered ball and RJ bent down to pet the dog gently and think quietly a bit. Sparky let the ball drop and crouched down to endure the petting. He was never anyone's dog after Randy had died; he just chose to stay nearby his master's family. RJ realized that if this was Sparky; Sparky number One that is, it was the same dog that been with his brother when he got that fatal tick bite. RJ had never bonded with a pet after that, especially dogs and cats. He kept to fish, frogs or hermit crabs; animals you couldn't touch or relate to really. He looked into the expressive brown eyes and felt his heart melt.

"You've been waiting a long time haven't you boy?" Feeling his throat tighten and his aunt's silent presence he suddenly whipped the ball back thru his legs and turned to watch Sparky dash off into the grass after it, just as spry and quick as he had been when they both had been much younger.

Chapter Twenty-One: A bad Breath.

A light blue Buick rolled up into the yard and RJ's cousin LindaKay waved to him thru a backseat window.

"RJ hon! I'm so glad we caught you! Hi Aunt Chrissy, what's goin' on?"

LindaKay was 4 years older than RJ but seeing her like this with her parents taking up the front seat made her seem so much younger. The trio bundled out and gave RJ and his aunt hugs. Uncle Bill stole a kiss from Aunt Chrissy and she gave him a critical look and clucked her tongue un-approvingly. LindaKay passed her baby boy to RJ in way of introduction and said, "You haven't met my youngest, Leonard. Come to think of it, you haven't met any of my kids. We didn't bring them to the funeral cause they caint be trusted to behave. You know how kids are. Where did you say your kids and wife got off to? Its just tragical they couldn't be here for your momma's funeral..."

There was an awkward silent moment as RJ tried to come up with an answer while juggling baby, blanket, and rattle all at the same time. Uncle Bill rescued him on one point and said "They're at Disneyland down in Florida LindaKay. I don't blame them, can't disappoint the kids just cause someone dies. You'd never hear the end of it isn't that right Eleanor?" RJ's Aunt Eleanor, the eldest of his mother's sisters looked over from where she was standing with Aunt Chrissy and said "Lord LindaKay, remember how you and David wailed when you couldn't go to Busch Gardens cause I had to have an operation? You'd had thought the whole clan had died. Besides, they can stop in and pay their respects on the return trip, can't they RJ?"

RJ nodded, still holding the child out from him a bit and trying not to drop it. The baby wriggled and squirmed without making a sound, its tiny hand gripping the rattle and banging it rapidly on RJ's arm. Aunt Edith took mercy on him and reached for the child "Tsk tsk! I haven't met a man yet who knew how to hold a baby and here you have raised three of them!" RJ smiled his gratitude and passed child and accessories over gladly. Baby Leonard chose that moment to let his rattle fly and it went sailing over RJ's shoulder. RJ followed its arc too surprised to make more than a halfhearted attempt at catching it and braced for the sound of the rattle breaking on the sidewalk.

But before the toy could hit the ancient stone sidewalk Sparky ran out of the tall grass and grabbed it midair, dancing backward with the rattle in his mouth and leaving the half-chewed red ball in its place. Everyone started calling to the dog and slapping his or her thighs, gesturing and even clapping for obedience. Aunt Chrissy used her sternest voice to call him to her without result. Baby Leonard chose that moment to start crying loudly and RJ and his Uncle Bill rushed forward in a flanking movement but Sparky was having none of it. He dodged several attempts at recovering the toy, letting RJ's hands get within inches and then bounding off into the grass. No one could make out where he was but they could track the toy's rattle. Moments later Sparky burst from the grass and crouched just out of reach. He shook his head wildly and was rewarded by even more manic noise from the baby's rattle. The dog's eyes shone with the attention this new game was getting him and his tail wagged furiously. It was all great fun as far as Sparky was concerned but not so much for the adults and certainly baby Leonard thought it tragical.

On RJ's third attempt he got a finger on the toy before Sparky ran the long way around the house, shot back thru Uncle Bill's legs and then came to a sudden stop just under the porch. RJ walked up speaking softly to Sparky who responded to each step RJ took with a short retreat of his own. Soon the dog's shiny black coat blended with the shadows underneath the house and RJ wasn't certain exactly where shadow ended and dog began. He caught a glint off the plastic here and there and the sound of the rattle as the dog shook it and chewed on it. RJ paused, not wanting to crawl under the porch after the dog and he looked back to where everyone else stood watching. He looked from face to face but there was no mercy and his uncle just shrugged and said "Looks like you're elected though I'm not sure baby Leonard will want it back after that dog's been at it."

RJ braced himself on the stack of cinderblocks that formed one corner of the porch and duck-walked in. He saw remnants of toys and bones that Sparky had brought under there over the years strewn about in the dust or half buried. They were gnawed, discolored, and only half recognizable. Some of them looked like toys that might have belonged to RJ long ago. He remembered playing in the shadows under the porch with plastic soldiers and marbles and bits of plastic packing material as building blocks. He shook the memory from his head and waited for his eyes to adjust, looking up thru the cracks in the porch for hidden cobwebs and spiders. He could hear the dog panting and its teeth clacking on the plastic as Sparky tried to get a purchase on the smooth baby toy. RJ called out to him and patted the ground encouragingly but a cloud of dust was all he got for his trouble. He half waddled half squirmed himself further under the house and said "C'mere Sparky you dumb dog, I gotta have that toy back!"

Of course there was no answer and RJ's scalp started itching just thinking about the layers of dust he was now swimming in, breathing in. He tried to peer beyond the dancing motes where the sun shown thru cracks in the porch above but it didn't help him see anything it just had the effect of killing his night vision. The old house seemed to be exhaling cold damp air right into his face. It reminded him of leaning over the edge of the well in Granmaw Wellman's back yard and feeling the coolness from far below wash up over him. Except this was getting colder and more uncomfortable by the second.

Reluctantly he let one knee touch the ground and leaned further in, inching forward guided by sound alone. Sparky's panting suddenly stopped and became a growl and RJ froze, squinting and leaning forward on one hand as he tried to make out what was going on a few feet in front of him. Didn't his aunt say something about snakes living in the rocks at the back of the house? Maybe Sparky scented one of them under here? RJ had heard someplace that a nest of snakes smelled like cucumbers and he took a slow deep breath searching for the slightest hint of vegetables in the air. He had decided to back out when the dog made a startled yelp and fell silent. He leaned forward again and softly asked "Sparky? You OK boy?"

RJ was acutely aware of the vulnerable position he was in. He stretched a leg back behind him to get a purchase on the ground before sliding backwards when he saw or thought he saw a point of light and the shiny pink curve of the baby's rattle. Apparently Sparky had abandoned it and left it lying just a foot beyond RJ's reach. RJ didn't want to return empty handed or spend a second longer in this closed in space than he had to so he hefted himself a bit forward and reached for the toy. It moved backwards just out of his reach exactly as it had when Sparky was toying with him out on the sidewalk. RJ cleared his throat and loudly said "Sparky, Stop it!" and made another attempt on the toy, stretching out completely in the dust. His hand again missed but he thought he felt the dog's fur this time. He made a mad scramble for dog or toy and tried to pull whatever he touched to him. He heard a grunt of surprise and a second pink point of light appeared next to the first and he heard a gruff hissing exhalation. It sounded like his own words being repeated back to him with a slow, heavy slur; "Ssssparky sssstopiiiittt!"

RJ made a sound of shock and surprise as he scrambled backwards as fast as he could from under the porch. He tried to cry out but all that would come out of his mouth was a noise that sounded like "Gaaaah!" He bumped his head sharply on the porch as he rushed to get out from under there and if he heard a distance echoing repeat of "Sssssparky, sssstopiiiittt" he didn't pause to make sure. He bolted upright soon as he could and turned around in circles, blinking in the sun and suddenly unsure of his footing. He put a hand out and grabbed a stout limb of the dogwood tree and pulled himself into it, almost hugging the trunk. He tried to call out a warning to his relatives, coughing and spitting while things spun around in his vision threatening to knock him to the ground. He couldn't see his aunts or his uncle anywhere in the yard but the cars were still there and he took a step toward them. He caught movement back toward the porch and froze, slowly rolling his eyes in that direction, dreading what he might see crawling out into the light.

What he saw was his Aunt Chrissy and Uncle Bill sitting in the two big rocking chairs on the porch and looking at him owlishly in surprise. They made no effort to help him or even speak to him. He looked at them as if they were cardboard cut outs of his actual relatives and then looked back down the sidewalk where he had last saw them, half expecting to see his real family still waiting for him to retrieve the baby rattle.

"Wha....what the HELL is under that house??"

His uncle looked to his Aunt Chrissy and then looked back. "Nuthin."

RJ rigidly pointed into the darkness and said "Something just SPOKE to me under there Dammit!"

"RJ!" his Aunt Chrissy snapped back at him. "Mind your language young man!"

RJ blinked and coughed once more, spitting on the sidewalk. "Don't 'language' me, what in God's name is going on here? You must have heard it, you were sitting right over my head!" He took a step forward and then froze, unable to move any closer to the shadowy darkness. The skin on his head crawled and even his face felt tight and hot as he tried to dust himself off as rapidly as possible.

"We heard you hit your head RJ..." Uncle Bill volunteered, "You were under there a while and we thought you were playing with some old toys or something. Sparky came out with the rattle a while back. LindaKay and Eleanor are inside showing the baby to your granmaw. Why don't you come on in and visit with us?"

RJ's anger rose at the matter-of-fact tone the two were using with him. He was still trying to clear his head and leaning heavily on the tree. "Wait, came out? The dog came out with the toy?" Aunt Chrissy stood up and held out her arms, gesturing to him. "C'mon on up here RJ, I'll put some ice in a rag and you can hold it against that bump you've got. C'mon on now, don't be so foolish."

RJ stepped backwards; she was using the same tone with him she'd used on the dog. He took one more look at the house and the black pool of shadows beneath it and turned toward his car. "No way, I'm not coming near that...that thing, that place ever again!" When his aunt tried to reply he cut her off with a wave over his shoulder. "No Ma'am, No Way!" He opened the door to his Honda and started the engine, the radio immediately squawking at him as he put the car in gear. His aunt and uncle were on the sidewalk now but he couldn't hear what they were saying over "Coal Miner's Daughter."

He gave the dial a frantic twist and turned around to back the car onto the road. It was a tight squeeze between the end of his uncle's car and the stones that marked the driveway but he didn't care. He pulled into the road and lined the car up in the lane without even looking to see if it was clear to pull out. A pickup truck buzzed around him and the driver shouted something rude in passing. RJ gunned the engine and the car leapt forward just as his aunt got to the end of the sidewalk and waved frantically at him to stop. He waved back automatically even as the car picked up speed and sped away from his grandmother's house. He'd had enough, he'd heard enough, and as his friend Indiana Bill would say, it was time to get the hell out of Dodge.

Chapter Twenty-Two: The long way round.

RJ watched thru the rear view mirror as long as he could. His aunt and uncle were both standing in the road and waving at him to come back. Not much chance of that he thought, there's already been too much too fast. Even after he made a turn and his grandmother's house was lost to view he was distracted to the point of ignoring his lane and almost rear-ended the pickup that had passed him a few minutes ago. It was stopped dead in the road and the blinkers were on but they were barely visible under the bright afternoon sun. He watched for a few moments but couldn't see anyone in the truck so he got out and went to see what was going on.

Soon as he could see around it he knew why the truck was jack-knifed in the road. The tiny stone bridge that crossed this branch of Wilson's Creek had slipped and dropped about a foot and a half below the surface of the road. Its foundations had effectively dammed up the stream which was visibly rising to overflow into the field beyond. RJ's memory of this place was sketchy but he seemed to remember visiting the nearby house with his mother long ago and that the people there were named Spaulding.

"Don't see that everyday, do ya?" came a voice from the other side of the truck. RJ looked around and squinted at a tall young man of slim build who came up from the water's edge. He carried a steel bucket of water and grinned at RJ as he squinted thru the sunlight.

"Nope, considering how dry it's been since I got here I am surprised there's been a washout."

The man's features changed soon as he heard RJ's accent and he said coldly: "You're not from around here, are ya?"

RJ smiled in spite of himself and said "Not anymore but I was raised here. I'm Gerry Wellman's son RJ."

The man nodded, his posture relaxing as he sat his bucket down. Offering his hand he said, "I could've guessed as much. I'm Doug Jr. You went to school with my dad Douglas Spaulding."

RJ nodded and shook the man's hand. It was wet and cold. He pulled his hand back in surprise and then glanced down at the bucket. Several dark eel-like things were swimming around at the bottom. RJ tried to ignore the bucket and pushed on with his questions. "Yes I did, I remember him well. Say, is there any way around this bridge? I was headed back into Wayne. His curiosity overwhelmed him and before the man could answer Rj said, "Wait, what have you got in that bucket there Doug?"

"DougJr...Doug's my dad see? This..." DougJr plunged his hand into the water and quickly pulled out one of the creatures. "This is what caused this bridge to sink in. They're Niaads...ugly sons of buck aren't they?"

RJ looked closer. The body of the creature was very eel-like and smooth but it had two little front legs and none in the back. It looked a bit like a catfish in the face and its mouth gaped and stretched wide as it tried to breathe out of water.

 "Niaads? Like the water spirits of ancient Myth? "

DougJr dropped it back in the bucket and wiped his hand on his jeans. "Naw naw they're really just salamanders I guess...not much more than eels. You've heard of mud puppies right? "

"Sure, I hooked one in Twelvepole when I was a kid. Put up a helluva fight."

DougJr nodded quickly. "Yeah these are like those only they burrow into the mud in between the rocks and under dark wet places...there's hundreds of them down there and they've loosened the support around the rocks at the very bottom of the bridge and now its slipped down a foot or two."

RJ looked into the bucket again, trying to imagine how he'd never heard of such a creature and how they were able to cause a bridge that must weigh tons to shift and settle. He imagined there were more than a few hundred at work down there under the bridge. "What...are you going to do with them?"

"I am going to take these back to the house and have mom fry them up. And while I'm there I'll call down to the police station to let them know there's been another subsidence."

RJ looked across the span. The other side was still mostly on level with the road, sloping downward across the 100 feet or so of bridge till it got to his side. There was another pickup on the other side in the middle of a three-point turn. He pointed at the truck and said, "Someone knows a way around?" Leaving it as a question and suddenly looking back down the road the way he had come, wondering if his uncle would come after him.

"There's a way around but your car won't make it. Gotta cross Wilson's Creek and you'd stall out before the water got up over your rims."

RJ did not want to go back to his grandmother's house and he didn't want to sit here any longer. "No other way huh?"

DougJr squinted back down the road and tilted his head. "I guess you could go all the way back thru Cabwaylingo then go up route 5 to Wilsondale or even further down to Breeden. But that's a helluva long drive from here."

RJ remembered the name Wilsondale and nodded "I think I saw that on the map. Just seems a long way around. How long before they fix this?"

"This, oh it won't take them long. They've got some heavy-duty equipment up at the military base. They'll probably throw a steel sheet across this for now and then get their boys on making something permanent before year's end. "

"That's right, there's a microwave tower or something on one of these hilltops, isn't there?"

DougJr pointed up the hillside roughly along the course of the stream. "Yep, right up there. Too bad you don't work for the Government; they'd let you cross the base to the other side. Then its all new road down to Asbury's Market and on to route 52."

RJ offered the man his hand and said, "Nope, I work for Notre Dame and that's not quite close enough." He shook DougJr's hand and got back into his car. He watched as the young man locked his truck and started to walk across the bridge and over to his house. RJ rolled his window down and shouted: "You're not afraid the rest of it will fall in too?"

DougJr just waved and thumped his bucket. "Nope, the niaads wouldn't let that happen. They're a plumb nuisance but everybody says they're good luck! See ya!"

RJ put his window up, sat back and took a deep breath. "I wish Mulder and Scully were here, this place is just too weird!" Looking at the empty seat beside him he took a second deep breath and let it out slowly. "Well maybe just Scully."

He drove back the only way he could, back past his grandmother's house. His uncle's car was gone and his grandmother was sitting on the porch rocking rapidly back and forth. He thought she turned her head towards him as he drove by but couldn't watch long enough to be sure. The road turned sharply to the left after her property and the cut thru the hillside barely had room for two cars to pass at the same time. Beyond that the road cut thru a short straight stretch of bottomland where an old sawmill once stood. RJ could still see the mounds of decaying sawdust though most of them were overgrown with weeds. That meant that the next driveway on the left was his uncle's house. The one where his mom had lived while Uncle Forrest was away in Germany.

RJ shook his head and made a face in the rearview mirror. I should have known things were weird back here, who would actually name their son Forrest anyway? He leaned his head out of the window and slowed down, trying to get a look up the hill at the house. There didn't seem to be a house standing there anymore or perhaps the kudzu had covered it so completely it had disappeared from view.

The road took his full attention again as it began to twist and turn, following TwelvePole Creek. He saw a sign for Cabwaylingo State Park and slowed down; the few cars on the road here weren't in any hurry. RJ wondered if they'd heard about the bridge 'subsidence' already. Maybe he should stop someplace to tell people? He watched for a gas station or a public building of some kind but did not see anywhere that didn't look like it was just somebody's house or like it was completely abandoned. The years hadn't been good to the economy of these small towns and they hadn't been left untouched like much of Wayne seemed to be.

He passed a sign for "Moses Asbury Road" and smiled remembering his father's claim to have known him. Or maybe Moses Asbury Jr. he couldn't remember which. While RJ did remember an old man living in Wayne by that name he thought it unlikely that he was the same one that the road was named for. More likely a Civil War personage like Mad Anthony Wayne who had his name all over everything in the area.

RJ drove for 20 minutes or so and it wasn't until he approached the entrance for Cabwaylingo that he recalled that he hadn't come in on 52 the day before, he'd come down the hillside on some meandering road leading from the cemetery. If he could get into Missouri Branch by driving along Wilson's Creek he should be able to get out the same way. He pulled onto the roadside and recovered the map from where it had fallen into the floorboard days ago. Was it really only three days? It seemed like so much longer after all the things RJ had seen and heard since first arriving in Wayne County.

He found Wayne on the map, followed the line of 152 down to Missouri Branch where he could see another road labeled 40 seemed to follow the ridge-line where the cemetery was marked and made its way sharply down the hill to connect with 152. He wondered why DougJr hadn't mentioned that road? RJ also noticed that the road thru Cabwaylingo went for miles thru the park before coming out the other side, all of it no doubt zoned 20mph or less. It would take an hour just to get to Kermit and then he'd have to find his way back up from there to Wayne. RJ was not sure he could find his way before dark and besides a lot of the roads in that area of the map didn't even have names. He rubbed his eyes and thought for a long moment before turning the car around and going back to the junction of 152 and 40. It involved back tracking but he thought he had a better chance finding his way back into Wayne following the ridge line than going thru the park and ending up even further away.

Chapter Twenty-Three: Lost in familiar territory.

RJ was lost.

He was high up on some ridge following a road that seemed to have been paved only as an afterthought. There was no sign of anything the least bit familiar. Actually it was all looking familiar and he wasn't sure he hadn't just crested a hill only to drive back down and start the same route all over again. It seemed an endless progression; hill on the left and on the right a drop down a steep ravine. And in the center potholes that a truck would have trouble crossing. There was the occasional mailbox with no numbers and rarely even a name. He met a few people coming the other way and he had to move his car way over into the brush almost dropping one wheel off the edge to allow them to go around. They drove past and stared at him with owlish eyes and open mouths. RJ was damned if he was going to wave any of them down and ask them how to get back to the real world.

He came to a wide spot on top of one of the ridges where a small grey church stood on a bit of land barely wide enough for itself and parking for a dozen cars. He slowed to a stop and looked hard for some sign, an address, or even a name of the road he was on so he could try and find it on the map. The road dipped down from this spot and looked like the it had been cut by following a cowpath; zigzagging down the hill with hairpin corners at each turn. Unexpectedly there were quite a few cows on the hillside and even a couple of goats.

RJ shook his head and said to himself "I could be anywhere...this looks more like Scotland or Ireland than it does West Virginia. IF it weren't for the occasional house trailer..." That thought reminded him why he was here and what he was trying desperately to get away from. He opened the car door and stood on the edge of the floorboard giving himself a few extra inches of height. He could see the shadow cast by the setting sun on the hillside opposite and already the lowlands ahead of him were lost in shadow, experiencing an early dusk. "The shade has come over!" as his mom would have said. RJ wished he'd listened closer to what his mom had said because then he might have heard a clue about where he was now or even what direction he should try to go. RJ had no confidence in his sense of direction and looking down at the twists and turns of the road as it continued on he realized it really didn't matter. He couldn't see where the road ended up and there was at least a fifty percent chance it was right back where he started.

There was the sudden roar of a truck's motor being gunned and a pickup slid in next to his car bringing with it a cloud of dust and gravel. RJ blinked and coughed as someone on the passenger side called out: "Thinkin' of becoming a Snake Handler are ya Big Bro?" Thru the slowly clearing dust RJ made out the grin of his middle brother KellyRay. "Don't know where the hell you are do ya? This here is Mathen's Ridge and that church has been closed all year...right after Brother Declan got bit for the third and final time."

RJ waved his hand thru the dust and leaned his head down to see his younger brother Ron behind the steering wheel. "They're all praying he'll get the use of his right side back but I don't think they'll be open to the public for a while if you catch my drift."

"I...never knew they had a building all their own. I thought they met at a member's house or something. Either way I'm not interested in getting anywhere near a snake, poisonous or not!"

KellyRay shifted his dip from one cheek to the other and spat, the juice landing near the front tire of RJ's car. He made a face like he was disappointed in his aim and said, "I ain't never been bothered by snakes and I live out in the woods with rattlers and copperheads, all sorts. If you don't go sticking your hand into their nest and just make a bit of noise when you come up on one they'll move off no problem."

RJ nodded like this was advice he'd ever want to use and there was an awkward pause as each brother tried to think of something other than what they were all there for.

"Your instincts are all wrong if you're trying to leave Wayne county." Ron offered as he pointed towards the road ahead of RJ's car and down into the valley. "You're gonna end up near Radnor and there's no roads thru that part of East Lynn lake. Now if you'd taken the right fork off Mill Creek back down at the bottom of the hill you might have had a chance to hit Ft. Gay and that's just a stone's throw from Louisa...Kentucky that is."

"There's a good spot to 'sang near here." KellyRay said. "And maybe if you're really really lucky we can show you something that will make you crap in your jeans...or cream in them!" Then he laughed harshly at his own joke and showed RJ his tobacco stained teeth. Ron punched him in the shoulder and that just made him laugh louder. "You are a doofus Kell, but that's is a good idea actually...might help clear things up a bit."

RJ looked from brother to brother not seeing any clue to what they were proposing in their faces. Ron nodded encouragingly and KellyRay took another shot at RJ's car expertly nailing the sideways H on the front hubcap. He looked up from under his ball cap with its camouflage pattern and said, "Well lock up your P.O.S. rice burner and get in the back. You won't be able to keep up where we're going and you sure as Hell ain't sitting on my lap."

"This isn't just an excuse to separate me from my only means of leaving here is it?"

"No one will bother your car and I promise I'll bring you right back to it when we're done."

KellyRay banged the side of the truck and said "Suck it up Big Bro and get yer ass in the flatbed!"

RJ closed his eyes and shook his head "I can't think of a single time that listening to you two ended well."

"Awww, we're all growed up and stuff now Big Brother, you can trust us. Besides, what you gonna do, tell dad on us?" Another punch from Ron. "That didn't help KellyRay."

"Well hell." RJ said letting his shoulders droop in defeat. "I don't see as I have much choice."

"C'mon then. You might want to park your car so the Indiana plate doesn't show to people driving by."

"Why? You said no one would bother it."

"Well mostly they won't but there's some around here that might see it as a gift from the Gods."

KellyRay snorted and almost swallowed his snuff. "Gods!" he managed to say as he expertly coughed, spat out the contents of his cheek and reached into his pocket for a fresh dip. "Now who's not helping?"

RJ gave his car a long look and didn't see anything in it that would encourage someone to break in. There wasn't anything of value in sight and the glove box only held a repair history of the car, an insurance card, and several cassette tapes his wife kept there. He backed it up to the porch on the church and then awkwardly climbed up the tailgate of Ron's pickup. Ron pulled out before he was seated and he plopped down hard on the tire well. More dust was thrown into the air and over RJ as Ron performed a tight donut in the parking lot and sped down the hill the way they had come.

Almost immediately they hit a pothole that made the truck bed buck and toss RJ dangerously close to going over the side. He gave up trying to balance himself and sat down with one arm braced against the tire well and the other gripping the side of the truck. He could see his brothers talking to each other but even with KellyRay's window down he couldn't make out what they were saying. Ron beeped and waved at someone in their front yard and they waved back and pointed at RJ in the back as they drove past. RJ gave a weak wave and figured that the rumor mill would soon be alive with the news that he had been re-captured at the border.

Chapter Twenty-Four: Salt Lick.

The forest around him looked dusty and mottled like the empty shell of a terrapin.

RJ was trying to understand how he ended up crouching here deep in the West Virginian woods when his goal this morning had been to get out of Wayne County as fast as he could. He shook his head and looked down at the too tight hunting clothes he was wearing and their muted camouflage-style patterns. The only thing that looked sillier than the clothes his brother had thrown together for him was his own face, which had been carefully painted to match the fabric's mottled designs. To top that off the whole ensemble had been doused with what could only have been deer urine. Just the way you want to smell for whatever this 'amazing thing' his brothers wanted to show him was going to be.

He tried to stifle a sneeze and managed instead to just sigh. He heard an admonishing tutt tutt from his brother Ron and he looked around to see where he might be crouched nearby. RJ could not spot him; the clothes he wore together with his sniper training from the military made him all too invisible. All RJ could make out were the slanting beams of sunlight cutting thru the dense growth of sycamores and maples around them. He thought he made out an eye and a toothy grin further down the hillside and decided that was his other brother KellyRay lying next to some rotted logs.

They had come unarmed though both of his brothers carried bags bulging with unknown contents. On the hour long hike into the woods RJ heard the slosh of liquid and had no doubt that brother KellyRay had brought along 'something to suck on' to replace the constant presence of a tobacco plug in his cheek. This had been RJ's only clue to what they were expecting to see or do, as KellyRay was hard pressed to give up his tobacco habit even for a little while. "Except when circumstances require a bit of decorum." RJ asked him what he meant by that recalling the scene at the funeral home but he just shrugged and said "If you've ever have a chaw forcibly jerked out of your mouth and stomped on you'd know not to bring it next time wouldn't you?"

The walk in from the truck had been largely silent between the brothers except for their muttered curses every time RJ tripped on a log or caused some shale to slip down the hillside. After a long heated struggle up a steep embankment he was ordered to crouch down and stay quiet. The object of their trek seemed to be a bowl shaped hollow just below them. It was tiny and too far from the road to be accessible by any other means and RJ couldn't see why it might be worth sneaking up on.

Several boulders the size of railroad cars were jumbled up in the hollow looking like a drunken giant's version of Stonehenge. They were riddled with lichen and holes made by erosion but RJ could not tell from where exactly they had fallen. The air here smelled musty, almost damp and it irritated his nose which was already running from the pollen and dust around him. He imagined there was a spring nearby, perhaps sheltered by the stones themselves.

He hadn't heard his brother move up next to him despite the fact that there were dry leaves all over the forest floor around him. Ron tugged his sleeve and RJ jumped and started to say something but Ron gave him a warning look and shook his head. He took out a small oval tin of the camo paint and dabbed some on RJ's nose where he had unconsciously wiped it. RJ could see he was suppressing a laugh and he stared stonily back at his youngest brother. Ron pointed down at the rocks and leaned in close to whisper: "Keep watching that dark patch and stay quiet you poor Summbitch."

RJ looked back at the spot and stared in silent agony. His nose itched and his legs were numb from being crossed up beneath him. He had been sitting that way since they had arrived here. He squinted thru the uncertain light and thought he saw some of the leaves stir in front of the cave. He looked back over his shoulder to see if Ron was looking at the same thing but his brother had left his side as silently as he had arrived.

Looking closer and trying not to snuffle or even breathe he saw KellyRay let himself down from the uppermost rock and deftly drop to the ground. He stayed crouched and unmoving long enough for RJ to wonder if he had hurt himself. Then his brother laid himself out flat on the ground and reached around to the bag on his back. He withdrew several items, placing them each in turn on a flat rock arranged in front of the stones. RJ saw him unwrap some sugar cubes, a long thin necklace of natural pearls, and a tiny metal hammer. He spent some moments arranging each item and then he scuttled and rolled further down the hill and out of sight.

RJ rolled his neck and then thought better of it, imaging the noise of his cricking bones would get him into trouble with his brothers. He leaned a bit against a nearby tree stump after inspecting it closely for snakes and resolved himself to jumping and rolling down the hill screaming all the way if one did appear. All bets were off if he came face to face with his childhood nemesis. He was already envisioning himself being medi-vacced out of the woods when a small sound or a change in the air made RJ look back towards the small clearing and he bit his lip to keep from gasping in surprise.

There was a deer standing immobile at the entrance to the enclosed space and a woman seemed to be kneeling beside it. She was brushing some leaves away to expose a small trickle of water. RJ turned his head to either side looking for his brothers and the woman rose up. She was not kneeling next to a deer but attached to it! The creature looked around and turned sideways to RJ scanning the hills to either side. He wanted to duck his head and look away but the sight mesmerized him. He could clearly see where the deer torso stopped and a woman's body began. RJ's heart was in his throat and his thoughts raced: "Oh God oh God oh God its a centaur! It's a centaur! A deer centaur...uh uh a deer-taur! Here in Muther Eff-ing West Virginia!"

RJ tasted blood as he bit his lip uncontrollably. He knew his breath was wheezing in and out of his nose in fear and awe but he couldn't help himself. He willed himself not to sneeze, to not even blink for fear of causing this vision to dash off into the darkening wood. He leaned against the tree stump and fought to comprehend what he was looking at. He couldn't quite take in the whole at once. He started to detail its features piece by piece as if judging some elaborate costume at a SciFi convention: "White tail, yes...hooves on all four legs, yes... very thin legs, OK...Overall color a warm leathery brown. You'd expect that wouldn't you? Yes... some odd curve of the spine just ahead of the forelegs. Muscles, re-enforced hipbones, or...I wonder if there's something extra there. Hmmm, very ah...athletic build from there up...supermodel looks if it weren't for the antlers and well the deer body. A tangle of hair down the back or is that a mane? Ahh...a bit of a roman nose there...can't tell if there's a division in it from here. No, I don't think so. But those eyes, those dark, dark eyes..."

RJ's inner dialog shut off abruptly as the creature locked her gaze on his. He saw her nose flare and she took several steps backward. He could see that she had a small metal hammer in her hand that she had just picked up from the pile of items KellyRay had left. She held his gaze for a long moment and RJ was certain he was going to wet himself and run screaming. And at the same moment he was sure he could spend the rest of his life gazing back into those eyes. He hardly moved at all when his brother Ron appeared at his side. He tilted his head in a sort of bow and whispered: "That strange and wondrous creature below you is the DeerLady. When you think you can move again lean forward as far as you can and spread your hands out to either side touching the ground. After that you're on your own." Then he added "You Poor summbitch."

RJ gave no sign of having heard his brother; it was the roar of his blood pumping thru his ears and his aching jaw that brought him back from wherever the gaze of the DeerLady had taken him. He blinked away tears and closed his mouth with a snap, his tongue painfully dry from being slack-jowled for so long. He leaned forward slowly, wrinkling his nose and trying to ignore the snot running from it. He spread his arms out touching the dry leaves and a puff of dust and pollen rose up to meet him. He shivered and gasped unable to stop breathing in and unable to hold back the building sneeze. He felt his heart cry out in despair knowing that when that sneeze came he would have chased away the most magical thing he'd ever seen in his sad little life. A second later he choked and sneezed with such force it blew several leaves up off the forest floor. He dared not look up and just pinched his nose and blew again, wracked with three tremendous rapid fire sneezes.

His first sneeze sent the DeerLady bolting away. She cleared several stones in one leap and disappeared into the shadows under the trees. RJ could hear the thump of the DeerLady's hooves first crashing on the rocks below then in the wood somewhere nearby. He heard one of his brothers cry out in warning. Then suddenly the forest was quiet except for the third and final ragged honk of his nose. A shadow shifted over RJ's bowed head as he wiped his nose on his sleeve and tried to focus in the last of the evening's light.

The DeerLady was standing before him. She looked a lot taller close up. She gazed at him with arms crossed below her breasts, one sharp hoof inches from RJ's outstretched hand. He wet his lips and looked at the outline of the figure before him unable to run or move or even stop his own heart. The DeerLady did nothing at first then leaned down and touched his tear-stained cheek with a clawed, four-fingered hand. She briefly rubbed finger and thumb together before bringing them up to her lips and tasting him with the dart of a tiny red tongue. RJ involuntarily snorted again and swallowed lord knows what before whispering "I'm sorry, I...I always sneeze in threes."

The DeerLady snorted back at him and showed her teeth. Then she looked around, her gaze clearly indicating the futile hiding places of his two brothers. They came out from cover and bowed silently where they were. RJ could see even his cynical brother KellyRay was in awe of this creature, or what was happening between them. The DeerLady put her hands out to the side mockingly returning the bow then reared back and let loose a loud laugh. The sound was somewhere between wind chimes and a baby's giggle. RJ straightened one leg and leaned forward on it while never taking his eyes off of the figure before him.

The DeerLady walked around RJ, coming much closer than a human would have, inspecting him closely. RJ returned the favor while she was still in his field of view. He noticed that her hide was not a uniform brown from waist up but had lighter speckles in it and bore little or no fur. Her hair or mane came to a sort of widow's peak in front framed by two mobile but normal looking deer ears and even thru his clogged nose RJ could detect an earthy scent about her. She exuded a different kind of beauty; otherworldly and primal at the same time. It felt like a looking at some natural wonder; a high waterfall or remote lake in the mountains. The Deerlady bit the top of his head when she walked behind him pulling out several hairs but by the time he cried out and turned it was too late. She was already gone.

Chapter Twenty-Five: Deer Lady.

His brothers hadn't stopped laughing the whole trip. KellyRay was turned in his seat looking out the open rear window of Ron's pickup and he just kept grinning at RJ then laughing and making rude comments. "Almost got ya some strange there didn't ya city-boy? Haw! There ain't none any stranger! How'd you know to snort like that? Like a goddamn buck in rut? If I'd known you could do that on command we could make some serious money renting you out to tourists!"

Ron eyed RJ thru the rearview mirror but he spoke to KellyRay sitting next to him. "Now Kell you know damned well RJ had no idea what he was doing." Then he glanced at KellyRay and continued "And he isn't the first dumb summbitch the DeerLady's singled out now is he?"

This just made KellyRay laugh all the harder "I got a damn site further than tricky Rick back there. But how was I supposed to know a little chaw would upset her so?" KellyRay made rotating gestures with his open hands "Got a firm little pair doesn't she RJ?" RJ didn't know how to respond to that and he felt his face and ears go red in a blush. KellyRay mimed rolling something between his fingers and said, "I'll never look at acorn crowns the same way, how about you?" It was Ron who answered though he was looking away uncomfortably. "I guess chewing tobacco while trying to mask your scent with deer whiz is what you'd call 'counter-productive to interspecies relations.'" He looked at KellyRay and shook his head "Just like you to brag about getting to second base with a woman who's a goddamn deer from the navel on down."

This set KellyRay to laughing loudly again. "A babe on top and an animal down below? Sounds like the perfect woman to me!" He looked between RJ and Ron and his grin faded. "At least she didn't laugh at me like she did RJ. Just like being back in school eh Big Bro? The only time women notice you is to laugh at you. Ain't that a bitch?"

RJ sighed and tried to re-direct the conversation. He wasn't enjoying his brother's jibes about being approached by the DeerLady. She wasn't human after all she was...legend. True he had felt something when she locked eyes with him and was still feeling it now somehow. His mind was in even more turmoil than it had been when the day had started. He felt full to bursting with questions and they had to bubble out sometime. "How long have you known about her?"

Ron spoke up to be heard over the pickup's motor. "Only saw her myself in recent years but there's talk she's been here since before the Indians came, before anyone came for that matter. That or there's been a series of them, Deerladies I mean. We can only get this close because we expanded the Covenant to include her." He paused while pulling out of the forest onto paved road. He quickly shifted up into high gear and elbowed KellyRay.

"Some people find it odd there's no gun hunting licenses issued in Wayne County. Ever. Not for deer anyway." KellyRay nodded and shifted his chaw from one cheek to the other "Damn straight. And sometimes tourists ignore the rules, the warnings. Those selfsame tourists find some other goddamned place to hunt."

"You can talk to her?" RJ asked, crouching down in the back so he could look in thru the truck window at his brothers.

"Not exactly."

"So how do you know she's anti-gun hunting but not anti-bow hunting? They're just as deadly."

"You looked into her eyes RJ, you tell me how you know Anything about a creature like that?"

"Well yeah I know but...no, I don't know. A lot happened in that short period. A lot...passed between us."

KellyRay reached thru the rear window and tried to thump RJ on the arm. He missed and said, "Other than snot and tears you mean?"

"Shut up. Yes other than that. I don't know how to grasp it. Its like...I don't know. I've never been that close to a real deer and only once been that close to a horse even. I was scared and yet there was something familiar. Like I was looking at a life-sized sculpture straight out of DnD. Another minute or two and I would have worked out her hit points and magic resistance."

Ron fished behind the seat without taking his eyes off the road and found a bottle of something, passed it to KellyRay who took a drink and passed it back thru the window to RJ. "Magic resistance is something you and I don't have. She could have taken you right then if she found you suitable. Ain't a damned thing anyone could have done to stop her either. So congratulations on being mediocre." KellyRay grinned at Ron's comment and added "Yep, just like high school."

RJ drank the drink--whisky, bourbon, moonshine--whatever it was because he was parched, headachy, and still a bit euphoric. He felt emotionally unsettled and susceptible. The fiery liquor burned all the way down and he made a face then handed the bottle back. "How do you keep something like her quiet? Forget finding Bigfoot; one camera crew and a few helicopters with infrared sensors and you'd see your DeerLady on every channel on the planet! Imagine how it would change things, what a difference it would make in the world if people knew something that looks like it walked out of 'Clash of the Titans' could actually exist?"

RJ's brothers looked at each other and there was a long silence. Finally Ron spoke up. "She's not like Bigfoot, not an animal at all. It's a mistake to think of the DeerLady like that. And maybe she did walk out of an ancient tragedy. Maybe she's tried to tell us but I don't remember Centaur-ese on the school curriculum." Ron fell silent in thought and downshifted as he mountain rose before them. "Hey yeah...It's like...You remember that Greek kid we had at school? Erik? Remember his mom? She didn't speak a word of English and when we went by his house she'd jabber at us and wave her arms about. Everyone thought she was bat shit crazy. Turns out she was just trying to act out the meanings of her words. A clever idea except she over estimated our ability to understand what she was getting at. "

KellyRay nodded and spat out the window. "What he said. Trying to understand the DeerLady is like trying to talk to a crazy Greek woman."

RJ could still feel his mind churning and he touched his cheek where her claws had wiped a tear away. He imagined he looked just as bad now as he had at his mother's funeral. But certainly things like that didn't matter to someone who lived in the woods. Who was a part of the woods? It would be like trying to explain what a computer is to a medieval peasant. Or like Ron said maybe it would be no more than trying to understand someone who spoke a different language, had different customs. He certainly hadn't meant to present himself as a potential mate and it still wasn't clear how that came about. RJ looked back behind him into the darkness and imagined her still standing over him expecting some response, to perform some ritual that he knew nothing about. That reminded him of something else that bothered him and he leaned his head thru the cab window again. "What were those things you put out for her; the sugar, the pearls, and the hammer? What was that all about?"

"They were fake pearls but how would she know? Its in the song RJ and if you hadn't run off this morning Granmaw Wellman might have taught you a few words of it. 'There's a Riddle and a Reason.'" KellyRay counted on his fingers and recited in a singsong voice: "The Riddle is 'What does the DeerLady wait for?' and the Reason is 'For her gifts to be returned in Kind.' That's how the song goes anyway. Makes me feel sad when I hear it."

"You're not telling me you go around singing about a half-woman half-deer and no one's asked you where you got the idea from?"

KellyRay thumped the side of the truck and shook his head. He spat out the window again and RJ was certain some of the spittle landed on him. "No Dumb Ass. I know some of the words but I don't go round singin' it. THEY sing it...Them Down Below."

Ron braked abruptly as he turned into the church parking lot and added "And if They know of her then she's a HELL of a lot older'n she looks." RJ stood up in the truck bed and stretched awkwardly before gingerly sliding over the side of the truck. KellyRay burst into laughter again and punched Ron in the shoulder. "Looks like the DeerLady's having a lasting effect on Big Bro back there!" RJ looked down and then turned away, glad for the darkness that hid his blushing face. He hadn't notice because at the moment his whole body felt like that. Ron laughed a bit too and said "It happens to everyone who gets that close to her son. I reckon its part of her strange way of picking a mate."

KellyRay leaned across the steering wheel and said, "Guess the Wellman boys just don't measure up to DeerLady standards. But she ain't going nowhere, you can always try again when you get back."

"Get back? Where am I going?"

"You are going to follow us to Pizza Hut and buy us each a large pizza pie for searching all over creation to find your sorry ass. And you're buying the beer."

RJ made a face like he was going to object and then just nodded. "That's exactly what I need right now. I just realized I haven't eaten since...since breakfast. I might even try some of your watered down 3% beer while I'm at it." He walked to his car and was relieved to find it untouched. Ron flashed his lights and called out "That's 3.5% and try to keep up!" Before RJ could get the key turned in his lock Ron spun his truck in a donut around the lot and then disappeared down the ridge.

Chapter Twenty-Six: Pit stop.

This wasn't the Pizza Hut on the west end of Huntington. It was not the one where RJ had spent many a night hanging out with his friends and playing 'name that tune' on the jukebox. Sure the exterior and decor where the same but there was more than distance that separated that Pizza Hut from this one on the edge of Wayne, West Virginia.

For one thing this place had no salad bar; just an extended area where the bar protruded into the room and allowed a few more people to squeeze in. And secondly the whole place had a haze of cigarette smoke hanging about 5 feet off the floor. RJ didn't think the Huntington Pizza Hut allowed smoking inside, if any of them did. Other than that the red vinyl tables were in exactly the same spots and the jukebox held the same place of honor by the door.

RJ ordered a couple of pizzas and three beers before walking over and examining the selections on it. The left hand row of songs had been taped over and new titles written with a thick permanent marker had been placed over the originals. He noticed that you could still see what the old labels had been thru the tape. In one slot "Dream Police" by Cheap Trick had been replaced with "All I ever need is you" by Kenny Rogers and in another "The Devil went down to Georgia" was now where an Elton John song had been. The last two entries both said "Amanda" and an arrow pointed up from the lower strip that said "Waylon" and a line was drawn thru the lower one that previously said "Boston."

RJ grinned and realized someone must have stacked the records in the wrong order. He was tempted to play them both when the lady behind the bar tapped her oversized ring on the counter to draw his attention. She slid the tray of drinks towards RJ and said "Don't bother looking' Honey, Free Bird isn't on there anymore."

RJ gave her a quizzical look as he turned back toward the room and tried to thread his way to the table where his brothers where talking to a rail thin man in his thirties who was dressed in a denim jacket and jeans over a red checked shirt. He had a half burnt cigarette in his mouth and nervously fiddled with his open pack of smokes as if he was afraid his last one would disappear. The man stood up and moved abruptly away from the table as RJ in-expertly settled the tray on the table. A tiny bit of foam spilled over the edge of one of the glasses and KellyRay said "Damn Son! I didn't plan on wearing my beer home! There'll be no tip for your sorry ass!" RJ ignored the comment, straightened up and looked sideways at the stranger. They silently regarded each other for a few seconds and then the man said, "You're the Older Brother? How long have you been gone from Wayne County?"

RJ was getting used to the directness of the locals around here and he searched for a spot to wipe his hand on his hunting clothes while he thought up an answer. He shot a closer look at his brothers and noticed they had both changed out of their camouflaged hunting gear and had even washed the war paint off their faces while RJ was ordering the beer. RJ settled for under his armpit hoping that it was mud free and then offered his hand. "I guess I've been gone eleven, twelve years or so. Call me RJ, and you're...?"

The man took his hand but there was no enthusiasm in his grip. "Long enough to forget your school chums then. I'm Dale Vernon, do you remember me? I bet you remember my sister LisaMarie! You were four kinds of lovesick for her all thru high school and she wouldn't give you the time of day."

RJ grinned and nodded with a chuckle but he had no idea who this guy was. Or LisaMarie. He tried to do the math quickly in his head and still couldn't place him. Still stalling he said "Its all coming back to me now. Lemme go to the bathroom and take this stuff off before the food comes. I'll talk to you in a minute."

Quickly he excused himself and without waiting for a response he turned and walked back to the toilet and quickly shed the smelly coveralls. His shirt and trousers where slightly sweaty and badly wrinkled but they were still more presentable than what he had on over them. He took time to try and wash off the camo from his face and hands noticing that his nose was the only place he could actually see his skin. There was a white streak in the green and black where he had repeatedly wiped his nose. The traffic thru the Men's room was brisk and he got more than one sideways glance and knowing chuckle. RJ decided to somehow get his brothers back for bringing him in here looking like this but he was exhausted and the smell of fresh baked pizza was making his stomach complain loudly. Revenge would have to wait till after supper.

When he returned he tossed the wadded up clothes at his brother Ron who caught them and tossed them back rapidly followed by the keys to his pickup. "Be sure to lock them in, those are special bought from the C. W. Fields Hunter's catalog."

"W. C. Fields is more like it!" RJ shot back and quickly made the round trip to the pickup and back. He started to sit down and KellyRay slid two empty glasses towards him "When you gonna learn to buy a pitcher--each--or you'll never get any rest yourself!" RJ looked to Ron for help but he just shrugged. "No wonder you never get drunk Big Bro, you spend all your time buying drinks and looking at yourself in the mirror."

RJ slid the glasses back into place, dragging the third unmentioned empty glass back in front of his seat. "Alright you moochers, I'll get one pitcher but then you're gonna have to tell me a thing or two about what happened tonight." Luckily he passed the waitress with two large pizzas on the way and asked for more beer as she was passing plates and napkins around. This didn't stop KellyRay from saying "OH waitress, there seems to be something wrong with my glass. I can see the bottom of it." She giggled half-heartedly and said, "I always give you a fresh beer KellyRay why don't you ever give me a fresh joke?" Now it was RJ's turn to laugh at his brother but he also noticed she didn't ask him what kind of beer to bring. RJ wasn't certain if it was because his brothers were regulars here or if it just didn't matter.

RJ's brother's were poised to dig in but looked at him expectantly. RJ picked up a slice that was hot but not too hot to handle and started to take a bite while eyeing his brothers. He paused and sat the slice back down. "Ok what? What's wrong with the pizza? Did you order anchovies or something?"

KellyRay grinned and said, "Do that thing. That thing you do with pizza."

"What?"

"You know, roll it up and suck out the sauce."

Ron nudged him. "Its all KellyRay could talk about. How you useta eat a slice of pizza like it was a taco or something. That's why we came here instead of some dive."

RJ panned his eyes around the room. He was definitely not ready to find out what 'some dive' might look like. "I don't remember...wait, oh right... thin crust. Right." RJ turned the slice pointy end toward him and rolled it up toward the crust. Then he made a loud slurping noise as he sucked the sauce out the end of the pizza 'roll.' It sounded like he was trying to get the last drops out of a milkshake. Then without pausing he popped the slice into his mouth and started chewing loudly. His fingers made short work of a second slice and with both cheeks full he mumbled "How's that?"

His brothers exploded with laughter, lifting their glasses in admiration. "That's the brother I remember! You could finish a large Gino's pizza in about 4 minutes flat!"

RJ shook his head at the exaggeration. "There's something I need to tell you about the Outside World boys. Out there they have a thing called "Deep Dish" pizza. You should try it sometime. You will never go back to this thin excuse for a pizza. Never!"

This brought more laughter and a short lived argument about how many slices each brother had consumed. The only solution seemed to be to order another one while they ate the second one. RJ lost count of how many times his glass was re-filled and worries of topping off his credit card were lost, somehow balanced in his head against the money saved by not staying in hotels or something like that. It had been after nine, nearly ten p.m. when they arrived so hours must have passed but RJ couldn't find it in himself to really care.

The restaurant half of Pizza Hut seemed to slowly empty out but the bar section had a steady business and showed no sign of closing. After the stress of the past few days it felt good to let go and BS with his brothers as if nothing had ever happened. During a lull in the conversation Ron got a serious look on his face and said "Son, I have some good news and some bad news. Which do you want first?"

"Give me the bad news first Bridge Keeper, I'm not afraid."

Ron paused for dramatic effect and then gripped RJ's shoulder. "Bro, your wife called this morning and said the kids had all gotten sunburns in Florida and she wasn't going to travel with them like that, funeral or no funeral. She's going to stay in that Disneyland resort over the weekend and then head straight home afterwards. She's not planning a stop in West Virginia."

RJ tried to process this for a minute or two, a wave of guilt passing over him as he realized he hadn't thought of his family all day. "And what's the good news?"

Ron slapped RJ's arm and sat back with a laugh, "I already told you son, "She's not coming to West Virginia!" KellyRay joined in with the jest and poured himself another full glass. "At least this gives you time to think up some good excuses. Can't tell her the truth can we?"

"And what is the truth, Brother O' Mine?"

KellyRay stood up abruptly, bracing himself on the edge of the table with one hand and waving vaguely at the rest of the room. "The truth is...that jukebox hasn't been updated since 1979 when we stole it from that other pizza place. Was there ever another pizza place in this sorry town to steal from? Hell if I know I was just a young felon at the time. Did I have a drink or two before we got here, again there is some truth to that. HOW-ever, the greater truth is I don't know who keeps ordering this cheap ass beer but I DO know one thing...one simple God's Honest Truth sort of...thing! I know I need to take a leak right NOW or y'all can have all this beer back cause I'mmmm done with it! Lordy my back teeth are swimming!" And with that pronouncement he leaned in the direction of the bathroom and the rest of him reluctantly followed.

RJ was speechless but Ron seemed un-phased. He poured half of Kelly's remaining glass into his and half into RJ's. Then he toasted to RJ one last time and said, "I guess there's nothing left for It." before downing it in one swallow. RJ followed suit and set his glass down loudly. He started to stand up but his legs weren't ready to obey him so stalling for time he said, "Nothing left for what?"

Ron stood up using RJ's arm as a crutch but once there he seemed in better shape than KellyRay and certainly better than RJ. "Why nothing for it but to go and see some gawd-daamned elves!"

Chapter Twenty-Seven: To the Bear Cave.

RJ hurried to catch up to his brother. He held his tongue till they were clear of the crowd and standing beside Ron's pickup. KellyRay was already there sitting on the tailgate and singing to himself. RJ tugged his brother's sleeve and said "Elves? You didn't tell me there were elves too?"

Ron looked at him and laughed loudly, joined distantly by KellyRay who couldn't have heard the whispered question. "Damn you're easy! And here I was going to let you drive. Hell I was! Ha Ha! Gimme back those keys! Betsy here don't take kindly to strangers behind the wheel. Especially those that are certifiably drunk."

"You were drinking too!"

Ron plucked the keys out of RJ's hand. "Yessir and the difference between you and me is I've been drunk before and regular like too. You drink like there's some reason for the beer to linger between your cup and your stomach. Waste of time trying to taste this stuff."

KellyRay thumped the truck bed and shouted "What he said...wimp! Now someone come here and close the tailgate! I don't want to slide out the back while I'm laying here." And with that he leaned back against the cab and stared up into the glaring parking lot lights.

Ron slid into the truck and turned to RJ, "I guess you're up here with me this time. Besides, I'm not certain he actually went TO the toilet when he left earlier." He gave nod of his head towards the back of the truck "Better walk around the front of the truck son."

RJ sat in silence while he tried to clear his head. The road was smooth for the first few minutes but soon they had turned off the highway and were bouncing and sliding their way up a steep hillside. RJ would have liked to close his eyes but after a nasty bump from the cab door he decided to try and brace himself against any sudden lurches. He was glad he wasn't driving at any rate because the road had given up any excuse at being paved or even well traveled. It looked to RJ as if they were just driving between trees straight into the woods.

"We're not going back to where the Dear...the deertaur...where the temple stones or whatever are? This looks like where we left the truck then except the fact that we're not on a road."

Ron didn't look away from the track he was following. "Other side of the holler from here, and further south. We would have stayed on the road a bit longer but the bridge is out. This was where a gas line went up the hill and down the other side. Not everyone has a primo vehicle like myself to even try this."

RJ nodded to himself, remembering the alternate route DougJr had given him this morning. "I'm glad I didn't find it! My little car wouldn't have gone this far."

Ron made a derisive snort. "Your little rice burner wouldn't have gone more than two car lengths. And I would have had to pull your sorry ass back onto the road if it didn't get hung up on a sapling or a tree stump for your trouble. But be glad Betsy can get you this far, we still have some walking to do after we stop."

RJ looked out into the dark, he didn't see as much as hear the closeness of the trees and considering how proud his brother was of his truck he didn't seem to mind that branches and saplings were scraping along the sides and the suspension complained more than once as they crossed ravines that were more narrow than the truck was long. After three of those in a row, each punctuated by cursing from the back where KellyRay still managed to hang on they hit a level patch and RJ asked "I thought there was a stream bed we had to cross?"

Ron gripped the steering wheel tightly and jerked it to the left and shouted "Coming up!" The trees along the right side gave way and the truck leaned at a sharp angle. RJ could see the headlights bouncing off water just a foot or two outside his window. "I'm both relieved and terrified that you inherited dad's night-time driving ability."

Ron laughed evilly and KellyRay cursed some more as the truck leveled out, turned hard to the right again and dived more than drove into the stream. Two huge gouts of water sprayed up around each side and RJ was hit in the face by the icy spray. The truck slid to a stop on a large sandbar in mid stream but the cursing from the back was even louder as KellyRay pounded on the rooftop and tried to reach in thru the cab window to get at Ron.

Ron leaned just out of reach and laughed even louder as KellyRay shouted: "You summbitch! What are you trying to do, sober me up? Come out here where I can kick yer ass!"

RJ's whole body shuddered with suppressed laughter. KellyRay had taken the brunt of the wave in the face and he was dripping wet. He was what Mom would have called "Mad as an ol' wet hen!" He climbed out and watched the two banter and curse at each other. KellyRay seemed genuinely angry but wasn't able to decide whether to threaten Ron or his truck. RJ gave it a few minutes just to enjoy the spectacle and then tried to distract them both: "Not to seem ungrateful, but why are we parked in the middle of a stream?"

KellyRay gave Ron one last dirty look and a muttered "You'll get yours soon enough." before answering RJ. "This is our land. Wellman Private land. We can park anywhere we want to."

Ron nodded walking thru the headlights and back to the cab where he flipped the passenger seat forward. He fished out a couple of flashlights and three bags similar to the one KellyRay had worn to see the Deerlady. He offered a light to RJ and the tossed a case to Kelly. He sat the other one on the seat and unzipped it, revealing a variety of items but RJ could only make out a foil blanket and a first aid kit before it was closed again. RJ tried the flashlight and played it around the tiny spit of land they were parked on and the thick brambles lining both sides of the stream. The truck would be hidden here day or night, visible only from the air and then only if anyone knew where to look. He turned back and saw KellyRay pulling his hunting clothes on Ron was doing the same. "Suit up, it can be chilly in the cave, and damp. At least at first."

RJ got his clothes from behind the passenger seat and turned his head at the smell. Time hadn't improved the combination of sweat, mud, deer musk and whatever else RJ had gotten on them. "Shouldn't we wash these or ourselves or something? I don't relish the idea of spending time in a cave with you two if you smell half as bad as this one does!"

KellyRay hitched up a belt around his waist and hung a water bottle from it "Shows what you know. Smelling bad is smelling good!" RJ looked at Ron for help but Ron had crossed to the further bank and was poking around in the shrubs for something at the base of a large oak tree. A short search later he straightened up with the end of a rope in his hand; it went under a log and up the side of the tree like a vine. RJ followed it up the tree with his light to where a black bag twisted, suspended in the very canopy of the tree. Ron took great care to lower it down without hitting anything but once or twice RJ heard the sound of glass clinking against glass. KellyRay was at his side and added his light to the scene. RJ kept watching the descent and asked, "Did you tie your food up in a tree to keep it safe from bears?" Ron kept silent, focused on his task but KellyRay elbowed RJ and said "Not because of the bears."

When the bag touched down it shifted again and RJ clearly heard glass bottles jostling against each other. Ron untied it and checked the contents. "I don't think Bears have a taste for moonshine RJ, but you're gonna have to try some of this, its the last of our departed father's final batch. Rare as Hen's teeth!"

RJ looked into the bag and could see several mason jars, some wine bottles and a couple of hip flasks mixed together with some cans that simply had the word "BEER" stenciled on the side. Suddenly RJ remembered the almost ritualistic way Ron had offered him a cup of coffee from Mom's cupboard and he said "I'd be honored Sir."

"Good, then you carry it up to the cave."

"Cave?" RJ echoed looking from brother to brother.

"Hell yeah the cave RJ, Granmaw Wellman DID tell you the cave story didn't she?"

"Oh, that cave" RJ said in surprise, looking around with his flashlight. "This is that place? Looks different than I pictured it...anyway I thought it was further away."

KellyRay fell in step behind Ron and RJ had to quickly shift the bag onto his shoulder and rush to catch up while trying to keep the flashlight trained on his brother's back. KellyRay paused briefly and looked back. "Didn't seem like we drove far enough did it? Well we did sorta take a shortcut across the county instead of following the roads like you did. It would take you a week to walk back even if you were lucky enough to find the road." He paused and pointed with his flashlight "Its downstream by the way. Always a good choice when you're lost. "

RJ nodded and shifted the bulky bag again. KellyRay shot him a disgusted look and turned to follow Ron, already out of reach of the flashlight's beam. RJ's mind was in turmoil, almost ready to believe yet still unable to make that final jump. He tried to play back all the strange things he'd seen in the past few days home but he still felt muzzy from the drink and it took all of his concentration to keep from banging the bag of alcohol on every tree and log they passed. Far up ahead he heard Ron call out "Don't break the hooch!"

RJ slipped and panted along as best he could. When he burst out of the trees with a loud sigh KellyRay thumped him on his stomach and hissed at him to be quiet. RJ looked around expecting to see the DeerLady appear in the little clearing and seeing nothing, let his bag down quietly. At first he could hear nothing then he heard the cry of some animal; high pitched and keening. He looked around himself in alarm and before he could ask about the call it was answered somewhere off to the left. This time it almost sounded like a woman's laughter or the sort of keening, broken laugh someone in deep despair might make. He watched KellyRay's face for signs that he was worried by the calls but KellyRay only shifted his dip from one cheek to the other and spat on the ground. "Sounds like they're getting further away, Ron's gone ahead to check the cave just in case."

RJ shifted his light around in a wide circle, the hair on his neck tingling as he imagined whatever it was that made that noise. KellyRay's assertion that it was getting further away did little to ease his pounding heart. He saw that the forest ended here though there were patches of trees ahead and further up the mountain. A cleared path twisted around the hillside and looked like it might have had water flowing down it recently. RJ imagined that was the direction Ron had headed. He didn't hear the animal call again though it was quiet enough around them to hear tree limbs rubbing against each other and something randomly flipping leaves around near the roots.

RJ had just about recovered enough to ask what they were listening for when Ron came slowly and quietly down the hill. He managed to move almost silently though RJ could see the concentration and the occasional flash of pain on his face. Ron waved at him and said "Quit shining that in my face and c'mon up. I don't feel like making this climb twice if I don't have to." RJ reached for the bag but it wasn't at his feet anymore, he turned his beam on KellyRay and found he had somehow taken it, silently removed a hip flask and was finishing a long pull from it while out of the flashlight's beam. He grinned and wiped his lips on his sleeve. "Its okay, this bottle's for me. Still plenty for...perusal." RJ shook his head. "You can quit being all mysterious. I remember this part of the story. We're supposed to take all this stuff up to the cave, get real drunk and wake up with a bunch of stone knives or something for our trouble?"

Ron took a deep breath and puffed out his chest "Blasphemy! You're not going to just get drunk, you're going to get Black Out Drunk." KellyRay joined him, cradling the bag of hooch as if it was a baby in his arms. "And don't knock stone knives, I once got 5 of them for a single pack of chewing gum."

"I'll give you a pack of gum and a bag of hooch if we just go back to Ron's place for the Black Out Drunk part."

Ron leaned to the side and mock whispered to KellyRay "Tsk tsk, no respect for time honored traditions anymore is there?"

RJ panned his light one more time around the small clearing then started up the path behind his brothers. Abruptly he stopped and turned the light back the way they had come. "Hey wait, what about those things we heard? What was making that weird cry like a woman being murdered?"

"We don't know what to rightly call them but whatever they are they're at least half wild hyena and half devil dog. Now do you want to stay here and debate till they come back or would you rather put your back to a wall? "

RJ did not need further prompting. He quickly if noisily closed the space between himself and the two receding backs ahead, his mind jumping from the present to the past and back again.

Chapter Twenty-Eight: Spirits and tongues freed.

The three Wellman boys sat a few feet back from the entrance of a large cave. The view out was of scrubby trees marching down to meet the stream somewhere below. Directly across from them were seemingly endless rows of mountains and somewhere amidst of them, the Ohio River.

But RJ could see none of this in the dark. It was overcast, cold, and windy up here on the ridge. They were sheltered from the teeth of the wind but a steady draft blew out of the cave from somewhere deep below and it chilled RJ even thru the layers of hunting clothes he wore.

Ron led the way forward only needing to duck a bit at the entrance and waved his hand in front of his face absently as several bats took flight around them. "Here's some Indiana Brown Bats for you RJ, you want to take them back home with you? Save them a long flight and all?" Ron chuckled at his own jest and then got louder as he saw RJ duck walking to keep his head as far as possible from the ceiling and panning his flashlight around every nook and corner. "You won't get far like that RJ. Besides, you need to watch where your feet are more than your head."

"That's easy for you two, you're both short bastards. I take after our mom and I'm a head taller than either of you."

KellyRay had passed them both during this and called out from ahead "C'mon ladies, the main chamber is just ahead and there's room to stand straight up in there." His light turned forward again and bobbed around a corner 20 feet or so ahead. Ron went next asking over his shoulder "You noticed he took the hooch with him didn't you?"

RJ turned the corner and felt the walls drop away around him. His light panned over the room. The ceiling was a good thirty feet above and the floor seemed fairly even if gently sloping toward the back where another dark void hinted at further chambers beyond. KellyRay was in the center of the room balancing his light on a rounded stalagmite and turning it on a rough blackened circle where bits of charred wood lay scattered about. Ron sat down his bag and searched about with his light. The beam struck a pile of dry wood and a paper bag with wood shavings and wadded up magazines sticking out. He set to building a fire and KellyRay lined up the bottles of drink by type on a natural shelf in the closest wall.

RJ was still turning round in full circles trying to find a spot where he felt safest. It didn't seem to exist. Soon as the fire caught on the kindling he moved up closer and spoke "Ron..." He stopped noting the peculiar quality of the sound as it echoed and almost amplified thru the chamber. He started again quieter, whispering as if he was in some great cathedral during mass.

"Ron, how far back does this cave go? It just dawns on me we didn't bring any sleeping gear but I doubt that matters. I see there are more bats in here too...and probably the godfather of all spiders judging from those webs over there. I doubt any of this matters but I don't think I am going to be able to relax enough in here to do you any good. Especially if the purpose is to fall unconscious so that someone or something can sneak up on us while we're out."

KellyRay walked over and looked RJ up and down "If you're done wetting your pants Granny have a snort of this." He handed RJ a shallow lid with some clear liquid in it. RJ studied it and watched the firelight flicker and dance on the surface. "You sure this is still good? Dad's 'shining days were over decades ago."

"Oh its Good RJ, its good!" KellyRay said, looking from moonshine to RJ's face. "How could it go bad, its 90% pure alcohol? Go ahead, toss some back to honor your dear ol' dad?"

RJ started to tip it back in one go but he caught the look on KellyRay's mischievous face. The yellow cast of the flames gave made his face even more grotesque as he gestured in anticipation. "Not afraid are ya? Don't be a Chickenshit, c'mon and drink it you summbitch!"

RJ gave KellyRay a defiant look and slurped some moonshine from the lip of the lid. The immediate burning sensation made him cough and the vapors burned his nose as he danced and gagged, pounding his chest and staggering toward Ron for help. Ron and KellyRay were both laughing and pointing at RJ then waving and trying to say something about the fire when RJ bent over double and coughed even louder, bracing on his knees.

Ron came over and forcibly turned RJ away from the open flame but couldn't get anything coherent out between gales of laughter. The sounds were echoed and distorted all around them and it sounded to RJ as if hosts of cackling demons were joining in just beyond the firelight. KellyRay sat down hard next to where RJ was still trying to catch his breath and said "They always told me Dad's 'shine would cut the hair off a wooden leg!" He laughed some more and when RJ punched him in the chest he just rolled his shoulder forward to take the blow and said, "That's you properly welcomed home finally!"

Ron had settled down enough to wheeze out "I thought you were going to set your face on fire when you coughed right next to the flame! I only stopped you cause I can't stand the smell of burnt hair." He reached out with a toe and kicked Kelly's boot. "You might have tested it first doofus."

RJ held quiet till he could talk without going into another coughing fit. Red faced, he just pointed at his two brothers with a shaky hand and whispered "Asswipes, both of you." Then he tugged the empty hooch bag behind him and sat down with a grump.

KellyRay felt around for the lid RJ had dropped and poured a small amount from the moonshine jar into it. He tossed it on the fire and it blazed up with a bright bluish tint. "See? You know our daddy never tainted his 'shine or used a car radiator to condense it with. Some birch bark for color and flavor but he wouldn't have lasted long if one of his customers got sick or blinded. Most of them were connected to the courthouse."

"You mean most of them worked IN the courthouse!" Ron replied, poking at the fire with another piece of wood before tipping it into the flames. "I remember that time Chuck Plymouth himself came down to the trailer looking for a sample. We sent him away with purity all right, pure water! That made him mad but he couldn't use us kids against Dad to get a piece of the action. Not that I think that threat would have gotten him anywhere with our ol' man."

RJ nodded, still eying KellyRay darkly. "I thought you hated him more than any of us. How is it you're talking so reverently about the man who nearly beat you to death on several occasions?"

KellyRay lifted up the partially empty bottle of moonshine and turned it so he could see the flames thru the liquid. "Two reasons Big Bro. One: He's dead and I'm not so that just shows who was meaner. And secondly..." Here he paused to take a drink and whistled in appreciation "Secondly when he died the recipe for this magical elixir passed to me. And it has been the solution for and cause of all the ills in my adult life. Bet you didn't know that did you?"

"He always claimed it wasn't written down any place, had it all in his head. How did you get him to tell you? You two weren't exactly drinkin' buddies."

"It was in his will."

"His will? Dad didn't have a will."

"Not a legal registered with the county type will but he let his wishes be known."

RJ turned to look at Ron's face "Is this true?"

Ron nodded and looked uncomfortable "I got his last working still and plans on how to build one to his exact specifications."

"You got his still and KellyRay got his recipe. What did I get?"

There was a pause as each brother stared into the fire and finally Ron replied. "You got to leave."

RJ stood up and walked a short distance back into the cave. He didn't need to speak up to be heard anywhere in that domed space. His voice had a sarcastic edge to it when he repeated, "I GOT to leave eh? That's just great. You know what? This is one cocked up family business we've got here."

Ron said "Well, its not like we inherited a vast alcoholic empire. If it weren't for selling the stuff we get in here to collectors around the state neither of us would make enough from 'shining or 'sanging to live off it."

RJ wasn't consoled by this fact. "Yeah, we each did sooo much with our inheritance. I wish I'd known what was at stake; I might have done things differently. And I probably wouldn't have come back here for any reason. I should have taken Mom with me when I went too."

"She wouldn't have gone. You already know the reason for that."

"Yeah and it killed her too, didn't it?" KellyRay said between sips, "Not leaving the state, I mean, or the county even. She could have gotten treatment in New York City, or out West but she wouldn't leave the Covenant. She gave that option to you, made Dad write it down with his brothers all in attendance. It was the last time they spoke to each other in this life."

RJ turned back to the fire and started to apologize. He gripped KellyRay's shoulder and said "I didn't know...I" but KellyRay cut him off and crossed to where the rest of the drinks were lined up. "Forget it, they're just words now anyway." He picked up a medium sized bottle and passed it to RJ. "Start with the rum, its sweeter than most of the stuff here. You can work up to the Gin and vodkas if you're still awake by then." He spat into the fire and sat back down, making it clear from his posture that the discussion was over.

Chapter Twenty-Nine: Into the Drink.

RJ's brothers seemed more at ease in these surroundings than RJ ever would. He guessed it was because both of them have been here before. In fact KellyRay seemed to be looking forward to the coming alcoholic binge.

To RJ the cave was only now taking on a sort of "Cabin in the Woods" feel and he still couldn't find a place to stand or sit where he felt comfortable, safe. Once or twice he stood up and dusted the seat of his overalls but all that did was transfer some of the fine dust coating everything to his hands. RJ looked at them disappointedly and then shoved them into his pockets. He turned off his flashlight now that his eyes had adjusted to the dim light cast by the campfire. He could see OK as long as he didn't look toward the flames. KellyRay was still sitting on the floor two bottles into his booze supply and humming some unrecognizable tune. Ron was off to one side holding his flashlight close to the wall. RJ walked up to see what he was looking at and saw the wall was marked with a list of about thirty names carved or painted onto the rock wall.

"What's this?" RJ asked noticing that he could only recognize the last couple. The very last name was his mother's though she had signed herself Gerry Wellman instead of Geraldine. "No don't tell me. Its the list of the uh, what's the word you used to describe us? The...Covenant Keepers?"

Ron pointed down to where several names had been scratched or painted over; three in a row were unreadable, half covered over by a large painted name that looked like "Zeke." Another one beyond that had been completely blotted out. "I'm betting those guys didn't consider themselves Covenant Keepers. I have always wondered what happened back then that made them abandon their position? But hang on a sec RJ...you think this is interesting? Come into the next chamber or as I like to call it, the "Scripture Room."

RJ followed Ron down to the lower end of the main chamber and along a narrow shaft that his potbelly barely fit thru. He grunted and scuffed and got hung up on a protruding rock at one point but eventually came thru into a roughly rectangular and narrow room that looked like it might fit inside the trailer of a semi. Immediately on the wall to the left were carvings of a different sort. Rows of nearly straight hash marks and arrow points mixed together. It looked to RJ like Roman numerals and some random directional symbols mixed together. "Good Lord!" was all RJ could get out. In an instant he knew what he was looking at. These were the carvings Granmaw Wellman had told him about; the Nativity Story written in old Irish script by Brother Wellman himself.

He looked closely at each line though neither brother understood any of it. RJ tried to will understanding into his brain, wishing that somehow enlightenment would jump off the wall and land in his subconscious. At the bottom of the text was carved a hand, its palm open and a heart outlined in the center. The mark of the carver, or a final amen?

Ron waited for the awe to sink in and then said "This looks like the real deal don't it?" RJ whistled softly and nodded, stepping back a bit in order to illuminate the whole chamber with his flashlight. There were other bits of text on the wall separated into little rectangles and in one section the text was underscored by a series of holes and tiny bumps about 3 feet off the floor. RJ had no idea what those were and he kneeled down to take a closer look. "Is this where the monk kept track of the days?"

"No, that's on the outer cave wall. You couldn't see it in the dark and besides he'd need to see the sun when it hit the Christmas Notch wouldn't he?" RJ nodded folding his arms to resist the urge to reach out and touch the centuries old carvings. Ron turned his light out and said, "Put out your light RJ, you need to see the coolest thing ever."

RJ secured his grip on the bulky light then thumbed the switch. He was immediately plunged into deep darkness. He looked about for his brother but could see nothing. He lifted his hand in front of his face but there wasn't even a variation in shadow before him. He could hear his brother breathing nearby and said, "What am I supposed to be seeing? I can't make out the nose in front of my face."

Ron kicked the wall with the toe of his boot and the resulting thump and crash was deafening in the small room. RJ turned toward the sound and saw faint little dots suddenly appear on the wall. It was so dark they seemed to float in the air and he moved towards them feeling out with his hands. He jumped when he came in contact with his brother's back. "Good you can see them too, can't you RJ? They react to vibration or sound of some kind. I find it easier to just make a big bang instead of trying to figure out what exact tone they react to."

"But what is it?"

"Some form of algae I think, or glow in the dark paint made from some. I think its something Them Down Below put here, though why or how long ago is anyone's guess. You can sometimes see stuff like this glowing in the very tips of tiny rock straws in the caves but I don't know if they're alive or just minerals."

RJ knelt down and looked as closely as he could at the tiny glowing spots. They were already fading away and he would have lost them entirely if Ron hadn't walked between him and the wall. Ron said "Lights coming up!" and then pointed his flashlight back beyond the room and slowly brought it over to shine on the markings. RJ blinked and closed his eyes till they adjusted, then he looked up the wall from where he crouched and wondered if "They" might be little folk like in the old Irish tradition. He hmmmed and frowned to himself, something about the evenly spaced runes above and the dots below bothered him deeply. Standing up he dusted his knees and asked "Do you have the translation Uncle Jack got from the University? The exact translation?"

"KellyRay might have brought a copy. He had some wild idea of setting it to music like a hymn. You should hear how he tries to preach when he's really drunk. I'm guessing you probably get your chance before this night's over."

"I thought it already was a hymn of sorts, the way Granmaw Wellman tells it."

"Damn straight. If Granmaw Wellman said it, its gospel all right. People come from all over to hear our Granmaw talk. Mostly though she just tries to teach them to listen."

RJ looked at his brother's face in the beam of his flashlight and said, "I heard her talking to Randy last night you know. Our dead brother Randy?"

Ron snorted, "Doesn't surprise me any. Why not too long ago a guy in a horse and carriage came by to chat with her. Said he was a re-creationist, whatever that is."

"Now who's not taking who seriously? I heard her talking to the dead Goddammit!" Ron flinched and said "Mind what you say, sound carries a long way here. Curses even further." He brought his flashlight close to shine right on RJ's chest. "How come you believe that but you don't believe anything else we've told you?"

"Looking at this makes me think I've been wrong about a lot of things recently."

"But how do you know KellyRay and I didn't do all this just to mess with your head?"

"Like someone once said: 'Rednecks aren't this creative.' Besides, you didn't make up the DeerLady though you know or think you know a lot more than you're letting on."

"Haa haa. Here's something do I know. There was serious discussion of breaking your legs and just leaving you here. That sound creative enough for ya?"

RJ shrugged. "Its the most believable thing you've said since I got here." He looked back behind him at the second chamber and into the next bit of tunnel. "Well where do we do this? Shouldn't we get on with it? Aren't we burning midnight or something?"

"Back in the front room and unless I miss my guess, KellyRay is already a bottle or two ahead of us. I usually let him start first, he pouts if he doesn't get first crack at the good stuff. But look here before we go back." Ron shined his light into the next bit of tunnel; it ceased being level, slanting downward and to the right. "There's half a dozen shafts that lead off this one. Goes on forever and at least one of them has a pit in the middle of the room so don't go running off wild or you'll take a nasty fall." He passed RJ who took one last look at the wall of characters and then followed his brother back to the main chamber.

"That other room and the tunnels between, they don't look all that natural? I thought Brother Wellman found this cave already here. It wasn't part of a coal mine was it?"

"No, but remember how long ago Brother Wellman's story took place. There's been 30 generations in and out of here since then and at least a few of our forefathers thought it should be made more comfortable if they had to spend so much time here. And one of them kept his family here almost a year after getting involved in that mess over at Gallipolis."

RJ didn't want to start another line of questioning but he made a mental note to himself to ask later whether Ron meant Gallipoli the town involved in the mining strikes or the city on the other side of the Silver Bridge up by Point Pleasant. RJ only knew one thing about that area and he wasn't going to invoke the specter of the Mothman while spending the night in a cave.

KellyRay said nothing as RJ joined him next to the fire; he just tapped the abandoned bottle of rum and shook a finger in his direction. RJ tried another sip of the rum and it was definitely going down easier than the moonshine had. He tried to take bigger swallows though his common sense was telling him to slow down. He had never consciously decided to get drunk though he had woken up a few times painfully surprised that he was hung over.

KellyRay had already lined up several additional bottles for him to finish off and a small plastic cup with moonshine in it. RJ was certain that was a bad idea. His first taste had seemed strong enough to melt plastic! A third drink of the rum and the warmth in his belly did not fade away. It was having a calming effect and making him uneasy at the same time. He tried to refocus, to remember the questions he was going to ask. He looked critically at the near empty bottle of Rum. It took some effort to focus on its tiny ingredient list.

"The alcohol must serve a purpose." He announced to KellyRay. "Otherwise just falling asleep would work. Perhaps it deadens part of the brain so that more of the subconscious part can take control." Kellyray spat into the fire and said "Son you're talking a helluva lot for someone who's supposed to be passed out drunk by now."

"OH I'm drunk. I assure you sir. But I am not "Black Out Drunk." I am however worried about alcohol poisoning setting in before that happens."

KellyRay laughed harshly and nudged RJ's single bottle with his toe. He gestured to the growing pile of exhausted spirits at his side and said "Yeah, ain't it great?" He took another pull of whatever it was he was drinking from a hip flask.

"Maybe I should have brought some cold medicine or something that will knock me out faster. I had some allergy relief stuff in the glove box for emergency use and it always makes me groggy even though it says it won't on the box."

"RJ, you can experiment with drug abuse another night. Ron wanted to get you some good stuff at Asbury's Market but seeing as you're a novice an' all I told him to save his money. Anything would do to get you drunk and besides, we already have the best hooch in the county! Why don't you take another swallow of Dad's recipe? It'll get you there quicker than all this other stuff."

RJ eyed the untouched plastic glass and said "Maybe some of the gin first, I still have some sensation in my tongue. Or maybe I should mix it with something?" KellyRay pulled back his arm as if he was going to backhand RJ and said, "You do and you'll lose a tooth!" Then he grinned evilly and said "On second thought go ahead, its your funeral."

RJ squinted at his brother's outline against the fire and kicked KellyRay's boot with his shoe. "You're just as full of bullshit are you ever were Kelly Ray Wellman."

KellyRay started to say something but it slurred a bit and instead he laughed hoarsely. Turning to look into the fire he started to whistle tunelessly, started again and got a little further, then stopped and thumped RJ on the top of his head. "Well, drink up!" Then with a deep breath he got out enough of the tune that RJ recognized it. "Scorpions...nice."

"Do you know any of the lyrics?"
"I've heard that song hundreds of times but not in the last ten years or so. Do I know the lyrics? No, just the chorus part about Winds of Change and something about Gorky Park."

KellyRay rolled his eyes and said "Every time I make an effort you slap it away." RJ looked hurt and confused. "What the hell are you talking about?"

"I didn't think you'd know any gospel, so I learned a few random rock songs."

"Is that what you listen to? Gospel music? I had you pegged as a good ol' country boy."

"You've been away a long time RJ, don't go making assumptions about people, it'll just piss them off."

"Okay okay! What other songs do you know?"

"Try me."

"I mostly listen to 80's stuff, some 70's. It's all that's on every station in my area. Except Country and you know how I feel about Country music."

KellyRay gave him a blank stare then silently took another drink and smacked his lips. "I bet you I know more 80's songs than you do."

"I dunno, I'm pretty good at that one hit wonder stuff. We have a music trivia game at home and I usually win at it."

"Alright then, you guessed my first song, try this one. If you get it wrong you have to take a big swaller of hooch."

"Whenever you're ready Maestro."

KellRay shifted his back against a stalagmite and whistled for almost a minute. He paused "Got it yet?"

RJ shook his head. "You gotta give me more than that." KellyRay whistled some more but very little of it sounded like music to RJ.

"Are you whistling the lyrics or the melody?"

"NO clues! Here I'll do it all in one go for you."

Again RJ listened and heard nothing recognizable. He thought hard but came up blank. "I have no idea."

"You don't? That was a big song in the 80's sung by a very popular guy. Make one guess, c'mon."

"Was he a one hit wonder?"

KellyRay scoffed and spit into the fire "One hit wonder? Not unless you consider one of the goddamn Beatles a One Hit Wonder."

"Uh...George Harrison?"

"Bzzzt! One out of 4 chance and you pick George. Drink up loser!"

RJ sighed and picked up the plastic cup. He figured he could get half of it down before it killed him and said "Well? What was it?"

"Drink first, answers afterwards."

RJ took a deep breath, let it out slow and tossed the drink back, trying to get it past his tongue before the potent taste hit him. He failed in that too. A repeat performance of his earlier encounter with moonshine took place though it lasted only half as long. RJ braced on the stalagmite wheezing and coughing while KellyRay kicked his legs in joy and howled in delight. A great plume of sparks and ash rose from the fire and he said "Just like starting over."

RJ eyed him thru blurred vision and said "What? What's like starting over?"

"Its the name of the song Dillweed. John Lennon sang it."

"I know how that song goes and you sounded nothing like it!"

KellyRay grinned "My performance was flawless though nothing in the rules said I had to make it easy on you."

"You never did play fair you rat bastard."

KellyRay chuckled to himself and pointed his bottle at RJ. "Played you like a drum! You want to bet on the remaining half of your drink?"

"What do I get if you can't guess what song I'm singing?"

"I'll match you drink for drink."

"That's no bet! You're going to drink that stuff whether you win or lose.

"I can't think of a better reason to play than not being able to lose."

RJ tried to think of a witty comeback but it was getting increasingly harder to think. He leaned over and placed his empty rum bottle with the others and said "This strikes me as the pinnacle of folly."

KellyRay stared at him uncomprehendingly. "Boy where did you learn to talk? PBS?"

"I give you points for even knowing how to spell PBS."

KellyRay looked confused for a moment then got mad. He stood up slowly and said, "Shut the hell up and keep drinking." He moved toward the exit tunnel and RJ called after him "Where are you going?"

"To take a leak and see what's become of that no good brother of ours."

RJ picked up a flashlight and panned it around the room. He hadn't noticed exactly when Ron had left the fireside drinking circle or even heard him announce where he was going. For the first time since coming here RJ was alone in the cave and the only sounds that came to him was the occasional bat flying thru and the distant exhalation of air from somewhere below. RJ's own breathing sounded thunderous to him and he turned to put the fire at his back and re-scanned the room.

His light kept playing on the tunnel entrance to the Scripture Room and he wondered if Ron had gone back in there? He took another drink, the taste of gin bitter and lemony after the sweet rum he just finished. He had no idea how he was supposed to drink enough of the foul tasting liquid to pass out and he was already regretting getting even a little drunk. All sorts of emergency situations came to mind along with how difficult it would be to get help. If there was help to be had. He took a step toward the exit and then came back looking around for a weapon of some kind. The most portable thing he could see was a can of generic beer. He passed that over and picked up a burning stick from the fire. It wasn't ideal but perhaps just the fact that it was burning might be a good deterrent for whatever he might encounter.

He leaned against one wall of the exit tunnel and flashed his light ahead of him then went out calling KellyRay's name. He heard nothing but soon as he was clear of the tunnel something knocked the fire from his hand and kicked it back into the cave. RJ flashed his light around trying to see what was attacking him and caught a glimpse of his brother KellyRay crouched down below the lip of the cave. He whispered angrily at RJ "Jackass! You want to let them know we're up here? Get down or go back!"

RJ crouched down cupping his flashlight to his chest and turning it off. He looked around trying to adjust to the sudden darkness but could see nothing but the distant moon glowing behind thick clouds. He turned to look where his brother was looking and caught the glint of a large knife in KellyRay's hand. RJ waited till he couldn't stand it any longer and said, "What the hell's going on? Where's Ron?"

KellyRay hissed at him to be quiet and then leaned in next to his ear. "Ron's down there someplace, near the clearing at the base of the trail. And he ain't alone."

RJ started to ask "Who?" but KellyRay clamped his grubby hand over RJ's mouth and said "Just...Shut...Up!" He gave RJ's face a squeeze for emphasis and then let go. Silently he moved forward and looked over the lip of the entrance cocking his head to listen. RJ heard nothing at first, then he heard the keening, stretched out scream they had encountered on the way in. It was a lot closer than before. What did Ron say it was? Hyenas? Half-hyenas? The call was answered again by a something making a sound that was half chuckle and half yelp. There was a pregnant silence and then a flurry of howls and someone calling out "Die! Die! Die!" RJ jumped and rolled over when he heard something scrabbling in the rock and gravel to his side and he turned just in time to see KellyRay slipping over the lip of the hill and out of sight.

RJ was alone again, straining to see anything beyond the dim silhouettes of the trees. He decided to risk a better look and shifted as silently as he could to the edge where KellyRay had descended. He couldn't see anything more than before though he thought he heard the occasional crunch of rocks or a footfall on the trail. The cries of the animals were constant now and definitely getting closer.

There was a scream of pain followed by several growls and then a large dark figure-- a deer or horse maybe-- ran quickly around the base of the trail thru the clearing and back into the darkness on the other side. No sooner had the clatter of hooves faded than three dog-like shapes raced along the same path, sniffing the trail as they ran and calling encouragement to each other in their near human voices. RJ could see no markings on them just their shapes and a glint of eye or fang. They looked to RJ like lean hunting dogs with short hunched up bodies suspended on long legs. In a flash they were gone and RJ ducked down covering his mouth in fear. If even one of those animals came up here he had nothing more than a bulky plastic flashlight to protect himself with. The silence around him was almost as terrifying as the distant calls of the creatures and he tried to will himself to breath shallowly, failed miserably and just bit his lip, bracing for a quick dash in the only direction he could go, back into the cave.

The tension in RJ built till he had to act. He shifted to get his feet turned under him and started to crawl on his hands and knees back into the cave; the ring of fire would be the safest place he could get to. He cursed the tiniest of sounds; his belt scraping on the rock, the noise the flashlight made as he nudged it ahead of him, still afraid to turn it on. He was halfway into the tunnel with just his legs sticking out behind him when something grabbed his ankle and pulled! That same something said "Gotcha!" and then laughed evilly as it stepped over him. He recognized the smell of sweat and moonshine and cursed at KellyRay who just kept laughing and disappeared around the turn. RJ got up and angrily said, "Dammit KellyRay I almost wet my pants thanks to you! Where's Ron?"

"Right behind you."

RJ whipped his head around and saw his younger brother come up behind him and into the firelight. He pushed a long satchel into RJ's arms and slapped a plastic map case down on top of it. "Here's the translation of the Script," he growled, "And a few other odds and ends for tradin'. I usually just pick up random things at flea markets or whatever a traveling salesman might have to offer but this trip there's at least one thing special that needed to be brought along. Open it."

RJ took the bag over to the fire ring and unzipped it. He could see some beer towels on top, a pair of salt and pepper shakers shaped like the two halves of a cow, a bottle of bubble soap and a pipe, at least a dozen knives and underneath it all a now familiar box with a sled depicted on the side. Ron watched as RJ freed the box from the bag and opened it briefly. The crystal caught the firelight and flung it around the room like submerged lights in a pool.

"Granmaw would have left you have it this morning if you hadn't driven off half cocked like you did. I hope it was worth my getting chewed up for." RJ looked at his brother in concern and saw that he had kept his left hand tucked under his armpit. Ron slowly held it out and RJ could three nasty gashes across the top and a tear in the skin between forefinger and thumb. Blood was slowly oozing from the wound and trickling down his fingers. KellyRay silently passed the mason jar of moonshine to him and Ron doused the wound with it.

Ron hissed, "Hurts almost as much as getting' bit!" then he traded the jar for a strip of checkered shirt KellyRay had torn from someplace. It looked almost clean to RJ. He slipped Mason's Crutch back into its box and set it aside. While he quickly inspected all the other items he asked, "Would someone please tell me what the hell just happened?"

"I remembered I had a copy of the translation in my glove box from our last trip up here so I went to go get for you. And I'm ashamed to say it must have been the events of the day or the drinking afterwards but I had also forgotten the swag bag locked in the toolbox. Granmaw Wellman insisted the Crutch be here with you, though I should tell you I'm not in the habit of bringing it up here, none of us are. I think this morning was the first time it has seen the light of day since Granmaw passed the Covenant on to our mom. Anyways, I was on my way back up here when our canine friends from before decided it was too much work to chase deer and came after me. I didn't hear anything till one jumped out and tried to pull me down. Damned thing forced me to break my favorite flashlight on its head. Then I got this love bite blocking the second one. The odds were plenty against me but I had one down and the other three were reconsidering their life of mischief before Ol' Kell here showed up."

KellyRay grinned and patted the empty sheaf at his belt. "Remind me to recover my knife in the morning. That dawg couldn't have gone far with 8 inches of German steel stuck in it." RJ shivered at the image of Kelly Ray Wellman with a knife in his hand and that evil grin on his face and then shook the memory away. He watched Ron expertly bandage his own hand without any help. "I saw them run past, three of them anyway. They were chasing a deer. Do you think they'll come back again?"

"We're safe enough up here in the cave with the fire. Plus that particular deer will lead them on a fool's errand to Far and Away before she tires of the game."

RJ sat up erect shifting forward anxiously. "You saw Her again? The DeerLady saved you? Why'd she do that?"

"I'd be careful trying to guess her motives, she is beyond any simple understanding. But I can tell you this, she has no love for those bastard hounds out there and I was mightily glad to see her choose my side in this fight."

RJ put his head in his hands. He had longed for another look at the DeerLady since she left him on the hillside and he hadn't even recognized her when she ran right by. It wouldn't do to admit that to his brothers though, he had taken enough ribbing from them about the first time.

Ron looked past RJ to KellyRay who had flipped open the box and was silently fingering Mason's Crutch. He said KellyRay's name a bit loudly and it made him jump and sit back. "KellyRay! There was something out there that wasn't part of the pack. I saw it lying under the truck on the sandbar. Ran off into the woods before I could get a close enough for a good look."

KellyRay nodded solemnly and eyed RJ who had looked up just in time to catch the exchange between brothers. RJ reached over and flipped the box closed again and said "This is just too much. Would one of you please TELL me when we're in a dangerous situation? I'd like to know exactly when to panic."

KellyRay got some tape from one of the bags and stretched out about two feet of it, bit it off with his teeth and passed it to Ron. "Consider that skirmish your one and only warning."

"And you're still planning to go thru with this, to get drunk enough to pass out knowing there's wild dogs just outside and Lord knows what to come up on us in our sleep?"

"Now more than ever, It's getting early and we should rightfully be fully lit by now. Stuff just keeps happening to ruin our quiet slide into unconsciousness."

RJ looked from brother to brother "Ron you too? You weren't even drinking earlier." Ron patted his shirt pocket with his good hand "I have a friend right here named Major Painkiller. Once I wash a couple of these bad boys down with anything alcoholic I'm out for hours."

RJ piled more wood on the fire which had faded to a few orange coals and the tiniest of flames. "I wish I were more drunk so this wouldn't seem like a huge disaster about to happen. And boys, if I live DO thru this night and get back to civilization I am never ever coming back to this little hell hole you call Wayne County."

KellyRay laughed and said, "I'll drink to that. We don't need you around here upsetting the local fauna with your girl-like screams and hand wringing."

RJ picked up a stick of wood thinking he might whack one of his brothers with it to get some answers. He still felt left out and he waved the end of it around like an old man with a cane. "Wait a second. Ron here was nearly eaten by wild dogs a minute ago and now neither of you are that bothered? You sure looked bothered when it was happening. Why aren't we barricading the entryway with something or piling up the burning wood to keep them out? Have either of you realized what can happen while the three of us snore blissfully away in a drunken stupor? I don't know about you but I don't want to wake up with my arm gnawed off just because I was too drunk to feel it!"

Ron nudged KellyRay. "I think you were wrong Kell, he HAS wet his pants. Stop obsessing about it RJ or you'll make it happen. Wellmans have been sleeping it off in this here cave for centuries. I reckon we can survive one more night."

KellyRay spoke up as he re-distributed the remaining alcohol. "City Boy here has stumbled onto one point that can't be ignored. It seems like something is trying to interrupt us, to keep the Covenant from happening tonight." Then he grinned at RJ and made ghostly noises. "OooooooOOoo really scary ain't it boy?"

"You can stow that noise right now mister or none of us will get any treats from the...from Them! The only thing that scares me more than being eaten by dogs in my sleep is thinking about having to spend another day up here so we can try it all again tomorrow night!"

Ron said, "RJ I told you..." but then gave up. He picked up a squat bottle shaped like a crown and opened it. He lifted it in his brother's direction with a wide wave of his hand. "A toast: To Oblivion!" then he popped two pills into his mouth and washed them down. His hoarse declaration of "Smoooooth!" was almost anticlimactic as he leaned back against the rock wall using his rolled up bag as a pillow. "You girls can lead the sing-along I'm worn out from the dogfight."

RJ dropped his shoulders in defeat. "Great, leave me with him why don't you?"

KellyRay made a rude slurping noise from his drink. "You can always leave RJ. HA! No wait, you can't." Then he smacked his lips loudly and said, "Ready for Round two?"

RJ reluctantly agreed and once he convinced KellyRay to play seriously he actually got into the competition. It was hindered by several arguments over what qualified as a 'hit' which was only resolved by a compromise Ron offered from behind closed eyes that what was a hit in one region might not be recognized as such in the other.

KellyRay launched into an elaborate conspiracy theory about the music industry and eventually slipped into his impression of an old time radio preacher. RJ knew he was trying to make a point of something but he'd lost track of what it was exactly. Still he helpfully added his own "Amen Brother!" and "Yes Lord yes!" at what he thought was the proper lulls and both were surprised that they remembered the chorus if not the whole lyrics to several songs their mother had sung when she thought no one was around to hear.

All the while RJ could feel the dark creeping into his subconscious. The quiet, the shadows, the little tingling at the back of his neck. He thought he was seeing things--spiders maybe--move along the walls wherever the edge of his vision was. They were making him edgy and he could feel an unknown fear coming on. He kept turning his head quickly trying to focus on the illusion of movement caused by the flickering firelight. He didn't know what he was going to be afraid of yet but he felt certain it wouldn't be long before he did.

"Hey KellyRay, sing that song about the DeerLady. You only hinted at it earlier. Gimme the whole thing."

KellyRay looked pleased to be asked but said "Naaw that makes me sad…would make you feel sad too."

"Well if you don't know the words just say so. I'll bet they know it at that Snake Handler's Church where we left my car."

"Did not, will not, do not…erm didn't."

"Yes we did. You all made me hide my plates remember?"

"You're drunk you stupid bastard! That was before we went into the woods. We left your car at Pizza Hut."

"No…oh, we did didn't we…Damn. I got further to walk than I thought."

KellyRay laughed harshly and said "You're nearly out for the count now. What you're experiencing is what we career drinkers call "Short Term Memory Lost…er Loss."

"C'mon KellKell, sing me to sleep willya? How am I ever gonna learn stuff if you don't tell me? You're sooo smart I bet you can sing it all in one go…"

"F--k it, anything to shut you up. But if you call me KellKell again in this life I will stick a sack over your head, beat you with a tire iron, and throw you out for the dogs."

"Big words for a man who can't even stand up."

"Can too." KellyRay stood up, braced on the wall for support then pushed off. He over-balanced and nearly fell into the fire. RJ tried to laugh but all he got out was "Yuk Yuk Yuk!" KellyRay ignored him and laced his fingers behind his back as if giving a recital at school. "I warn ya right now, this doesn't rhyme in English." Then he ceremonially spat his tobacco into the flames before beginning:

"There's a Riddle and a Reason.'

"What does the DeerLady wait for?'
"For her gifts to be returned in Kind.'
Her reason is her own curse to bear.
Though it be simple in the telling.

The DeerLady paused, when others rushed thru.
The Deerlady paused, and in pausing was lost.
The DeerLady paused, when others would do.
The DeerLady paused, and in pausing was cursed.

This form that you behold shall come to your land.
A journey is fated for me to meet a woman from my kingdom,
In the country far across the sea.

Though I bring you sweets, you are not sweet to me.
Though I bring you silver, you do not value me.
Though I bring you pearls, your neck is un-adorned.
Though I bring you love, your love does not see me.

She shall stand in for the stag, She shall be the seal and the salmon.
She shall live, as the Living would not,
In the tomb upon the hill.

She shall be the Pursued,
She shall be the Uncaught.
She shall be the captured,
She shall be the Unsought.

Some riddles are not undone by being answered true.

Some curses not lifted though the gods will take their due.

"What does the DeerLady wait for?'
"For her gifts to be returned in Kind.'
Her reason is her own curse to bear.
Though it be simple in the telling.

RJ's mine drifted while he listened, and begrudgingly acknowledged his brother's vocal talent, though only to himself. The song reminded him of a painting of a hunt he once saw in a museum; a valiant horned stag cornered by hounds but still fighting on till the last. His imagination locked on that image and substituted the DeerLady for the stag and the hunting hounds were replaced by cruel looking dark things that only distantly bore any resemblance to actual canines. His heart ached when he thought about her dying. Now that he knew such a being existed he couldn't imagine how great the loss to the world would be if she died. His mind wandered as he tried to think about how long she must have been here? Maybe she was immortal, immortal but not invincible? Or was she? It was no matter though, no consequence on the here and now. He longed for unconsciousness to take him but it would not come. He struggled to pick up the thread of the song again, something was missing from it and he knew it was important. Just like KellyRay to leave out the best parts. And almost before he formed that thought, he was out.

KellyRay:

KellyRay dreamed he was preaching before a large crowd at some outdoor revival. A bonfire lit the scene and figures danced lasciviously around it. Loving worshipers repeated his every word back to him and he knew there was an equal chance of an orgy or a sacrifice; he need only let his whim be known.

A large dark figure strode into the crowd, a head taller than everyone and massively built. The crowd fell back before it crying out to him for protection, to be saved. Its evilly slanted eyes dismissed the worshipers and focused solely on him. KellyRay shook off his preacher's robes to show his perfectly tanned and toned body. He raised his arms to his crowd and they roared for their champion. The light glistened off his oiled and muscular arms. He was pumped like a wrestler and the stage had become his ring. The dark figure slipped effortlessly thru the ropes and was booed by everyone. KellyRay grinned and spit over his shoulder. He assumed a wrestler's stance and said, "Let's get this dance started!"

Ron:

Ronald Glen Wellman awoke in his bed alone. He squinted at the time: nine am? He was late! He threw the covers off and stretched in the sunlight coming thru massive and ornate windows. He sighed to himself "If only it was Saturday!" And then realized it was. He debated lying back down but he could hear the sounds of cooking downstairs. It made his stomach rumble in anticipation. He crossed the well-appointed bedroom to a walk-in shower. The water was just hot enough and he let it pound his back and shoulders longer than he should. His back felt good for the first time in ages. He looked for the scar on his left bicep and couldn't find it. Maybe he just dreamed he had a scar? He looked in the mirror and grinned, deciding he didn't need to shave. He brushed his teeth till they were as bright as the fixtures around him and then he dressed in loose casual clothes of an understated quality.

His son dashed past him on the stair and out the door in a flurry of sport equipment and bundled up football jerseys. He managed to ruffle his hair before he was gone. He turned toward the smell of coffee and looked at his perfect wife. "G-good morning Bea-utiful." His voice choked every time he saw her. Even with two children she had not aged a bit. He sat down with a smile on his face to a huge breakfast exactly like he liked it. The coffee was sweet and hot and washed over his being like a magic wave. He reached down under the table to scratch his old coon dog's ears right where he knew them to be. His wife smiled at him and crinkled her nose cutely, a promise of more later? His baby girl tottered in and held her arms out wanting to be picked up. He sat her on his knee and stroked her curly auburn locks. He offered her a bite of honeyed toast and sighed. It was going to be another great day, just like everyday.

RJ:

RJ felt the cold seeping into his bones. He turned on his side still half asleep and smelled something musky near his face. He opened his eyes to see a big lumpy shape in the dark right next to him. He thought it was KellyRay and tried to push the offending lump away from his face. There was a muffled growl and RJ jerked his hand back, recoiling from the touch of fur. He bit his lips to keep from crying out realizing that some animal was lying on the cave floor next to him. He tried to suppress the panic rising in him, willing himself to be calm. He rolled his eyes as far to the left and right as he could without moving his head. He caught a glimpse of the coals from the fire and a shape he took to be one of his brothers reclined against the stalagmite in the middle of the room. His brother was snoring loudly but there was also a constant murmur, a susurration of voices from somewhere nearby. RJ could not make out more than the occasional syllable but at least the voices sounded human.

He tried again to focus on the dark shape next to him. The dog or hyena if that's what it was seemed much too large for either, more like a mastiff or Great Dane. It had stiff greasy hair that stuck straight back along its spine like the quills on a porcupine. RJ watched it fearfully for long moments but its only movements were the slow rhythm of its breathing. It too was out unconscious like his brothers. Questions and panicked answers rushed thru RJ's mind. What was going on? Did he dare get up and try to run? Would it wake the Hyena-hound? Where were those voices coming from? He chose and discarded a dozen escape plans in seconds till suddenly a hand grabbed his shoulder and rolled him onto his back. A demonic face hovered over him, suspended on a spider webbing of bluish lines. Contour lines defined the edge of the specter's face but it lips and jaw did not move. RJ thought he saw the dim firelight reflected somewhere deep in the demon's eyes but it could just as easily been hellish fires sustaining the phantom.

The creature whistled curiously at him and when he didn't respond it spoke in a guttural tongue: "Et cito? Nulla mora somniare." The disembodied chanting beyond RJ got louder and more agitated. It was as if a large invisible host was nearby in the dark, focusing its malicious intent on his every move. The demon reached out a bony finger outlined in blue and its touch on RJ's cheek was cold and death-like. Its grotesque face did not show emotion as a cloud of dust or something viler billowed from its lips and hit RJ square in the face. RJ sneezed so loudly he was sure the DeerLady could have heard it miles away but there was no DeerLady to save him here. He snorted again, deeply inhaling against his will. He felt the top of his head immediately burn and itch like he'd just snorted hot British mustard. The room began to spin and he was sucked back into the blackness.

Chapter Thirty: On the Way to Dick's Place.

I don't know why no one ever told me that Dick was short for Richard. I eventually found it out on the playground like all the other kids did. Either by shouting it at someone or having it shouted at me. But I never considered going by the name Dick, not just because of the obvious nickname but because there already was one in our family. I never knew exactly what his relationship to me was; I just assumed he belonged in that category of vague relations that is either a Great Uncle or an Elderly Cousin. I only knew that he shared a last name with us and that was good enough for everyone involved.

Dick Wellman was already an old man the day my dad took me to see him. Not that being social was the point of our visit mind you. He (my dad that is) had this idea of towing home a broken down "Deuce and a half" that had been abandoned in the little patch of garden Dick worked on his property with a mind of repairing it and selling it off for profit. But he didn't know what condition it's engine was in or even if there was an engine. I recall hearing that it was a '56 model and that someone from the local mining concern had gotten it stuck in Dick Wellman's field one day and just left it, never to return.

It was not revealed to me what the mining company wanted with a former military vehicle or why they didn't take it with them when the mines petered out and everything else of value was hauled away. "More trouble than it was worth!" is the most likely reason.

My dad thought Dick might have the keys to it and well it was just going to waste and rot out there in the field ain't it? The whole thing sounded like a bad idea to me and I really wanted to ask him what sort of shape could it be in after nearly three decades in a cornfield but I knew better than to say anything. It wasn't my place to ask questions as I'd been told often enough. I don't even remember why I was along for the ride or where my brothers were. I guess I was the only one home at the time so I won the lottery. So there I was squeezed into the front of my dad's flatbed truck between him and his drinkin' buddy Lloyd Maynard. Lloyd was a thin, dark-haired character who had a little black mustache like Gomez Addams. That was about all I could find to like about him. He talked constantly which was a habit that made my dad insane when other people did it but for some reason he put up with it from Lloyd.

We hadn't gone very far from our house when Lloyd proceeded to share with me the reason why he only drank peppermint schnapps. I hadn't asked actually, he was just trying to include me in the constant stream of dialog he generated or possibly continuing some conversation he was having with my dad before I got in the truck.

"Cause then boy if the Fuzz pulls you over they can't prove you were drinkin'! They smell peppermint breath mints instead of schnapps or that rotgut your daddy makes." My dad reached across me to whack Lloyd in the chest and elbowed me in the mouth at the same time. My head banged back against the rear window and I tried real hard not to say anything but my eyes started and I sort of just growled out "Owwww" and stared straight ahead. Growled as well as a 16 year old might I guess.

My dad pulled his arm back like he was going to hit me on purpose this time but Lloyd suddenly pounded the dashboard so hard that dust flew around the cab and he let out a raucous laugh. I didn't know which of us he was laughing at but my dad apparently did cause he joined in and they spent the next half hour taking turns pushing me into the other one or reaching across my face or behind my head in order to thump or pinch the other one.

Lloyd concluded his lesson with: "Just remember to have some peppermint breath mints in your car to show them!" An outside observer might point out Lloyd's lack of a car or even a license but there was no way I was going to say anything. Just being within arms reach of my dad made me leery of anything that might set him off. As it was I couldn't dodge their blows or so much as deflect them. I'd never seen this sort of behavior from my dad before and didn't know if I should encourage it, join in, or express any emotion at all. I already had a sour stomach from the herky-jerky suspension on the truck and from sitting between my dad who smelled of gasoline and Camel cigarettes and Lloyd Maynard who smelled of peppermint schnapps and whatever other liquor he was drinking before we got on the road. I wasn't big on praying but I had a sort of silent litany in my mind that I repeated over and over about how bad it would be to get sick right there in the truck and I promised my stomach if it would just hold on I would empty it at the earliest acceptable opportunity.

We were caught by the one stop light in Ceredo and while we waited a car with three girls in it pulled into the turn lane on the right side of us. Lloyd rolled the down his window and proceeded to grin and wriggle his tongue and eyebrows at them. This set off peals of laughter from the girls and he nudged me hard in the side as he proclaimed "Oh yeah, they know what that means, they're young but they know!" My dad actually seemed a bit put out that his buddy was hanging half out the window of his truck but he couldn't resist looking around us to see who was in the car.

"Why that's your girlfriend in the back seat ain't it boy?" I had been trying to change the light to green with the sheer force of my mind so I could get out of this situation before it got worse but at that comment I turned my head and looked over Lloyd's shoulder. I'm not sure why because I didn't have a girlfriend of any sort to actually be in a back seat. I guess I couldn't resist seeing what my dad thought girlfriend material looked like. I didn't recognize anyone in the car but they immediately recognized me and the laughter got even louder. They called out "Well Man! WelllMaaaan Honey! Who are your handsome friends? That's a nice set of wheels you have there Wellman, all seven of them!" And then they broke up into more laughter.

I turned and looked out the rear window to hide my embarrassment and to pretend to check the spare tossed in amongst the sawdust and tools on the back of the truck. Someone was behind us and beeped his horn, which only made my dad cuss and flip them off. He refused to move forward "Until I'm good and goddamned ready to." Then he said, "You can get out here if you want boy those ladies look like they need some lovin'!" Next to slowly being eaten alive by ants that was the last thing I wanted to do right then. I just nodded forward at the green light and said "No thank you sir, I want to go with you on your mission."

There was a brief silence in the truck then even more laughter erupted from both sides as my dad finally put the truck into gear. "A mission? Did you hear that Lloyd Maynard? We're on a God-damned mission!" He deftly worked thru all the gears as we left the girls behind and then he looked at me in the mirror. "Well listen up swabbie, you aren't going on any F--king mission. You're going to sit right there and not get out of the F--king truck unless I tell you to. Got it?"

I quickly nodded and then said "Yes sir" barely suppressing the urge to salute or throw up. I cursed myself for putting my dad in a military mindset though he might have already been there just thinking about the Deuce and a Half he was about to see. I tried to put the whole thing out of my mind and instead tried to recall the names of the three girls in that car. I was certain I'd hear about this incident at school the next day but couldn't place whether they were in my class or if they were upperclassmen. I stared forward and up, occasionally seeing my dad's perpetually stubbled face reflected back at me as he changed lanes. I thought a lot of dark things at that reflection before settling on my usual game of calculating the percentage chance of surviving a crash with him at the wheel.

Long before Han Solo said, "Never tell me the odds" and even before I held my first pair of percentile dice in DnD I was working out the odds of a being in an accident with my dad and my potential survival rate. I had a list of things that deducted from the base chance and then tried to add back in the conservative driving skills and quick reflexes of strangers. Strangers who moved quickly to get out of my dad's way, to let him thru amber or even red lights or to give him more than his half of the narrow country roads just so he could fly past without hitting anyone.

It was minus 10 points for each drink he'd had, minus 15 for not wearing seat belts, and the ability of the truck to survive a roll over? Minus another 20. My dad sometimes raced people in cars or drove in the oncoming lane to pass someone--traffic or no traffic--then stomp on the brakes to watch their reaction. Once he even passed someone on the access ramp to Highway 64 by going over the berm and gunning it up the hill and into traffic. Later I revised my debit system for alcohol tolerance but still often ended up with less than a 10% chance of surviving. That I didn't die or even get into an accident while riding with him I could only attribute to Fate's whimsy and its overall desire not to complicate other people's lives.

I explained my system to my mom once and she told me not to worry none, that my dad was too mean to die by accident. There was always an awkward silence after that declaration and I would go on to say I just couldn't wrap my head around that sort of "devil may care" attitude. I lived my life like I wanted to stay alive. I wanted most of the people around me to stay alive and I even wanted to do minimal damage to property in the event that I did die. It was my belief that most people felt that way but my dad didn't seem to waste any time thinking about it. It was never about living or dying for him it was always about the moment. He valued things like cars and women and good booze, but the longer I was around him the more I was convinced he didn't value Life itself, not one whit. So why would he value mine? I don't know how I was supposed to develop a sense of self worth in such a situation.

My dad went about his life untroubled by immaterial concepts like this and more than once professed a real pride in his ability to live his life like he wanted to without the need of a "long-haired education.' Sometimes I envied that and secretly wished that I wasn't smarter than he was or just better educated if it meant I had to go thru life aware of what was I was lacking, of what potential there was in the greater world, and how far down the Great Pecking Order of Life I was starting out.

Dick Wellman's place sat in a hollow between two low hills with a train track running across it. The very bottom of the valley was boggy and once long ago a stream ran thru it. It looked to me like the most useless bit of land around which probably meant he got it for a bargain. His house was modest in size but looked much bigger because of the wrap around porch that covered three sides. There was a circular gravel driveway that curved up to his door and next to that was a platform built of railway ties that stuck out from the hillside so you could drive your car onto it and work underneath whist still standing up. Both hillsides had crops growing on them; corn on this side and tobacco on the other.

Wayne County was not the right climate for tobacco and a lot of people pointed that out to Dick Wellman but he grew it all the same. There was a barn behind his house so old and unkempt that the wood had faded to a greyish silver color and thru the wildly canting doors you could see dark things way in the back hanging from the rafters. To my eye they looked like man-sized bats slowly swinging in the shadows and I did not care to go inside. I knew from my time in Virginia that this was how they dried tobacco on the farm but my mind also suggested that if there were man-sized bats in West Virginia what better place to hide during the day than in an upside down forest of brown tobacco leaves? For once I was glad to be left in the truck though the question of why I was even there still played at the back of my mind.

Dad called out to the house without getting out of the truck. Perhaps because all anyone in the house could see was Lloyd Maynard's head, still stuck out the window and pivoting around as if he was assessing for the county or something. Neither of us could see the Deuce and a Half from where the truck stopped nor any sign that anyone was home besides the front door being open. The screen door was the only barrier between the bright sun and the dark interior. My dad stood on the running board of his truck so his head would be visible over the cab and yelled "Heigh Oh Dick! It's Ray Isaac, you in there? You still alive you stubborn old summbitch?"

I gave Lloyd a questioning look and he just shrugged and grinned, finishing his hip flask of peppermint schnapps and letting it slide down to the floor between his legs. I had never heard my dad call out "Heigh Ho" to anyone before. I suppose he was trying to sound friendly. Maybe he didn't know to approach an elder any better than I did. He stepped down from the truck and slammed the door loudly. He called out again, "Hey Dick its Ray Isaac, Jack Wellman's boy. Don't meet me at the door with a shotgun like you did last time. I'd hate to have to kick an old man's ass you know."

There was some noise deep in the house and then a shadow darkened the already dim area behind the screen door. Whoever it was started making a dry rasping noise I took to be laughter. A pale gnarled hand pushed the door open a bit to show it was unlocked and I heard the figure say: "That'd be the day. Long as I still got you fooled I got nuthin' to worry about." Then the figure went away and dad walked around the back of the truck and spoke to us in a low voice: "Lloyd stay here and keep the boy quiet till I've been in there a while then come up to the porch and stand there with your hands in your pockets. Don't come up the steps till you're asked to unless you want a gut full of buckshot." He looked at me and gripped my shoulder thru the window. "I may not even need you but you listen for me callin' you and then you come in and be respectful." He let go and turned back to the door and said under his breath "Don't let that old fart get ahold of you boy, don't let him touch you or there'll be hell to pay."

"Is this guy supposed to be crazy or something?" I muttered to Lloyd Maynard as we watched my dad's back as he talked thru the screen door to someone inside.

"Hell no, I guess not!" Lloyd replied. "Just old which is crazy enough."

I mulled this over and it did not escape me that my dad had pulled the truck up so that his friend Lloyd Maynard was between him and the front door. Or maybe that's just the way it happened. I jumped at a loud slam when the screen door closed with my dad on the inside and even Lloyd Maynard looked nervous. He kept reaching down and fingering the empty bottles at his feet, running his hands over each as if to coax more liquor from them. I took advantage of the extra space to my left and scooted over towards the driver's seat. I was careful not to brush against the stick shift knowing my dad never used the emergency brake and I doubted it was hooked up anyway. The horrors that would befall me if I knocked the shifter out of gear and the truck rolled down the hill into the corn patch or even thru that and into the stream bottom were just too terrible to contemplate.

There was no sound coming from the house and none around us except the ever-present drone of insects. I looked at the tracks and could just barely make out a railroad bridge at the far end, the closer end obscured by trees and the hillside. I had no idea where I was or which direction home lay in. With no other homes nearby and only a dirt road leading in and out it was as isolated as anywhere in the world. I decided this was must have been how "Man" West Virginia got its name. Was there also be a town called Woman or Wife? Ex-wife, West Virginia? I decided to look closer at the state map the next time I ran across one.

The tedious heat in the truck was interrupted by a visit from two dogs, large and looking as old as anything around them. They had loose, rust colored hides and regarded us thru red-rimmed eyes. We watched as they crawled out from under the porch, shook the dust from their coats, and slowly loped over to the truck. I got the impression that barking would have been too much effort for them. They stood at the end of the drive and looked up at us, ignoring Lloyd Maynard's attempts to get one to come over. He called and patted the side of the truck but failed having nothing to really offer a couple of coonhounds. Together they turned, walked around the truck and down the hill towards the stream.

"What kind of dog was that?"

"Hell if I know, looked kinda like a bloodhound but their legs were too short like they were part wiener dog or something." I looked back but it was too late to confirm what Lloyd had said, the dogs were long out of sight.

"I didn't notice that but I did notice that one of them looked like she was nursing pups but I don't see them around anyplace."

"Nursing pups from her bitch's teats!" Lloyd chuckled to himself and added "Bitch's teats, Witch's Tits!" He found that word combination funny on some level and laughed loudly, then abruptly cutting himself off as he remembered my dad's orders. For a bit he just sat there shifting his feet and watching the empties clink and tinkle against his shoes. "I reckon it's been long enough. I didn't hear any gunshots so they're probably into the good stuff by now."

Lloyd opened the door and slid out, taking a moment to tug on his shirt and jeans as if that would hide the fact that he was still in yesterday's clothes and had spent most of the morning sleeping it off on our living room carpet. His lanky stride took him to the porch step quickly but there he paused, leaning his head to the side and trying to see into the darkened house. A shadow moved inside and my dad's unmistakable bellow called him in.

"Where the F--k have you been? Get in here and try some of this hooch! Dick Wellman this is my no good, rotten-assed, stupid summbitch of a friend Lloyd Maynard..." I heard a harsh laugh in reply as Lloyd ducked his head and went inside, closing the screen door quietly behind him.

I scooted over to the passenger window and tried to find room for my feet in the pile of empties on that side of the floor well. I didn't want to make too much noise and miss my dad's call. I unbuttoned my too warm shirt a bit and closed my eyes, still hoping my stomach would stop complaining and hoping even more I'd get a drink of water or a soda pop out of the trip.

Something the size of a buzzard was riding the air over the cornfield and I squinted and watched it loop and turn as it tried to gain altitude. I didn't think buzzards were common to West Virginia but had no way to actually tell what it was.

Chapter Thirty-One: Interrogation and more.

Suddenly there was a loud bang when my dad slammed his hand against the side of the truck right beside me. He reached thru the window and grabbed my collar pulling abruptly and actually ripping it a bit from the shirt.

"Are you deef boy? Get the F--k in there!" My dad jerked the truck door open and I had just put my hand in the handle to open it myself. The door swung wide and twisted my hand hard to the side and I barely had time to free it before I was dragged into the house. Dad opened the door and pushed me in then elbowed past me and disappeared back into the dark. I was still trying to adjust my eyes and hadn't been invited to sit down so I just stood there blinking as my dad said "This one we call RJ, he's currently the oldest of my good for nothing children."

I thought I could make out someone in a rocking chair directly in front of me and I looked in his direction. "Good to meet you sir."

The still dis-embodied voice said, "Why didn't you come in with your pappy?" I had a feeling "Cause he told me not to" was the wrong response so I told a half lie. I said "Uh...I was looking at your dogs."

"And what did you think of them eh?"

"I thought they looked a bit strange, I couldn't tell what kind they are. And one looked like she had pups but I didn't see any around."

Lloyd Maynard blurted out "Staring at dog tits!" but no one laughed so he just sat back on the couch and shut up.

"Not so strange, they're just mixed bloods. And not even my dogs...just showed up one day and stuck around. I tried to chase them off but they aren't afraid of nuthin'. I think there's still a pup or two under the house if the bitch hasn't eaten them."

I am sure I looked disturbed by that comment but couldn't think of a response. My dad said "Don't you dare think you can bring home another mutt RJ. You ain't capable of taking care of a dog are you boy?"

I tucked my head down and replied "No sir I...I'm not." Though in my head I was trying to figure out what he meant by that. We hadn't had a dog around the house in years and that one my dad had shot for being an egg sucker. Which was not any fault of mine or the dog's but the worst thing I could have done was to contradict my dad in front of his friends.

Dick Wellman leaned forward in his rocking chair and said, "You're supposed to be the smart one ain't cha?" He had on a sleeveless t-shirt stained down the front and trousers so old they had slick spots on the thighs and bare spots on the knees. He was rail thin and looked to be about a thousand years old. The only thing about him that didn't look like it was carved out of an old oak tree was his eyes. He had the same steely blue eyes my father had and I immediately wished he'd politely lean back into the shadow where I couldn't see him.

My dad made a popping noise as he took a pull from a bottle and said in dismissal. "Takes after his mom. Always talking about f--k all that matters to anyone."

Dick Wellman folded his thin arms across his chest and said, "Say something smart." And when I looked confused and unable to answer he added. "What is it they're teaching smart kids these days?"

"Mmmm, I don't know what you mean sir? I have the same curriculum as everyone else. I'm not even in the advanced classes. "

"Curriculum! That's a big word. Sounds Latin to me. What else? Do you like science boy, or do you follow the Bible?"

I was really squirming here, torn between answering honestly and getting into trouble with my dad. And I was still favoring my hand, rubbing my wrist as I stood there and flexing my fingers to try and relieve some of the pain. I could see Dick Wellman looking at me critically, waiting for my response as he lifted a tin can to his lips and spat into it.

"Dinosaurs!" my dad barked out. "He doesn't believe in the Bible cause he likes dinosaurs. Tell him what you showed me last summer." I couldn't tell if that was a condemnation or a point of pride to my dad. I tried to read his face and failed then turned back to Dick Wellman, slightly preferring his visage to my dad's.

"I...um, there's a spot below the flood wall in Wayne where I dug up some fossils. I had five or six of them before the summer was over."

"Fossils you say? Fossils of what?"

"I don't know exactly I only found what looked like tail bones. They ranged from thumbnail size to as long as my finger. There was a lot more of it but I couldn't break it free from the rock."

Dick Wellman shifted in his seat. He rubbed the grey stubble on his chin and said: "Take an educated guess. Let's hear what your amateur fossil hunting skills tell you."

I looked at Dad who wasn't giving me any kind of sign good or bad so I carried on. Lloyd Maynard was sitting back on the couch enjoying the show. The now half empty Mason jar at his side might have had something to do with that.

"Well sir the thing is... there aren't supposed to be any big vertebrate fossils in West Virginia. It was mostly a shallow inland sea back then and you usually only find trilobites-they're like a cross between cockroaches and horseshoe crabs-- and plants of course. And then nothing more elaborate than prehistoric coral. Then everything died off and turned into coal. I guess there had to be bigger things living in the sea but you don't hear about them much. Science Digest had an story in it about someone finding cave bear bones down in Mercer county somewhere but that wasn't long enough ago to make real fossils out of them. I guess they were just bones. "

"And the things you're calling fossils, couldn't they have just been bones too?"

"I might have thought so if they weren't made of stone and if I hadn't chipped them out of solid rock myself, sir. I'm pretty sure they're as old as everyone says."

"That may be young man. So what happened to these rare discoveries? Part of some extensive museum display with our family name emblazoned on it?"

I looked at my dad again who didn't look happy with where the conversation was going. He was puffing and blowing hard on his Camel cigarette and his eyes held the same dark warning they always held. I knew I was in dangerous territory but I didn't know where the exit was. I couldn't help but notice Dick Wellman was talking to me differently than he did my dad. I think it was the first time an adult actually asked me something and listened to the answer. This confused and intrigued me but there was still a hint of melancholy in my voice when I continued.

"I...took them to school so my Science teacher could see them." I didn't mention that the shoebox and its contents had been stolen from me on the school bus and dumped out the window somewhere between my house and the school building. I hoped against hope that Dick wouldn't ask to see them. Fortunately or unfortunately my favoring of my right hand caught his eye and he said, "What did you do to your hand boy?"

I didn't want to lie about something else so soon after the last one but more and more I was envisioning a long and painful ride home ahead of me so I tried to be as obscure about things as I could. "It got hurt when I got out of the truck."

Dick Wellman was looking at my dad and gestured for the bottle of Wild Turkey they were sharing. "And how'd that happen exactly?"

"I...was unfamiliar with how the door opened sir."

"Unfamiliar with how a door opens? Do you ride in cars without doors very often young Mr. Wellman?" He seemed to be enjoying this way too much and I wondered what his motivation was in tormenting me. He might not have known if I was lying but he knew I was holding something back.

"Oh no sir its just that I wasn't sitting next to the door on the way here and didn't give it a good look before trying to open it."

"Call your dad Sir he likes it. I'm out of the Sir business. Call me Dick. That's an order."

"Yes...I will do that."

"Now come over here and let me see your hand close up. It looks like your little finger is bent the wrong way from here."

Again I looked at my dad and he was sitting on the edge of his seat, teeth grinding on one side, cigarette perched on the other. He looked poised to jump up and hit someone. It was probably going to be me. I slowly held my hand out and rotated it where I stood. Dick Wellman leaned forward too and said, "Yep, looks like your pinky finger is out of socket. I can fix that."

He held his hand out to me and gestured for me to give him mine. I was frozen where I was and I felt my stomach roiling again. Maybe throwing up would distract everyone from any physical contact. "No I'll be fine, really...Dick." My dad's feet hit the wooden floor loudly and we all turned to look at him. I saw actual worry flash across his face but it was quickly replaced by anger. He cuffed me on top of my head and then pointed out the door behind me. "Get yer ass back in the truck and stop bothering Dick with your goddamned finger!"

I turned to obey immediately but Dick had risen too. He grabbed my hand in his and pulled me closer. In the patch of light I had been standing in I could see his thin and spotted hands gripping mine. His skin was loose and heavily wrinkled like he'd once been heavier or had lost a lot of weight all at once. He caught my eye and pointed down to the base of his thumb. There was a tiny white scar there standing out against the acorn brown of his skin. Another tear-dropped shaped one started at his wrist and disappeared up his sleeve. He made sure I saw them and then gave my pinky a mighty tug. I yelled loudly and jerked away from him, stumbling out the door onto the porch. I shook my hand and tucked it under my armpit. I could hear shouting and Lloyd Maynard's laughter coming from inside. I looked at my hand closely as I walked back to the truck, pausing while I awkwardly opened the truck door with the wrong hand. My hand still stung and there looked like bruising was forming near the wrist but I had to admit it most of the pain had stopped immediately.

I waited what must have been another hour before anyone came outside. I risked slipping around the side of the house to take a leak in the tall weeds. I could hear voices rising and falling inside. A hot debate was going on about something. Eventually my dad and Lloyd Maynard re-appeared, looked surprised to see me in the truck and passed a guilty look between them.

I was full of unanswered questions and it was well past dinnertime. I spent a lot of time around my dad hungry because mentioning food made him rant about my being fat and how he could survive in the woods with just a pocketknife. I found it easier to stay silent and sneak food later. He was of the mindset that if my body was hungry it would automatically 'eat up' some of the fat. I'm pretty sure his science was a bit vague on that point but it might have worked if I'd been starving in a cave somewhere, I dunno. His body seemed to run on alcohol, coffee, and cigarettes. He smelled of all three when they got in the truck, squeezed me in-between them, and started back. I got a glimpse of the forgotten deuce-and-a-half as we completed the loop of the driveway and figured whatever deal my dad had offered Dick Wellman it didn't involve immediate possession of the ancient truck.

On the long drive home there was an odd bit of dialog between my dad and Lloyd Maynard that went something like this:

"Be a real pain to drive all this way every Sunday."

"Won't be a pain for long, two trips later he'll forget what he asked for."

"Crazy old bastard. I wonder what he's up to."

"Don't matter. A free truck's a free truck."

Then my dad looks at me in the rearview mirror. "Let me give you a piece of advice boy. If I ever make the mistake of taking you somewhere again..."

I waited to hear what he was going to say and after an awkward moment I responded, "Yes sir?"

"Sometimes, and I mean sometimes, it pays to shut the F--k up and stay shut up than whatever the price of staying silent is. You got that boy?"

"Yes Sir. Understood sir." I was sure he was talking about the scene in Dick Wellman's house but I wasn't sure where in the conversation I should have shut up. He probably would have preferred that I was a deaf mute with a preternatural skill at repairing cars and stout, load-bearing legs. I sat silently running this nugget of wisdom over and over in my head as we bounced and banged our way back to the trailer on Airport road. I really didn't understand most of it but I got the shut up part. That was a no brainer.

When we stopped at the same light where we had encountered the girls my dad broke the silence with a loud question aimed at me: "You got a pocketknife don'cha boy?"

I thought hard to recall if my dad had ever given me a pocketknife at any point. "Yes?" I ventured hoping he wouldn't hear the hesitation in my voice. I thought this might be a time when he wanted me to employ the nugget of wisdom he'd just given me so I didn't volunteer anything further.

"Well where the F--k is it?"

"I remember having one last summer but I haven't seen it for a while."

He angrily shifted into gear and floored the truck. "Goddamn kids don't know how to take care of anything! What happen to your F— king knife boy?"

"I...when I last saw it KellyRay had it. I think he got caught with it at school."

"What the Hell? Why did you let him take your goddamned knife to school?

"I didn't let him have it, he just took it. "

"Did you kick his ass?"

My dad was always asking me if I kicked someone's ass and I always disappointed him by answering in so many words...no. I didn't want to mention KellyRay had used that same knife last summer to stab me and I still felt a bit guilty about blaming the whole broken arm thing on him. Bringing that up again wasn't going to do either of us any good but then again he wasn't here in the truck to take his share of abuse either.

"He got beat by the vice-principal for bringing it to school. I figured that was revenge enough." I'll spare you the rest of my father's ranting and declarations of impending discipline. Lloyd Maynard was no help; a glance at him and I could tell my dad had cowed him too. I was glad it was getting dark and Dad couldn't see the miserable look on my face. One of his favorite rants was about our lack of gratitude and how much worse he'd had it growing up. I often imagined those dark un-informed years and myself never living to see 18. I wasn't sure about reaching eighteen in these modern times either. You could pile a lot of pain and darkness into the remaining two years.

Chapter Thirty-Two: Uncle Wellman and Aunt Millie.

I stood on the sidewalk outside Aunt Millie's restaurant waiting for the bus to pick me up. It was the first time I'd tried to ride public transport I was very nervous. I couldn't count the school bus as practical experience but I imagined it was pretty similar except that you paid for the pleasure and you got to say where you wanted to get off.

I had one dollar and 35 cents in my pocket. Which believe it or not was enough for a round trip to Dick Wellman's place. I wasn't supposed to be riding the bus there but my dad was too busy to take me as promised and instead sent Lloyd Maynard to take me.

Lloyd Maynard showed up and confessed to me he was 'Three sheets in the wind" and besides he didn't have a driver's license and the car my dad had loaned him didn't have plates and had been freshly painted and there'd be hell to pay for both of us if anything happened to it and couldn't I just ride the bus?

In the face of all that evidence and not wanting to take a chance on his driving abilities I agreed and he dug around in his pockets for enough change. There was a brief distraction when he produced a thick fountain pen from a shirt pocket. It had a girl on it that lost her clothes when you turned it upside down. I looked at it and tilted it over a couple of times before he sheepishly admitted it was broke but you could see her panties if you held it up to the light just right.

I sighed and gave it back to him loudly counting the coins as they appeared. I had twenty-seven cents to my name and held that info back in reserve should he have to give me excess. I told him I'd never ridden the bus and he just waved his hand "Its easy, you put the money in get a transfer and you're there."

Around eighty-nine cents I went to get my quarter and two pennies while Lloyd Maynard dug around in the glove box of the car. He found some smokes and a checkbook but neither was helpful to my cause. I was a kid and no one was going to cash a check for me and Lloyd Maynard said he was 'known' all over town and couldn't cash a check with someone else's name on it no how.

I was getting a bit anxious as we realized we weren't going to make the golden amount of $1.35. Lloyd looked really distressed and that made me really distressed. I was sure this was important to my dad and his planned acquisition of the Deuce and a half so I really didn't want to disappoint. The only things of value in the house were a couple of soda bottles. You could get 5 cents each for returnable bottles at Asbury's grocery. This made Lloyd's face light up and he immediately hatched a plan; he'd give me a lift to Asbury's market and I could cash in the bottles then catch the bus from there. It was on his way and would save me part of the trip.

I had been saving those bottles for more soda. A bottle of Pepsi was 35 cents and there were 6 bottles in a carton. I only needed two more bottles and I could walk them up to the store and cash them in then get a bottle of soda to drink on the walk home and be left with one bottle to the good. I would look for them on the walk home from school and sometimes my step brother Ricky would leave them— empty—as a sort of calling card to show he'd been in the house while everyone was gone.

I got in the car with Lloyd still unsure how to get to Dick's place but at least we had a plan. Lloyd Maynard drove very slowly because he did not want to scratch or wreck the loaner car. I think he was just about as afraid of my dad as his sons were though I don't know what made him stick around. I asked him if he knew Dick Wellman's address and he admitted he did not. I asked him how the bus driver would know where to drop me off and he said "Hell's bells boy, just tell him you're going to see Dick Wellman! Everybody knows where that old bastard lives. He's been holed up in that house since I was a pup!"

No further clues were given me and so I had to be satisfied with that. Lloyd let me out in front of Asbury's market and said "I'll park in the back so no one notices the plates are missing." I wanted to point out to him that everything was missing on that car; all the chrome and trim had been removed or taped over for the paint job. He didn't give me an opportunity to reply though; he buzzed thru the light at the corner and bounced the car up into the parking lot behind. (My dad was a body and paint man; he didn't do shocks.)

I took my empties thru the magazine aisle so I could look at the comic book covers and while I didn't have enough for one of those I thought I might manage a piece of candy and still have $1.35 left over. The candy rack was right by the check out so that it could be monitored for shoplifting. There was a huge mirror overhead so old man Asbury could stand in the next aisle and look up and watch what you did when you thought you were out of sight. I picked up several different candies but nothing fit my rough estimate of 19 cents change after bus fare.

I gave up and caught a movement as Mr. Asbury dashed around the aisle, having to both observe my potential candy purchases and work the till at the same time. I lifted the carton onto the belt and it rolled forward. I watched him look at the empties skeptically and then back at me. He cocked his head and said, "Did you buy these here boy?"

"I found them on the road sir."

"Well I don't know if I can take them if I didn't sell them."

This unexpected complication upset me and I said "Please! I need the money for bus fare!"

"Looks to me like you need it for comic books and candy."

"No, No Sir! I was just looking. "

"Then do you have enough money to pay for the candy YOU HID IN YOUR POCKET???"

I looked around me and even back at my pockets in the rear "What where? I haven't got any candy!"

Mr. Asbury leaned across the check out lane and eyed me closely: "I just wanted to see how you'd react. If you had tried to run I'd know you were guilty."

"Oh." I said in a small voice. I was sniffling a bit from the shock of being yelled at and being called a thief. I think that might have softened him a bit. Old Man Asbury wasn't known for being unfair but he still scared every kid in town.

"Where did you say you got these bottles?"

"I find them on the roadside. I look for them when I'm walking home from school."

"Where do you live?"

"1101 Airport road."

"You walk to school and back from there?"

"I have to. We live on the wrong side of the bypass. If I lived on the other side of the road I could catch the No. 7 bus but the driver told me he wasn't allowed to pick anyone beyond that point."

"Old man Asbury seemed to find this even more doubtful than my story about the bottles. "That doesn't make any sense, are you sure that's what he said?" I guess I was picturing the beating I had coming up and it must have shown on my face because he relented and opened his cash register, took out some change and passed it to me. "I reckon there's no store between Airport road and here so they must be from my place."

"Thank you sir!" I said and started to leave. He shouted after me "Tell your daddy not to send you in here by yourself again. I'm watching you kids all the time!"

I didn't reply. I walked around back to find Lloyd Maynard smoking a cigarette with a kid from the senior class. He was on break and talking about drinking and girls to Lloyd. Lloyd Maynard was trying to convince him to slip him a beer or two but as he had no money to back it up that transaction wasn't going so well.

I proudly presented my newfound wealth and Lloyd Maynard loudly bemoaned the fact that it wasn't enough to get a beer and a bus token but it would have to do. I watched him climb back into the freshly painted Cadillac. I don't think I mentioned that before but it was a late 60's Cadillac. Which knowing my dad and his buddies at the paint shop made things even more suspicious when you pictured Lloyd Maynard and some high school kid riding around Ceredo in it. I tried to convince him to take me the whole way by offering to give him the bus money but he couldn't see any percentage in it and besides even if he drove me it wasn't enough money to get a grown man drunk.

I said OK and waved as he bounced the car over the curb and back into the street. I took up my post at the bus stop and mostly stood around looking at the gas station across the street and a few people going into Asbury's. I saw several people that I recognized but I was a bit embarrassed to be out in the open like that and didn't wave or talk to anyone.

There weren't any bus schedule posted but eventually a bus came by and opened its door for me. I told my whole sad story to the bus driver who told me what a nuisance it was for kids to get on and not know where they are going and he wasn't responsible if they ended up in the back of nowhere and besides I didn't need a transfer anyway.

After the encounter with old man Asbury I was feeling a bit tough skinned and determined not to get upset so I asked him if he knew the place where Dick Wellman lived, if not the man himself. I described the train bridge and the Deuce-and a Half in the field and the big old barn with the tobacco that looked like bats. He seemed to find that funny and told me to sit down and keep a lookout the window. If I saw anyplace that looked like what I described I was to pull the bell cord. I thanked him and sat down and soon realized I didn't know what side of the road to watch so I spent the next 40 minutes or so whipping my head back and forth.

A lady got on with a bag of groceries and asked me whose boy I was? I told her my name was Wellman and she rolled her eyes and tutt-tutted at me. She had a lot to say about Wellmans but not much that was flattering. Then she asked me what church I was going to and I misunderstood her, thinking that she thought I was headed to Church right that minute. "Oh no ma'am. I'm supposed to be headed to Dick Wellman's place but I don't know what side of the road its on."

"Why he owns the field right behind ours! You can get up to his place by going along the path and across the tracks. Otherwise you'd have to ride this rickety ol' bus out to the VA hospital and back. "

I thanked her for that info and she sniffed and pointed up at the bell cord. "Pull that when we go thru the next stop sign please. I don't know why they don't make the cords so you can reach them without getting out of your seat. I reckon it wouldn't be any fun for DEMONIC bus drivers would it?"

I followed her gaze forward when she stressed the word demonic and saw the bus driver grinning back at us in the rear view mirror. He started braking even before I pulled the cord and the lady whose said to call her Aunt Millie pushed her bag of shopping at me and started carefully down the aisle, bracing on each seat. She spoke to the driver and he smiled pleasantly to her and when I got off he paused and asked me why I was going to see crazy Old Man Wellman anyway? I told him I honestly didn't know but my dad promised I would so here I am. He didn't have a reply to that and it struck me that he must have heard of Dick Wellman after all to even have asked that question.

I followed Aunt Millie up to her house, holding the enormous bag and trying not to huff too much with the effort while she checked her mailbox and dug for her keys. I started to follow her in but she stopped me at the door. I could see past her into a brightly lit room with shiny hardwood floor and furniture still covered in plastic. I suspected she had just moved in or something. She took the bag from me and said goodbye and that I ought to consider showing up at church on Sunday.

I said I would consider it and stepped off her porch to look around. All the fields seemed exactly alike to me and I went a short distance down one side of the road and back up the other way trying to catch a glimpse of the barn or the truck or the railway bridge. On my third trip back past her house Aunt Millie stepped out onto her porch and said "Don't you know where it is? Ain't you ever been?"

"Only that one time when my dad and Lloyd Maynard brought me out. I didn't really pay attention to how we got here...there."

"Lloyd Maynard? You know my boy Lloyd?"

"Yes ma'am. He was supposed to drive me out here but...I guess he had other things to do."

"Other things like not coming to see his momma!" She made a face and I blushed, suddenly realizing that Lloyd Maynard and Aunt Millie were related. No wonder she had opinions about the Wellmans. "Well..." she said, "Tell him to stop in next time he's so close by." Then she pointed back around her house "Best go round back and follow the path past the well. Then turn left at the end of the field and walk up to the railroad tracks. You can see his place from there."

I thanked her and started off immediately. It had already been several hours since I left home and I still had no idea what it was I was going to do once I was there. I imagined it was probably yard work or crawling around under the front porch and other fine activities I wasn't dressed for.

I gave the well a wide berth like Granmaw Wellman always warned me to and I noticed that the path between fields led to a wider spot that must have been for tractors or harvesters to get on and off the road. A rusty car body occupied the spot and I could just make out the word "Studebaker" on the side. It seemed to me that abandoning cars in fields was a tradition many families in the area observed. I didn't know anything about cars and had no guess how long this one had been sitting there but it looked at least as old as the truck my dad was interested in. It gave me lots to think about as I walked around the edge of Mrs. Maynard's field and I almost missed the path up to the railway track.

I arrived at Dick's place and performed my own version of my dad's cautious approach. I cupped my hands and called out "Hello!" to the house from the driveway and the two hounds belted out from underneath the front porch and came running at me barking something awful and flaring their nostrils at me like they'd been shot from the very depths of hell. I had no cover and no weapon so I just stepped back from the drive and covered my face.

The first dog hit me in the chest and knocked me down. The second arrived a heartbeat later and I was roughly licked and sniffed and slobbered on. I tried to push them away but soon as I got one head turned away the second was licking my face or putting its huge paws up on my shoulders. I cursed and shouted and half laughed relieved I wasn't being eaten alive but at the same time I couldn't stand up. Each time I tried one of the hounds would growl and the other would head butt me down or push me back into the dust with its paws. I don't know how long this went on before I could hear hoarse laughter coming from the house. Dick Wellman seemed to think this was the funniest thing he'd seen in many a year. I spit and sputtered a bit and called out loudly "Could you call your dogs off please! They won't let me be long enough to stand up!"

"Oh they won't hurt you none, just give 'em a good boot in the ass and they'll leave you be."

"Right…" I thought that was bad advice and I half crawled half tumbled to the porch with Dick Wellman laughing his head off the whole time. Once I set foot on his porch Dick took mercy on me and shooed them off with a wave of his cane. He sat down in his rocking chair and looked at me while I tried to wipe dog spit off my face and said "Don't you look in a right state!" And before I could reply he said, "I expected you hours ago, its already late afternoon boy. What have you to say for yourself?"

I wiped my face on my shirttail and tried to catch my breath before I told him the whole sorry story including the help I got from Mrs. Maynard. He looked off in the direction I came from and said, "I went to her church, years ago. Beautiful women there…only reason I ever had for going. The rest seemed a bit too…superstitious. She didn't happen to say who's running her church these days did she?

"No sir, I thought a church was run by the people who went to it."

He made a derisive snort and said, "You've got an eye opener or two coming your way boy, just you wait."

The room was slightly better lit than before and I could see old framed pictures in black and white along the walls, some faded postcards under glass and what looked like ribbons or lace hanging by a faded mirror and wash basin. It reminded me of a room in my granmaw's house and had about the same smell too, minus the lilac water. My look around was interrupted when Dick said "Well? We might as well get started. Where is your notebook? Your pencil?"

I blinked back at him for a few seconds and said "What? No one told me to bring anything. I thought I was coming over to mow your lawn or something."

Dick got up and brushed past me; rummaging in some drawers of a dark wooden chest and said "They didn't eh? You do eh? Is that what you want to do RJ? Do you want to mow my law now that you're here?"

"If that's what's expected of me. I don't exactly want to but its something I know how to do. I mow the lawn for a friend of mine every couple weeks."

"How much do they pay you?"

"Five dollars usually. And sometimes they throw in a soda or ice cream when it's hot."

"Five dollars? Is that all? You're being foolish to mow someone's lawn for 5 bucks and the promise of icey cream."

I shrugged and looked away. "Well sir, it IS their mower. And it's a friend of mine so I wouldn't charge top dollar anyway."

Dick chuckled at that and handed me a small spiral notebook and a pencil that said "First National Bank of Charleston" on the side. "You have an arrangement then. I see how it is." I followed him back out onto the porch and he indicated a folding chair next to the bannister. "Have a seat and let me tell you our arrangement. I think you'll like it a bit better than mowing the lawn, especially if you had to push it all the way from Ceredo."

I made sure my feet didn't dangle down in front of the hound dogs and then waited for Dick Wellman to start.

You and I are going to tell each other some stories. And you're gonna write down the good stuff. I want to talk to someone and you are smart enough not to ask stupid questions. And to listen. You are gonna tell me stuff too and I'll decide if you should write it down or not. When that note book's full, your daddy can have the keys to the truck. What do you think about that?"

"Just one question sir. How do I know what the good parts are?"

"Well hell boy, you'll just have to write everything down and decide what was good later won't you?"

"Yes sir, I guess so. What do you plan on doing with it when it's done? Are you going to submit it to a book company or a magazine?"

"We'll decide that when we've actually got something on paper eh? And didn't I tell you not to call me Sir?"

"Yes ...Mr. Wellman. I'm ready when you are."

"'About time too. Put this down on page one: Composition task...no, just 'Writing Assignment No.1'"

I hurried to write down what he said, stroked thru it and wrote it again. I was in an awkward bent over position with the pad on my knee but I was very curious about what might come next so I held my tongue. Dick Wellman took a deep breath and spit his chaw over the bannister before saying anything. He produced a small bottle of whisky from somewhere and took a swallow. He grinned in appreciation and smacked his lips with an "Ah Chaaa!" sound. I was pretty sure he didn't want that written down but I made up my mind to negotiate for a drink of my own soon.

SECTION THREE:

Below.

Chapter Thirty-Three: Letting in the Dark.

I woke in darkness.

I looked about cautiously after waking the last time to find a beast lying next to me. For a long time I sensed nothing but the darkness; it felt thick and wrapped about me with an intimate embrace. After a bit I thought could see a distant point of light. Perhaps it was just an artifact of my vision like some nerve in the back of my eye misfiring, I really couldn't be sure. As it drew closer it grew in size till it looked like a striped, undulating line. I was fascinated more than afraid; the lingering effects of the drink and whatever else I'd been exposed to made my mind feel detached. As the image got closer it looked more like a snake but one made of sharp angles and built of triangles and cubes. I recalled seeing a toy snake like it in at a fair once; yellow with bright orange markings. But that one didn't move or have sharp, almost diamond-edged twists and corners along its body like the one approaching me.

When it was very close it raised its head and looked at me. Origami wings unfolded from its back and I moved a bit to the side to let it pass. At the last second it lunged at me opening its mouth wide, wide enough to swallow me whole! The teeth looked sharp, sharper than a shark's. They were isosceles triangle sharp.

I cried out and awoke. Sitting up I noticed three things almost immediately. It was pitch dark wherever I was, very humid, and I was naked. There was something beneath me that felt like chamois or sponge and overhead in the dark there was a looming sensation of weight as if a large overhanging shelf was just inches from my skull. A cool hand touched my arm and I flinched casting my eyes about for the slightest hint of light but I could still see nothing. At least I thought it was a hand but it could have been anything. It left my forearm and slid down to my left hand, grasping it tight.

A voice said "Exsisto procul pacis veneratio hospes."

"Ron? KellyRay?"

"Quis colo colui cultum mos vos exsisto hodie?"

It sounded like a garbled mix of words and syllables but there was no menace in the tone. I rubbed my head in the dark and said "Oh yeah, "Them." I thought back to what I had been told of Brother Wellman's visit here over a thousand years ago. He probably preached to them in Latin and possibly Celtic as well and since then they have been exposed to Hillbilly. I despaired at even the thought of attempting a translation. The fact was I had flunked basic Spanish in high school, twice. Just about all I knew about foreign languages and accents came from TV. There was no way I was going to be able to decipher what they were saying to me. It might as well be Elvish or Aztec to my ears.

I put my other hand on top of the one holding mine and followed the arm up to a shoulder. My fingers brushed hair and a breast and I pulled back quickly, embarrassed. Whoever was sharing this close space with me was female!

"Sorry!..um, Hello?" I was acutely aware of my nudity and I felt around for something, anything to cover myself with. The only thing that came to hand was something about the size of a pumpkin that gave a bit when I squeezed on it. I decided this must be a pillow or cushion of some sort and I placed it over my lap. There was a touch of hair on my face and I heard a giggle very close by. Then whomever it was shifted away from me and a large figure covered in blue glowing paint bobbed into view. I couldn't see anything else in the dark and the figure seemed to float and grow closer, too close! I began to feel around frantically for my clothing, a torch, for Mason's Crutch! It was gone! I groaned at my failure to protect it, and its failure to protect me.

Cold rough hands grabbed me and slid me forward off the ledge and onto my feet. I could see a dim blue glow around the muscular body of the man before me, details beginning to resolve themselves this close up. I could see now that he didn't wear a mask so much as had his face painted in garish detail. His body was coated in something that gave off a dim blue glow all over with jagged lines or lightning bolts outlined within the sea of blue. The only things he wore was a long necklace made of stones and small carvings which wrapped around his neck several times and a wedged shaped bit of weaving at the waist providing a tiny bit of coverage front and back. He grinned a wide smile with multicolored teeth and extended his arm to the right. I looked where he was pointing but I saw nothing.

"Progredior illic si vos postulo ut evacuate."

I squinted and blinked but saw nothing in the direction he gestured. In fact the only way I could tell I wasn't still dreaming was that the blue giant disappeared when I closed my eyes and he was back when I opened them. I shook my head not realizing the futility of the gesture and tried to say, "I'm sorry but I don't know what you want?" I felt chagrined and muttered an apology under my breath. " I don't suppose Starfleet issued you a Universal Translator?"

I cursed my brothers wherever they were for getting me swept into this situation with no preparation. I was clueless and blind and on my own but I would have to try. Something about Starfleet made me think I should start by leaving contractions out of my speech in case he could catch something of my language so I repeated myself in soft tones, careful not to infer any sort of challenge: "I do not know what you want? I can not see what you are pointing at."

The blue giant pointed again and nudged me in the same direction. I felt out with my hands till I found a bit of wall and followed that to an opening. I couldn't tell if it led to a tunnel or another room. I followed the wall around with my left hand the right one waving around in front of me. My feet bumped against a lip of rock and beyond that the smooth floor turned to sand and gravel. I bent down to feel outwards, imagining this might be the edge of an underground lake and got a hint of dampness in the sand. It was only a few inches deep though and the whole space was perhaps a 5-foot circle. The figure behind me said something in a warning tone and I stopped, standing back up slowly.

"Noli manum illic Quod vastata sit!"

There were some grumbling noises as the figure came closer and I felt him squeeze into the space next to me. Moments later I heard the unmistakable sound of water hitting sand and the accompanying scent left me no doubt. Even in the dark I felt my face turn red in embarrassment and I pretended to look up and off to the side till I felt him pass by me again. I knew he was still nearby and I heard what I hoped were words of encouragement. If I hadn't felt the burden of all that drinking we did earlier that night I might have tried to convince him I didn't need to go but I really did need to and so without further ceremony I made my best guess at finding my target and dampened a few rocks myself. I hoped there weren't any decorations or sacred beads in that space because once the decision was made it wasn't going to be unmade. I still felt embarrassed by having to do a private act in the presence of some other person, in the dark, in the nude, and with a female someplace nearby.

I listened for a chuckle or some other recognizable comment around me but I was allowed to finish in silence. A vessel of some sort was held before me and I tried to take it from him and take a drink but my right hand was roughly pushed into the water and swished about. A little light came on and I put my other hand in, laving them in the tepid water for a few seconds. Then it was pulled away and I heard it dumped onto the sandy space behind me. This first lesson was one I wouldn't soon forget. I wished I'd paid more attention to the story of Helen Keller. There might have been some good survival tips in there. I hoped I didn't have to learn sign language or something before I could ask to leave. That was my main goal now and a vision of crossing the 14th Street Bridge into Ohio and never looking back hovered in my mind while I stood there waiting for more instructions.

My host or guard or babysitter's dim blue outline moved away and was partially obscured by a turn in the wall before coming back and presenting me with three squat pottery jars. I could see their outlines in small tracings around the bottles and my hands were once again guided to them. One by one they were opened for me and I could see they were filled with glowing paint: Yellow, Blue and Green.

The blue giant dipped a finger into the blue pot and put a bit on his face, leaning in close so I could see. He said something that sounded similar to what the girl before had said: "Quis colo colui cultum mos vos exsisto hodie?" I still had no idea what it meant but I decided I was meant to choose a color and paint myself. This felt like it had serious implications and would probably affect how these people reacted to me from here on out. I put a dot of each color on my left hand and then spread them out into stripes along each finger to get a feel for how far each color would cover; if it could be rubbed off easily; and part of me worried I'd be allergic to whatever it was.

Nothing in my experience recommended one color over the other but I figured if the man before me wore blue I'd better do so too. I dipped two fingers into the blue pot and smeared it under my right eye like I was prepping for a football game. The blue giant seemed satisfied with my choice and took the other two colors away. I heard him speak to someone in that chamber beyond and a murmur of responses carried to me. Sounded like there were a lot of people out there waiting. I spread the paint over my face while he came back to watch. I didn't put any on my beard because that didn't seem practical and I noticed my observer was clean-shaven and bald, save for a braid down the back of his head. It wasn't dyed but had strands of something woven into it that gave off a glow of their own. I looked up at him when I'd finished and he whistled something. I'm sure it wasn't in appreciation because he thumped his chest and mine and then my stomach, his hand gesturing to everything below that.

"Illic. Et hic. Aliquam omnia hyacinthino."

Again I thought I caught a word or two in his speech that was recognizable. Maybe I didn't deserve that D in Spanish after all. "illicit ? Omnia?" Omnia sounded like Omni… maybe he meant all? I should paint it all? No other thought occurred so I started on my arms and chest. I was running out of paint and skipped to my legs, doing just a streak down my thighs and again on my shins. I ran my finger around the inside of the pot dramatically and handed it back to him. He hummed something to himself and then made me jump by shouting out to someone over his shoulder. I didn't see who arrived till they moved in front of him and the giggle that followed convinced me that it was the person who had been sitting beside me while I slept. I could only make out an outline of a slim body and long hair pulled back in a ponytail like the blue giant's. She put her arms around his waist and I could see she was a good head shorter than he was. Daughter maybe? They exchanged some whispered words and he left me with her.

A chant went up outside and I thought I could even hear some drums and tambourines mixed in. I had clearly made the blue giant mad or perhaps just impatient. He had a crowd waiting to meet me and I was still un-presentable, even in the dark. The girl did not wear any glowing body paint but had strands in her hair and around her wrists and ankles. Earlier she didn't even have that much on, or at least nothing that glowed anyway and in the dark I couldn't tell if she wore anything else at all and it was making me very nervous.

My anxiety went up several notches when I felt her hands on my shins, spreading the paint out with a practiced hand. I could see her fingers at work and tried to remain still as a statue while she practically massaged the paint into my skin. She hummed a tune to herself and didn't seem bothered with the task making short work of one leg, then the other.

Her hands moved above my knees and I tried to push them away. She still managed to make an effort before I caught both her hands and lifted them to my stomach. First contact or not I had my limits and I was glad I wasn't a brightly glowing outline at this moment. She made that giggling noise again and I was certain the whole scene was amusing her immensely. She paused in surprise when her fingers contacted my chest hair and I wondered if her people did not grow body hair or just removed it to aid in body painting? I flinched expecting to have it plucked out but that didn't happen, her humming stopped and became whispered words. It wasn't clear whether she was singing to me or to herself.

I tried to thank her, searching my memory for the bits of Spanish floating to the top. It was the only latin based language I had any experience with and even so it would have been a more modern Latin than they were using but I gave it a try anyway. I said "Gracias...mi chica?" She stopped trying to touch up my paint job here and there and said "Gratias? Gratiae meae puellae? Mei Puella!"

After that came a rapid-fire stream of words I had no chance of following. I tried to slow her down and capture the words as she repeated her outburst. I was certain I heard Gracias or Gratias so I tried a simple affirmative. "Gracias, si. Mucho gracias." Again I triggered a barrage of questions and when I didn't respond she disappeared into the dark.

I cursed myself for being so casual with a language I barely understood. If they didn't think me an idiot before they had plenty of reason to think so now. I could have just agreed to be dinner far as I knew. At least I didn't try raising my voice and speaking slowly cause that always seemed to work in movies.

I wished for a mirror but the best I could do was stick my arms out where I could see them and then do the same with my legs. There was a handprint on each shin and a void from there up to my stomach. The handprints weren't mine. My upper torso was covered, at least in front. I had noticed that the blue giant was painted front and back so he must have had help too. I tried picturing what my face paint must look like and how the gap where my beard was must make it look like I had a huge open mouth.

The blue giant came back from whatever he had been doing and gestured, whistling at me. I guessed enough time had been wasted on prepping me for the crowd. When I started feeling outward with my hands and feet to avoid tripping on something he came over and took my arm like I was an invalid and led me out into the 'open.'

A blast of sound hit me when we stepped out a roar rose from thousands of voices echoing around and focused on me. I could feel every syllable in my chest. The song was much clearer now and mixed in with it were the sounds of people speaking, chanting, pounding on drums and those frequent piercing whistles that carried over everything. My breath was taken away by the size and scale of what I saw before me and I thought "I would love to see this in daylight!" Then I laughed a bit out loud; there was no daylight here, an unknowingly vast distance below the surface. Just this sea of glowing faces painted red, yellow and blue.

The ambient light here was no brighter than half dead coals in a fire but it seemed so bright by comparison that I was able to look around as we crossed the open space towards a large ornate archway on the opposite side of the cave nestled between two natural columns.

Picture the shell of a gigantic chambered Nautilus outlined in glowing dots and dashes. Add to that a border of Mayan pictographs and intersperse a few heraldic designs here and there. Now scale it up till it can hold a several hundred people on the main floor and many more on each level leading up to a ceiling spiked with stalactites and more randomly glowing areas. Picture all that and you have a small idea of the cavern I found myself in.

Now the crowd was chanting long verses of song in their own language--at least it didn't sound like the stuff my hosts had used toward me--and occasionally they were interrupted by whistles from a few other blue painted giants who were overseeing the whole scene. My personal blue giant took a step forward and the crowd opened a few paces ahead for him but when I followed I was mobbed. Garishly painted faces pressed in from every side and hands reached out and touched me. My hair and beard seem to draw special attention and some actually yanked on it to see if it would come off. Every few steps I was stopped from moving forward by a child or young adult who grabbed my hand and stepped in close, sniffing dramatically. I bore this as best I could but I also tried to stay close behind Blue Giant. Even though I had on paint like everyone else I still felt naked and exposed.

Words were sung at me and hands beckoned me from all directions. I kept trying to turn and slide thru groups of people to remain in the wake of my escort, hoping that turning my backside to people wasn't considered some sort of insult here because there was no direction for modesty. Soon several more large men with blue painted bodies fell in around me and they kept up a singsong chant that must have contained some sort of warning because it immediately minimized the number of curious people actually able to reach me from the crowd.

Chapter Thirty-Four: King of the Underworld.

We went up steps that had been polished so smooth that they looked like a shallow frozen waterfall. We entered a chamber lit with some actual torches and I began to think that light was a strict commodity for these people or a rigorously controlled one in any case.

I glanced around the walls and ceiling of the huge cavern and could see that the naturally ruddiness of the stone had been covered with more 'glow in the dark' graffiti. Everywhere that wasn't painted with some form of picture or pictogram was covered by line after line of those dots and holes I'd seen in the Scripture room. It dawned on me too late that I must have been standing right next to a partial translation! The whole thing could have been a sort of Rosetta Stone left un-translated for centuries. Again I damned my brothers for not letting me in on the whole story or for being too lazy to seek it out themselves.

The tone of the song changed from place to place but never seemed to cease. I was pushed to the front of the assembly and I looked up to where the frozen waterfall apparently emerged from the wall to form a high seat or throne. A man sat there, his body was covered in geometric patches of all three colors and between those he was covered in pictograms or tattoos. His perch put everyone in the room at his feet and the significance of that wasn't wasted on me. I stood quietly looking up in awe, trying to take it all in. There were two more blue giants standing to either side of his throne. They were standing on small risers that elevated them a bit but still kept their heads lower than the leader's. The King or Chief of these people could reach out and pat one on the head if he wanted or just as easily smack him with his scepter.

One of these "senior' giants lifted a stack of shelf fungus towards his chief who took the top one without looking at it. His gaze met mine and I could see keen interest there but I also felt an air of superiority. Whatever I represented in his world, I was no equal and perhaps only a resource to be used and discarded.

I didn't hold his gaze for long; in fact I didn't realize I had been looking back at him at all. The Chief was the first well-lit person I'd seen since waking up here and I could see that his face was craggy and rounded but with a strong square jowl. He would have fit in perfectly with people from the Southwest, from Mexico or Peru maybe. Except that his skin--what little of it remained unpainted-- seemed as pale as mine, perhaps more so. I wondered how many generations it took for melanin to become recessive. Or perhaps this was a trait they looked for in their Chiefs. I took in the details of his illustrated body; the cloak of feathers and flowers draped over his shoulders and the patchwork cushions lining his seat. I could swear there was a square or two of denim mixed in there. I looked to the left and right at the blue giants around me and couldn't decide what their normal skin tone was, the lighting there wasn't as bright. I wondered if the fact that his subjects were kept in the dark was a cliche' that both our worlds shared.

When he spoke the song immediately became a murmur, a mere backdrop. And each sentence was spaced out so that it could be echoed by the crowd and spread like a ripple on water thru the people massed outside. I wondered if this method was all that effective or if the furthest group of listeners might suffer from a "Blessed are the cheese makers" effect. I had little time to think on it as the Chief pointed at me and I heard the word Wellman clearly mentioned. The flattened bit of shelf fungus had those same dots and holes on it and he ran his fingers over the surface lightly as he spoke. Everywhere I looked there was a new amazing thing and I wondered how my ancestors could have kept this place quiet for centuries?

Again the name Wellman was mentioned and the Chief paused, looking at me expectantly. I thought of about 10 things to do at that moment but I did none of them. I just looked around confusedly and held my tongue. Again he spoke, his voice rising and his words sounding sharper, less friendly. When he got to the word Wellman this time he pronounced it with great emphasis. I tried to communicate my distress with my expression but nothing got across to him. He stood up and the chanting became a whisper. The blue giant on his left handed him a scepter. At first I thought it was Mason's Crutch but it was different in its design and when it passed into his grip it lit up from within. The swirling shifting contents of the crystal on top making everything take on a shimmering fire lit quality. I knew I had to do something now, to respond to him somehow but I did not know his words and Mason's Crutch was lost to me.

The Chief did not need to refer to his text this time. He spoke again gesturing to his scepter then pointing it at me. I would have searched my pockets like a mime if I'd had any, but I did my best "laugh clown laugh" imitation and knelt down to pick up a pinch of sand from the floor. I sprinkled it from hand to hand and then dusted them around as if looking for something turned to dust. I turned back to the Chief and pointed to his scepter. "Lost. Wellman has lost Mason's Crutch." Then for drama I dropped to my knees and hugged myself. I felt childish and glad for the darkness. My words were echoed back thru the crowd and I could hear the word "lost" fade away like an echo. Then my big blue guide wedged his hand under my right arm and stood me back up. He spoke to me while eyeing the Chief and I hoped my dramatic performance sparked some understanding in him.

His attitude was anything but understanding. "Suspendisse Wellman ubi sceptra vestra? Populus qui non huc sine sole ligatis."

I still didn't know how to respond to this and was out of ideas. I shrugged and said "Nada" in half hope that something would get across. A look passed between the chief's advisors and they whispered to him urgently. He sat back down and sang a few short phrases to the blue giants around me. Without another word I was grabbed under the arms and force-marched out into the crowd. They weren't so anxious to touch me now. I was taken into another room by 4 of the guards and two of them forced me down onto a pit of fine sand, edged with small stones and several flat rocks. The humidity in there was heavy but I didn't care. I thought I was about to die. I babbled and pleaded with them, knowing they could not understand me. I kept this up while two of them held me flat and the other two scooped sand onto my legs and chest. It was very warm but not hot enough to burn and I laughed a bit hysterically imagining myself about to be slow cooked in a sand pit for my crime of snubbing the chief.

The four men spoke to each other and from their gruff tones I could tell this was a distasteful task for them. Once my legs were covered they rubbed the sand into my skin, scrubbing and scratching away. I complained bitterly and tried to shift and wriggle away from them. I thought their goal might be to scrape the paint off my body and I would have helped them if my hands were free. My stomach and chest were next and I cried out in pain when their efforts pulled out several chest hairs at the same time. When they got to my face I was sure I would be blinded.

At that moment the giant holding my legs let out a cry of surprise and was flattened to the sand by a large dark animal standing on his back. It growled and showed its sharp yellow teeth before moving forward and snapping at my captors. I recognized its spiky midnight black fur and evil smell in an instance. It was the creature that was sleeping beside me in the cave just before I was brought here. The four blue guards were backed up against the rear wall shouting and whistling in alarm. They may not have known what it was but they were certainly afraid of it and I was too. I didn't dare move or take my eyes off the creature. It was barrel chested and had short legs covered in shaggy fur. Where its pupils should be was just pinpoints of bright pink light. At first I thought it was one of the hyena hounds I had seen chasing the DeerLady but it didn't match what I remembered from their fleeting forms. It stalked around me in a circle and I could see a black harness with a long leather tube suspended from it. It made another loop around me and then dropped to its belly, still growling. It turned its muzzle towards me and spoke in a guttural voice: "Sssssparky, sssstoppiiiittt!" I am sure I fainted a bit after that because my vision swam and the darkness beat at my mind like moths trying to get at a burning flame. My head dropped back onto the sand and I covered my eyes praying to either wake up or for the world to make a bit more sense please? I thought I might have been saved from having the flesh scoured from my body but by what?

I let my hands fall to my side and my fingers touched the harness around the creature's torso. It growled but made no other response. I felt around for the catch and opened the case and reached in. I touched the top of something and the interior of the case began to glow in a greenish light. Grasping the top and pulling it free Mason's Crutch lit the chamber with a hundred shades of green from neon lime to a dark mossy color. One of the blue giants gave out a whistle and cry then dashed for the door. He disappeared from view and when "Sparky" made no effort to stop him the other three quickly left too. The light and the swirling moving fluids within the geode transfixed me and I momentarily forgot the massive beast at my side. I wedged the tip into the sand and stood up, dusting myself off and examining the deep scratches on my legs and stomach by its light. Sparky looked at me and I turned away, disconcerted by its unflinching gaze. I felt I should say something in response to my rescue so I said "Good dog...er, boy. Nice Sparky."

This seemed to satisfy the beast; it closed its eyes and immediately ignored me. I thought I detected a smirk in its canine features but wasn't going to interrogate it when it seemed content to lie on the warm sand.

I looked around the room I was in still cast in the greenish light from Mason's Crutch. There were pots of hot water and stones but no sign of food. I dipped some water out and sipped it. It was heavy with mineral aftertaste and I risked drinking several cupped handfuls. What I really wanted was food. I still had no idea how long I'd been unconscious since the cave but my stomach seemed to think it had been days. That pizza was long gone and my stomach growled loudly.

I looked out of the opening into the square and there was a circle of people standing way back looking in my direction and doing that humming singing murmuring thing. When the light from the staff spilled out into the open they shifted further back and several of the blue giants moved between them and the light, briskly whistling and interlinking their arms. I tried to show them my distress by rubbing my belly and then gesturing to my mouth. The crowd noise took on several high notes of alarm and more people slipped away into the dark. I had a sudden thought of the ending scenes of Close Encounters and wished I could do more than blow a few notes on an ocarina, maybe I could get thru to these people.

I turned around and startled to find Sparky silently standing behind me. It looked past me at the guards and the guards thinned out almost magically. I guessed I wasn't going anywhere without an escort now. I was still leery of the beast but so far it hadn't made any violent actions against me. I said, "I don't suppose you have any trail mix in your pouch do you?" Sparky continued to regard me with its pink eyes but said nothing. "You can talk, I heard you say "Sparky stop it" earlier.

Sparky took a step closer and its gravelly inhuman voice said "Ssssparky, sssstopiiiittt." Suddenly its body seemed to tense up and get bigger, more muscular. It began to resemble a wolverine more than a dog and I could see it sniffing the air and scanning the crowd of people outside with keen interest. This was just about the most disturbing thing I'd ever seen or heard even though I'd now heard it three times. It was one thing to watch "An American Werewolf in London" it's a whole another thing to be ringside when the Rick Baker transformations begin. I shook my head quickly, "No No! There's nothing to stop here. Sparky lie down…er sit! Sit Sparky Sit!" Sparky let out a long sigh of stinking, fetid breath and virtually deflated before my eyes. Then it looked at me in disappointment and went to lie back down near Mason's Crutch.

I asked myself what the hell was going on but nothing I'd been told in the past couple of days prepared me for being here among these people. If I was supposed to have a trade agreement with them then they already had everything we'd brought along on this trip. If it was a "meet the new ambassador" situation then the decision had been made for me and I was stuck. But Ron had pointed out several names on the list that had been removed later so the choice was somehow revoked in their cases. Or terminated. Then there was Mason's Crutch and Sparky and whatever relation tied the two together. No one had mentioned that the Crutch had a protector--of sorts--and no reference to it spraying out green magical beams whenever I touched it. It hadn't done that at Granmaw's house so maybe it only worked down here in the Dark, wherever here was in relation to the surface.

I was still half convinced that I was dreaming, and the one thing that was convincing me I wasn't was the constant growling of my stomach. I sat in the doorway where I could see the people outside as they nervously looked back, still humming and singing to themselves. I hoped to catch sight of someone coming out of one of the side caverns with food or even the smell of cooked food that might lead me to something to eat. I was feeling so hungry it was giving me a headache and I think I would have snatched food from a child if he came in range.

No one did though. The guards, as I'd come to think of the blue giants, stayed between the crowd and me. I thought about trying my mime skills again but was debating how to convey the difference between "I want to eat something" and "I want to eat you." I scanned the faces of the guards trying to find the familiar one of my earlier host but I could not see enough detail in that dim light to tell one from another. Several now bore additional paint, accenting around the face with white stripes and jagged lines. It was an almost a comical representation of anger. It would be very comical if it had not been aimed at me.

I stood up deciding that if I wasn't going to be immediately stopped or killed I'd go explore for food. When I could see across the crowd I noticed a glow moving in my direction. A ring of blue guards were making their way toward me with steady drumbeats and whistling. In their middle was the chief on a suspended hammock of some sort. He reclined on pillows but he didn't look relaxed. His scepter was in his right hand and its blue light arced and danced angrily. I felt that exact sinking feeling you get when a police car suddenly appears behind you on the highway.

When the line of guards opened in front of me and the chief's bearers turned his hammock so he could see me up close I stepped back into my room and picked up Mason's Crutch. Instantly the Sparky creature was awake and on its feet, sniffing the air and growling toward the Chief. I said, "You better stay back, he might not be an animal lover like me." I hoped the meaning got across to Sparky if not the sarcasm. I also hoped that the Chief didn't have plans of taking Mason's Crutch away from me because I had a feeling Sparky would not like that at all. I didn't feel I could control the creature if it decided to attack someone but I took hope from the fact that earlier it hadn't bit or even scratched the guard, just used its own bulk to knock him off me.

No one entered the room so I gave up waiting and stepped back outside. The Chief was sitting up in his hammock and listening to his two advisors who stood behind him whispering. I watched quietly and noticed that my head was higher than the Chief's so I leaned forward a bit using the crutch as a support and bowed just to the exact height to match his. I wanted to acknowledge his position without diminishing mine. I felt a lot more confident with the Crutch in my hand; its swirling green colors seemed equal to his blue ones and that suited me just fine.

He said a couple of words to one of his advisors who disappeared into the crowd and quickly re-appeared with one of the blue guards. I recognized him as my host and he dropped onto his knees to lower his head below the Chiefs. They exchanged words and he stepped toward me very cautiously and spoke again in that strange half Latin half Celtic speech I'd heard before. It was of no use of course; the hours in between hadn't improved my ability to understand him. He moved to take me by the arm but I refused to go with him. I tugged him down to my level till my stomach made a loud rumble. I thumped my stomach and put his hand on it, holding it there till he could feel the rumblings himself. He looked confused for a moment and then turned back to the Chief almost laughing in his relief. An excited staccato went up from the crowd beyond and my guard looked almost paternal, patting my stomach and smiling as he went back to the crowd.

The Chief gave a command and my blue guard whistled a long series of tones which was repeated by another guard nearby, then one in the back and so on off into the distance. I was again struck by the size of the place and wondered just how many people were down here? I was pleased with finally getting my meaning across but Sparky chose that moment to slide silently to my side. He looked at the Chief and his scepter and bared his fangs. His appearance caused a lot of sudden murmurings in the group and the blue guards moved to come between us. I looked at Sparky and frowned, choosing to grab the harness across his shoulders instead of actually touching the animal. The Chief stood up out of his hammock and pointed at Sparky. He clearly objected to its presence but I couldn't do anything about it so I just watched, straightening up to again to be at the same height as he was.

The Chief sang a few words and capped it off with a whistle and I saw the sand at his feet shift and ripple, taking a shape I dimly remembered. It was the crystalline snake from my dream, rising several feet from the floor and flaring its diamond edged hood. I guessed it was twelve, fifteen feet long as it coiled and twisted at the Chief's feet like a tightening spring. I thought I might laugh to relieve the stress of the situation but that could be misconstrued as derision just as easily. I didn't want to see whose beast was the stronger; any fight between them would no doubt end the Covenant between the Above and Below. I stood my ground and pretended to stroke Sparky's coat. His hackles were up and the spiky hair felt hard edged as nails. I could feel him shifting beneath my touch and I whispered, "Stay boy. Stay. We're not here to start a fight."

The Chief's snake was rising up on its tail, its body shifting and spiraling in an almost hypnotic pattern. It flickered a glassine tongue in our direction and I thought I could see its beady gemstone eyes looking us over, seeking weak spots, places to attack. The Chief continued to hum and sing to it and the light from his scepter blazed and reflected off of everything around him.

I thought I might have to change tactics and was ready to utter, "Sparky Stop it!" when a young girl bearing a bowl broke from between two guards and ran up to me. She slid on her knees before me and I heard one of the Blue giants calling out sharply to her. All at once people were shouting and singing and whistling. She placed the bowl on the ground, selected something that looked like a grey zucchini and offered it up to me. I looked at her for a second in the flickering lights then took her offering. I made a bit show of biting the end off and chewing dramatically.

It was like a spongy raw potato inside but I knew spitting it out would probably be deadly for both of us. Making what I thought was a sound of appreciation I chewed loudly and sat down on the sand next to her. She giggled and I realized this was the girl I'd first encountered in the dark. The chief barked a few words and everything dropped to a whisper. His words cowed the girl and she slipped away back to the crowd. I called out "Thank you!" and remained sitting. I put Mason's Crutch on the ground pointed back into the dark stuffy room behind me. Sparky walked around me still eyeing the snake and sniffed at the items in the bowl. He picked up a couple of hard round things in his mouth and retreated into the humid darkness making loud crunching noises as he went.

I was silently thankful a crisis had been averted and felt I was just a little closer to communicating with these people. What happened next was a steady parade of food and entertainment as the Chief called for something, took a small taste of it and then had my "Girl Friday" carry it over to me to eat. Most of the items tasted musty and some had sharp tasting goo in the middle like Brie cheese. A cup of something that looked like broth or thin gravy arrived and I found it tasted like cocoa and peppers whizzed together. It was delightful and I finished it all in one go. More than one of the foods offered me smelled or tasted rotten but I forced myself to sample everything the Chief sent to me.

One of the last items delivered looked like a huge roasted centipede all curled up and charred along the edges. It was still warm from the cooking fires. I noticed this item was brought directly to me and I looked it over skeptically. I broke off a leg and looked at it dubiously for a second. Squeezing it produced a small creamy pile of goo on my hand and I stuck my tongue out to taste it. Immediately I spit out the bitter tasting stuff and coughed while the Chief roared with laughter. The old boy had a sense of humor but he must have taken mercy on me because he waved my hostess back over and he used a knife to cut it down the back and peel it open like a lobster tail. He tilted his plate down so I could see the white pieces of meat inside the shell then he picked out a huge chunk and sucked it down with relish. I grinned and nodded and when Friday had brought me half of the remainder I did the same. I made a mental note to include a bucket of crawdads in the next Covenant exchange package.

The girl I was now referring to as Friday seemed pleased with her new position and sat proudly beside me and talked non-stop. She might have been talking about the food or my coming sacrifice but she seemed friendly enough and a welcome barrier between the unknown social protocols I had been stumbling over.

On one trip she brought me a large shapeless cushion to sit on. It smelled of mold and had a dusting of spores on its surface that came off on my hand when I touched it. I could only assume it was a fungus of some kind but it was much more comfortable to sit on than the sand and pebble floor of this huge cavern. I thanked her and she seemed emboldened to try and sit on it with me. The puffball rolled and shifted because I didn't have the knack of sitting on it and she ended up much too close. I tried not to look at her directly as I passed her the empty bowl and covered my embarrassment by begging for more food.

Even in the lowered green glow of Mason's Crutch I could tell she was a healthy young woman who was somewhere in her late teens or early twenties. But who knew if they measured years down here at all, let alone how? Her closeness reminded me of my nakedness and of the half scraped off blue paint. I wondered how that left me in their eyes but long as they were happy to feed me I was happy to eat. I decided that a safer place to look was over at the Chief and his scepter. The winged snake had shrunk to a thin rope-like form barely 3 feet in length. It spiraled around the scepter and interlaced thru the Chief's fingers. I was struck by how much it reminded me of a Caduceus or physician's staff and I hoped that the inferred motto of "First Do No Harm" applied here as well. I really was at his mercy and that of the whole tribe.

Chapter Thirty-Five: A Small Start toward Understanding.

After the feast I struggled to stifle my yawns and two more cups of the warm sweet drink was all I could manage. I decided to indicate the end of the feast by sliding off the puffball I was using as a beanbag chair and just prop my head on it right there on the ground. The Chief and his advisors watched for a while then his bearers turned him toward the patient crowd behind. He spoke briefly, breaking into a song that was echoed by everyone and then he was carried off to his glowing chamber.

Friday and her father (I guess!) remained near me as people faded back into the shadows. We were by no means alone in the open space but the few left hurried thru the square eyeing us from a distance.

I stood up and looked around as best I could, noticing the ambient light was dying off with the crowd. I mimed laying my head on my folded hands and snoring softly to Friday but she just looked between her father and me. I was feeling the weight of the food and drink and thought seeking out that toilet or cat box or whatever it was I'd been to before would be a great idea right about now.

I picked up Mason's Crutch and it sprang to life. Holding it over my head helped me see better but it did not help as much as a true torch would have. Sparky came out of the room behind me like a shot and rushed to my side. Friday and her father fell back, averting their eyes from its green glow. With my free hand I picked up the puffball and passed it to Friday; my plan was to watch where she took it and follow her into what would hopefully be living quarters. She took it and fired off some rapid-fire words punctuated by her father's brusque reply. He took the puffball back from her and dropped it on the ground in front of me, raising his voice in clear disapproval while gesturing to his daughter. I didn't have to be a father myself to understand what he thought I intended. I'm sure he was feeling the same frustration I felt in not being able to get our exact meanings across.

These two seemed to be the only ones who spoke to me in Latin and that indicated to me that they were chosen for the job of talking to whatever Wellman ended up down here among them. I was pretty sure few if any of my predecessors would have known Latin to start with and I couldn't even assume they learned any from these people. Situations like this repeated throughout history but I didn't recall reading any details on how it sorted out. Usually the conquered people learned the language of their invaders but that hardly applied here. I stepped back and knelt beside Sparky muttering, "I wish I could understand these people, the movies always skim over this part." Sparky's impassive canine face lacked any sign of comprehension. His eyes followed me everywhere and glowed with an intense pink fire when Mason's Crutch got closer to him.

I decided I the next move was up to me so I started off into the center of the cavern. Friday and father fell in behind me and I looked over into the softly glowing chamber where the Chief lived and wondered if I should try to bluff my way into sleeping in his space tonight. My confidence wasn't quite that strong so I put his chamber to my back and looked at the row of cave openings along the far wall. One of them was where I had first emerged and if I found that I'd find the sandbox I now desperately needed.

I picked one I thought was directly across from the Chief's chamber since I didn't remember veering to the left or right when they had escorted me across the main chamber before. When I got close Friday started talking again pointing to each one in turn. Across the arch of each roughly oval opening was a series of characters and dots. The first one I stopped in front of had singing drifting from inside and after a moment Friday's father stepped past me and leaned his head inside giving a sharp whistle. There was a brief verse of song in reply and then four people came out, an elderly couple and two young boys.

They were afraid to look directly at me and held their hands up to shade their eyes from the Crutch while they hummed and sang their questions to the blue giant and Friday. The two boys hid behind their elders and gave out a cry when they saw me and started to run back inside. I looked around for Sparky but he was nowhere to be seen, it was clearly my presence that terrified them. Each one was grabbed in turn by the old man and pulled back in line. Friday gestured to the now empty abode but I could see this choice did not make her happy. I realized she thought I was evicting the foursome and taking their house as mine. I waved my hands in denial and shook my head. There was no comprehension on anyone's face so I went over to the elderly lady and faced her back to the cave. One by one I guided them back into their home and before anyone could argue I stepped over to the next door.

Here too I detected singing inside and quickly moved on before Friday's father forced whoever was inside to come out. The third one had a curious musty odor not unlike some of the food I had been fed and I started to go in but Friday took my arm and steered me toward the fourth door. She led the way in and it immediately turned to the side just like I remembered. It must be their house...cave...space? I could now see alcoves and benches carved into the rock and holes in the wall stuffed with various items. I did not see a candle or torch or even something that passed for a fire pit. More carvings and dots ran along the wall at about knee height, curved up to the ceiling and back down around various shield shaped designs that reminded me of heraldic crests.

The largest one depicted a dome with a hexagonal pattern in it and a figure half in and half out of the uppermost hex. The figure was blue and there were lightning bolts or jagged lines in the space above his head. It looked like a drawing of "Thunderdome" to me but it could have just as easily been a tortoise shell or a beehive. I decided to call Friday's father "Max" and pointed to his chest and then to the crest and said, "Max...Mad Max!" Of course this meant nothing to him and I had to wait several minutes while he sang and whistled and spoke rapidly about something. I felt like I was on a tour of Stonehenge and had picked up the Latin audioguide instead of the English one. It might have been rude to interrupt so I waited till he ran out of steam and then looked around for the room I awoke in.

I found the sandbox room first and could see a lot more detail this time with Mason's Crutch as a torch. I stopped with one foot in and looked at the two of them expectantly. Again father and daughter exchanged words, which ended with Max going back outside and Friday giggling as she passed me, disappearing into the chamber beyond. There was no curtain or door, who would need one in pitch blackness? But now I had the Crutch with me and didn't know how to put it out. I looked around the outer room and stuck it into the first empty cubbyhole I could find. It faded to a dim glow but did not go completely out. I didn't wait long to see if it would because my need was on the verge of becoming an accident and I didn't know how long Max and Friday would give me privacy.

I did what I needed to as quickly as possible and hoped the sounds did not carry very far. I came out to find Friday staring deeply into the geode end of the Crutch, a bowl of water forgotten in her hands. I cleared my throat to interrupt her soft humming and she turned to me, offering the bowl. I washed my hands thoroughly and lacking someplace to dry them I just shook them rapidly and retrieved the Crutch from the wall. I could see the amused look on Friday's face as she walked past and I hoped my smile conveyed the same thing to her. Without further words I followed her into the side chamber choosing to look at the faint shadow her curves cast on the wall rather than their source.

I found that if left untouched, Mason's Crutch would settle down to a very dim glow. It would also react to certain places in the walls of the room as if there were hidden minerals or magnetic fields in those locations. But for all I knew it was reacting to pixie dust. I had no way to scientifically define its uses and limits other than casual experimentation. It still seemed odd that I would be down here carrying around a magic staff but it seemed to somehow fit in the whole surreal landscape around me.

Friday watched me wave the Crutch around and try to balance it on my palm then I tried rubbing it to make it brighter. I even tried saying "Seem Seem Salabeem" and "Abracabra." I looked back at Friday and shrugged. "I guess I should have played more magic users in DnD." She refused to touch it when I offered it to her so all I really knew was that it glowed brightly when I touched it and that the swirly liquid on the inside sometimes seemed turbulent and sometimes seemed like a fine mist. I also knew Sparky seemed bonded to it in some way though he had not returned since I'd left the steam chamber.

I walked back thru the living area and stood in the doorway. I could not see Sparky anywhere. There were just a few people moving around on errands and I could still hear chanting and song coming from the Chief's area. I was now convinced that the music never stopped and it had been wrong of me to assume there were clearly defined periods of activity here. It would be interesting to see what sort of sleep cycle people who lived in darkness all their lives actually needed. I tried to recall research I'd read on the subject when I worked night shift but all that came to mind was that the cycles of sleep and activity slowly spiraled out of sync. A person's sleeping period got shorter and their activity period longer as the conscious mind lost track of its time sense. Would there still be some sort of effect created by the moon despite it being thru solid rock? Gravity was a Law back home but I probably shouldn't even assume basic physics in the light of my present predicament!

Abruptly I shook my head and chastised myself for doing lame experiments and aloofly observing a society that might be planning on keeping me a prisoner or boiling me in a pot tomorrow. I admitted to myself that I had sensed no lasting threat and had even felt a bit cocky with Mason's Crutch in my possession. But that was no reason to assume I knew enough about what was going on around me to make any solid conclusions. I was certain things weren't going as smoothly as anyone expected it to but having no other guide I would have to live for the moment, try to communicate my desire to be non-threatening and most of all, survive long enough to be taken back to the surface world.

A movement behind me made me snap out of my reverie and I saw Friday standing there watching me. She was a constant reminder that I wasn't in Kansas anymore. I stepped thru the doorway and put my hand down at about Sparky's height and said, "I don't see Sparky. My dog...or whatever he is? You know...woof! WOOF!" She shook her head and I put my fingers up at my ears and growled. Still no comprehension and so I mimicked his throaty voice: "Sssssparky Stoppit." With a cry of alarm she ran back inside and I followed her trying to get her to understand. She disappeared into the other half of the living space and I gave up the pursuit. I was not going to go into sections of their home I hadn't been invited into. I called out "Hello um...Friday?" but got no response. I followed it with an "I'm sorry!" knowing she wouldn't understand that either. Dejected and distressed I went back into the sleeping chamber.

I lay down on the bed of moss and lichen that formed the mattress and slid the Crutch in between the wall and me. The cushion I had used to hide my nakedness was still there but it seemed little more than folded layers of some soft spongy material that probably doubled as a blanket when spread out. I tried to sleep but couldn't stop thinking about the primitive conditions I was in. Even Granmaw Wellman's spare bed with the deer skulls above it would have been more comfortable to me. I checked every inch of the bedding and the overhang for insects though I hadn't seen a single one all day. I decided I was better off in complete darkness so I wrapped the head of Mason's Crutch up as best I could and managed to close my eyes for a while.

Friday did not return but after a while I felt someone watching me and I lifted the coverings off Mason's Crutch to bathe the room in its green glow. With its help I could see Max's head looking around the wall at me. His expression was unreadable. He squinted in the sudden light and left. I could still hear the distant song of the village all around me, even thru the walls. My mind ran in circles trying to guess what was going to happen later and it eventually exhausted itself. I did not dream of a snake this time but of walking on a still shoreline at night with no breeze. The sounds of the world swelled all around me; the surf, the birds, the mermaids in the waves, all calling out to me to come play.

Chapter Thirty-Six: Topside.

Ron was the first to awake. The combination of pain relievers and alcohol always hit hard but never lasted as long as his brother KellyRay's binge drinking. He looked around for his flashlight belatedly remembering that he broke it the night before. He gingerly felt along his wrapped up hand. It was throbbing and could use a clean bandage but only hurt when he tried to flex it. There was a dim glow coming from the direction of the cave entrance and he went that way to relieve himself and see what weather the day was bringing. He kicked at KellyRay's boot as he went by knowing enough to avoid his flailing arms but all he managed to do was interrupt the steady snoring coming from KellyRay's open mouth.

Outside the fresh air helped him wake and the grey skies promised rain; a welcome break from the dry autumn weather they'd been having. October useta be cooler than this he mused to himself. It useta start crisp and sharp like a slap in the face. He heard bottles clinking together and called back into the cave "Kell is there enough of that jet fuel left to start the fire? I would thumb wrestle the devil himself for a cup of coffee right now and me with this bad hand!"

There was no answer so Ron went back inside to see KellyRay sitting up, panning his flashlight around the room. His beam lingered over the pile of empties, the cold fire pit and the empty bags of swag. "Sommabitch! They took everything. Didn't leave a G'dammed thing!!" Ron joined him in the search and did not discover the usual pile of goodies and bumpy fungus, only a pile of clothes that belonged to RJ.

"Well not quite everything. They left us RJ's laundry to do." He picked up the various pieces and when he got to the underwear he stretched the band out and shot them at KellyRay. "Here's that emergency shelter you always wanted!" KellyRay batted them aside and cursed at Ron for a bit. "All the hooch is gone too, every drop. I don't understand it. I figured we'd get something in trade for Big Bro...he's gotta be worth something." KellyRay stood up and started toward the exit. "You don't think he woke up early and took off with everything do you?"

Ron waited for him to disappear and then called out "Not naked he didn't!" KellyRay came back and searched the room again with his light. There was a scraping noise as he slid RJ's light across the floor to Ron. "Go check the Scripture room, I'll start the fire."

Ron took the flashlight and quickly looked around the Scripture room. There was nothing in there, there never was. He had only been gone a minute when KellyRay whooped in surprise. "Found it! Found something anyway. Summabitches left their trades in the fire pit. How stupid was that? I almost didn't see them."

Ron rejoined him and added his beam to KellyRay's. In the fire circle were two squat pots and something shaped like a shallow teapot. KellyRay picked it up and it sloshed around, half full of some liquid. "Hot damn, we finally got something to drink!" He lifted it up to his lips intending to drink from the spout and Ron punched his arm. "Hey dumbass what if that only looks like a teapot? What if it's an oil lamp and you're about to chug down kerosene?"

KellyRay looked sheepish and then sniffed the opening. "I dunno, it doesn't smell flammable. " He bent down to examine the other two bits of pottery. "If there's tea in the pot this should be the milk and sugar but no such luck."

Ron looked inside as KellyRay displayed the contents of each pot. "Looks like paste or spread of some kind; one yellow like mustard, the other one's green like relish." KellyRay laughed and stuck his finger into one of the pots, the yellow pigment glistened in the flashlight's beam and he said, "What do you think? Kinda looks like mustard..."

Ron picked up the other pot and looked into it, sniffed it, and shrugged. "You think everything they leave is food when you're hungry. But I'm not carrying you out of here if its cream of bat whizz soup or a primitive form of Sterno."

KellyRay nodded and wiped his fingers on his coveralls. He stood up, returning his attention to the oil lamp and said, "Why would they leave this stuff on the cooking fire if it wasn't meant to be cooked?"

"It wasn't a cooking fire when they were here. But I think it was still lit. Maybe something happens when it's warmed up?" Ron looked closer at the circle of ash and charcoal to see if it had been changed at all during the night but other than seeing where the pots had been left he could not find anything significant. He turned to find KellyRay had put his flashlight down and was going thru the empty liquor bottles and tipping each one over his open mouth for the last precious drops inside. "Hey! Lookit your hip there son, on the right where you smeared that stuff, it's glowing!"

KellyRay half turned and then turned back the other way. He put out his flashlight and cursed in surprise when his coveralls lit up in two stripes as well as the fingertips he'd dipped in the paint pot. "Well that's right nice but we already have glow in the dark paint up here. I was hoping it was some sort of medical miracle that cured cancer or let you hump all night long!"

Ron turned his light on KellyRay and said, "You're lucky it didn't eat thru your clothes and make your wiener drop off. But you have a point. We'll have to give this stuff to Uncle Jack and see if he can get it analyzed. Glowing in the dark might be a side effect of whatever it's supposed to do."

KellyRay gave him a dejected look and said, "That'll take too long. I say if it looks like paint, glows in the dark, and hasn't grown hair on my fingernails then its probably just glow in the dark paint." He put the lid back on the pot and sat it down on RJ's abandoned clothes. "What do you think the other stuff is? "Paint remover?"

"Maybe."

"It smells a bit earthy, like musk and freshly turned soil."

"I reckon everything from that far down smells earthy like.'"

"Hey Ron, how far down do you think they live anyway?"

"I don't rightly know. I heard coalmines could go a couple miles back into the hills and at least a mile deep. Must be beyond that or there'd be lots more places like this." Ron reached over for the pot and gave it a sniff. "I get musty book and sour milk."

"Then I'm doubly glad you stopped me from drinking it."

"Something you said earlier has stuck in my mind son. Why did they leave it in the fire pit if it wasn't meant to be heated up?"

"Well...the little pots weren't actually IN the fire pit, they were just on the edge. The teapot or whatever the hell it is was though. Smack dab in the middle."

Ron looked closely at the bottom of the oil lamp. "Do you think those burn marks were there before? This piece of pottery has been heated up at least once. Maybe last night."

KellyRay came over and looked closer at the bottom of the pot and shook his head. "Doesn't look fresh. If it was I'd imagine there'd be bits of ash and cinders still stuck to it."

"What do you say we heat it up and see? I was going to start the fire anyway, won't hurt none and if nothing happens Uncle Jack can have it too."

KellyRay piled up some kindling and bits of wood. "Well, if it gets all steamy hot and a genie comes out, I'm going to wish for Kathy Ireland to run naked thru this cave and jump into my arms!"

Ron chuckled and threw a stick at him "That's what your first wish would be? You'd use it to see Kathy Ireland naked?"

"Depends."

"On what?"

"On whether or not the genie is hot. If she's hot I'd wish her naked instead! Wouldn't that just get you hard? Having a beautiful naked woman who could grant wishes?"

"The genie in that Aladdin movie was a guy and he sounded like Robin Williams. That's the kind of genie we get these days not the Barbara Eden kind."

"Well hurry up and cook that muther, let's see!"

"Now don't get your bloomers all in a knot granny, there's a science to these things."

KellyRay stuck his toe under RJ's discarded underwear and kicked it in Ron's direction. "Here burn these. Probably smoke out all the bats and bugs if they don't just explode when they hit an open flame."

Ron didn't even have to dodge the projectile; it was wildly off course and disappeared into a dark corner. "Good thing you can shoot straighter than you can kick son."

"I'm damned good with a knife too. Which reminds me, I'd better go out and retrieve my knife if "Them" ain't carried that off too."

"Uh, you know They never leave this cave, even in the dark. So if the knife's gone the dog is too. Don't waste a lot of time looking for it. Get the cooking gear and the coffee from the truck while you're at it. I'm not going anywhere without some java juice in me."

KellyRay stomped down the hillside to where the confrontation with the hyena hounds took place. There was no sign of any dead dogs where he expected one to be though his keen hunter's eyes found traces of blood on the stones nearby.

The air was heavy with the promise of rain and he cursed to himself as he searched. Once the rain fell it would be nearly impossible to find his knife assuming it had fallen out of the hyena and almost as hard to find the carcass if it hadn't. He gave the area a quick second pass and then went to the lock box on the back of Ron's truck. He grabbed up the cooking utensil bag and dug around a bit looking for the coffee. He found a jar of instant and more importantly, a small bottle of Yukon Jack. He shook it and grinned though there was no one around. "Just about enough to compensate for the loss of one knife."

He hefted his burden to his back and zig zagged up the hill on the off chance that the hyena had crawled up there to die. There was no sign of a dead dog here either and the thought that maybe the DeerLady had come back and taken it occupied his mind on the climb up. He dropped the bag next to the fire and let it clang loudly. "I see you're still here and Kathy Ireland isn't so I guess it's not the wish granting kind of lamp! Am I right?"

Ron dug around in the bag and unfolded a wire screen. "I haven't put it on the fire yet, I was waiting for this wire rack to perch it on. Don't want it right on the flames. It might crack open and all the contents would be wasted."

KellyRay took a swig from his bottle and sighed. "I might have to wish for Kathy Ireland to come with her own brewery." He laughed at his own joke and sat down to watch the flames. "I hope its something we can make money from. I've gone damned near broke trying to cater this here family re-union."

Ron continued trying to balance his coffee pot and the oil lamp on the wire rack so that both got equal amounts of heat. "I see that didn't stop you from helping yourself to my stash." He sat back to check his work then leaned against the stalagmite. "I studied on the matter while you were out there son and I'm gonna bet you two bottles of Yukon Jack that this is just tea."

"You'll be sorry when I'm swimming in barrels of whisky with Kathy Ireland."

"Not in a brewery you won't. As painful as this conversation has become I can't help but point out that they make whisky at a distillery. They make beer at brewery. "

"Would I care if I was drunk? And if that's the case I'd be more interested in dressing her up as the St. Patrick's girl."

"St. Pauli girl. And keep your fantasies to yourself willya? I haven't eaten yet."

The cave got quiet and the sound of the fire seemed to settle a calm over both brothers. The simmering oil lamp gave off a stronger, pungent smell but no genie or wind spirit appeared.

KellyRay sighed loudly and stretched out, yawning in spite of himself. "So what's the plan, man?"

"We wait. With at least one of us here at all times. We don't know when RJ will return and if he tries to find his way home and we're not here he could wander around in circles till he mistaken for a deer and shot full of arrows."

"He makes too much damn noise to be mistaken for a deer."

Ron laughed as he fished the coffee pot off the fire with a stick. "That's not what the DeerLady thought!" KellyRay joined in and abruptly fell asleep with obscene visions of the DeerLady and his clueless older brother in his head.

Ron managed a half cup of black coffee and once he was sure KellyRay was asleep he quietly dug deeper into his cooking gear and came up with a small packet of oatmeal cookies.

He sat back against the wall dipping the cookies into his coffee and grinning with satisfaction. He didn't seem to be waking up though. The coffee was having no effect and he could barely smell it over the pungent earthy scent of the oil lamp. He roused himself enough to take it off the wire rack and mumbled to KellyRay "I think...I think something in that pot's making us sleepy. What a pair of dumb-ass hillbillies we are. Done fooled around and smothered ourselves..." His last conscious act was to tip the coffee pot over the coals and then slump down on the cave floor.

Chapter Thirty-Seven: A slug in the Dark.

I was startled awake when rough hands grabbed my shoulders and a heavy weight pressed against me, pinning me back into the alcove. I struck out with my right but my punches were at an awkward angle and had no effect. I had no way of knowing what or who had jumped me in the dark and my terror rose as hands gripped my head and jaw with a casual strength that surpassed any human I'd ever met. Maybe it was my panic but it felt was like the Hulk was sitting on my chest, pressing my head rigidly against the back of the stone alcove. There was no glow from Mason's Crutch and a wave of loss washed over me as I realized it was once again missing or useless to me now.

I struggled against the grip on my head trying to turn my face away and arch up enough to slip out from under whatever held me down. I feared the creature was going to force something down my throat so I clenched my teeth tightly and grunted in frustration as I bucked and tried to roll away. Then the thing sitting on me clamped its dirty hand over my mouth and held it closed. I could taste coal dust and a hint of some spice, cinnamon maybe? Part of my mind tried to place where I'd encountered this before even as I struggled to escape and identify my assailant.

I tried to ask "What? " but I could only make choked, back of the throat noises. I wanted to ask why, ask who, but my attacker was silent in its intent. I felt its grip on me shift and then things got worse. The hand behind my head slipped around and pressed a nostril closed, hard. I grunted as my head hit the stone wall and when I tried to take in a breath something wet and leathery was pushed against my open nostril. I struggled desperately fearing I was to die of suffocation but my assailant seemed intent on plugging my nose in this weird way. I could make no sense of it and I tried to use the half breath I still had in my lungs to blow whatever it was back out. I made a sickly bubbling noise around the foreign object but wasn't able to get it out. My free hand scrabbled and scratched at the creature and I arched up almost double managing to get both arms free and I flailed at the hands on my face to try and feel what was being held to my nose. Maybe it was some sort of inhaled poison or a dirty scrap of cloth? My fingers came away damp and sticky and I thought my nose had begun to bleed.

Again I tried to ask "Why?" tossing my head side to side like a wild thing. I could draw in enough air thru my mouth but inhaling was unthinkable. My fear reached new heights as I realized that whatever it was blocking my nose had begun to move on its own! It was making its way up my nose, into my sinus, toward my brain! Panic and revulsion gave me a sudden strength and I threw off my attacker and knelt against the wall, gasping for air, coughing and honking to force whatever it was out! I could feel something pressing between my eye and my nose bridge and I shook my head wildly as whatever it was tickled and pricked nerve endings inside my skull. I had never felt so violated and sickened as I did at that moment.

I tried to focus on the figure now standing over me. I wanted to pummel the smile off its face and pound it into a bloody pulp against the wall. Holding the right side of my face I was dimly aware that the foreign object had stopped progressing into my skull but I could still feel it blocking my breathing thru that side of my nose. I tried to apply enough pressure to blow it out, shouting at my attacker "What did you do to me you bastard?" I could see it better now; a dull green glow sliding over black, sinuous skin. Spiky hair fell down its back like a mane but the face I saw was too human to be perched on that short demonic body. The figure was looking at me, grinning a too wide grin full of teeth. Its head tilted a bit then it tapped the side of its nose by the eye ridge and said: "There...Sssparky, sssstopped iiiittt."

"What?? Stopped what?" I covered my nose with both hands as if I'd been struck and pinched the bridge of my nose to stop the tingling, the constant firing of nerves that were being assaulted by some slimy thing inside my head. The tingling coursed up between my eyebrows where it burned in a pinpoint of agony. I could see sparks at the edge of my vision with each passing breath and I cried in frustration knowing there wasn't anything I could do about this violation of my body.

I leapt up from my crouched position and tried to tackle Sparky but he just sort of melted down into a dog shape and slipped under my arms. I hit the wall hard and turned in time to see him trot out around the wall partition. His tail wagging in satisfaction was the last sight I had of him before he was gone and Friday and Max quickly came in. They must have been just outside, afraid to confront Sparky. I didn't blame them. Friday handed me a damp, spongy ball of fungus and I rubbed at my face, my nose. I felt unclean and violated even to the point of sticking my finger into my other nostril and trying to press on the thing in my head. All I got for my efforts was a bout of vertigo. I waited for it to pass and slid back into the alcove, my heart still racing and my fists clenching in frustration.

Friday took my hands in hers and told me to calm down. I panted and gasped out "I don't want to calm down! I want a cat scan and a long pair of tweezers! What just happened to me? Why did he do that?" I kept asking these two questions over and over. If I could have crawled out of my own skin I would have. Max disappeared and came back with a long necked jar. He took a sip from it and then handed it to me. I was hoping it was some my dad's moonshine; I would have poured it into my nose and damned the consequences. It tasted like soy sauce but with an alcoholic kick. I coughed roughly for some time and then took a second drink before handing it back to Max.

"Thank you. I don't know how this can help but thank you."

"No, thanks are to The Wellman."

I looked up at him and saw concern on his face, and on Friday's too. "Wait what? I heard that, I mean I think I understood that."

"This one said: No, thanks are to The Wellman."

I turned to Friday with a question on my lips and then realized I could see her better than before. Either the ambient light level had increased while I slept or my eyes were now completely adjusted to this dark place. I was embarrassed by the thoughts that went thru my head and I'm sure her father saw my appraising up and down gaze. I was relieved to see she was every inch human though she had these remarkably wide dark eyes that reminded me of the DeerLady's. I tried to focus only on those eyes and said, "I understood you when you told me to calm down but I was too freaked out to notice."

Friday gave me a skeptical look and it was clear she didn't follow all of that. I dabbed at my nose, which was running constantly, and looked around trying to locate Mason's Crutch. "Have you seen Mason's Crutch? The glowing stick thing I had with me?" She responded in a rapid-fire response that left me hopelessly lost. I tried again using simpler terms. I was getting some of what they were saying but total comprehension was still escaping me. It didn't help that every response was sung instead of spoken, as if each sentence had to fit to an elaborate melody I couldn't hear. "My glowing thing?"

"Your demon has it."

"Demon? Is that what he is? I don't believe in...well he's certainly not 'My' demon." I stood up to leave thinking I'd find Sparky in the sweat room but Max put out a hand.

"To appear in the outside before your color..." Then it was his turn to look embarrassed. "To see The Wellman unpainted is unclear. "

I sat back and said "Oh...yes... Bring me a color." Then I glanced at Friday. "Better bring two pots." She giggled and started to go then halted, waiting for her father to agree. He slowly nodded and after she was gone he gave me that measuring look from the night before. "I think there is more you would paint than just yourself."

I tried to assure him my thoughts had not gone there and that I held his daughter in the highest regard but he was either not understanding it or not buying it. I tried to divert his train of thought and framed a question as simply as I could. "Your daughter does not wear paint. Why?"

""So she may not be Seen. When she has color she may live alone, or with a husband." I nodded as if I understood and he continued to look at me as if to say "She won't be wearing your color anytime soon!" I held my tongue but in my heart I readily agreed. My mind was suddenly filled by images of Captain Cook and Magellan's ill-fated crews. Weren't they all killed when they started to fraternize with the natives? I tried again to take his mind off defending his daughter's virtue by clearing my throat and rubbing the bulge on my nose. "Do you know what this is? What did Sparky put up my nose? How is it making it possible for me to understand the gist of…the bulk of…a lot of what you say? Has it happened before?"

Max frowned and said, "The Wellman's words are scattered. That way is a direction that leads to cave-ins." He sang a bit more song and let it fade away when Friday returned with two pots of the glowing blue paint. She dipped two fingers in and started towards me but her father stopped her, nudging her toward the door. "The Wellman can wear his color well enough without your help." I took the pots from her and solemnly turned my back. After a moment the room was empty and I started by painting my face. It still tingled when I touched it and I saw sparks at the corner of my eyes when I pushed on the swollen side of my nose. Whatever was there was no longer moving around and I could almost convince myself it was just a blocked nasal cavity. Painting my forehead caused a shivering to run down my whole spine and I was reduced to holding onto the edge of the alcove while spreading the paint with the other hand.

I sent dark thoughts at Sparky while I worked and thought back to the last time I had seen him before he re-appeared in my room. My God! I suddenly realized I had asked for this! I had actually said to Sparky: "I wish I could understand these people, the movies always skim over this part." I guessed I was lucky he hadn't tried to shove a Latin-to-English dictionary down my throat. I thought I was being careful in my dealings with these people but I had made the mistake of assuming Sparky was dog-like just because he took on a dog's form. I didn't know what he was; devil, djinn, or Id monster, but it was becoming clear that he was a bigger and more personal threat than all the other things I'd seen down here.

I stepped out of Friday's cave and looked about. In the square were knots of people humming and singing among themselves. When my appearance was noticed a note of discord came into their songs and they moved off, just slowly enough to avoid giving offense but I noticed within minutes a circle of silence had formed around me. I looked back and Friday and Max had come with me to the middle of the 'square' but when I turned towards the sweat room they kept going forward and disappeared into the Chief's chambers. No doubt to report the strange events of this morning.

I stuck my head into the sweat room and surprised several naked men sitting in a circle. One was in the act of pouring water over the stones I'd seen at the back of the room and a large cloud of steam obscured his surprised look. The song they were singing faded and they looked at me terrified that I might join them. Sparky was not in there so I muttered, "Um, never mind...keep doing...whatever."

I looked around for more places he might hide. I saw several people carrying baskets slung at their sides or balanced on their heads going toward a tunnel just barely visible in the gloom of a far corner. I decided to follow them just to get an idea of where they were going and maybe find 'my demon' and give him a piece of my mind. And recover Mason's Crutch.

I hummed a bit as I joined the line of people, trying to blend in. The person just in front of me picked up her pace and hurried ahead, clearly not liking my proximity. I saw the tunnel curve slowly downward and the markings on the wall became further apart. The walls and floor were more natural looking here; they did not bear the worn, polished look of the central chamber. I passed people coming out with their empty baskets and when they recognized me they stopped singing and watched me pass. After several more twists in the tunnel I looked back and noticed that I had at least four people following me at a respectful distance.

A sharp turn to the right and my nose was assailed by the strong odor of decay. I saw dim figures ahead on a sort of jetty out into a shallow pit. In the darkness below I could make out thousands of mushrooms and fungi growing everywhere, on everything. The people ahead of me chanted some ritual words and then shook their burdens out into the dark space. I could finally see that it was baskets of sand and gravel they were dumping into the mushroom patch. Mixed in with that were clumps of things I recognized more from their smell than their shape. Suddenly I realized that I was looking at a colossal sized compost heap.

"Leave it to me to find the city dump!" I turned to find that the line of people had backed up behind me; all of them afraid to interrupt me or just curious as to why I was here. I smiled and nodded to them as I turned to follow my path back up the incline and met Friday on the way down. She was panting and out of breath from her rush to catch up to me. I was glad to see her but she was not glad I was here.

"Why did you come here? The People who Bind the Sun should not go to such a place."

"'People who bind the Sun?' Is that what your people call mine?

"Yes Wellman. Your people first came to us with the Sun bound in jars of flame. But once we narrowed the Covenant it could sing to us no harm. "

I thought she meant it was a rule of the Covenant not to bring light sources here. I wondered if that counted Mason's Crutch? "I came looking for my...demon. Has he been seen since this morning? Since he did this?" And I tapped my misshapen and bruised nose.

"Yes Wellman, in the chamber of our First. They are wrestling and there is no rest within his walls."

I didn't need to follow that completely to know I didn't like the sound of it so I let Friday lead me back up and out towards the Chief's--or First's chamber. On the way I tried to use my newfound comprehension to finally introduce myself. "By the way, my name is RJ Wellman, what's your name?" I saw several emotions pass over her face before she said: "I do not have a name in your tuneless tongue. In the Saga of my people I am MorningSong. But now that you are here our First has given me a new name. "

"What is your new name MorningSong?"

Friday turned her face away and did not answer till we were clear of nearby villagers. "He has named me "Wellman's Shadow.""

I hoped that I understood her words correctly. 'Shadow' could be interpreted as many things. I hoped it meant that I'd have to get used to her following me around. I was pretty sure only Friday and her father understood what I was saying anyway...and possibly the First.

I still felt confused and out of place and desperately needed someone who knew the customs of this society. My brothers were not here and I had begun to doubt they had any clue about what was really going on down here anyway. Friday's face was still clouded with emotion so I tried to coax more from her. "Is that a name you are happy with?"

"I can be happy or sad with it but it is now my name. "

I frowned and just before we walked into the First's chamber I touched Friday's arm. "I gave you a name too, in my tongue. Would you like to hear it?"

Friday looked upset and stepped back from the archway. "This is not a small thing! You must tell me what The People who Bind the Sun will call me!"

"Yes...Well, okay. If I ever meet another of my people I will tell them your name is 'Friday.'"

"Friday? Is that a word of meaning to your people?"

I despaired at explaining TGIF to her and there wasn't enough time to tell her the story of Robinson Crusoe. Even explaining the days of the week would be lengthy and largely futile. I had a feeling a lot of references involving time would not translate to her anyway, slug or no slug. I searched my mind for a suitable answer. Suddenly I remembered that I had once written a DnD scenario that involved the characters surviving a week with each day represented by its namesake God or Goddess. I thought I remembered enough of the research to paint a picture of 'Friday' for her.

"Among my people Friday refers to Freya. Freya was…is a goddess of love and fertility and even other goddesses think she is the most beautiful of goddesses. She holds sway over crops and childbirth. She loves music, flowers, and elves. Freya lives in a beautiful palace where love songs are always sung." I decided not to get into things like hit points or her magical cloak and chariot. I waited for Friday's reaction but it seemed I had upset her again. Her eyes welled up and she squeezed out the tears, pushing past me and abruptly announcing my arrival in the First's Chamber.

Chapter Thirty-eight: Wellman's Aplenty.

I expected to see the First rolling around on the floor with Sparky's dog form or that wolverine looking shape he briefly had. Instead I found him laying on the bottom most step of the First's throne. He was casually licking Mason's Crutch and ignoring the dive-bombing attacks of the crystalline snakebird as it swooped and beat its wings at him.

The First and his two advisors stood helplessly nearby and a crowd of others backed away from the scene unable to reach the door. The trio turned and rushed up to me when Friday announced my arrival and all three simultaneously attempted to explain the situation and demand I do something about it.

I didn't need a translator to realize things were reaching a boiling point. The First had lost all his good-natured patience with my 'demon' and by association me. I walked up to where Sparky was still lounging and said, "What do you think you are doing?" Sparky didn't respond he just eyed me for a long moment. His tiny forked tongue flickered over the globed end of Mason's Crutch and the roiling liquid inside responded as if he was lapping up water from a dish.

Eventually a ripple traveled over his body and he sat up, now in a humanoid form. He was bald, short but powerfully built and other than his glowing pink eyes he was the spitting image of my deceased brother Randy. I thought he had chosen this form to try and soften my anger towards him but it had the opposite effect. Referring to this creature, this demon as Randy or as my brother was immediately repugnant to me.

He regarded me with unblinking amusement but I did not give him the satisfaction of showing shock or fear. Finally he spoke in answer to my original question: "Cleaning Mason's Crutch, it smells of you."

"I see you speak better in this form, thank you for that but can't you clean the staff somewhere else?"

"The light is best here."

"There's a reason for that, its the Chief's throne room!" I watched as he opened the leather sheath and slid Mason's Crutch back into it. I noticed he only had three fingers and a thumb but there was also a dewclaw or spine a few inches up his wrist. I had a lot of questions for Sparky but I wasn't sure I wanted to ask them in front of the First and his followers. I still suspected they understood more of my speech than they let on. "I think you just did this to annoy the First and his... glass snakebird."

Sparky grinned and showed off rows of tiny sharp teeth. "The Quetzal and I have wrestled many times but always to no result. However she has not learned as much from those fights as I have."

"You certainly haven't learned manners! I'm a guest here and your behavior reflects on me. An ambassador to a new land would not turn his dog loose on his hosts!"

"Ambassador? Dog? Why do you continue to make assumptions about everything you see here?" He paused and looked past me at the frightened faces of the crowd. "Is this all you wish to talk about? It bores me to hear it. I only respond because I can see it makes you uncomfortable."

"Well then I have a couple of other questions you might try answering! Why didn't you speak clearly to me before? Do you know what's going on? Why are you and Mason's Crutch bonded together? And mainly, where in the hell do you get off sticking a slug up my nose in the middle of the night?"

"I'm hurt that you aren't finding my gift useful. I traveled to the Second Circle to get it. Maybe I should pull it back out." Sparky made a step towards me and I jumped back putting my hands up defensively. Instead he grinned even wider and shoved the case into my hands. "This is Your Crutch now, bear it while you can." With that he slipped into his hound form and bounded toward the exit. I saw the First watching me closely, fear and concern flashing across his face. I called out after Sparky: "You didn't answer any of my questions!" but the only response I got was that keening laugh that so chillingly reminded me of a woman weeping.

The First took his seat and some order returned to his throne room. He spoke to one of his advisors and the advisor leaned over and stage whispered so that all present could hear: "Demon servit sua natura atque tenebrarum Wellman." The First placed his scepter in a sconce carved in the side of his throne and the quetzal landed on it, diminishing its glow and snaking its tail around the shaft. He looked at me and then gestured to his advisor. The advisor stepped down to be on level with me but continued to address Friday. <Does Wellman's Shadow believe that Wellman is the master of the demon or is the demon the master of Wellman?>

Friday closed her eyes and hummed to herself little snippets of song and repeated several phrases before answering: "There is discord, Second Speaker. The demon hears its new Master but the song of its ancient master still rings in its ears." I think I understood this exchange to be for my benefit more than the First's. Sparky seemed to be truly chaotic in nature and only did what it amused him to do. I chose to ignore the Second Speaker for a moment and asked Friday "What do you think Sparky meant by "Bear it while you can?"

Friday dipped her head and solemnly spoke in a dirge like manner: "You did not sing at the feast last night and you did not learn any of our songs. You cannot control your demon and the Covenant nearly broke between our people. When you were found with the Offering there were two other Wellmans there and much confusion came into our song as we tried to decide which to bring to our circle. The decision was made because the demon slept at your side and it bore the Crutch. The Speakers and the People are not in harmony in this and some are thinking that you were not the right Wellman to bring here."

This was a lot to accept but it was essentially true. "The other two are also Wellmans and they are my brothers. They did not speak of demons to me but they certainly know more about the Covenant than I do."

Friday gave me a pitying look as if I'd admitted to being impotent. Then she spoke to the Second Speaker: "The First's wisdom is clear in this. It is as he foresaw. The Wellman speaks of two other Brother Wellmans in the Above. I happily sing about my father's journey to bring them here." Startled I asked Friday for clarification. "Your father's gone back up there to get my brothers? What for?"

"The Covenant speaks of only one Brother Wellman, but not which one. The First will decide which Wellman is best for his people."

I realized that this situation must not have occurred before; one where the direct successor to the position of Covenant Keeper wasn't chosen by the previous one before they passed over. I was reminded of Sparky's comment about making assumptions and clearly we Wellmans had assumed that the right to chose the successor was ours to make. Now the First had seized this situation to exert his will over the choice. The First was right to bring into question the balance of power but how this would change it I couldn't see.

"My brothers…the two other Wellmans? They've…never been here before have they? How long ago was the last Wellman brought before your First?" Friday cast about for some way of answering me. "I had not seen a Wellman before you came. My father had never seen a Wellman either but his father taught him the song of your people and that of demons so that we may sing as one under the Covenant." She paused and her eyes glanced up at the Chief before whispering. "Our First was Third Speaker when last a Wellman performed in this chamber."

I closed my eyes and sighed. My family who seemed to have all the answers had actually just been blindly trading with these people for hundreds of years based on random luck and whatever good will the first Brother Wellman had laid down. This culture was changed forever by his contact and it was unclear to me whether they have benefited from it at all. I supposed my culture had been changed too or at least the culture of my family since they've spent centuries putting all their energies into trying to keep things secret. I wasn't sure if that was for selfish or altruistic reasons. It seemed to me it was a balancing act no one person could manage.

Friday moved toward the door and gestured for me to follow. "Your voice will be stronger once you have eaten." I followed her gaze around the room and saw everyone present whispering or singing in small groups except us. I slung Mason's Crutch onto my back and nodded. "I have a feeling I will need my voice later."

Most of the food I was offered was a repeat of the choices I had made during the feast. My favorite of those presented to me tasted like a dish of rice pudding. I was halfway thru my bowl before I thought to ask Friday what it was. Almost as quickly I stopped her from replying, fearing it might be termite soup or something just as appetizing. I liked most of what I was served except a dish that tasted like a stew made from oyster mushrooms.

Afterwards she took me to an empty chamber to wait for my brothers' arrival. The whole apartment was dark and looked abandoned when we arrived but Friday sang a high trilling song and slapped her palm on the wall. This caused a myriad of tiny lights and dots to spring to life and I clapped my hands in surprise and appreciation. "More magic! I could spend my whole life trying to figure out how all this works. With your help of course Friday."

She tilted her head to the side as if she didn't trust my words and then sat down on a bench height ledge protruding from the wall. I was surprised that the stone was always warm here and said so. Friday giggled for the first time that day and said "Are your homes kept cold and unfriendly?" I felt I wasn't going to get anywhere explaining that in detail so I just replied "In some homes friends and family are welcome in others they find the air cold and stale. We have not found harmony among all of our people."

"That is because you do not sing enough. You put meaning on a few notes where a whole song would be preferred..."

"There are more than Wellmans where I come from, and many other peoples. They do not speak with one voice and rarely sing the same songs. Only a few of them speak the words of the First Wellman anymore."

Friday gave me another sad look. "Was there no one who knew his song who could have taught it to you?" I looked uncomfortable and thought about my sad academic record. "Well, there were some who might have taught me those words. If I had listened."

"What song did you listen to? Didn't you want to come here and meet me?"

I had to chuckle helplessly at this. Talking to girls was universally difficult! "I'm sure if I'd been told our paths would cross someday I would have tried harder to learn those words."

"Our paths would cross?"

"Um, our songs? If I had known our songs would intertwine I would have tried harder to sing." Friday stumbled up and turned to look out the doorway. I thought she was blushing and didn't want me to see it.

"Our songs are not so intertwined yet Wellman. But surely you realize that a Wellman's Shadow must go where a Wellman goes." I fell silent trying to understand the meaning behind this and what I'd said to embarrass her. She came back over and gave me a hug then quickly stepped out of the doorway. She turned again so her face was hidden from me and I saw her back straighten, tense up. I moved to where I could follow her gaze toward a gathering crowd in the Square. "There are now three Wellmans in our circle and I am but one Shadow!" I realized I still had a mountain of questions and very few of them were going to be answered by the arrival of Ronnie and KellyRay Wellman.

Friday heard the song change before I did when we stepped outside. I saw my brothers being escorted toward the First's chamber and called out to them. Ronnie was guarded but walking on his own and KellyRay was resisting and had to be lifted by a couple of the blue giants that had first greeted me. His toes barely touched the ground and he kicked out viscously. I could hear him cursing and yelling "Give me back my clothes you summbitches!" Ronnie was quiet but alertly looking around. He caught my eye and lifted his head in recognition. I noticed his wounded hand was wrapped in a huge ball of something that looked like silk or spider web.

Once we were closer I could see Ron was covered head to toe in green paint and KellyRay had splotches of yellow dabbed all over him. Some of the places looked like they were bruised underneath. I was suddenly reminded of my nakedness and tried not to stand next to either of them. I swung the Crutch's case in front of me as discretely as I could and tried to think of something clever to say. Ron spoke up first over the rising music and said "Looks like we've been invited to your hootenanny son. I hope you didn't tell them Wellman's are good eating?"

"Damn your hide I can barely say anything to them at all! Why didn't you tell me they spoke some weird combination of Latin, Indian, and Gaelic? And what about Sparky? Didn't tell me about him either! Guess everyone back home keeps a demon under their granny's front porch?" I noticed none of this was making sense to him so I paused to catch my breath and asked a bit more calmly: "What happened to your hand?"

"My hand was bit by one of those damned hounds last night, remember? What happened to your nose? Did you bump against the wall wandering around down here in the dark?"

"I'll explain about the nose later."

KellyRay had stopped struggling and looked me up and down. He kept his hand clamped over his crotch and tossed his head in Friday's direction. "I see you found the native guides to your liking." I blushed and said, "Shut up and Focus. From what I've gathered the Chief up there, the one they call the First, wants to pick one of us to be his Wellman, his Covenant Keeper. I don't think we have the luxury of picking one ourselves anymore. Whatever you do don't let him force you to express a preference between us. I'm not sure what will happen to the other two. Now tell me, how much time has passed since we fell asleep in the cave?"

KellyRay hadn't taken his eyes off Friday; his frank appreciation was making both of us uncomfortable. "Same day far as I know. We found some paint pots and an oil lamp of some kind." He leaned forward and asked Friday "You don't happen to know Kathy Ireland do you sweet thing? Doesn't matter, I bet you could make me forget her..."

"Try to think with more than your weiner willya? Have you even looked around you? You have no idea how big a deal this is! Magic works here dudes, Magic with a capital M. Check this out!" I retrieved the Crutch from its case and it glowed with a bright green light and the liquid inside looked like a tempest in a bottle. KellyRay reached for it immediately and I pulled it back "I want to see if it glows when you hold it but there's a catch."

Almost as quickly, Sparky appeared from behind me as if he'd been there all along. He was in his humanoid form and grinned at KellyRay. "If you become the only Wellman here you can have your pick of the lovelies." I nudged him aside and said, "This is a demon I'm calling "Sparky." I don't think he's the same as Granmaw's Sparky, at least not always, but he's a trouble maker in any form."

KellyRay was speechless, his mouth hanging open in surprise. "You're "calling" it a demon but is it a demon? That's not some sort of costume he's wearing?" Sparky wriggled his eyebrows and showed KellyRay his teeth. "Yes I'm answering to Sparky right now. Nice ring to it don't cha think?" and he put out his clawed hand for KellyRay to shake. "You've got a killer throw with that knife arm of yours. Remind me to give it back to you sometime. But hey, no hard feelings right?" KellyRay reached out to shake his hand but jerked his back pointing to Sparky's three-fingered hand and made a squealing sound as he backed away. Ron didn't offer to shake his hand either and Sparky shrugged and slipped back into the crowd. "Y'all have this munged up enough without my help. I'm just gonna sit back and watch a while."

Ron watched him go and shook his head. "I just don't know what to think about that. Or this glowing rod you have there. I've been told what Mason's Crutch looked like but Granmaw would never let us even see it. Made me promise not to take a peek till I brought it up to the cave for you." He let his eyes slide sideways and said "And who's this, your new wife? She seems be following our every word."

"That's Friday; MorningSong, known as Wellman's Shadow. She's my—our interpreter. And she's not getting every word but from the way she just elbowed me I'd say she understood the word 'wife' well enough, thank you."

KellyRay was still grinning at her lasciviously "Wellman's Shadow huh? I bet that means she gets real close sometimes don't it Big Bro?" Then he lowered his gaze. "Not so Big Bro."

I made a half serious swing at him with the Crutch and he laughed evilly. It reminded me of Sparky's laugh and I grimaced thinking of the mischief those two could cause here. "She's not the only woman here but she's one of the few that can understand even half of what we're saying. Her father probably knows more but he doesn't talk much. He was one of those blue painted giants that brought you down here. And he definitely doesn't like his daughter hanging out with outlanders like us but the First has given her the job of learning our song." I stepped in front of her and gave KellyRay my best Ray Isaac Wellman stare. "Try to show a little respect."

I turned to Friday and gestured to my brothers. "These two Wellmans have not had the pleasure of learning from you. Please forgive their...bluntness. Even among Wellmans there are different songs." Friday looked at me and I could tell the exchange she's heard so far was not making any of us her favorite. She said, "When words fail, the singer must sometimes hum." Then she stepped back a bit as if to give us a bit of privacy and started singing to people in the crowd.

I stepped in closer and huddled with my brothers. " Let me couch this in DnD terms so we can cover things quickly: For me maybe two days have passed, no way to tell here. In that time I've seen some low-level magic or unknown biochemical things going on, I just can't tell you that for sure yet. I believe its magic cause I've seen big stuff too. The Crutch seems to be a key artifact here as is the scepter that the First has. I have a hunch there's more such items, or were. That glass snake thing on it can move around and generate magic effects like Sparky can. I've seen it shape change a bit and it can grow in size. Could be its magic is of a different nature than the magic in the Crutch. Sound or music affects them both. The Crutch glows and seems sensitive to pockets of magic or other magical items. It may do other things, again I don't know. Sparky is linked to it somehow and will follow whoever carries the Crutch.

"I referred to him as a demon because that's what Friday's people call him. Oh and they refer to us as the 'People who Bind the Sun.' A big part of the problem is that I don't know how to control Sparky and they see that as a sign that they might need to replace me as "The Wellman." There are probably political reasons I haven't even touched on yet. The big chief up in the chair was friendly enough last night though Sparky forced a show of magic between us and I don't think he liked the result. I know his advisors didn't. There was a feast afterwards to try and cool things down. Don't know how successful that was. The food here is edible though its largely mushroom based. Oh, and if you get offered something that looks like giant centipede. It is giant centipede. I don't know much more than that. I was asleep for an unknown length of time so I've barely scratched the surface. They seem to sing all the time in a sort of operatic undertone to every conversation. Friday knows how to talk to us in our language and the two old guys next to the First up there are known as "Speakers." I assume that's an advisory role. The color paint everyone wears has some significance though I'm guessing they didn't give you much of a choice, sorry about that, probably my fault. "

Friday came back and said "The First has presented some questions to the Second and Third Speakers that will aid him in his decision. But now that there are three Wellman's here how should we address you separately?"

"Well I told you I'm RJ Wellman, this is Ron Wellman, and that one with his tongue hanging out is KellyRay Wellman. RJ, Ron, and KellyRay should work, right?" Friday shifted her lips side to side and shook her head. "Those words are too hard to give any meaning to my people. I will tell them you are Wellman Blue, he is the Green Wellman, and that one Yellow Wellman." KellyRay made a face and Ron snickered and said, "I always thought you were Yella." Friday gave them both wide-eyed stares for a long moment, decided not to reply and turned away to speak to the Third Speaker. Who in turn nodded and started to converse with the Second Speaker. This must have been some sign that they were about to begin because the singing faded to a background noise and conversations in several groups became a complementary humming noise.

Chapter Thirty-nine: Life is a Mystery.

I looked around to see where Sparky had gotten to but could not see him; the quetzal was flying around in the upper parts of the chamber among the stalagmites that jutted down from the ceiling. I assumed the demon was up there too from the aggravated way it was buzzing and flashing its colors. I hoped it didn't reflect the mood of the First. We gathered at the base of the First's throne and I was relieved to see Friday still standing with us. I looked thru the crowds to either side and tried to find her father among the blue guards. They were all gathered together and chanting as one. I couldn't help but notice there were a lot of them and they were between the only exit and us.

"Friday and I will try to translate the questions as best we can. And she'll translate the answers back to the Speakers. Don't speak directly to the First unless he comes down to our level. I think that was one of the mistakes I made last night. Oh yeah, try not to use words that refer to the sun or the passage of time. I haven't worked out how time is measured here, or even if it is." KellyRay looked like he was finally taking this seriously and he said, "What if we give an answer they don't like, are we f--ked?"

"I don't know. They've been good to me so far but I haven't pushed it, haven't tried to openly defy anything I was asked to do. I think we could bluff the average citizen here but don't try to BS the First. He's got some plan behind all this and remember what I said; don't indicate a personal choice over any of us. I figure it's the best way we all stay safe and sound, got it?" KellyRay nodded and I saw his tongue push the side of his cheek where his dip of snuff usually was and I was glad he didn't have anything to spit out just then. I looked over at Ron who was looking a bit shell-shocked. He whispered: "Son I'm not sure I can take all this in. I think I feel like you felt when you first came back to West Virginia. Now I can see there was a whole lot of second level shinola going on. I never dreamed the stakes would be higher than losing our supply of Indian artifacts. I'm willing to do whatever to keep that going for our whole family but I might need a nice quiet place to freak out after this is said and done."

My reply was cut off as the First speaker gestured and the one known as Second Speaker sang a short burst of song. It sounded like a proclamation of some kind. Friday was the only one who responded and she put the flat of her hand over the top of each of our heads and stated our new titles. When she said Wellman Blue I noticed that only some the people in the 'chorus' around us repeated the name. Then when Ron was introduced as the Green Wellman a different group repeated his name. The same thing happened when Wellman the Yellow was named and I realized that each group that responded was painted in the same basic color. Apparently we had our built in cheering sections and I hoped that whatever happened to the two of us who weren't selected didn't also happen to the people of that color. I had chosen my color simply because the first guy I saw here was wearing blue. Ron and KellyRay hadn't had a choice at all far as I knew. I caught my brother's looking at me for some re-assurance. I had none. I put my hand on my chest making a fist; our childhood signal that Crunch Time had arrived.

Second Speaker pointed to KellyRay "Quaestiones sunt ad te, Wellman dui." KellyRay looked pale and his eyes darted around for an exit. "Don't start with me! I got nuthin to say to naked bald men!"

I hissed at him to be quiet and pleaded with Friday "Just say ummmm, say he sincerely hopes his answers will please the First." Words were exchanged and the Second Speaker didn't look offended so I assumed Friday was being politic with her answers. Maybe the First should send her to the Above instead of picking one of us clueless hillbillies? I shook my head and re-focused as the first question was finished and translated to me by Friday. I hadn't told my brothers about my enhanced vision and understanding but they seemed willing to accept my role as co-translator. I reminded KellyRay to look at the Second Speaker instead of me and repeated the question in a droning voice. I admit it was a bit melodramatic but I hoped that the listeners would believe I was doing a better job if it sounded a bit more operatic to their ears.

"The first question is: <An unquam carbones effodere de terra?> "Have you ever dug the coals from the earth?"

KellyRay looked relieved and shook his head "No sir, I have not." Friday and I conferred a bit and then passed it on back to Second Speaker. I was thinking of what my own response might have been. So far we agreed; there hadn't been enough coal left in Wayne County to keep a mine open in decades. However long that was to the People.

<"Cum sol est, te, quid facis?"> "When the Sun is full upon you, what do you do?"

"What? What do I do when the sun is up? I do what everybody else does. I get up, I eat something, I go to work, I have lunch, I take a dump, I go back to work, I come home. Then I have something to drink and I watch TV. Same as those other two losers."

I covered my face and sighed, looking at Friday. She was still trying to translate all that into something relevant. I offered: "Tell the Second Speaker the Yellow Wellman labors with the common people at whatever task he finds before him." Friday looked happy with my version and passed it on. When she was done she said softly "Did you ask me to speak a falseness, or just a less lyrical answer?"

"In the circle of my people both answers might have been given. The gap between our peoples is larger than the Second Speaker realizes."

The Third Speaker stepped down to our level and with a nod to the Second Speaker he spoke to Ron. <An consonat omne Wellmans cantare?> "Is your song harmonious with the other Wellmans?"

Ron thought about his answer but before he came up with something KellyRay spoke up "Yeah everybody gets along with Ron here. He's a good ol' boy if there ever was one."

Second Speaker looked ruffled and waited for Friday's translation then he puffed up his chest and said, "I no longer need to ask the same question of the Yellow Wellman."

Ron looked annoyed at KellyRay but nodded and said, "Yes, I try to get along with everyone. If I have a problem with someone I try not to make it my opening round in the negotiations."

I tried to help Friday with this one but she touched my arm to silence me. "The Green Wellman and the Yellow answer your question in harmony." I looked at my brothers and then nodded. I hoped it was close enough because I wasn't going to be seen arguing with Friday in front of the whole court. We had to present a united front even if we disagreed on the details. She was looking at me for approval and I said "In harmony, yes."

The First leaned forward and touched Second Speaker with his scepter. They spoke quietly to each other and then he returned looking grim. It didn't surprise me that the next question was directed to me. <Numquid et alia tribus in foedus populi, qui honorem?> "Are there other tribes who would honor the Covenant?"

I looked at my brothers and Friday who bit her lip waiting for my reply. The background song dropped to a hum and the only other thing I could hear was Sparky laughing out loud from somewhere up against the ceiling. He wasn't helping. I took a deep breath and sighed, turning formally to the Second Speaker in such a way that I could watch the First's reaction when my words were translated. "There are many tribes and as many songs but I have never heard another tribe sing of the Covenant. I am a Wellman and I only know what songs a Wellman can sing." Friday looked in awe at me. "So you can sing!" and I even caught her father nodding in approval. The First was eager to hear my response but wasn't quite as pleased as the others when the translation came across. Ron leaned in and said "Nice move, I hope you can follow it up."

Third Speaker turned to KellyRay and asked him <Cum Wellman est homo, quid fecisti populum tuum superstes auxiliator?> "When you became a man what did you do to help your people survive?"

"What the hell? Didn't they already ask me what I do for a living? Tell them I hunt for furry little animals and do a bit of car repair on the side. " After a long discussion with Friday in which I tried to explain what a car was we decided to say that the Yellow Wellman sought out food and things to make his home warm when he wasn't helping his neighbor's to sing better." I felt pretty good about that answer even if it was dripping with obfuscation. The next question was asked of Ron and it snapped us all back to remembering how serious our answers were.

<Quid multiplicia dona 'Oblatio'?> "What happened to the many gifts in the "Offering?" I was glad Ron got this one because I couldn't answer it and I was afraid KellyRay would answer something like "Traded them for booze." Ron was giving his answers a lot of thought and at least this time KellyRay didn't try to answer for him.

"I tried to share them round the family. Sold some of them sure but there was always a mystery item or two we either stored or sent off for study. A lot of them ended up on a shelf in my trailer. "

Friday shortened this answer too and I hoped it was not too objectionable to the listeners. "The gifts were shared among the people according to their need."

Suddenly the First reached forward and stopped Second Speaker from asking me the next question with a touch of his scepter: <Verba vestra parvi et tuneless. Cantus Primus Wellman ut ostende nobis fecit.> "Your words are short and tuneless. Teach us a song as the First Wellman did."

I looked around helplessly and said "Me? I can't sing...uh, without my choir. The brothers Wellman will have to help me. The more the merrier as we say in the Above."

Friday saw her father coming over thru the crowd and she backed away. "I cannot help you with this question Blue Wellman. I will translate for the People, and my father will translate to the First and his Speakers." I looked pleadingly at her but she was prevented by some unspoken rule. I wondered if she'd known all along the questions would lead to this? Perhaps she did but either she was prevented from saying so or had more confidence in us than I had.

I turned to my brothers and let them in on the First's request. "I wish they'd asked for something else! What song can we sing to these people? Remembering that it'll have to be translated. I can't sing at all, KellyRay can but only when he's drunk and Ron your twang is so bad that it can curdle milk in the next room!"

Sparky stepped up and joined our little huddle. He was still trying to look like our brother Randy but all that was doing was making us even more nervous. "How's it going boys? The chief isn't going to wait forever for you to start. I've been listening in on what he and his Speakers have planned and if this doesn't go well...Let's just say you can forget about seeing the next sunrise."

I tried to ignore him but I could see he was getting to KellyRay. He kept looking at the First and then over at his guards. I was worried he'd try to grab a knife and bolt. Sparky looked around at our blank faces and said, "Guess I should go topside and start over with another family. Maybe there's an Atkins kid who can carry a tune and won't ask too many questions."

KellyRay's face got stormy and he blurted out "The Atkins boys can suck it! One of those idiots set fire to a railroad tie and then pushed it down the hill behind our trailer!" He looked like he was going to take a swing at Sparky so I snapped my fingers in front of his face. He struck my hand away angrily but looked back at our group.

"Ignore him KellyRay. I told you he's a troublemaker. We can do this as a group, as brothers, OK?"

He still looked agitated and I knew if Sparky stuck around we wouldn't be able to agree on anything. I opened the Crutch's case and slid the top out where he could see it. I gripped it just below the globe and said "Hey! You there, Sparky! Go find a dark corner and stay there till I call you." He flinched as if he was going to dash off immediately but then just waved as he slowly walked away. "Give me something hard to do why don't you? Find a dark corner in this cave? You can do better than that. Or can you? I know KellyRay can...." When he was out of sight and hopefully out of earshot I turned back to my brothers.

"Country music?" Ron suggested. He had gotten all serious and grim as things progressed around us and I wondered if his military training included anything about dealing with native peoples. There was no time to ask but at least he wasn't on the edge of freaking out like KellyRay was.

"We don't want to permanently depress these people do we?"

"Hey Kenny Rogers is good music. Ask anyone around."

"Plus it should be something they can relate to. No one down here is gonna understand riding on a train or poker."

"Sheesh. I suppose you'd like some Guess Who?"

"Who?"

"Don't start that! "

"No I'm just thinking of songs we might know about non-modern things. What's that one they have about Mother Nature? "

"I think its called Mother Nature."

"Do you know the words?"

"Thinking...thinking...No. Not all of them. And neither do you."

"I was thinking we could just 'do wop' behind you and you could lead the choir like you said."

"Way to cop out Ron. And let me get us killed? Christ! We need something really simple that we all three know."

"Well he only asked you to sing, it was your idea to make this a three man band."

"You can't back out now. I can't tell you how serious this is. These people live music twenty-four seven. Imagine being boo'ed off the stage at Woodstock."

Silence.

"Except at Woodstock no one ate the lousy acts did they?"

"They're not cannibals! In fact the only meat I've seen is what looked like a giant centipede though meat might have been mixed in with some of the stews and things."

"Maybe they only eat their honored guests. Or the tone deaf ones anyway..."

"C'mon, focus! How about The National Anthem?"

"Yeah... 'Oh say can you see...? ' How's that go again?"

"We don't know our own national anthem?"

"I know O Canada but I can only sing it with a silly voice."

"We're not singing O Canada. Why in the hell do you know the Canadian national anthem? Wait, now I'm not focused, tell me later! How about something religious?"

"Well not too religious. They've had a little exposure to that already and look where they are now."

"Riiiight."

"Something kinda religious but not really and something we all three know."

"What's popular? What was on the radio when you drove down?"

"I stopped listening to the radio just north of Columbus. Nothing but static and farm reports after that."

"Ok you can Shuuuuut the F--k up!"

"Ok Ok! What did you listen to then?"

"A cassette tape."

"What tape?"

"Oh...I think it was Madonna."

"Christ! And you were making fun of Kenny Rogers?"

"Please, pay attention! We're going to have to get something together quick. Who knows there might be a death penalty clause for delay of concert."

"Rich, which Madonna album was it?"

"The Immaculate Collection."

"Son even I know that's a greatest hits album but its like 10 years old. How often do you BUY music anyway?"

"When it goes on sale. Besides it was a gift. How about Jimmy Buffett?"

"You're the only one here who knows the words and I doubt these people have ever heard of a cheeseburger."

"I know that song."

"What the Cheeseburger in Paradise song?"

Both of us looked at KellyRay blankly. "I know 'Like a Prayer.' It played everywhere, even down here. Gets stuck in your head and you can't stop singing it."

"Ok, how's it go?"

"Like a little.... no....I don't...somebody get me started... all I can think of is the chorus."

"Sheeee-it. This isn't going to work. We're dead meat my brothers."

"We have to try something!"

"Mmmmmmmmnnn mmmmnnnnn little prayer... mmmnnn something something."

"Stop trying to help me will you? I know how to figure out how it starts you just picture the video."

"The one with Black Jesus in it? "

"It wasn't Black Jesus it was...Well just leave that part out for now. We're not going to be acting out the whole video anyway. I'll start but if you guys leave me hangin' I'll kill you both!"

"I have a serious feeling that if we screw up you'll have to get in line for the killing thing."

"OoooooK. I'm thinking video...church...Madonna...she's singing...Got it! "Life is a mystery!" That's how it starts."

"Oh I think this'll work. It almost sounds like a hymn or something anyway."

"I think that was the idea... damn my stomach hurts."

"The chanting's stopped, we have to go do this NOW."

"Lord Lord Lord...You sure we can't sing "Picked a fine time to leave me Lucille?"

"YOU can do that as an encore, now stay focused."

"Riiiight."

"Is it too late to get drunk? I always sing better when I'm drunk."

"You mean you think you sound better when you're drunk, but you don't, trust me."

"What's the first line again?"

"Life is a mystery!" And sing it like its a meditation or something."

"Yeah yeah and you guys come in and follow my lead, do the choir thing, not the Do Wop thing."

""Riiiight."

"Uhmmm, what's the second line?"

"We've got to get started now!!"

"Wait wait, what do we do when it comes to the instrumental part?"

"Just keep clapping and singing...go out into the audience like you see some choirs do. Get all charismatic with it."

"Got it...Ad lib but don't get too showy."

"I feel sick..."

"Who told these people we could sing anyway?"

"You did!"

"I admit now that was an Idiot move in a society where everyone can sing!"

"Go time. Been Nice knowing you. But not very."

"Save it for later. We still have to get thru this and get out with our skins."

"Just one thing before we go."

"You picked a fine time to leave me..."

"Asshole!"

The crowd was silent for the first few minutes of our performance and I'm sure most of them didn't know what to make of it but once the chorus came around a couple of times we actually had some of the Yellows singing along. KellyRay's voice being the stronger he took over singing once I got him past the first few words. He liked being the focus of the crowd's attention and it didn't hurt that he moved out from the oval space around the feet of the First's throne singing and clapping much like he would have at church back home. If I didn't know better I would have thought he was drunk but I guess he realized there was no need to hold back, we might not get a second chance. We were literally singing as if our lives depended on it.

Afterwards I realized we weren't in that much danger to start with but I blame Sparky for putting that thought in KellyRay's head and letting it build up between us. The demon laughed and made faces at us from behind the crowd but for some reason avoided taking direct action to interrupt us. In my case he just made me get goofier. I followed KellyRay as he walked around in a big circle and when he got to where Friday and her Father were standing I got her to clap and sing with me while doing a bit of a side to side shuffle. These people really liked music and it didn't seem to matter that they couldn't directly understand the words. Enough of the lyrics were repeated that they quickly caught on, phonetically anyway.

KellyRay faltered on the second set of lyrics but I came over and let him harmonize with me as I sang them. Ron was more reluctant to join in, barely doing more than swaying and clapping along. I put my arm around him and guided him over to where some of the people had drums or possibly they were just pots they'd turned upside down. He tried to use it like a bongo and it didn't take much encouragement for several of the drummers among the people to follow the beat. I guess our whole performance was more primitive than anything Madonna had ever done on stage but honestly how were they going to know we were doing it wrong? They hadn't heard it before.

When we finished there were high five's all around. I think that might have been the first time "Them that Live Below" saw a high five in action but it immediately caught on. Breathless, we waited to see the First's reaction. I saw the slightest smile curl around the corner of his mouth and he said one of the few words I ever heard him speak directly to us. He gestured with his scepter and said "Again."

KellyRay didn't get to sing "Lucille" to the People because after going thru "Like a Prayer" twice we begged off asking for drink and food. We were led outside with everyone in high spirits and I'm sure I heard the chorus from the song being repeated about a 100 times during that night.

Everyone wanted high fives from us as well. My hand was sore from the repetitions before the evening was done. I was worried that we'd changed a lot of things with one song but at least we were alive and had sent a positive message to these people and their chief.

KellyRay worried me a bit with his crowd of yellow painted fans. He was enjoying his sudden rock star status and especially the attention of several young females in the group. I caught him staring at them with lusty eyes and he gave me thumbs up. He didn't seem to need a slug up his nose to communicate his intentions. I shouted to him to remember his manners but he waved me off, an arm around a girl on each side. The lack of light didn't seem to be bothering him much and at some point during the night he disappeared. Part of me envied his cavalier attitude and I wondered how different our arrival here might have been if he'd been in my shoes. Been the first to make contact? What would we be doing now? Would the other brothers have even been invited down?

I looked around for Friday and was told in vague gestures by one of the people bringing food that she had remained with the First and his Speakers as they discussed our fate. I hoped that her report of my behavior would reflect well on us. I hadn't exactly made a devotee of her but I felt that if we were tossed out or sent away in shame it wouldn't be for what I did but what I didn't understand.

It occurred to me that I had understood the server's speech much more fully than just a day ago. I was certain that I wouldn't need Friday to help me over the tricky bits at all in a few days and that thought gladdened my heart immensely till I saw Sparky moving thru the crowd with a group of Yellows. It reminded me where my newfound talent for language came from and I couldn't help but wonder what else it was doing to me. The bump on the side of my nose had almost gone away but I still couldn't breathe thru my right nostril. Poking at it caused little sparks at the edge of my vision and if I kept it up I got a bit dizzy. I couldn't do anything about it medically and I still needed the beneficial aspects so I tried not to think about it too much.

Ron sat nearby unable to chat with anyone without my attempts at translating. He kept asking what each food was made of and I tried to council him to just try things and see what they were like. He seemed oddly ill at ease, as typically he was able to navigate any social situation, even when it was one over his usual station. I asked him what was bothering him and he pointed at the Crutch guarded by Sparky, again in his dog form.

"Two things aren't sitting right with me Big Bro. First off, that represents something very scary to me. You might have wasted your youth playing DnD and secretly praying for a world full of magic but I only played a few games and moved on. You've also had at least a day or so more than I have to get used to the idea of magic actually existing. But what does that mean for us back home? Why does magic work here and not on the surface? If it is magic that is. None of the objects I've taken from the cave ever glowed on its own like that. Nothing ever flew or levitated and nothing ever helped me understand the speech of some lost Aztec tribe. I worry what the First would do if he knew he had access to energies that we couldn't also control. And I've been thinking about all those questions he asked us, what he might have been fishing for? Its one thing for us to give them flashlights and fire starters but have you seen anything from our world here? Any jewelry? Anyone chewing gum? Anything at all? I haven't. What has he done with it all? I can't see very far in this light but I'm pretty sure I'd know a jar of dad's moonshine if I saw it. This is a celebration and no one's getting drunk! Did the chief drink it all himself or has he squirreled it all away someplace for study like we've done with a few of the more obscure items?

"Here's something else you can think about. Our family's been trading with these people for a couple hundred years giving them booze and worthless items. If the boss man figures out the imbalance in the trade relationship don't you think he'll do something about it? To us?"

Sparky shifted into his human form long enough to chuckle and slap Ron on his back. "I like this one. He's trying to think ahead now, at least a little. Should I go tell the First that magic doesn't work in sunlight and that Mason's Crutch is only a walking stick up there?"

"Is that true? Magic can't work in sunlight?"

Sparky shook one of his clawed fingers at me "Can't make it that easy on you boys, what would you learn if I gave you all the answers?"

"You're a bastard, you know that? Why don't you go down to Georgia and fiddle about, leave us hillbillies alone for a while?"

Sparky laughed that disturbing laugh of his and said, "That would have been a good one to sing here! But seriously RJ, let me tell you two things before we go any further. One: It's not nice to call your demon names, especially if they involve dubious lineage. And Two: The biggest difference between you and me is that I know the rules and I've been playing this game a Hell of a lot longer than you have. Best remember that when discussing how to walk this maze."

Ron made a face like he'd smelled something bad and said "Just tell me one thing; Where are we, exactly?"

Sparky said "Why Son you're below the Dark and into the Warm. And when you understand what that means you'll be ready for the Big picture." Sparky slipped back into his dog form and ran off laughing even harder. Ron sat back down and pulled me down with him. "I'm with you, that dog is a bastard by any standard."

Chapter Forty: Missing Rota.

I took Ron down to the refuse pile I found earlier and asked his opinion. We decided it was a combination of midden and compost pile. We looked closely to see if anything other than organic waste was being thrown in and saw nothing.

"I half expected this to be their graveyard as well but there's no sign of what they do with their dead."

"Or if they even die."

"I think we can assume they do. They obviously age so I think they die. But I'm not sure I want to find out firsthand." I quickly guided him away after our brief look remembering Friday's words that People who Bind the Sun shouldn't come here. I was hoping we had time to do a bigger tour of the place and see where some of the larger tunnels led to but it had been several hours since the feast has started so we headed back assuming we could expect an answer to our fate sometime soon.

"What do you think of that name: "Populus qui ligatis Solis?" "The People who Bind the Sun?"

"I think its pretty good choice considering they don't have a sun in their world. I could do with some strong flashlights down here; everything seems to be in a greenish grey twilight. Was it like this the whole time you've been here?"

"Till I got a slug shoved up my nose, yeah. Then shortly afterwards things looked lighter and I started grasping concepts in their speech that had eluded me before."

"Must be nice, except for the slug part. You can start a new career when you get home if it sticks with you."

"I had thought of that, and if we're down here too long I might have to. There's a nightshift job back in Indiana that is starting to miss me."

"Did you tell these people that you also had a family back there who might miss you?"

"I didn't, no. It's been pretty whirlwind since the funeral and all the stuff Granmaw tried to tell me. Then you guys and then the DeerLady and remember I didn't expect to be whisked off to a faerie mound after getting drunk. Plus I've been busy checking things out here too."

"I saw you checking some things out earlier!" Ron grinned and made a curvy shape in the air. "Your girl Friday will be my girl Friday if they pick me won't she?"

My face clouded up and I said, "Now don't start that again! I haven't even touched her except accidentally and I'd expect you to do the same. KellyRay won't listen to reason but I'm hoping you see that blindly joining into this carnival will get us all in hot water."

"You two that close? What would your wife say?"

I paused in mid step and said "I'm telling you It's not like that but its ALSO not like I could explain away a couple hundred nude body paint enthusiasts to anyone who hasn't been thru what we have."

Ron grinned. "They ARE a healthy bunch, aren't they?"

By then I'd found my way back to my chamber and was secretly relieved I picked the right one on the very first try. I did the wall slap and song thing like I'd seen Friday do and the wall lights responded to me. Ron gave a low whistle but I stopped him cold. "I wouldn't do that if I were you, whistling seems to be reserved for the blue guard and they use it like traffic cops to issue orders. So it can be heard over the singing I guess. We don't want to be misunderstood by the locals especially where it comes to the warrior caste."

Ron nodded and stumbled a bit trying to sit down. I took out the Crutch and held it aloft till he had a look around.

"Looks like a set from the Flintstones. Think they have a pig under the sink instead of a garbage disposal?"

"I haven't seen any sort of plumbing here. There's a toilet alcove over there but it's really more of a cat box than anything. Friday brought me a finger bowl to wash my hands in afterwards but I don't know where she got it. I'm not even certain it was water. I saw steam in a sauna room of some kind but I didn't see whether the water was carried in or if it came from a hot spring. The walls here are always warm so I'd say we're far enough below ground to get the benefit of magma activity."

Ron gestured for me to hand him Mason's Crutch. "C'mon, I want to see if this glows for me too. I think I'm ready to find out if I'm a wizard or not."

I turned Mason's Crutch -- The Crutch -- around handle first and passed it to Ron. The globe of liquid swirled and sloshed but I was sure it was just from the movement. When he grasped it the green glow didn't diminish one bit but he gasped and leaned forward stroking the globe as if it was a crystal ball. "Lord Lord Lord! I can see...I can see it all... Jesus H. Christ what's that!" And then he slumped back on the bench.

I jumped up and cried out his name, shaking him hard till I saw the grin on his face and he broke out laughing. "Just messing with you Big Bro, you seemed to put so much stock in this magic stuff I knew I could pull your leg. Guess it's still just a chemical light to me."

I frowned and thumped his shoulder as I sat back down. "Good one Ron, when I figure out how to cast fireballs with it I'll keep you in mind. And maybe it's just a continual light staff or maybe it's more than that. It did more than just glow before. When they had their first feast for me the chief's quetzal got all agitated with Sparky and they had a little stand off. The Crutch got brighter and...well got a lot brighter. And it changes intensity when its near magical things like Sparky or certain mineral seams in the wall..."

"Quetzal?"

"Yeah, the crystal snake bird thing perched on his throne. Surely you noticed it."

"You mean that glass sculpture he has on his scepter? Didn't look alive to me. I noticed it was gone later but I thought he'd just took it off or picked up another scepter."

"No it was alive, it flew up to the ceiling when we were being questioned. It doesn't like Sparky but he delights in tormenting it. The First's scepter is like the Crutch and the Quetzal is bonded to it like a familiar somehow. How did you miss it? It was flapping and throwing off sparks the whole time."

"You sure you really saw that? Was Sparky there then too? And the Crutch? Maybe Sparky was doing it to you or maybe there's things you can only see or detect when holding the Crutch or when you're the Chosen One. Things that others can't."

"The crowd seemed to react to it."

"Who says they can't do that naturally? Doesn't mean we can."

"But...but what about Sparky? You saw him shape change, you saw him talk one minute and run off like a hound on the scent in the next!"

"I admit that a shape changer is pretty strong evidence when it bites you on the hand."

"Assuming it was him and not just one of the hyena hounds. But you're right; I totally forgot that little detail. Let's peel that webbing off your hand and see how bad a demon dog bite is."

Ron sat the Crutch down and tugged on the wrappings. Under the silk like exterior was a webbing of white, flossy material that reminded me of cotton candy. I sat back a bit and watched him unwind and peel off the layers "If a bunch of spiders come running out I'm taking my dice and going home."

He gave me a sheepish grin and said, "This hasn't hurt one bit since we woke up here and I kinda forgot about it. This bandage is as light as a feather and didn't bother me none while we were out there clapping or eating. I was tempted to take it off sooner but I was kinda waiting on someone to tell me that it was OK to do so."

Ron's hand was perfectly normal that I could see. He was squinting at it up close where there had been tears in the skin and puncture wounds but nothing was visible any longer. I held the Crutch up close to his hand to help him see and tiny lines of silver appeared thru his skin like he'd waved it thru a cobweb. I passed the Crutch to him and said "Can you see the little lines where it looks like it was stitched back together? Tiny ones thin as well, spiderweb?"

He nodded and flexed his hand. "Yeah! And it's good as new."

"Just Like Magic!"

"Just 'like' Magic is exactly it. Whether its Magic, Faith, or Pharmacology I'm not gonna look a gift horse in the mouth." He gave the Crutch a closer inspection and said "Remember the story about Mason's baby boy Jason being cured of the croup by these people? It may not be magic, but if there's medicine here that can work this fast above ground there's a fortune to be made in the drug industry alone."

"Which is why we can't let other people know about this place. That's been one of our family's rules since the beginning. "

"Yes, its part of the Covenant and I won't be the one who rats them out to Big Business but even in that story the "healing" took place underground. "

"We'll have to test it somehow. How about I whack KellyRay on the head with the Crutch and see if he still has a bump when we get topside?"

"If he's doing what I think he's doing, he might not ever want to go back."

"Of the three of us he'll be the one least missed. Even his ex-wife won't come looking for him. She knows he doesn't have a dime to his name and actually, she's supposed to be paying him child support or he'd be in county jail over it right now."

I nodded soberly. "I have a wife and family but I'm not so certain I'll be all that missed. Still I'd like to tell my kids that magic actually works somewhere in the world." I laughed bitterly as a realization hit me. "Guess I got to visit the Magic Kingdom after all! I'm sure they would have handled all this better than I have. Not to mention they can sing better than I do."

"Everyone sings better than you do. If they're picking ambassadors on that basis you might as well pack for home now." Ron stopped flexing his hand and gave me a serious look. "Magic Kingdom is exactly right. But don't knock your own instincts; I think you've done a good job of adapting. So our best bet is to keep doing that. Going forward from here we have to have faith that regardless of whether or not these things work in our world we're currently NOT in our world. We can adapt to it or rattle around in the dark pretending things don't work differently here. Besides, don't you think it'd be fun to believe in magic for just a little while?"

"You amaze me sometimes Ronald Glen Wellman. Just when I think you're just a redneck vet with a pick up truck and a kick ass stereo you show me there's a bit of the ol' mountain wisdom in you."

Ron shrugged and gave his trademark grin. "Whatever makes sense at the time, that's how I make my choices."

"Speaking of choices, we should hear something soon. I have no doubt that it'll be a big decision but I no longer fear for our lives."

Ron chuckled and put his feet up on the bench. "Long as we can sing for our supper eh? What do you do want to do for an encore?"

"I have to admit I've spent a little time thinking up other songs that have universal themes. I want to be ready in case we're called to do another command performance."

"KellyRay turned out to be a showman didn't he?"

"Its not that much of a surprise to me. He's always had it in him but he's been too busy being ornery to do anything worthwhile."

"Do you think they'll pick him?"

"There's at least a dozen of the yellow painted ones that would vote for him, if this was a democracy that is. I wonder if the First wouldn't see his charisma as a threat. We don't really know what holds these people together yet."

I nodded and put the Crutch back in a cubbyhole. Its light waned but did not fade altogether. "Do you want to stay?"

"I don't rightly know RJ. I spent a lot of time learning about the family business if you catch my drift, but I was content to have it fund my truck payments. I don't think I want the job of full time ambassador. I like that truck though and just a few hours ago I was looking forward to off-roading it home to some biscuits and gravy."

"Wait till the caffeine headache kicks in. Though come to think of it, I didn't have one when I got here, or a hang over. The only thing I've drank besides water was some of their cocoa drink. It was good but I didn't get a buzz from it. Still it must have stopped the craving, that or whatever's in the water. Granmaw Wellman swears by it."

"Or maybe it's Magic?"

I chuckled and said, "Imagine how rich we'd be if we had a caffeine based hangover cure that was also chocolate flavored? We'd walk among men as gods you and I..."

Ron laughed with me this time and said "And think of the slogan: "Hand prepared by topless native women from sources deep in mother earth!"

"Better not point that out to KellyRay, he would think you're serious. Our first priority is to protect these people from the evils of our society as best we can then to keep the trade agreement going--exclusively if we can. Then and only then can we start trying to share our findings with the rest of the world."

Ron stopped smiling and looked past my shoulder. I looked back and saw Friday standing there. How much she'd heard I didn't know. She didn't look upset but she wasn't smiling at me like before either. Blushing, I stood up and she stepped back out of the doorway. "Come. The First would make his wisdom known to the Wellmans."

I quickly grabbed the Crutch and kicked Ron's boots off the bench. "We're on amigo."

KellyRay was already there looking very satisfied with himself. He waved and sent the two women next to him off to the crowd beyond. He swatted one on the rump and I noticed there were places on her where the paint had worn off. It made me angry to see evidence of his foolish actions and I wished I could talk a couple of those big blue guards into dragging him into the sauna room and scour the smile off his face.

Ron didn't look too pleased either but he didn't say anything to KellyRay. He looked around the upper reaches of the chamber for the Quetzal and over at the First still on his throne. Second and Third Speakers were on the ground level with us, apparently ready to deliver the verdict. I noted a difference in the crowd's tone, its mood, and guessed they knew better than I did how important the next few minutes were going to be for them.

Friday stood apart from us though I could see worry in her face as she looked from one brother to the next. I hoped I knew who she would have chosen but I also knew her role was interpreter for these people; it didn't mean she even got a say in who she spoke for.

Suddenly I wondered where Sparky was and if he'd told anyone about the lack of magic in my world. I started to take the Crutch out of its case to summon him then decided we'd all be better off without a demon hanging around and besides I didn't think I could do anything about it if he had. It was clearly too late now. The Second Speaker went up one step to be able to see over us and sang his intro song. I didn't need Friday to translate him anymore but I still wished she were at my side.

"The First observes that many mushrooms look alike but they often taste different and are useful for different things. Thus it is true that each Wellman brings with him a different tone, a different approach to the Song. Even though they claim little knowledge of the Covenant we have all heard their song and the First is content to know that the Covenant is contained in the melody, if not in the actual verse."

I turned to my brothers and said "Translation: he liked our song and thinks we're OK."

Third Speaker joined the Second on his step and ran his hand over a fresh stack of shelf fungus. It made the noise of playing cards being riffled and he split the stack in two and 'finger read' from the fresh one.

"The Yellow Wellman sings well, and the people of the Yellow paint have accepted him. He is free to leave or to join with them as his song leads him." A rising chant went up from the Yellows present and KellyRay looked at me. "Well? Did I win?"

"Sorta, he says you're a sweet yellow songbird and you're free to hang out with your yellow friends over there." KellyRay started to go over there but I held his arm. "I think we need to hear the whole thing before you go off with your girlfriends don't you?" He pulled his arm free roughly and said "Just tell me the part where I'm put in charge of the booze." The Second Speaker started again and I ignored KellyRay's comment to concentrate on the translation.

"The Green Wellman seeks peace between our peoples and his song is loudest within himself. Because he has not found it among his people he is not bound by it to them, or to us, or to the Covenant. Neither are we bound to him. In his wisdom the First has decided that he should be allowed to travel freely Above or Below until he finds a strong song to sing."

I turned to Ron and said, "That was about you. He says you're free to stay or go for as long as you like. Says you're looking for inner peace or something like that and good luck."

Ron grinned and said, "Are you sure that's all he said? I can't tell if that means I've got the job or not."

"I think that means you're free to help with it or to help yourself as you see fit. But I think it also means you don't get to 'bear' Mason's Crutch either."

"So you're the one they picked? I always knew you would be."

"He hasn't said for sure yet."

"Who else is left? Kelly's got his groupies? I've got my freedom and you get to stay here learning ancient Latin and performing opera with topless natives. Sounds like a good gig."

"Hang on hang on. The Third Speaker is starting to speak." I looked at him and then over to Friday who still looked uncertain. Her father was right behind her and his face was still unreadable. I knew a catch must have been coming.

"Wellman the Blue is trying to swim in dark waters. He flounders and needs help doing everything but he has not yet failed to try. His song is uncertain but we saw moments of brightness in the depths. The First believes he will be our Brother Wellman once he's properly taught how to sing."

I laughed at that a bit and stopped abruptly when I saw how solemn everyone was. Third Speaker was pausing for effect, obviously proud of the reaction his joke got. "The First's wisdom is paramount in this. He has perceived that though the people in the Above can bind the Sun to their will they do not always feel its warmth. Thus he has decided that the Blue Wellman should seek out the Wellspring of Songs and bring the gift of light and warmth to his people and the gift of a better song to ours."

I closed my eyes and shook my head in disbelief. Had I heard right? Ron was tugging on my arm and asking what had been said. It was clear by my look and that of Fridays that this was not a result I had anticipated. "Beg pardon?" I asked, trying to get the Third Speaker's attention. It was no use; he had turned and ascended back up the throne, the Second speaker matching him step by step. I guessed the First wasn't used to having to repeat himself, even thru his secondary's.

"I think…I think I've just been told to go off someplace and improve myself. I'm not sure what was meant by his words. I think the boss wants me to get more training and to do that I have to go to "the WellSpring of Songs" and learn how to sing to his satisfaction."

"Lordy RJ, you'll be here for years. I'll give your regards to your wife and kids."

"This isn't funny Ron."

"I'm not laughing."

"Well who is?" I looked around and KellyRay was in a huddle with his Yellow friends. They apparently didn't need further explanations. Beyond him was the doorway to the First's chambers and I could see Sparky out there, rolling on the ground and holding his sides. He was laughing so loud and continuously he hardly stopped for a breath. I really didn't like him much at that moment.

I started to go out there and shut him up but I was tackle hugged by Friday who cried against my chest. I looked around helplessly and saw her father staring at me, his eyes even colder than they usually were. I patted her shoulders awkwardly and said "Don't worry Friday, I'll be OK. I just gotta make this side trip for your First, then I can be the Wellman for your people."

Friday hit my chest with her fist, her words coming out in broken gasps between weeping fits. "I am not worried for you Blue Wellman! I am sad to leave my father!"

"What? Who said you had to leave your father? Don't they like the job you're doing?"

She hit me again and looked up at me, her wet face streaked by the paint from my chest, by her tears. "Thick skinned mole! Have you forgotten already that the First named me Wellman's Shadow? I have to go with you to the WellSpring of Song! You and your brother and the demon you call Sparky!"

"Holy Crap! I didn't realize that. I'm so sorry!" I looked over her shoulder trying to find Sparky in the confusion but the crowd had started leaving and blocked my view outside. "Do we really have to take him too?"

"He is bound to the Crutch and thus to you. You will take the Crutch with you to the WellSpring and he will follow." There was more crying, her face felt hot against my skin and I tried to awkwardly console her at the same time being aware of her father's stony gaze over her shoulders. "Well how far is it to the WellSpring? Your people can't be without a Wellman for too long can they?"

"I do not know, it is not my song to sing. I do know that no one who has gone there has ever come back. Not in my memory, or my father's." Then just as quickly as she had arrived she dashed off thru the open doorway. I thought I saw her try to kick at Sparky and then shy back. He was leaning against a wall still holding his stomach and laughing hysterically in my direction. I made a promise to myself to get rid of him as soon as we got to this WellSpring of Song. If we got there at all.

The End.

Some of the scenes in this book were inspired by real events but the people aren't the people you think, the things aren't the things you think, and I admit freely that I don't know the first thing about Latin, ancient Irish priests, or coal mining.

To see the image that inspired this whole novel go to this website: http://cwva.org/controversy/ogham_intro.html

And think "Yeah but What if?"
-R. Allen Jervis
South Bend, Indiana
June 24th, 2012

Printed in Great Britain
by Amazon.co.uk, Ltd.,
Marston Gate.